A Brother for Sorrows

A Brother for Sorrows

Anita Tiemeyer

Shawm Publishers

Genre: Historical Fiction
Geographic: (N.Y.)--History--(1945-1965)--Fiction
(I.N.)--History--(1945-1965)--Fiction

LoC: PS3620.A31 T2020, DCN: F TIE

Paperback: ISBN 978-0-578-79242-2
Ebook: ISBN 978-0-578-79244-6
Library of Congress Control Number: 2020921504

Cover art by Creative Publishing Book Design
Layout by Kim Autrey
Author photograph by Demico Southern

www.anitatiemeyer.com

for Dennis

Sorrow comes in great waves . . . But rolls over us, and though it may almost smother us, it leaves us. And we know that if it is strong, We are stronger, inasmuch as it passes and we remain.

--HENRY JAMES

For with much wisdom comes sorrows; the more knowledge, the more grief.

--ANONYMOUS

CHAPTER ONE

Irene pulled open the battered entrance door to the two-story brick apartment building and stepped inside. The empty stairwell was warm on this last Monday of June. At mid-morning, no sounds emanated from behind the apartment doors. Tenants must be at work, she presumed. She stepped down the short set of worn linoleum stairs. Joe's apartment was on the right. She looked at the wooden mezuzah nailed on the right side of the door frame. Without thinking, she reached up and touched it. Being Catholic, she didn't need to do this. But it gave her courage.

"Joe?" she called as she quietly knocked on the door. She heard nothing. She knew he had to be home because she had seen his Ford Falcon in a parking space right outside the apartment building. The back door of the stairwell banged open with a sudden gust of wind, making her clutch her faux leather shoulder bag. She knocked again, this time louder. Finding a key among the fistful on her key ring, she unlocked the door and felt resistance as she opened it.

As she opened the door, three brown paper grocery bags of garbage fell over. "Joe? Are you home?" Again, no answer. The airless, still apartment reeked of cigarettes.

The darkened living room appeared as if an Indiana tornado had struck. A soiled T-shirt and a pair of blue jeans had been flung over a chair. A pair of loafers, men's slippers, and a dirty pair of white sweat socks peeked out from under the couch. Next to the navy corduroy sofa lay a used paper plate that held the remnants of moldy barbecue sauce. Three Time magazines, bulging file folders, and notepads with disorganized scribbling were scattered around the floor. She peered at the date of an unopened Bloomington Daily Herald—June 7, 1963. That was three weeks ago!

In front of the sofa in the middle of the room, the antique, marble-topped coffee table (fondly donated to Joe by his Great Aunt Harriet) was laden with a sickening glass of old milk, watery catsup on a greasy paper plate, stale French fries, a half-eaten hamburger still in its wrapper, an overflowing ashtray, an unopened box of Alka-Seltzer, and this month's copy of Indiana Magazine of History. A half-full coffee cup that had a disgusting cigarette butt floating in it completed the repulsive display. An undershirt, gym shorts, a pair of brownish tennis shoes, and a blue and white-checkered wool blanket with some crusty spots on it lay partially imbedded in the sofa cushions as if someone had lain on top of them. A telephone with the receiver off the cradle sat precariously on top of the couch. Irene slowly replaced the receiver and stared at it. And, curiously, everywhere, on the spot-stained carpet, on top of the portable TV set with a bent antenna, in the ugly Goodwill-quality armchair, and crowding the glass lamp on the cheap wooden end table were stacks and stacks of books.

Irene pulled open the beige curtains at the window to see the room better, dust scattering into the air. Examining the books closer, she discovered that all of them were about German history. In a haphazard order were volumes on post World War I; the Cold War; the rise of Nazism; Germany during World War II; Germany after World War II; Germany during the time of Bismarck, the Holy Roman Empire; Germany during the Crusades. Most of them were from the Indiana University Lilly Library. Some were from the libraries at the University of Chicago, University of Illinois, University of Michigan, Boston University, and even Yale University. She knew this wasn't the subject of his dissertation. Joe had chosen big business and labor disputes in America at the turn of the century. He had finished his doctoral coursework and had passed his written exams just a couple of months ago. Since then, he devoted his time to his paper. But there was enough material here for a major thesis.

A thin book on top of the stack in the easy chair lay open, revealing a famous black and white photo of a youngish Adolph Hitler, dressed in a military shirt and staring out with stony black eyes. A red ink pen had been used to draw several boxes around the picture. Irene recognized Joe's notes in the margins. However, the handwriting was much worse than his usual crooked left-handed penmanship. She gave up trying to read his notes. But seeing that picture of Hitler disturbed her.

Next in her search was the second bedroom that served as Joe's office. In the windowless room, she turned on the light switch. A black metal music stand stood next to a dusty brass floor lamp still lit in the middle of the room. A four-drawer metal filing cabinet stood in a corner; a thick music book lay open on top. The middle drawer was ajar with some music pulled halfway out. A stack of sheet music lay carelessly on the floor. Joe's hefty-sized oak desk nearly groaned with the amount of office paraphernalia on it. Situated in front of it was a 1930s-style swivel chair Joe had bought at an antique store in Nashville, Indiana. But what alerted Irene was Joe's clarinet lying in its case on top of his new IBM Selectric typewriter. She knew Joe would never leave his instrument out like that, especially on top of his beloved typewriter. "Dust would get on it and make the keys go out of adjustment," he had told her. Something was not right.

In the bedroom, a blue lamp on the pine dresser shone with a low wattage bulb. Car keys, aftershave bottles, an unopened package of undershirts, a watch, and a pile of loose coins were all casually scattered on top of it. The room smelled rank as if someone had slept in the worn-out double bed for weeks. The curtains were tightly closed. Socks, boxer shorts, a roll of toilet paper, pillows, another filled ashtray, and used tissues littered the bed. That unmade bed especially bothered Irene. She knew Joe had always made his bed since he was eight years old, thanks to the demands of his Aunt Mil, her father's older sister. Sheets wadded up on the floor were spotted with faded brown splotches. Coffee spills, perhaps? The tiny metal reading lamp on the bookcase headboard sat askew.

Looking in his half-empty wall closet, Irene wondered how Joe could have been so busy that he would allow his apartment to get this bad. Didn't he even have enough time to hang up a shirt?

She cringed at going into the bathroom. As she walked in, her shoes cracked on mirror shards on the pink-tiled floor. She found a tiny aspirin tin in a corner. Then she looked up and gasped. The medicine cabinet mirror had been smashed. Some larger pieces still clung to the bottom frame, ready to fall. Mirror chips littered the sink; fragments large and small lay among his toothbrush, electric razor, a bottle of Old

Spice, comb, hairbrush, and even the crusty soap dish. There was a half-full glass of water with tiny bits of silver floating in it. With her heart racing, she immediately flung open the white plastic shower curtain, expecting to see Joe lying in the tub, expired from some violent attack from an intruder. Thank God, it was empty, albeit dusty as if it had not been used in weeks. She exhaled.

Irene thought she heard something and hurried to the kitchen. She heard a scrape under her shoe as she slipped and fell hard. She felt a bright sting on her elbow, but she ignored it when she saw Joe.

He lay on his right side under the kitchen table, his head resting on the filthy linoleum floor. His eyes, ringed in a frightful gray hue, were half-opened as if in death. Glistening in his weeks-old beard was a single thread of saliva from his parted lips. His right arm was splayed awkwardly, and congealed blood spread on his hands, wrists, and inner arm. His T-shirt was drenched.

"Joe! Joe! Wake up!" On her knees, Irene shook him hard by his shoulders. She paid no attention to the blood that was dripping down her arm. Looking up, she saw on the kitchen table an empty bottle of drugstore sleeping pills next to a half-glass of water and three overripe bananas. Several envelopes and a bloody newspaper lay unopened. She shook the bottle in his face. "How many pills did you take? How many, Joe? Answer me!"

Joe's face was sallow. "I dunno. Leave me alone," he mumbled as he opened then closed his eyes.

"Joe, you have to wake up." She shook him again. "C'mon, let's get you up!"

"No."

"Joe, you've got to get up. You can't stay here on the floor. You've lost a lot of blood, and I've got to get you to the hospital." A quick examination revealed that he had made three deep vertical cuts, two at his right wrist and another longer, much deeper one on his inner arm. Yet, three more jagged cuts began to bleed on his left wrist. As was her occupation, Irene's doctor's stance took over. "We have to stitch these cuts. Do you have some ice?" With effort, she pulled him out from under the table, knocking a kitchen chair. Any sudden move would start the blood flowing again. While he lay on the floor, she opened a cabinet drawer and grabbed several dishtowels. Trying not to panic, she hurriedly broke out ice from the freezer tray in the refrigerator and wrapped it in a towel to make a pack.

"Why did you do this? What happened? Did you have some kind of altercation with somebody?" Tears were not what she wanted right now as she lightly pressed the dishtowel against his arm. Blood from the cut on her elbow that had flowed down her arm now dripped on her skirt.

Joe watched her although he couldn't quite focus. He blinked as if trying to keep the kitchen from spinning.

"Here, hold this." Irene shoved a towel under his inner arm. As she worked, she felt her elbow throb. She saw a bloody, palm-sized piece of mirror on the floor. It must have dug its sharp corner into her elbow when she had fallen. She held it up to Joe's face. "You used this, didn't you?" She threw it into the sink. Glancing around, she saw more filled ashtrays, half-empty Coke cans, dirty coffee cups, an opened package of Oreo cookies, and more stacks of magazines and newspapers on the countertops. Dirty dishes sat in the sink.

Joe turned over slowly on his left elbow and knees as if he weighed three hundred pounds. He protectively held his right arm to his chest. "I'm gonna throw up." As Irene held a dishcloth under his mouth, he heaved twice, three times. Tears and snot dripped from his face. He spit saliva.

Irene said as she quickly went to the refrigerator to get more ice. "Maybe you can get rid of those pills. Otherwise, they'll have to pump your stomach." She tried to put the make-shift ice pack in his hand to hold against his arm. But he wouldn't hold onto it. The whole slippery mess slid away.

"No, I'm not going. Where're my glasses?" His words slurred.

"Can you get up? I'm calling an ambulance."

"No!" Joe whined, collapsing on his stomach. Although he was dead weight, Irene managed to pull him up to his bare feet and sat him in a kitchen chair. He leaned over and covered his face with his arm that had begun to seep blood again. "Oh, God. Oh, God." He groaned through clenched jaws. "It hurts!"

"Stay with me, Joe." Irene wiped the blood from his arms. "Stay awake."

With bloodstained hands, she put his loafers on his feet, and finding his glasses on the blood-streaked floor, she put them in her purse. "Keep this ice pack on your arm," she said as she put a towel under his armpit. She called an ambulance from the kitchen wall phone.

While they waited, Joe kept heaving between his knees. When the hearse-like ambulance finally arrived, the two policemen clumsily got him into the back. Irene had to keep throwing towels at them to try to staunch the copious amount of messy blood.

At the Bloomington hospital, Joe was put on a gurney and quickly rolled into an intake room. Hospital staff began their work cutting away his shirt, placing a blood pressure cuff on his left arm, putting a stethoscope to his heart, and inserting an IV line into the back of his left hand. A nurse called the resident doctor.

Irene stayed even though she was told to go into the waiting room. "My name is Dr. Irene Pierce. I'm a resident at Marion County General in Indianapolis. His name is Joe Kaufmann. I'm his sister. He's lost quite a bit of blood, so I think he needs a transfusion. His blood type is B-positive."

A nurse spoke. "We don't have that on hand. We'll have to use O-neg." She turned and went out of the exam room.

A short, heavyset physician wearing thick glasses appeared and looked over his new patient. As he shone a penlight into Joe's eyes, Irene continued. "I don't know exactly when he did this. I found him on the kitchen floor of his apartment about thirty minutes ago. He took OTC sleeping pills, but I don't know how many. The bottle was empty."

The doctor looked at Irene. "You have a lot of blood on you. Are you hurt too?"

"Oh, I fell and cut my elbow." Irene twisted her arm but couldn't see her injury.

"Do you want a nurse to look at your elbow?"

"Sure."

"How did Mr. Kaufmann cut himself?"

Irene frowned. "He smashed a mirror and used a piece of it. It was on the floor when I fell."

While a nurse tended Irene, the doctor forced charcoal into Joe's stomach instead of pumping his stomach since he refused to say when he had swallowed the sleeping pills or how many he had taken. Because he wouldn't answer when repeatedly asked when he had cut himself, he got a penicillin shot to prevent infection, plus a tetanus shot. A lab tech took a sample of his blood.

The doctor checked Joe's hands to see if he had cut any nerves.

Fortunately, Joe had missed them. He left, and Irene and Joe waited. After what seemed an eternity, a nurse came with a suture kit. As she began her work on Joe's arm and wrists, Joe shouted out in pain. "Sir, please lie still," she said. To calm Joe, Irene stroked his thick, oily black hair. "Just look at me, Joe," she said, holding his face in her hands.

When the nurse finished her work sewing up his wounds, she said, "We'll come back shortly." She went out.

"I need something for the pain," Joe whined. He moved about on the gurney, trying to sit up.

Irene said, "They can't give you anything yet until the sleeping pills are out of your system. You're not helping yourself, Joe. Just lie still."

With eyes closed, he turned his head on the pillow. He looked exhausted.

Irene stayed with Joe for an interminable amount of time. She looked at her watch. They had been at the hospital for nearly three hours.

Finally, the doctor came back. "I want to call a psych consult," he stated, clicking a pen over a clipboard holding a thick stack of papers.

Before Irene could respond, Joe shouted, "No! Are you done now? I'm ready to leave. Irene, help me get this needle out. It hurts." Holding his heavily bandaged arm, he weakly tried to sit up again.

"I know what's wrong with him," Irene replied, although she had no idea what had brought on this self-inflicted disaster. She took Joe's hand away from the IV catheter he was trying to pull out.

The bespectacled doctor pressed further. "He needs follow-up care. I can call Central State up in Indianapolis and make a referral. We'll keep him overnight to get him stabilized. Would you be able to take him up to Central State Hospital tomorrow?"

Irene said without thinking, "That won't be necessary. I know I can handle him." She pushed Joe on his shoulders to get him to lay back on the gurney. "Joe, you're staying here for the night."

"No. I want to go back to my apartment."

"Mr. Kaufmann, we think it would be best to watch you until tomorrow," said the resident. "Are you still feeling like you're going to hurt yourself?"

"Go screw yourself."

That comment sealed his fate. Two orderlies raised the gurney's safety bars, unlatched the brakes on the wheels, and began rolling him toward an elevator. Irene followed them, her mind and body numb with weariness.

CHAPTER TWO

Back at his apartment the next morning, Joe eagerly swallowed the pain medicine and promptly hit the sofa on top of his clothes.

Irene sat in the ugly, corduroy armchair and watched him. "You're lucky there was no nerve damage."

He made no reply. After making a phone call to her supervisor at Marion County General saying she had a family emergency, Irene began the monumental task of cleaning the apartment. As she worked, she kept checking the motionless heap on the couch, fearing that Joe would suddenly get up to do more harm to himself. Looking through the stacks of library books, she speculated that Joe's self-inflicted wounds might be connected with all these books, particularly the ones on Nazi Germany. But she would not ask him about it yet. No sense in "poking the bear."

In the mid-afternoon, she sat at the kitchen table to rest and munch on some Oreos. She started to go through his mail and overdue bills. It was a wonder that his lights hadn't been turned off, and he hadn't been evicted for not paying his rent. She would have to clean up this mess as well. *You are going to owe me a lot of dough, she thought angrily.*

Later, getting him into the bathtub was a battle. "Don't get your arm wet. Yes, I know that hand hurts. Don't you have any more shampoo?" As she bathed him, she noticed how thin he was. His shoulder bones pointed out of his skin. His collar bones looked painfully fragile. She could make out the ripple of ribs through the plentiful black hair on his torso. His face was as gaunt as an Old Testament prophet.

Irene put a towel around him before helping him sit on the closed toilet lid. "Joe, you should have called me or called somebody if you were feeling down. You didn't have to do this." She reached for his hairbrush. But first, she made sure there were no stray mirror fragments in it.

"Don't you think I know that already?" Joe raised his voice impatiently. "That's not the point. It just happened."

As she brushed his hair, Irene said, "You'll have to replace the mirror, you know. You're going to lose your security deposit if you don't. And I guess I'll have to take care of your rent and your other bills."

"Oh, okay, thanks. I'll pay you back, and I'll get the mirror fixed. Don't worry about it. Irene, will you give me a script for some sleeping pills?"

"What?"

"No! I mean it! I haven't had a good night's sleep in weeks. All I do is pace the floor for hours, and then I'm so tired during the day I can't stay awake, and I can't get any work done. And my arm and my wrists hurt. Please!"

"Are you out of your mind? You just had charcoal rammed down your throat because you took an overdose of sleeping pills. You think I can trust you with prescription pills that are ten times stronger, so you can finish the job of killing yourself? And besides, taking sleeping pills with your codeine, which already makes you drowsy and suppresses your breathing is a lethal combination. Do you think I'm that stupid?"

"No, Irene. I won't overdose on them. I swear, I promise. I can't function like this. I'm even afraid to go to bed at night. I get these terrible nightmares, and I wake up and can't fall asleep again."

Irene shook her head.

"Please, Irene."

"I said no."

Irene stood over Joe and watched him rub his upper left shoulder awkwardly with his bandaged right hand. "Does your arm hurt?"

Joe frowned. "Yes. I have a headache too."

After changing the sheets, Irene got him into bed with his bandaged arm propped on a pillow. She turned out the lights and left, leaving the bedroom door half-open. The bottle of codeine was put safely in a zippered pocket inside her purse. Still shocked at this incomprehensible deed, she sat on the couch to think.

Why? Why? Joe would not have created this situation on his own. He had been too happy, too involved living his life to attempt suicide. He had too much going right in his life. Joe had finished his bachelor's degree in history in three years at Cornell University back in 1959. Getting his master's degree at Indiana University had only taken a year and a half, and he had moved right on to his doctoral program, finishing his coursework in twenty-four months. He had passed his written and oral exams easily. Now, he was knee-deep in his research for his dissertation.

Moreover, since he had wanted to become a college professor, he had been required to teach some undergraduate courses. He had loved it, even when he had to grade the not-so-grammatically correct term papers and finals by his giddy freshmen. On top of that, his brilliant writing skills had helped him publish scholarly articles in regional and national historical periodicals. Future job openings were being discussed with his professors, who had recognized his scholarly genius.

Irene had caught her breath at the potential of what Joe could do with his life. So, what happened to derail his trajectory toward completing his doctorate and starting a successful career?

But reality brought Irene back to this dreadful apartment. The landscape was total devastation, like the aftermath of an all-out assault on a perfectly innocent village. Bombs that had downed trees and had created huge craters in the earth; tanks that had destroyed green fields, civilian bodies strewn in muddy creek beds, their blood seeping into the water like the blood spreading into the dining room carpet from the kitchen. Everything was the empty colorlessness of annihilation.

Nothing had been left alive except the near unconscious victim on the kitchen floor. The heap she had found wasn't Joe. In her brother's face, Irene saw the paralysis of total defeat to whoever or whatever that had caused him to try to take his life. How serendipitous that Hitler's face stared out at the carnage from the top of the books.

****

"Don't you dare call Grayson!"

"Too late. Daddy called me last night while you were sleeping, wondering why you hadn't contacted him about when that Civil War

article you wrote for that history magazine was coming out. I told him
you had to go to the hospital after an accident. I purposely didn't tell
him anything else. Naturally, he got upset. He and Ruth are arriving at
the Weir-Cook airport at four o'clock tomorrow afternoon, and then
they're taking a rental car down here to Bloomington. I told him I
would have picked them up at the airport, but I couldn't because I had
to stay here with you."

"I don't need a babysitter."

"Yes, you do. Joe, I don't trust you. When you tear open your arm
and wrists and overdose on sleeping pills, that's a suicide attempt.
Don't tell me what you did was anything but a suicide attempt. You're
lucky I talked the doctor into not writing a consult for Central State
Hospital in Indianapolis. Stop rolling your eyes. And stop smoking.
This apartment smells like you've smoked a whole factory of cigarettes.
It stinks to high heaven in here."

"That's none of your business. Leave me alone."

"I can't, you fool!"

Silence.

"Joe, just tell me what happened. Please."

Silence.

"You can't keep this bottled up. There's no shame here. You need
help, but you have to open up and talk."

Silence.

Irene sat next to him on the sofa. She put her arms around him and
kissed his cheek. "I love you, Joe. I am so worried about you. I wish
you would tell me why you did this." She stroked the back of his neck
even as he turned away his head. "Okay. Maybe we will just wait for
Daddy. He'll get it out of you."

****

Irene lifted her head from the sofa pillow.

"Ugh, ugh . . . ah!"

She quickly turned on the lamp on the end table and reached for
her robe which wasn't there. Since she was staying at Joe's apartment
for the night, she had no bedclothes. On the floor in his bedroom, she
had opened a package of new undershirts to wear one over her panties.
Still, in her socks, she hurried to Joe's bedroom.

In the faint light from the living room, Irene saw Joe, lying on his side, crunched in a fetal position. She heard him moaning.

"Joe, wake up," she said softly, turning on the tiny blue metal lamp on his headboard. She lay next to him and put her hands on his face. "What's the matter, Joe? Did you have a bad dream?"

Joe sat up. He yelled out in pain.

"Oh, be careful. You don't want to pull out the stitches."

Through wet eyes, Joe said, "I can't remember. I can't remember."

"Remember what?"

"It hurt so bad. They were pulling on my hands, twisting my arm. I tried to get away from them."

"Who, Joe? Who were you trying to get away from?"

"I wanted to run back to the barrack and hide in the hole. It was what my father had dug behind the bottom slats of the bunks so that nobody would see me. I didn't know where he was. But then I remembered he was still working in the kitchen." His breathing stopped. "She was there! She was kneading dough in a huge bowl."

"Who, Joe? Who was there?"

He shook his head. "It's gone now. I can't remember any more."

Irene kissed him and stroked his face, wiping his tears, knowing that he had had a nightmare about Buchenwald. But she didn't know how to comfort him, to make things right for him. She thought about what had happened so many years ago. Her father, Grayson Pierce, had been an army surgeon during World War II. He had rescued Joe when he was six from this Nazi concentration camp at the end of the war and had brought him home to Ithaca to rear as his ward. Her father had had to deal with these same nightmares. She could still hear Joe's terror-filled screams through her bedroom walls. She knew he had always rushed to hide in his bedroom closet or under his bed. Night after night, his guardian had to get out of bed to comfort him. He often had given him midnight baths as Joe had wet his bed. She knew the strain her father felt, had seen the weariness in his slumped shoulders for lack of sleep, the exhausted frustration in his face because he couldn't stop Joe's nightmares and the hallucinations.

Now it was her turn.

"I can't remember her face! I can't see it. I don't know what she looks like!" Joe put his face in his hands and sobbed.

"I'm so sorry, Joe. I'm so sorry. I'm here. I'm not going to leave you.".

CHAPTER THREE

Grayson and Ruth Pierce could count on one hand how many times they had visited Joe in Bloomington in the four years he had lived there. Grayson was Chief Surgeon at Thompkins County Hospital, and Ruth was a general practitioner, so their work commitments made the trips difficult to organize and execute. Of course, they also had to stop in Indianapolis to visit Irene, but as a resident at Marion County General Hospital, her schedule was restrictive, too. But Grayson's phone call two nights ago alarmed him enough to move mountains to make the 700-mile trip to Joe's apartment as quickly as he and Ruth could get there. Grayson had heard the anxiety in his daughter's voice.

As Joe camped out on the sofa with his bare feet on the coffee table and smoking a cigarette, Irene watched from the window. When she saw a large sedan pull into the apartment building's parking lot, she quickly went out.

"Honey, how are you?" Grayson hugged her and kissed the top of her head.

Irene tried to keep her tears at bay. She said, "Daddy. I came out to prepare you."

"Irene, what's going on?" Ruth came around to the driver's side of the car.

Irene looked at her stepmother's kind but worried face. "Everything is wrong. It's . . . it's been awful the past couple of days."

"Then let's go inside." Grayson took a step forward.

"No, wait." Irene looked back at the apartment entrance door, fearing Joe would somehow escape. "Daddy, brace yourself. Joe did some terrible things to himself. He's—"

"What? Is he hurt?" Grayson's voice rose. He clutched his daughter's arms.

"Yes, he hurt himself." Tears dripped down her red cheeks. "Daddy, he tried to commit suicide. Something's happened that's made him crazy." Irene's voice was hoarse. She twisted her fingers. Lowering her voice, she said, "He's acting like he's afraid again. You know what I mean . . . ." She looked up at her towering father.

The big man pushed past her and rushed into the building. With Irene and Ruth right behind him, he burst into the apartment. "Joe!"

As Grayson moved toward him, Joe pushed himself up on the sofa to evade him, protecting his heavily bandaged arm. "Go away. I don't want you here."

Joe's guardian stopped. He stared at the piteous shell of his ward. Joe's T-shirt hung so loosely over his jeans he could have easily slipped out of them like a pair of pajama bottoms. Although reasonably clean, Joe's hair hung over his ears and down the back of his neck, disheveled and in need of cutting. Because of the risk of a razor blade, Irene had not allowed him to trim the heavy black beard that covered nearly half of his face. His heavy, brow-framed glasses were smeary.

But it was the bandages on his right arm that upset Grayson. The thick gauze dressing started from his armpit and stopped right at the base of his thumb. His left hand and wrist were bandaged as well, although not as bulky. Despite the thick wrapping, a little blood had seeped through under his arm.

Grayson set his mouth, trying to restrain his emotion. "Tell me what happened." He towered over Joe, his hands on his waist.

"I hadn't heard from him since finals week," Irene said after closing the door. "I called him a dozen times, but he wouldn't pick up. So, two days ago, I came down to the apartment and knocked on the door, and when he didn't answer, I used my spare key to come in."

Ruth sat on the edge of a straight-back chair, her arms crossed tightly over her straw purse. Leaning forward, she said, "Joe, you look awful. Are you in pain?"

Irene said, "I've got some codeine to give him, but I think he's had too much already."

Joe threw a hateful glance at her.

Irene went on. "This place was a mess." She paused, looking at Joe to see if he would stop her. He slumped into the sofa, his face impassive. "When I went into the bathroom, I saw that the medicine cabinet mirror had been smashed."

"Was there an intruder?" Ruth inquired anxiously.

"No, no." Irene shook her head. "When I came to the door, it was locked. I found him in the kitchen."

Grayson sank into the ugly Goodwill armchair next to the couch. The smelly living room was stifling, so he leaned over and turned on the dusty portable fan.

"He . . . he was on the floor, bleeding and almost unconscious. He had cut his arm and both his wrists. And there was an empty bottle of OTC sleeping pills on the kitchen table."

Joe snapped, "Shut up about that!" He fished a cigarette out of a pack on the coffee table. He lit it furiously.

"Joe, they have to know. Daddy, he was semi-conscience. I put ice on his arm and called an ambulance." Irene didn't like the whiny pitch in her voice.

"What happened at the hospital?" asked Grayson.

"The doctor forced charcoal into his stomach. He asked him how many pills he had taken and when he took them. Of course, being the stubborn dope that he is, he wouldn't say." Her anger flared.

Grayson's face was a rock, his severe eyes on his ward.

"The doctor planned to keep him overnight for observation. But, of course, Joe wanted to leave. When he asked him if he might hurt himself again, Joe practically took his head off. So, they kept him overnight, and I brought him home yesterday. The doctor was ready to write a consult for Central State Hospital in Indianapolis, but I talked him out of it. I said I knew what was going on, even though I didn't."

"Why, Joe?" Grayson's deep, gravelly voice resonated a little too loudly.

"I don't want to talk about it."

Grayson blinked. He sighed, relaxing his broad shoulders. "All right. Maybe we can talk about it later." Concession curbed his voice. He took off his summer fedora and threw it on the coffee table.

"We don't have to talk about it at all." Joe put down his feet and stubbed out his cigarette in a plastic ashtray on the end table.

Grayson said, "Let's take a breather."

Ruth said, "We've had a long morning. Maybe we should get something to eat." To Grayson, she said, "We should find a hotel room, too."

Joe looked at her. "Hotel room? You're staying here in Bloomington?"

Grayson retorted, "We didn't travel seven hundred miles to get here and then just turn around and go back to Ithaca!"

Under his breath, Joe muttered, "I don't need anybody here."

"Huh? What'd you say, boy?"

"Nothing."

Irene said, "There's no food in the apartment other than a package of Oreos and some pickle relish in the refrigerator. I'm starving."

Ruth gathered her gloves and purse and stood. "Then lets you and me go to the grocery store."

Irene offered, "We can take my car." The two women left.

Grayson fidgeted in his dismay. "Joe, I know you're angry. You're probably a little ashamed, too. It's difficult to open up about this. But I'm here. It's just you and me. Tell me what's going on."

Joe lit a fresh cigarette. Defiantly, he blew smoke toward the low ceiling. "You gonna try to commit me again?" he asked with narrowed eyes.

Grayson tightened his big surgeon's hands into fists. But his voice was even. "I would if I thought it was necessary."

"What's the rule about that? Don't you need a court order? Convince a judge that I'm a danger to myself? Since I'm an adult, three days in the looney bin, and then I can check myself out."

"Don't mock me, Joe! Can't you understand how worried I am about you? You've got your sister in knots, and my wife was crying on the plane all the way from Ithaca." He gestured to the kitchen. "What did that kitchen look like when Irene found you on the floor? Did she get all the blood cleaned up? You're smoking like a chimney, and you look like crap. You're as thin as a scarecrow. And your hair and your beard are so long you look like an Orthodox Jew!"

Joe continued dragging on his smoke. There was a slight tremor in his bandaged left hand.

Restless, Grayson stood. He ran agitated fingers through his slick, coffee brown hair. He paced. "This isn't you, Joe. You weren't like this when you came home for Christmas. Please! Tell me why you did this!"

Softly, Joe said, "I can't talk about it right now. It's too upsetting. I don't even want to think about it."

"Of course, it's upsetting. I know you, Joe. You're covering up whatever the problem is by lashing out. You're putting up a defense by being angry. Now you're in denial. I'm trying to help you, son. You know I've always tried to protect you."

Joe leaned forward and stared right into his guardian's clear grey eyes. "And you always fail, don't you?"

Grayson threw up his hands.

"It's all about you!" Joe's voice rose. He managed to get on his feet. He held his right arm away from his side to not to put pressure on his painful wound. "You've never been able to protect me! Let me count the ways! I threw myself out of a second-story bedroom window when I was seven. I got beat up by three hoodlums when I was fourteen. I ran away for eight days when I was fifteen. And then I nearly starved myself to death in that Havensbrook Psychiatric Hospital. And on top of that, I was terrorized by two old women growing up in the mansion." He said with bitter sarcasm, "Yeah, I've done well with my life since you rescued me from Buchenwald." He inhaled his light. "Is it that crazy that I cut my arm and my wrists to pieces and took an overdose of sleeping pills? What's next? That I'll hang myself?"

Grayson went to him, his arms ready to collect his ward into his broad chest.

But Joe backed away, holding out his bandaged hand to repel his guardian. "Not this time, Grayson. You're not going to smother me with your well-intentioned love. It doesn't work anymore." He quickly wiped his eyes under his glasses. "You can't help me now. Nobody can." He shook with rising emotion. "I have to face this myself or . . . succumb to it."

"No!" Grayson roared. "We can face this together! We've had to do this ever since I brought you home nineteen years ago!"

Joe walked about the living room, still smoking. He was getting dizzy, and his arm throbbed. Grayson's eyes bore into him like a drill. He didn't want to say out loud what he and his guardian had had to face all these years, the unceasing horror of Buchenwald. "I have to lie down. I need my pain pills."

"Okay, you should go to bed and rest. Where did Irene put the codeine?" Grayson looked around.

"I don't know where she's hiding it. I haven't figured that out yet."

"Well, thank goodness for that." Grayson pinched the bridge of his long nose. "Maybe I can get you some Tylenol. Do you have any? Maybe in that medicine cabinet you busted?"

Joe gave a short cynical laugh. "I wouldn't go in there to look for it if I were you. Irene may not have cleaned up all the glass." He headed toward the darkened bedroom, touching the walls and doorframes to steady himself.

Grayson followed him and helped him to bed, carefully arranging his arm over the pillows. "Would you like a cool washcloth for your head? That might help you relax."

"Sure." Joe closed his eyes.

****

At the A &P grocery store, the aisles were crowded with customers. Serenaded by Mantovani's music over loudspeakers, Irene pushed the grocery cart, and Ruth walked beside her. They said little as they filled the cart. Ruth had told Irene when they had entered the store not to worry about paying for the food. She and Grayson had planned to help as much as they could. Irene murmured her gratitude. She thought about the bills she had stacked two days ago on Joe's kitchen table. She'd talk with her father about those later.

"What about a pot roast?" Ruth suggested at the meat counter, although she had no idea how to prepare it. Ruth never was good at cooking. Thank goodness the Pierce family's cook, Rose, helped out to keep the family well-fed.

"No, I think that's a little too complicated," Irene replied. "If we get some ground beef and tomato sauce, we could have spaghetti. Joe likes that, and I can make it pretty well."

On impulse, Ruth put a small pair of scissors in the cart. She commented, "These are so we can try to make Joe look less like a caveman and more like a modern man about town." Irene said nothing but thought, How am I supposed to keep these away from him?

They stopped at the cleaning supplies aisle. "I did the best I could to scrub down his apartment," Irene said, her voice wooden. "He didn't have much." She stared at the row of carpet-cleaning products.

"Irene, what's wrong?" Ruth stepped nearer.

"We . . . we need to buy something to clean the blood . . . on the carpet. When the emergency guys came, they didn't bind his wounds very well, and they started to bleed again. Some of it dripped on the floor." She squeezed her eyes so as not to cry.

"Oh, my dear." Ruth impulsively took Irene into her arms to hug her. She stroked her stepdaughter's cropped, thick blonde hair. She felt Irene's body shake, her tears dampening her dress as Irene pressed her face into her arm.

"There, there. It's all right, Irene. You can cry." Ruth lightly rubbed her back.

Swallowing hard, Irene said, "But I shouldn't get upset about this. I see blood all the time but . . ." She whispered, "But it was Joe's blood."

Ruth glanced around to see if anyone saw them. An elderly couple stopped and watched as if trying to look concerned. Ruth gently pulled Irene closer to the shelves. She gave a hard look at the intruding couple, willing them to move on. "It's hard, I know. I'm worried, too, Irene. You know how much I care for Joe. I've loved him from the moment I met him when he was just fifteen." A wave of emotion made her green eyes bright with wetness. "And you know what? I've never said this, but I have always loved you, too. You've had such determination and courage to get your medical training, and I'm truly proud of you!"

Irene stopped crying and pulled out of Ruth's embrace. "Do you mean that?"

"Yes, sweetheart. I've been your cheerleader always, if only from a distance. You seemed so independent and strong-minded that I didn't want to get in your way. But I was ready to help you if you ever asked."

Irene fingered the grocery cart handle, thinking. She began to regret the blatant animosity she had shown when Ruth had married her father. Already being a resentful sixteen-year-old still didn't excuse her behavior.

"Irene, just like you, your father gave me the self-confidence I never got from my own family, least of all from my three older brothers. After my first husband died during the war, I got a lot of pressure to find a new husband and settle down with a home and children to rear. But I wanted to follow in my husband's footsteps and become a doctor. He was a cardiac surgeon.

"Years later, when I met your father at that medical convention in New York, it was love at first sight. He gave me the courage to start my own practice and build my career. And it didn't hurt that he gave me a lot of referrals."

Ruth reached down to arrange some of the boxes of food in the cart. "It's not easy being a female doctor. I get resistance from many of my patients. They keep assuming I'm the nurse. Some male patients refuse to let me examine them." She saw a look of understanding on Irene's face. "I've been in your shoes, honey. I know what you're going through. And I want to support you all I can. But it's difficult with seven hundred miles between us."

Irene spoke with resentment in her voice. "I had to fight my aunt and my grandmother when I was growing up. I've always wanted to be a doctor, but they said absolutely not. They expected me to get married and have a family. It wasn't my place to do a man's job." Irene didn't want to think about her cruel grandmother, Nina Cassandra, or her wicked Aunt Mil, her father's older sister.

"Yes, they didn't treat you well at all. You're lucky you had your father to support you and encourage you." She smiled gently. "Your father is the kindest, most considerate, most generous human being I have ever known. He is the rare kind of man who isn't afraid to cry or to feel compassion. He doesn't have to protect his ego. He knows he has nothing to prove to anybody. He listens to his patients. He doesn't pass judgment. People who are hurting and feeling vulnerable come to him because they know they can trust him. He will do whatever it takes to heal them. He is truly a great man."

Irene said, "And he has a sense of humor, too."

Ruth laughed. "Yes, his dry wit can be entertaining."

"He's made wisecracks to Aunt Mil and Grandma that are so subtle they don't even notice. But then, they don't notice anything but themselves."

They turned back to the shelf of cleansers. Ruth said, "Would you like me to clean the rug?"

Irene nodded.

Ruth reached for a box of Arm and Hammer carpet cleaner and put it in the cart. She also selected a scrub brush.

After the women returned with the groceries, Irene drove back to Indianapolis to pack a suitcase, and she stopped by the hospital to request some time off.

Back at Joe's apartment, the Pierce family ate a late supper. Of course, Joe did more smoking than eating, much to the predictable consternation of his guardian. Nothing more was discussed about his suicide attempt. Afterward, Ruth and Grayson left to find a hotel.

There was some argument as to whether or not Irene would sleep with Joe in his full-sized double bed. No matter where she slept, either with him or on his sofa, she feared falling asleep and waking up to find him on the kitchen floor again bleeding out or, having found the pain pills in her purse, passed out from an overdose. She decided to sleep with him, one hand draped over his waist to hold him in the bed.

CHAPTER FOUR

10:05 p.m. Grayson swallowed the rest of his water and wiped his mouth. After setting the glass on the hotel bathroom vanity, he padded to the double bed in his undershirt and pajama bottoms and sat. He briefly thought about turning on the TV to watch some news but decided he didn't have the mindset. Instead, he reached for his timeworn Bible he had put on the nightstand and began turning pages. Putting on his half-glasses, he found a familiar passage:

Hear me, Lord, and answer me, for I am poor and oppressed. Preserve my life, for I am loyal; save your servant who trusts in you. You are my God; pity me, Lord; to you I call all the day. Gladden the soul of your servant; to you, Lord, I lift up my soul. Lord, you are kind and forgiving, most loving to all who call on you. Lord, hear my prayer; listen to my cry for help. In this time of trouble I call, for you will answer me. Be my rock of refuge, a stronghold to save me. You are my rock and my fortress; for your name's sake lead and guide me . . . Into your hands I commend my spirit; you will redeem me, Lord, faithful God.

He took off his glasses and closed the Bible. He clasped his hands—hands that God had given him to save hundreds of lives. These hands had penetrated stomachs and bowels, carved out tumors and spleens and appendixes, tied off countless blood vessels, and stitched gaping wounds. He healed people who were suffering from pain. And that gave him great joy and personal satisfaction.

Broken parts of the human body that he could feel in his skilled hands—he could fix those, as a repairman could fix a car or a furnace. Alas! Ailments of the mind were beyond him. Such disorders were the intangible diseases that he could neither see on an X-ray nor put under a microscope like a spot of blood. But he couldn't relieve the suffering of the one patient who meant the most to him. If he could only slice open Joe's chest on the operating table, cut out that blasted childhood memory of Buchenwald, and throw it into the waiting metal pan held by a nurse, to be discarded like a malignant lump. Then he would carefully stitch up his ward and watch him being wheeled into the recovery room. He would be at peace, knowing that Joe would be free of this Nazi-saturated disease. His ward could look forward to a happy, productive life!

He imagined seeing Joe on the kitchen floor. This torment, this nightmare was starting all over again.

Awkwardly, Grayson lowered himself on cracking knees on the side of the bed. He put his hands together and closed his eyes tightly. He crossed himself and prayed. "Lord, my God in heaven. I beg You again to help me. I need Your strength. My boy is lost, and I have to help him find his way again. Please, help me! I am Your humble servant. I will do anything You ask of me. Just help me bring my ward back!"

As his tears flowed, Grayson finished. "In Jesus Christ's name, amen." He crossed himself again and collapsed on the carpet. Unbeknownst to him, Ruth had stood next to the vanity in her bathrobe, listening to her husband's pleas to the Almighty. She sat beside him and put her arms around his shoulders.

"We'll get through this, Grayson. I know the Lord will answer you. He will be your anchor."

Grayson's sobs turned into heaves of anguish. "I've tried so hard, Ruth! I've done everything I could to keep him safe and whole."

"Yes, Grayson."

"I took him out of that stinking hellhole at Buchenwald. I saved his life! I gave him a home, food, warm clothes, a good education. I stayed with him when he was a child, screaming his head off after waking up from his nightmares. For years, I fought my family to keep him in the Jewish faith. I watched him graduate valedictorian of his high school. I watched him graduate from Cornell summa cum laude. I've thrown money at him like there's no tomorrow. He's wanted for nothing. I've given him every opportunity to live a normal, successful life!"

Ruth rubbed his arm. "Of course, you've done your best for him, sweetheart. You've stood right next to him all his life. You love him like he is your own flesh and blood."

Grayson shook his head and wiped his nose. "Yes, but I've let him slip through my fingers. I've failed in keeping him safe." Groaning, he arose. "Try as hard as I can to keep him on his feet, he keeps falling down!" He paused, thinking about the afternoon in Joe's apartment. "He told me that this afternoon when you and Irene were out grocery shopping. He said even though I've shown him all my love throughout the years, I haven't been able to protect him. And he's right."

The big man rose and sank on the edge of the bed. Ruth sat on the other double bed facing him.

Grayson put his fists on his knees. "It was so hard to hear the truth from him. He said, 'Let me count the ways.' He talked about how he jumped out of his bedroom window, not three weeks after I had brought him home from that orphanage in Switzerland. When he jumped out of that blasted second-story window, he was crying for help. Those old women were torturing him, and I was too busy with my patients to see it. I was blind! I thought he'd be taken care of by my own mother and sister!" He shook his head in angst. "And getting beat up by those hoodlums from his school when he was fourteen. After that attack, I saw the signs. For months afterward, he wasn't eating or sleeping, shutting himself away from everybody. He was in a depression, and I stood by and did nothing. I should have gotten him into therapy right then. Then a few months later, he ran away and was missing for eight days. You remember that. He'd still be gone if the state police hadn't have found him. When he ran away, he was crying for help again!"

"Yes, Grayson."

"Then I put him in a psychiatric hospital where he refused to eat, and then I had to put him in that hospital in Albany and watch the nurses stick a feeding tube up his nose. Even with all the psychotherapy he had with that psychiatrist, Dr. Montgomery, he nearly starved himself to death. He wanted to die, you know. He told me that. He said he couldn't live with himself being a survivor when there had been thousands of victims piled up around him in the camp." Grayson lowered his head in exhausting defeat. "I let him put himself in harm's way.

Grayson rubbed his eyes. His shoulders sagged. "Now this." As if the words were too agonizing to speak, he said, "Yesterday, Joe seemed to say he might make another attempt. He said, 'What's next? That I should hang myself?'" Grayson put his face in his hands, his sobs renewed.

Ruth moved to his side and hugged him. "Honey, this suicide attempt came out of nowhere. We still don't know why he did it. Besides, you can't expect to stay with him and watch him twenty-four hours a day. He's an adult, although I am frightened for him right now."

"I know how fragile he is." Grayson closed his hands in vexation. "It's as if he's this . . . palm-sized Tiffany figurine that's made out of brittle glass. It's so beautiful, so precious. Yet it's going to break no matter how carefully I hold it."

Ruth countered bravely. "But he has resilience. He overcame those setbacks. Look how much he's accomplished! He's fought his way out of those terrible times and survived. And he'll survive again. We just have to get his head back on straight."

Grayson gave a bitter chuckle through his tears. "You sound just like his Aunt Mil. If she were here, she'd have him by the ear and sitting him down at his desk and telling him to forget the past and get cracking on his schoolwork, or rather, his dissertation. I have to admit she's had as much influence on him as I have. Maybe not in the most kindhearted way, but she got her point across to him."

The two of them sat in silence.

Grayson mused, "I don't think I ever told you this, Ruth. Back when I had told my mother and Mil that I was going to marry you and move out of the mansion, I had an unpleasant conversation with Mil. I was packing up my study, and she came in. She asked for Joe."

"What? I don't understand."

"She wanted Joe to stay with her at the mansion instead of him moving with Irene and me into our new house. At first, I was shocked that she would make such an outlandish request, and naturally, I said 'no.' But she was serious. She said she could take care of him, keep him focused on his studies, and keep him out of trouble."

Ruth spoke slowly, choosing her words carefully. "Meaning, she could watch him better than we could."

Grayson nodded forcefully. "Yes. But I said she hadn't been watching him very well when it was twelve hours before anyone knew he was missing when he ran away. I shouldn't have said that to her. She admitted she would regret that mistake for the rest of her life."

"Well, from her point of view, asking for Joe made sense. After all, we'd be busy at work, and Joe would be coming home to an empty house, and, dare I say it, Irene wouldn't be able to watch him."

Again, Grayson nodded.

"Mildred truly loved Joe, didn't she?"

"Ruth, she was as committed to him as I was from the day I brought him home. I haven't told her yet about Joe now. I just said we were going on a visit and not to worry. She seemed to accept that, although she might have wondered why we left in such a hurry."

Grayson pulled down the bed covers. "Now, he tried to kill himself yet again. I tell you, this suicide attempt has something to do with Buchenwald. I know it. There's nothing else that would push him to do this." He looked at his travel clock on the nightstand. Sighing, he said, "It's late. I'm tired. We'll have to deal with this tomorrow when we go back to his apartment,"

"Do you think he'll talk about it?" Ruth climbed into the bed on the other side.

"That's the big question. Joe can be pretty stubborn."

Ruth settled into her husband's arms. "Grayson, we'll help him together. I will do anything you want me to if it will get Joe back on his feet. You know I love him, too."

"I know you do. I know it's been a tall order for you to deal with my children. I've always appreciated your patience, Ruth. What would I ever do without you?"

He turned out the light.

CHAPTER FIVE

Sleep for Grayson and Ruth had been fitful at best. They rose at seven-thirty and had breakfast at a local restaurant near the hotel. Ruth had the good forethought to call Joe's apartment before they showed up at his door. Irene had answered in a tired voice, saying that he was still asleep. She told Ruth to come no earlier than eleven o'clock. That gave her father more time to wring his hands.

They arrived with more groceries. While Grayson sat at the kitchen table pretending to read the newspaper, Ruth and Irene set to work shaving off Joe's weeks-old beard and giving him a tentative haircut in the bathroom. Inexplicably, he told them to leave the mustache.

"Well! You look like a new man, Joe!" Grayson said when his ward came into the kitchen. He folded the paper.

Joe dropped into a kitchen chair. Grayson brushed the corner of his ward's new mustache. "A little dirt under your nose, eh? Now you look really look like a college professor!"

"Shall I prepare lunch?" Ruth began taking groceries out of the bags.

"How about some cold cuts and chips? What do you say, Joe?" Grayson rose and took a generous-sized bowl from the cupboard. He tore open a large bag of Ruffles potato chips. Ruth opened a can of green beans to put on the stove to heat. Irene busied herself cleaning out the bathroom sink of the mountains of black hair.

Lunch was quiet. No one commented on Joe's disinterest in his food. He pushed the potato chips around (usually his favorite) on his plate, and he didn't touch his bologna sandwich or his green beans. He took a small bite of an Oreo cookie and casually dropped it back on his plate.

"Joe, I never heard from you about that Civil War article," Grayson said. He munched on a carrot stick. "Did you get it published?"

"Huh? I dunno. The magazine was on the counter over there. Irene might have moved it when she cleaned."

"Was it that Indiana History magazine with the picture of an Indiana president on it?" asked Irene. She found the magazine and began flipping pages.

"No, that was Vice President Schuyler Colfax. He was in office with Ulysses S. Grant from 1869 to 1873."

"Oh." She handed the magazine to Joe. He found his article and began reading.

Grayson and Ruth covertly smiled at each other.

Ruth stood. "Why don't you boys move to the living room while Irene and I clean up. Joe, I'll wrap up your sandwich and put it in the fridge if you want to eat it later. Grayson, shall I make a pot of coffee?"

"No, thank you, my dear." Grayson and Joe went into the living room. Joe handed the magazine to his guardian.

Grayson turned the fan on again and settled on the sofa. "It's plenty warm in here. I guess the new central air conditioning has spoiled us in the house." He looked for Joe's article.

Joe turned on the TV. Finding only soap operas and an annoying local variety show, he turned it off. He plopped into the Goodwill chair and held up his bandaged right arm, his elbow resting in his lap.

Putting aside the magazine, Grayson studied him after he lit a pipe. "I assume you'll get your stitches out in a week? Is that what the doctor said?" He threw a spent match into an ashtray.

Joe shrugged nonchalantly. "I dunno. Ask Irene." He would not meet his guardian's eyes.

Grayson puffed away, his face showing veiled annoyance. "Is there anything you do know?"

Joe let out his breath forcefully through his nose. "I know where this is going, Grayson."

Ruth and Irene quietly entered and took seats around the men.

Irene asked hesitantly, "Joe, I want to ask you something."

Joe looked at her, his face blank.

"When I came into the apartment, you know, when I found you, there were all these books on Germany everywhere." She gestured to three tall stacks she had put along the wall. "They're all from different libraries. Are you working on a special project?"

Twisting his mouth to give himself time to think of an answer, Joe replied, "Where're my cigarettes?" He rose.

Irene crossed her arms and glared at him. "Go find them yourself."

After opening and closing drawers in the kitchen, Joe went into his office. More slamming drawers. He returned with a crushed pack of Salems, a plastic ashtray, and a book of matches. Everyone watched him as he lit up and sat back in his chair.

Grayson shifted on the sofa. Ruth put a steadying hand on his knee.

Joe looked at the others. "What? What are you all waiting for?"

"Your sister asked you a question, Joe," Grayson said evenly.

Time seemed to stop. All that could be heard was the slow ticking of the metallic wall clock. Joe got up and went to the window, studying the busy sparrows chirping in the redbud tree as he smoked.

A scene came into his mind. He was sitting in a big leather chair in the office of his psychiatrist, Dr. Montgomery, at the Havensbrook Psychiatric Hospital for adolescent boys. The doctor had been patiently waiting for an answer, too. Joe had watched the chirping birds outside the window behind the doctor's huge desk, the green Adirondack mountains in the distance.

"No. I'm not working on a special project on Germany."

Irene started, "Then why—?"

Joe tightened his face, closing his eyes, and then opening them. "I'm a historian. I have to know history, not just American history but European and other places. And I have to teach it. I can't ignore Germany's history or make excuses to my profs as to why I don't want to study it the way I did when I was an undergraduate. I have to force myself to read it and know it." He didn't look at the skeptical faces around him.

"But haven't you already taken courses in German history? I'm confused."

"No. I started my research before that happened."

Irene asked, "What is 'that'? When? Where were—?"

"All right! I'll tell you, Irene! Just don't push me." He quickly extinguished his smoke.

Grayson and Ruth exchanged looks.

"I . . . . You remember at Christmas when I showed you those pictures?"

"I think so," replied Irene. "They were photographs of your I. U. friends, weren't they? I recognized Frank Oneida. He was a doctoral student in music whom you knew from Ithaca. He was a bit eccentric, wasn't he? You said you could hardly carry on a conversation with him."

Joe opened a slender drawer in the end table and took out several pictures. He passed them to Irene. "Here they are."

Irene studied the pictures carefully and then gave them to her father. He pulled out his half-glasses.

Joe lit another cigarette. "He's the one who set this whole goddamn thing in motion. You remember me talking about one of Frank's students, Robert Stangarden? He was in that photo of those four French horn players taken right after their band concert last November." He picked an imaginary speck of tobacco from his tongue.

Grayson snapped his fingers. "Yes! Seeing those pictures, I told you how much you and that kid looked alike. The resemblance was uncanny."

"Oh, yes. I remember," offered Ruth. She leaned over to look at the photos in Grayson's hands. "He looks like he could be your younger brother."

Joe blew out smoke. "Frank thought so, too. That's why he introduced us after watching Fidelio being put on by the opera department back in October. Robert was playing in the pit orchestra . . ."

****

Since Frank Oneida had bought the tickets at the last minute, he and Joe could only get the balcony seats where the air was hot and close, making it difficult to concentrate on watching the performance. Joe had loosened his tie early in the first act and had taken off his suit coat at the intermission. Now, he had to wave his program in his face to cool himself in the third act. From time to time, he looked through his old binoculars, a high school graduation gift from his Aunt Mil.

At the present moment, Joe studied the esteemed Professor Emeritus Jonathan Blakey singing the part of Don Pizarro in

Beethoven's Fidelio. The venerable singer wore a bulky, straw-colored wig, an early nineteenth-century German prison guard costume, and enough make-up to fill a department store. His voice resonated like a toiling church bell, and his flamboyant antics belied his age of seventy-one. He opened his mouth so wide that when he sang in the low register, Joe could actually see the fillings in his back molars through his binoculars. His red, sagging face was awash in gullies of perspiration mixed with black mascara. Sanguine rouge saturated his cheeks, turning them into a sickly brownish hue with the pancake make-up. However, none of it mattered. This was Beethoven!

Joe moved his sights to the pit orchestra. The forty-five-member student music group sawed and honked and beat the finale under the disapproving eye of Tibor Kozma, Indiana University's orchestra director. Frank had said before the opera had started that there was a love-hate relationship between the Hungarian-born conductor who had come to I. U. by way of the New York Metropolitan Opera and the student musicians. "Those kiddos are getting a taste of the real music world," Frank had said knowingly. "Kozma's a pussycat compared to some conductors." Although Joe couldn't see the music director's face, he watched the lively maestro, imagining him scowling at the woodwinds and glowering at the second violins. When he pointed to his left ear, shaking his finger violently, Joe knew he was trying to tell the strings to listen to the intonation. The white-haired man waved his left-hand palm down at the low brass. They had been told before not to play so loud. They were drowning out the singers!

"What part does your student play?" Joe whispered to Frank.

Frank strained his neck, trying to see around a heavyset woman wearing a hat. "He's on third. Do you see him?"

"Shhh!" somebody said behind them.

"I'm not sure," Joe replied in a low voice.

"Give me those binocs."

Without taking the strap off around Joe's neck, Frank grabbed the binoculars, almost choking Joe. He had to lean over not to get strangled.

Oblivious, Frank exclaimed, "I see him!"

"Give me some air, you—"

"Quiet! Or I'll call the usher!"

Sighing, Joe endured the strap digging into his neck.

At 4:35 p.m., the final chords evaporated up to the auditorium ceiling. The audience gave instant applause and, of course, a standing ovation. Roses and carnations flew onto the stage. After several minutes, the clapping and the "bravos" dissipated, and the house lights went up. People began to file out slowly.

Joe and Frank pushed their way through the crowd to reach the orchestra pit. Dressed in his custom-tailored navy suit and dove-gray silk tie, Joe made quite a contrast to his friend, Frank, who looked as if he shopped for his clothes at the Salvation Army store. Today, he wore a too-tight tweed jacket with frayed patches on the elbows, an open-collared dark yellow shirt, and black pants, two sizes too big.

As they leaned over the brass railing, Frank waved to a student. "Hey, Robert!"

The slender, brown-haired young man dressed in a black suit and tie looked up from his instrument case to see Frank Oneida, his French horn instructor.

Looking at the other three horn students who were putting away their instruments, Frank said proudly, "Sounded great! You guys nailed that finale. I'm proud of my boys. Did you guys have to pick up your lips off the floor? Ha! Ha!"

The students moved away with eyes averted, trying to ignore their tall, frightfully skinny teacher. Looking embarrassed, Robert closed his case and stood, music folder in hand. He looked around as if looking to find someone. He waited for some cello students to move their big cases so he could take the left side stairs out of the orchestra pit.

"I want to introduce you to a friend of mine." Frank motioned to Joe. "Robert, this is Joe Kaufmann." Frank jerked a thumb at Robert. "Joe, this is my boy wonder, Robert Stangarden."

Joe shook lukewarm hands with Robert. *Why does he look so familiar?*

"You did such a terrific job today, Robert, that I want to take you to dinner at the Gables." Frank turned to lead the way back up the center aisle.

"Um, I don't know. I've got a lot of homework to do, and I'm supposed to meet a friend in a practice room. We have an ear-training test tomorrow." Robert glanced up behind him, seeing busy theatre students the opera set on the stage.

"Oh, c'mon! Since when are you gonna turn down a free meal? We have to celebrate your debut with the I. U. Opera Company. I promise we won't be more than forty-five minutes." He tapped his tarnished

Mickey Mouse watch. "We'll even skip flirting with the waitress."

Reluctantly, Robert followed the other two. Joe noticed the kid's worried face. He remembered the low-grade panic he had felt all during his first year at Cornell University, not knowing what the professors expected, trying to keep up with ocean waves of material they threw in every class. Plus, there were countless tests, pop quizzes, term papers, final exams, and the complete lack of time.

Inside the dimly lit restaurant, the only other customers were a gray-haired gentleman in a fedora drinking coffee reading a newspaper at the counter, and a well-dressed young couple sitting in their own little world in a booth. Hank Williams crooned *The Great Speckled Bird* on a radio, and a blonde waitress in a tight pink uniform chewing gum and filing her red-painted nails as she leaned over the counter.

"God Almighty, I swear, we're in Nashville!" Frank pointed a knowledgeable finger at Robert. "That's Tennessee, not Nashville, Indiana. Let's sit here." He slid into a booth.

Frank and Joe sat on one side, and Robert sat across from them. The blonde waitress whose nametag said "Hilda" sashayed her way over with an order pad and menus. The look on her face showed what she thought about college boys. They only had one thing on their mind, and it was not eating.

Frank gave her his best condescending grin, showing big crooked teeth. "Hello. We're running a little short on time, so what do you recommend that's quick and easy?"

"Not me." Hilda, the waitress, popped the gum in her mouth.

Frank giggled. Robert shifted his weight in the booth and tried to focus on his menu. Sensing the younger man's confusion, Joe bent his head down to hide a smile

"Well, what'll it be, Mr. Third Horn?" Frank asked. "Order anything you want. Money is no object." He gave a mocking sneer at Joe. "You pay for your own dinner."

Joe rolled his eyes. He knew who would be paying for all three of them.

"Ah, I guess I'll have to pay you back sometime," Robert said meekly.

Before Joe could answer, Frank fingered the lapel on Joe's suit coat. "Look at this, Robert. This finely-tailored Brooks Brothers suit came from New York."

"That's because I'm from New York!" Joe retorted.

The waitress exchanged looks with Robert. She gave him a big, "it's okay" smile.

"Don't worry about paying, Robert. I do this all the time." Joe stared hard at Frank.

Robert looked back at the menu, still not sure who would be paying for his meal. "Okay. I'll have the cheeseburger plate, no tomato. And a chocolate milkshake."

Frank said, "I'll have the same, no onion, add the tomato. And a Coke instead of a chocolate milkshake."

"And you, honey?" Hilda looked at Joe over her order pad.

Joe cleared his throat. "I will have the cottage cheese and fruit plate, a toasted cheese sandwich, and coffee."

Frank nearly jumped out of the booth in mock surprise. "What? What kind of an order is that? That's what my grandmother would order."

"I happen to like cottage cheese and fruit. Lay off, Frank."

Frank vigorously shook his head in mock dismay. All this was a ploy to try to get Robert to smile. But the kid only nervously fingered his napkin, looking more confused than ever.

Hilda left with the menus.

The front door opened, and four sorority girls came in and sat at a table far away from the "boys."

"Hey, there they are, Robert. Just for you!" Frank whispered. His close-set blue eyes twinkled. "Take your pick!"

Joe said through gritted teeth, "Settle down, Frank."

But Frank just kept a stupid grin on his face. He pulled out a small plastic comb and ran it through his wavy brown hair. "How do I look?" he asked Joe.

"You look like a scarecrow who thinks he's a movie star."

The waitress came back with drinks and Joe's cottage cheese and fruit plate. He laid aside the maraschino cherry to which Frank helped himself. "See, Robert, Joe is of the Jewish persuasion. That's why he ordered the cheese sandwich."

"Does that mean he's a vegetarian?" Robert sucked his milkshake through a paper straw.

Joe answered, "No. That means I follow Jewish dietary law, such as not eating meat and dairy products at the same meal."

"Why?"

Frank jumped in. "Something in the Bible about not boiling the calf in the mother cow's milk." He dumped an overflowing spoon of sugar into his Coke.

"Oh, that's sick."

Joe said, "It's in the Old Testament—"

"I'd rather not know." Robert watched Joe pour a generous amount of sugar into his coffee.

"They make the coffee too strong," Joe remarked as he stirred.

"Let me tell you why I asked you to have dinner with me and 'Curly' here." Frank motioned to Joe. "I think you two are related."

"Huh?" said Robert.

"When I saw you come into my studio for your first lesson, I said to myself, 'Is that kid some relation to Joe?' I swear. The two of you look like brothers." Frank waved his spoon around for emphasis.

Joe and Robert met eyes for the first time. Joe lit a cigarette to break his gaze.

"It's true! Look at the two of you. Same eyes, same shape of the head. Even your hands look alike." He grabbed their hands and turned them over palm-up to make his point.

"It's just a coincidence, Frank." Joe lost his smile and took back his hand. Despite wanting to dismiss Frank's observation, he knew he was right. Both of them had a bookish face, square jaw, and a straight, prominent nose. Both had wide-set brown eyes so dark they were almost black. Their eyebrows were smooth and slightly curved. However, Joe wore glasses, and Robert did not, and Joe had black hair; Robert's was a deep chestnut. Joe distinctly looked older, with a heavier beard stubble. Nevertheless, the similarity was there.

"Even seeing you two walk is incredible. This ain't a coincidence!"

A brief awkward pause hung in the air. Fortunately, the food arrived, and the three busied themselves. Joe and Robert ate quietly. Frank, who had no self-control, hummed the last theme of the Fidelio opera as he poured gallons of catsup on his French fries.

After gulping his burger in three bites, Frank said, "Robert, I want you to know that Joe is one hell of a clarinet player." He eyed the second half of Joe's toasted cheese sandwich.

"I am not, Frank."

"Oh, yes, you are. Don't believe anything he says, Robert. He and I played together in Ithaca. That's in New York. I was at Ithaca College, and he was at Cornell, and we started playing together in pick-up groups. Mind you, now. I played the trumpet. Not too many requests for a French horn player at a New Year Eve's party. We got quite a few pay gigs. But I have to say the other clarinet students at Ithaca didn't like that. Man, can this dude jam!"

"I wish I could get some pay gigs," Robert murmured.

"We played mainly wedding receptions, banquets, parties," said Joe. "Have you ever heard of klezmer music, Robert?"

"Uh, uh."

"It's a Jewish version of a dance band, with a smaller combination of instruments. There's a violin, clarinet, trumpet, saxophone—"

"Sometimes a drum set and a bass," Frank added.

"It has its origins in eastern Europe, Poland, Czechoslovakia, places like that. There's an exotic style to it if you can get past the excruciating intonation. Our band was a pretty loose group, a lot of show-offs trying to make the worst possible sounds. The music was so bad you'd almost want to wear earplugs. Ha!"

"That was the fun of it, Joe." Frank ate the lettuce leaf from Joe's plate.

Joe looked at Robert. The young freshman music student turned his head, and when he stared back, Joe's heart jumped. He felt a familiarity in Robert's eyes that unnerved him. All this was too uncomfortable to keep up, and they both looked away again.

As he licked salt off his fingers, Robert asked shyly, "So, are you in music here at I. U.?"

Joe laughed. His easy smile filled his whole face. "No. I'm in the doctoral program in the history department."

Frank pointed his fork at Joe. "Listen, Robert. If anybody should make a career in music, it's this guy. He should be hired to teach clarinet at this school. His aunt tried her best to talk him into getting a music degree. Hell, he could have played his way into Julliard without even taking his clarinet out of the case!"

"No, Frank."

Frank shook his head in mock exasperation. "Such a waste of talent."

Joe wadded up his napkin and put it on his empty plate. "I've told you before, Frank. I like music as a hobby. If I tried to pursue a degree in it, it'd be work and not fun. I just couldn't see myself locked up in a practice room for four years. I'm quite happy as a doctorate candidate in history." He looked at Robert. "I also teach a couple of freshman and sophomore classes as a TA."

When he saw the young man's confusion, he added, "That stands for teacher's assistant. That's what Mr. Oneida is when he gives horn lessons to students like you."

"He just doesn't get it, does he, Robert?" Frank's eyes were bright, almost manic.

"Huh?" asked Robert.

"So, my dear Joseph, let me educate you again on the facts of music." Frank put a condescending arm around his friend's shoulders. "By making music, you're giving yourself to the heavenly heights of man's most profound expression of life. Music is God's most noble gift to humankind. There is no truer, aesthetically beautiful endeavor than creating music. The angels—"

"Shut up, Frank." At once, Joe looked around to see if any other customer had heard him. He pushed off Frank's arm. Another cigarette found its place on his lip.

Frank put a fake hurt look on his narrow, pocked-marked face.

Joe changed the subject. "Where are you from, Robert?"

"Indianapolis." Looking at his cheeseburger, Robert thought about the calf and the milk again. He had no appetite. He touched his mouth with his napkin.

"Oh? Were you born here?" Joe crossed his ankles tightly under the table.

"No. I was born in Argentina."

"So, you must know Spanish."

"No. When I was three, we moved to the United States. My parents are originally from Germany, and they had immigrated to Buenos Aires right at the end of the war."

Frank perked up. "I didn't know that. So, your parents are German? How 'bout that? I bet you know German. What brought them to Indiana?"

"My dad got a job as an accountant with Allison Transmission in Indianapolis. They make transmissions for heavy-duty trucks."

"That's the big company, isn't it?" said Joe.

"Yeah."

"Does your family have any relatives back in Germany?" He didn't realize how tightly he had laced his fingers.

"He's asking because he's originally from Germany, too," Frank explained. "He knows German."

Robert spoke a little slower. "I don't know. My folks had never discussed anything when they lived in Germany. So, I guess we don't have any relatives. None that I know of."

"What year were you born?" Joe asked.

"1946."

The waitress came back and placed three checks on the table. "You gents let me know if you need anything else."

After inspecting his bill, Frank covertly slid it toward Joe's check. Joe glanced at it and put the two pieces of paper together along with Robert's. He hoped the other two would not see his slightly trembling fingers. He crushed his cigarette in the ashtray with more force than he wanted to.

"Well," he spoke bravely, "this has been fun. Too bad we all have to go back to being students again tomorrow." He slid out of the booth, followed by Frank and Robert.

"You want to leave a tip?" Joe asked Frank, annoyance in his voice.

Frank made a show of digging into his Salvation Army-bought pants pocket to fish out a nickel and two pennies. Robert added two quarters.

After Joe paid the checks, they went out to Joe's car, a 1963 powder-blue Ford Falcon. "My chariot awaits," he said. "Robert, I'll take you back to your dorm room. Frank, you get in the back."

****

Joe said, "Frank started to come apart shortly after that encounter with Robert. In December, he showed me a letter he had gotten from the music school dean, Dr. Wilfred Bain, saying that he'd lose his stipend to teach the undergrads if there was one more complaint against him."

Irene asked, "What was he doing?"

"I found out from Robert. I met him in a practice room at the music annex building. I was there practicing my clarinet, and he offered to accompany me. He's a dynamite pianist. He said Mr. Oneida, as he called him, acted like a maniac during his lessons by dancing around in his studio and singing, and he wouldn't let him play his study material. At other times, Frank would be completely despondent, not engaged in the lesson, not listening, giving no feedback or instruction.

"But Frank just wouldn't or couldn't take the hint. I'd seen him plenty of times when he'd be on cloud nine, and other times so miserable, he couldn't even get up out of a chair. I felt bad for him. He always acted strange sometimes when we were undergrads, but at I. U., he got worse. Maybe grad school was too stressful for him. But the last straw was his finances. At the end of the second semester, he was forced to drop out of the doctoral program because he was behind his university bills. And this was after I had given him money."

Grayson cocked his head. "What do you mean? How much money did you give him?"

Joe shrugged. "Enough for him to pay his rent for a couple of months and pay his utility bills. I bought food for him, too. Otherwise, I think he'd have been out on the street and starving."

"So, what happened to him?" asked Ruth.

"He's from Washington state, so I guess that's where he went after school was out."

Grayson handed the pictures back to Joe, who looked at them, thinking, *I will kill Frank the next time I see him if I see him. I will make him beg God to take his miserable soul out of his skinny body. If it hadn't been for him introducing me to that kid—*

Ruth interrupted his thoughts. "So, tell us more about this student. What's his name again?"

"Robert Stangarden. Whenever I saw him on campus, he was always in a hurry, too busy even to talk over a cup of coffee. If he weren't in the music library or rushing off to class, he'd be in a practice room with his French horn. Frank and I went to his concerts. He plays better than the first chair players. Robert is the most disciplined student I've ever seen. I don't know any doctoral candidate who works as hard as he does. At the few times I saw him, he didn't seem interested in hanging out with friends or socializing. He was all work and no play."

"So, how does he figure into what happened to you three days ago?" Grayson asked.

Suddenly, Joe lost his smile. "Everything went to hell at the end of finals week."

****

"Mr. Kaufmann, you don't have to do this."

Robert Stangarden carried a full box of record albums down the dormitory stairs. He followed Joe, who was carrying a lighter box of clothes. They walked out to Joe's car that he had parked illegally in the drop-off area in front of Reed Hall. Students and parents crowded the dormitory entrance, loading vehicles with a school year's worth of typical things college kids collected.

"My pleasure, Robert," Joe replied, putting the box in the back seat. "I'm only sorry I don't have a bigger car. What we need is my guardian's old Ford Super Deluxe station wagon. Now, that car could hold the contents of a whole house with room to spare!"

Robert stared forlornly at the other students as they laughed and talked and gave each other farewell hugs, apparently excited about having finished finals week and getting ready for a carefree summer. "Well, I don't have that much. I never had a lot of money to spend on extra stuff."

"I know what it's like to have to live on a shoestring," Joe replied. But that statement wasn't true. Joe never had to worry about undergraduate expenses because he had been awarded plenty of academic scholarships at Cornell University. And having a guardian who loved to spend money on his kids was a bonus. But it was his Aunt Mil, his guardian's older sister, who had bankrolled most of his college education. Grayson had told him that since his aunt was getting along in years, she had wanted her considerable investments to go to a worthy cause, namely, her nephew. Joe had hesitated about asking about Irene's financial needs. Training to become a doctor took enormous funds. He wasn't sure if Aunt Mil had contributed. She had been of the most "reasonable" opinion that girls were supposed to grow up to become wives and mothers, not be gallivanting around doing a man's job like being a doctor. Maybe Grayson and Ruth had helped her.

"Got enough room?" Joe asked as he and Robert climbed into the car.

Robert had to squeeze his knees together because Joe had moved up the front seat almost to the dashboard. "Yes. I'm fine."

The last day of finals week, May 15, was perfect. No rain, lots of sunshine, and in the upper 60's. They traveled north on State Road 37, past thickly wooded hills and cornfields sprouting late spring greenery.

Traffic became heavier the closer they got to Indianapolis.

After driving several miles west on Interstate 465 and then north of Weir Cook Airport, Joe followed Robert's directions into Pike Township, an old but steadily expanding community with rows of new houses on nearly every street. Joe took the off-ramp at West 56th Street. Heading east, he turned again on Guion Road and then south on 46th Street. The neighborhood was filled with modest homes and young sycamore trees lining the street.

Joe stopped the car in front of a two-story, white-sided house with a detached one-car garage. Faded yellow awnings topped the windows and the front door. There were no trees around the house, but some overgrown boxwood shrubs hid the bottom of the front windows. A lone lilac bush stood on the east side of the front yard.

"Is this it?" Joe asked, putting on the emergency brake after cutting the engine.

Robert looked out the car window. "Yeah. I see my dad has waited for me to trim the bushes."

"The lawn looks good."

"Too good. I'll probably mow it later today." Robert got out. He pulled a set of keys from his pants' pocket and started up the sidewalk. Joe opened the trunk.

The two men made several trips to carry all of Robert's things into the house. After the last box, Joe watched Robert lock the front door. "My mom called me a couple of weeks ago saying there had been a break-in at a house down the street." He gestured to the door. "Can't be too careful." He grabbed his French horn case and climbed the narrow wooden stairs, presumably to his room.

Joe looked about. The cozy living room held two overstuffed chairs, a pair of lacquered end tables, and a somewhat worn rolled-arm sofa. A 1950s-style television sat close to a wood-paneled wall. Next to it, a fireplace was blocked shut with a white painted board. Brown linen curtains framed the living room windows. A clear glass empty bowl with a heavy air-proof lid sat on the oblong red oak coffee table. Seeing all this, Joe could not help but think how his Grandma Nina and Aunt Mil would have turned up their cultured, blue-veined noses at this cheap, low-brow furniture.

Robert returned. He said, "Would you like something to drink? A Coke or something?" He pointed to the next room, which was the kitchen.

"Sure," Joe answered. "Where're your parents, Robert?"

Robert looked at his watch. "I think my dad is probably picking up my mom from school. She's a cafeteria worker at one of the elementary schools. I wrote them a letter last week telling them I had a friend who was helping me move back home for the summer."

"Your dad's still not at work?" Joe looked up at the ornately-carved cuckoo clock hanging next to the doorway to the kitchen. Soon, the bird would come out to announce the time: 2:30. Joe remembered how much he hated cuckoo clocks. They were just too annoying.

"Being Friday, he might get out early."

"Huh?" Joe asked. He noticed the cherry wood spinet piano positioned in another corner of the living room. An old-fashioned wind-up metronome sat on top alongside a brass piano lamp. He opened the keyboard lid and played a chord. He was surprised at the tone quality of this humble instrument. He ran a quick scale. "I'm impressed, Robert. This piano is in great shape. Did you take lessons on this piano?"

"Yeah. When I was four, my mom started me. She loves music. I guess that's where I got my interest in it." Robert opened the piano bench to show his torn, dog-eared piano books. "It's all here."

"I think I recognize some of these books." Joe flipped through the music. "I took piano lessons, too, but I was eight when I started." He put the music back and followed Robert into the large, brightly lit kitchen. Smelling bread dough and cinnamon, he immediately liked this room. It boasted a Westinghouse refrigerator, turquoise metal cabinets, and a built-in wall pantry. The countertops were laden with a ceramic canister set, a toaster, and a fat cookie jar in the shape of a pig. A rack of serious-looking knives hung on the wall next to a wall calendar displaying a flower garden scene for May.

Joe sat at the kitchen table. He fiddled with the pig-shaped plastic salt and pepper shakers.

Robert looked inside the fridge. "Coke okay?"

"Sure." Joe took two paper napkins from a small napkin tray.

While Joe opened and poured the soda pop, Robert took out four walnut shortbread cookies from the cookie jar. The two quietly drank their Cokes and munched the cookies.

"These are good," Joe remarked.

"My mom is a wonderful cook." Robert beamed. "I love everything she makes."

"She must be quite the professional with all the equipment in this kitchen." He suddenly thought of Rose, the Pierce family cook who had made delicious meals for him as a child. She would have approved of this kitchen. "What's her specialty?" Joe studied his cookie, his brows knitted.

"I think baking is what she loves to do most. You know, pies, cakes, cookies."

"Robert, where did she get the recipe for these cookies?" Joe sat straighter in his chair, now frowning.

"I dunno. She has lots of cookbooks, and some of them are in German. 'From the old country' she likes to say." Robert took another swig of Coke. "Why do you ask? Is there something wrong?"

Joe hesitated, savoring the cookie. For an inexplicable reason, this cookie tasted familiar. "No, nothing's wrong. I guess I'm feeling a little déjà vu."

Robert gave a laugh. "I get that, too, sometimes but not from eating cookies."

Joe dismissed the curious sensation and looked out through the sliding glass doors. He observed the small backyard, devoid of trees and surrounded by a somewhat dilapidated wooden fence. A beat-up outdoor grill stood on a concrete patio, along with two lawn chairs and a metal patio table. A garden hose curled around a large black pot filled with meager petunias.

To Joe, this was a typical middle-class home, unremarkable but comfortable. He imagined a hard-working father, dedicated to his job and family, sitting on the couch with a newspaper and the TV set blaring the CBS evening news with Walter Cronkite. In the kitchen, a happy, nurturing mother who loved to cook, stirring a big pot of beef stew. She made hearty meals, kept her men in clean, well-mended clothes, and made sure the house was spotless (which it was). Inwardly, Joe contemplated how tranquil, how untroubled this home was. On this quiet street in an ordinary neighborhood in a typical Midwestern city, all that was missing was the white picket fence and the family dog.

They heard a muffled bang outside. Robert got up at once. "They're home," he said and went to the utility room off the kitchen.

Joe rose slowly. Déjà vu engulfed his mind again, but now he felt a sense of increasing fear as well. Something was very wrong. He waited in the kitchen.

The woman came first carrying a full grocery bag. The man was on her heels, carrying two more bags.

"Joe, I'd like you to meet my—"

Upon seeing Joe, the woman dropped her bag. Something broke inside it. Her hands flew to her face, and she gasped.

For less than a second, Joe saw shock in the man's eyes as he met them, but immediately that shock turned into threatening anger.

Joe couldn't swallow. He felt goosebumps on his scalp, and he could barely see. Without realizing it, his feet moved him out of that kitchen and through the living room. He pulled and pushed and rattled the doorknob. His fingers were so slippery he couldn't grasp on the deadbolt above it. He couldn't escape!

"Mr. Kaufmann, what's wrong?" Robert's voice cut through his terror.

There were shouts and wails from the kitchen.

Joe felt he was suffocating. He had to get that door open. He almost heard the gunshots. He almost saw the barbed wire.

Fingers finally turned the deadbolt, and Joe ran like the little six-year-boy he used to be.

****

Joe's shoulders trembled. "I had no idea. I had no idea."

Unaware how tightly his aching arms held his stomach, Joe rocked back and forth. "It was them. It was them!"

"Who, Joe? Who were they?" Grayson demanded.

Joe put his face in his hands. Even as he desperately wanted not to cry, the roar erupted from his whole body. "Nazis! They were those Nazis!"

"What?" burst the collective shout.

Joe stood and paced. He took off his glasses and rubbed his face vigorously, then put them back on. "His parents . . . I knew them from Buchenwald." He smoked furiously. "I just had to get out of that house as fast as I could. But Robert had locked the front door, and I was trapped. There was all this screaming and commotion from the kitchen. Robert kept asking me what was wrong. I kept pulling the doorknob, trying to get the damn door open. Then Robert must have unlocked the deadbolt, and I ran to my car. Then I tore out of that neighborhood. I hit a curb, and as fast as I was going, I nearly hit a tree. I was so upset. Since I didn't know Indianapolis very well, I got lost. I couldn't find a major freeway for miles. Finally, once I was on State Road 37, I gunned it all the way back to Bloomington. I almost had a wreck."

"Are you sure you knew who they were?" Grayson asked in disbelief.

"Yes, Grayson. You don't understand! I was scared out of my mind. I had to get out of there!"

Grayson said, "Son, you're not making any sense about all this. Can you start at the beginning, so we understand how you knew these people from Buchenwald?"

Joe closed his eyes, trying to get hold of himself. He took a straight-backed chair from a corner and sat. "I thought I would never have to talk about this. It was in the past, and it was over." He beat his fists on his knees, mindless of his injured wrists. "Why did I take that kid home?"

Ruth shook her head. "But you would not have known about his parents. You can't blame yourself for that." She frowned in confusion. "How are you so sure you knew these people from Buchenwald?"

He replied through clenched jaws, "You don't forget the face of the woman who kept you alive." He moved back to the armchair, taking the ashtray.

Irene said, "Joe, will you please explain all this? I am completely lost!"

"All right. Let me tell the story in my own way." He met Grayson's eyes. "This is something even you don't know about, Grayson. I never talked about it because I didn't want to drudge up any more memories."

He paused to organize his thoughts. "It started in June 1944. My mother and father and I were hiding in an attic in Berlin. I was six at the time. We were discovered by the German police and put on a train. We ended up at Buchenwald. My mother was taken away almost immediately by an SS officer. My father and I had to walk with the other prisoners to this nasty place in the back of the camp. There was barbed wire around these rows and rows of long shacks. The smell was so bad it was impossible to breathe. The guards took my father away for a while. I was shocked to see him when he came back. His hair had been shaved off completely, and he was bleeding from some cuts, I suppose, from the razor blade they used on him.

"A few days later, my father and I went out of the barrack during the night. A guard took us to a building near the big one at the camp entrance, which I believe was the headquarters. We went to a side door, and an overweight woman was there. She had food for us. We hadn't eaten since we had arrived at Buchenwald. We had to eat fast, and I remember how good it tasted. She gave us food every night through the rest of the year and into the early spring of 1945. My father was put to work in the kitchen, and he said she was the head cook for the SS officers. She always gave him food to hide in his pants and bring back for us to eat later. He made me crawl into a hole he had dug under a bunker, and there he gave me the food. That's where I hid during the day."

Grayson said, "This was the dirt hole I had found you in when my evac hospital came to liberate Buchenwald in April 1945. You never told me that it was your father who had put you there."

Joe turned his head away.

"So, tell us more about this couple," said Irene.

Joe paused, reflecting on the scene. "Many times, when we were at the back of that mess hall, a fat man was with her. He was her husband. I had recognized him from when we first arrived. He had been sitting at a table with prisoners lined up in front of him. He took down information about them in a big green ledger book. He was a civilian because he didn't wear a uniform. But he was still a Nazi because he wore a swastika armband."

"Joe, this is too incredible!" said Grayson. With agitation, he dug into his pants pocket for his pipe and tobacco pouch.

"I will never forget their faces at the camp." Joe closed his eyes. "I remember it got icy cold that winter. The snow was up to my waist, and my father had to carry me. The woman would be waiting with a kettle that had a lid on it. When she took it off, I remember seeing the steam rising from the noodles, beans, or the potatoes. Sometimes, it was cabbage with corned beef. It smelled wonderful! And she always had a treat for me, like those cookies Robert gave me in his kitchen." His mouth began to water. A moment passed, and he opened his eyes. "Almost every time we were there for the food, my father went off a little way with the woman while I was eating. I couldn't hear what they were talking about. When I asked him later, he wouldn't tell me.

"Eventually, the other prisoners figured out why we left the barrack at night. And they didn't like it that we got extra food to eat. It became harder to hide it. Everybody was so hungry they would have torn us apart to get it." Joe saw in his mind's eye the kapos, the Polish Jews in charge of the barrack, threatening his father, raising their fists at him. "But as soon as they tried to come near us, the Nazi guards would drive them away. I don't why. Usually, they would just stand around and laugh, watching the inmates fight over an apple core or a piece of moldy bread."

Joe held his right arm up, resting his elbow on the arm of the chair. "In the spring, she and that man, her husband, stopped coming right before all the Nazis left. I remember there was still snow on the ground, but it was getting warmer. So, my father and I began to starve, just like everyone else."

Grayson puffed furiously. "Joe, why did that woman give food to you and your father?"

Joe shook his head. "I don't know. She seemed worried about us. Her husband was always looking around, pushing us to eat faster." He paused, remembering. "That man. I was terrified of him. He looked so angry I thought he would attack my father like one of those police dogs. And when the woman and my father walked away to talk, I could barely eat my food with this brute staring at me. Even with it being dark, I will never forget seeing the absolute hate in his eyes."

Joe was unaware that he was clutching the arms of the chair where he sat.

"What happened to your mother?" Ruth asked softly.

Joe felt a wave of sadness. "I don't know. I never saw her again after that SS officer took her away."

"I'm so sorry, Joe."

Pointing his finger, Joe said, "That woman and her husband were the couple I saw in Robert's house. They were Robert's parents."

Ruth asked, "How did they get from Germany to the U. S.? Where did they go after the war?"

"I have no idea." Joe shrugged. "All I know is my father said one day that he wasn't working in the kitchen anymore. They must have left. In my research, I learned that German refugees by the thousands fled to South America, particularly to Argentina. Then some went on to the States. Maybe that's how they got here. Robert did say he was born in Buenos Aires."

"How did this man get a job? What does he do for a living?" asked Grayson.

"Robert said his dad works for Allison Transmission as an accountant, and his mother is a cook at one of the elementary schools in one of the townships."

Grayson thoughtfully laid his pipe in the ashtray on the coffee table. "This is a fantastic story, Joe. How could they have managed to hide who they truly were and get American citizenship and have social security numbers and have jobs and rear a kid like any other American family? What were their names again?"

Joe had to think hard. "I think I remember her name was Matilda Steghausen. I don't remember the first name of that Nazi husband."

Irene said, "But Robert's last name is—"

"Stangarden. They had to have changed their names, which makes sense if they were trying to hide the fact that they had been Nazis."

Grayson stood. He slowly walked around the living room, hands in his pockets. "Joe, do you realize what you are accusing these people of?"

Joe replied, "I know who I saw, Grayson. I wouldn't have forgotten the face of someone who had given me food to stay alive. Or her husband."

Grayson's face was pensive as he folded his arms.

Irene spoke. "So, seeing that couple at that house is why you started reading about Germany?"

"Yes." Joe put out his smoke. "It's just that the more I read and studied, the more I got upset, and things went downhill from there."

Grayson said, "So, you came back to Bloomington after taking this Robert kid home, and that would have been the third or fourth week of May?"

"Third week."

"And you started reading all these books on German history." He motioned to the books against the wall. "And you began getting out of sorts."

Joe was silent.

"And now it's the end of June. So, you've been stewing about this for more than a month. You put yourself back in that black hole of depression. Why didn't you call somebody? Why didn't you at least call Irene? Why didn't you call me? No, you didn't do that. Instead, you decided to hurt yourself."

Joe looked at his guardian with filled eyes. He felt like the seven-year-old boy he used to be when trying to explain his behavior—the nightmares, the bedwetting, the hoarding of empty vegetable cans in his closet for fear of going hungry. "I did it because I got scared again. Just like before when I . . . I ran away when I was fifteen. And when I was in Havensbrook. Remember when we first arrived at that psyche hospital, and you checked me in, and we sat in the dayroom? I told you how frightened I was. I didn't want to face those memories of the camp again."

Grayson's deep voice was soft. "Yes, I remember."

"I knew I was going to have to face it again when I was supposed to start psychotherapy. I had to talk about it with that psychiatrist, Dr. Montgomery. And I got so angry at him and with you. I told you how much I hated being alive. I should have died like everyone else at the camp. And I tried to be dead!"

Joe quickly wiped his damp cheeks. "But eventually I got over it. I got past it."

"And you went on to become valedictorian of your high school and graduate summa cum laude from an Ivy League school and look where you're at today. A doctoral student at a prestigious university working on your dissertation."

Joe shook his head once. "But now, I'm on my knees again. That old, stinking terror came back when I saw that couple. I-I just couldn't believe it when I saw them. I started having nightmares again. So, I bought sleeping pills. But I couldn't stay asleep. I started taking more, but they didn't work. I didn't want to eat. I stopped doing everyday things like paying the bills and answering the phone. Yeah, I know what you're thinking, Grayson. It's the depression again. I know that. I'm an adult now, and I understand what's happening.

"But I just couldn't be rational about all this. I was freakin' out, thinking that Robert's dad, this Steghausen character, would come after me. He could kill me. He's a Nazi. That's what Nazis do!"

"Joe, think about this," Grayson said. "First of all, how did that man recognize you? You were just a child in the camp."

Joe took a deep breath, steeling himself. "I look exactly like my father." He trembled. Seeing his image, seeing his father in the bathroom mirror had been the breaking point.

An almost imperceptible look of understanding passed over Grayson's face. Indeed, he had seen Joe's father lying dead next to a barbed-wire fence. But he pressed on. "Why would he come after you? Not only would he be caught, but he'd also expose himself as a Nazi. He and his wife would risk being deported."

"Grayson, you don't get it. The Nazis were brainwashed to exterminate the Jews. That was their mentality. That was the German culture. He wouldn't have cared. He'd kill me so that I wouldn't turn him in to the authorities. Not that they would have believed me. I'm telling you, Grayson, I'm scared out of my mind. Seeing that couple in that house brought me back to that hellhole. I can't live with it anymore!"

His body shaking uncontrollably, Joe lit another cigarette, barely able to strike the match with unsteady hands. The dressing on his right wrist started to show blood. "It's no use, Grayson, putting on this charade of living. I have an albatross, a ball and chain, a load of bricks on my back that's crushing me! Am I to live my life with memories I will never come to terms with? When I look over my shoulder, must I keep watching for another Nazi to pop out of nowhere? I haven't stopped thinking about that Steghausen bastard. I have this, this irrational premonition that he's going to try to kill me. If Robert tells him who I am and where I live, I'm dead. When he saw me in that kitchen, he would have shot me if he had had a Luger in his hand. I saw it in his eyes. The hatred was the same as what I saw in those camp guards. And that miserable S. O. B. lives only seventy miles away from me.

"I just wanted to make the fear go away. I'm tired of being afraid. The only way to stop this was to end my life. There. I admit it."

A tense silence held the room. Joe let his breath go out with exhaustion.

Irene noticed his wrist. "Joe, you're bleeding. I'll get some Band-Aids from the bathroom. Do you have any gauze?"

"I dunno. I'm tired. Can we stop this interrogation? I want to lie down for a while."

Grayson stood. "Okay. I think we've had enough conversation for now. Ruth, will you help Irene with Joe's wrist?"

In the bathroom with Joe sitting on the toilet lid, Irene and Ruth covered the bloody dressing with inadequate bandages as best they could. Irene said, "Joe, this isn't going to work. We need to go to the drugstore to get some proper bandages. Ruth, will you go with me?"

Ruth answered, "Of course. Let's get you into bed, Joe."

Once in his freshly made bed, Irene closed the door. While she and Ruth were off to the drugstore, Grayson sat in the living room and gave in to his presentiment.

Sitting at the kitchen table while Ruth and Irene prepared the evening meal, Grayson stared hard at his ward. "Joe, what do you want to do now?"

Joe sat across from him, slumped as if he was still exhausted after the three-hour nap. "I know what my gut tells me. I want to get away from here. I know it's a crazy feeling but—"

"No, it's not crazy. I think it's a reasonable reaction to these circumstances." Grayson played with the saltshaker on the table. "Come back home to Ithaca, Joe. Get your affairs done here in Bloomington, pay your bills, and your rent for the next couple of months. Go to the post office to forward your mail."

"That's just running away again, Grayson."

"Well, so be it."

Joe inhaled, returning his guardian's steely gaze. "You just want to keep an eye on me."

"Okay. Yes. Do you think you can be trusted to stay here alone in your apartment and not try to hurt yourself again?"

Joe did not answer.

Ruth spoke as she took the pot of spaghetti off the stove and drained the water in the sink. "Think of it as a break from your dissertation, Joe. You've been under so much pressure for the past two years working on your Ph.D. You've never taken a vacation, have you?"

"I'd be far away from that Nazi pig." Joe watched Irene set the table.

Startled at his response, Ruth replied, "Umm, yes. But wouldn't that give you some peace of mind? You could relax at the house for a while and get some rest. Maybe take some walks in the state parks." She put the pasta in a large glass bowl and put it on the table.

Grayson added, "That's a wonderful idea, Ruth. How about some hiking, Joe? We've not done that in ages. I need the exercise." He patted his burgeoning midsection.

Irene put out a water pitcher, "I'll help you get your things packed and close the apartment, Joe, although we would need to do it right away. I've got to get back to Indianapolis. My supervisor is expecting me back at work on Monday." She opened the refrigerator. "Do you have any Parmesan cheese?"

Joe could not calm his quivering stomach. Looking at dinner placed in front of him made him nauseous. Ignoring Irene's question, he said, "I'll have to contact my advisor, Dr. Reed. I have to report every couple of months."

Grayson dipped into the steaming bowl of spaghetti sauce. "Would that be a problem? Tell him the truth that you are taking a break for a month or two to clear your head. Surely, he'll understand. How many years do you have left to get your dissertation finished?"

"Four. I'm ahead of schedule. You know it's not very challenging work." Joe thought. "What about my . . .?" He held out his thickly bandaged arm.

"Do I need to remind you that I'm a surgeon? I know how to take out stitches. I've been doing it for over thirty years!" He gestured to Ruth. "And if I'm too busy, your stepmother can do it. Here's some salad." He put a bottle of French dressing next to Joe's salad bowl.

Joe stared at his plate as Ruth put the pasta on it. "So, what happens when the summer is over?"

Grayson replied, "Can't you continue working on your dissertation in Ithaca? Other doctoral students live somewhere else while working on theirs, don't they? They have families, jobs."

"Well, yes. I'd have to coordinate this with my advisor."

"Okay, then. It's settled." Grayson pushed Joe's plate closer to him. "Now, let's say grace."

****

The next day, a somewhat relieved guardian and stepmother drove their rental car to Indianapolis to take a plane back to Ithaca. Irene helped Joe pack his suitcases and close the apartment. To avoid the obvious questions about his bandaged wrists and arm, Joe called his advisor, Dr. Alfred Reed, rather than meeting him in person. Joe promised to see him in the fall to discuss the progress on his dissertation. However, he got into a heated conversation with Irene about when this would happen. "You'll have to come back to Bloomington sooner or later," she said. "You don't have to be here for more than a day or two. I'll even come down from Indianapolis and stay with you if you want."

Joe replied, "Oh, all right. I never dreamed this would happen."

Irene rubbed his shoulder and kissed his cheek.

CHAPTER SIX

With his hair freshly cut and his beard shaved off almost to the point of skimming the first and second layers of skin (the barber in Bloomington had been a guy from some Middle East country and very exuberant about his job), Joe started for Ithaca. His arm and wrists were still snugly wrapped, but his wounds were beginning to itch. Irene had left that morning to go back to her job at Marion County General Hospital with a few leftover codeine capsules still hidden in her purse.

His mind cleared of all the sleeping pills and pain meds, Joe was ready for the lengthy, 700-mile trip. As he turned onto North State Road 37 to Indianapolis, he forced himself not to think about the terrible incident with Robert's parents. He drove onto Interstate East 465 to pick up I-70 for Dayton, Ohio, staying clear of town's west side. He only stopped once for gas and an overnight stay in a motel in Erie, Pennsylvania.

The next day he climbed out of his car in the driveway of the Pierce's quiescent, two-story brick home in Ithaca, New York. Being the middle of the afternoon, he was not surprised that the house was empty, save for little Blueberry, who had yet to appear. Grayson and Ruth would most likely be in their perspective offices seeing patients.

He dropped his luggage at the foot of the stairs and collapsed in the closest chair in the living room. He hadn't the energy to carry his things upstairs to his old room. Staring at the inert fireplace, kept clean so thoroughly by Ruth, he closed his eyes.

He heard a short "purrumph" and felt tiny pressure points on his thighs with needle-sharp claws digging into his jeans. Blueberry wanted attention. Joe surmised she was lonely during the day when the oversized, two-legged "cats" were gone for so long. Joe rubbed and stroked her head and let his tears flood his eyes.

All he could feel was utter, bottomless sadness. His life had halted at the edge of an unforeseen, dangerous precipice. Up until now, it had been filled with academic pursuits in the time-worn, limestone buildings on the Indiana University campus. Joe had sat in cavernous lecture halls taking notes from world-famous historians and answering relentless questions from professors who looked as ancient and moss-covered as the campus buildings. But now the old Satan of his childhood had appeared again, still alive and still terrifying.

As he sat with Blueberry's placid green eyes staring up at him, he let his mind stumble back to the nightmarish place he had been able to push aside for so many years: Buchenwald. Inhaling deeply, he felt hoary, cold fingers tightening around his neck, choking him, squeezing his soul out of his body. Joe imagined himself being tossed on top of one of the countless piles of naked, stinking corpses. The devil would laugh—another dead Jew for the oven's fire that never burned out. And that abominable fiend wore a swastika armband.

Suddenly, his whole body jerked, and he opened his eyes. Blueberry leaped off his lap and headed straight for the fuzzy toy mouse lying next to the ottoman. Joe heard the rosewood clock with the Roman numerals ticking patiently on the mantle above the fireplace. He looked about the living room. Yellow, orange, and red pillows lay neatly on the Tudor-styled sofa. The drop-leaf mahogany coffee table with the cat's paw legs stood in front of it. On top of it was an array of magazines placed in perfect symmetry. Next to them stood a pink ceramic vase filled with fresh-cut yellow and red carnations that were most likely purchased at a local flower shop. The slick wooden floor gleamed with a blue, red, and yellow-striped accent rug in the middle. The room was as relucent and joyful as the June sun shining through the spotless picture window. But Joe could not appreciate the ambiance. The cheerful room seemed ironic.

Although knowing he should eat something, he decided to go upstairs to put away his clothes instead. He trudged up the polished black walnut steps. His bedroom waited for him like an old schoolmate. It looked quite different from when he had left it eight years ago when he moved out to live in an apartment near Cornell

University. Instead of wayward socks attempting to flee opened dresser drawers, and girlie magazines pressed securely between the mattress and box springs, now it was immaculate and as annoyingly pristine as a guest bedroom—a far cry from the gloomy, airless bedroom in Bloomington, Indiana. Joe set down his suitcases and closed the door.

Seeing a half angle of his body in the mirror that hung over his freshly dusted dresser, he slowly walked to it. He stared at his reflection. He hadn't looked at his face since he had broken the medicine cabinet mirror. The mustache made him look older. But even with that and his black, brow-rimmed glasses, the similarity was there—the square shape of his face, the smooth, gently arched brows, the well-proportioned straight nose, the generous lips, the firm chin, the five o'clock shadow. His father gazed back at him with gentle, liquid brown eyes. Joe would never be able to get away from this reflection of his father.

He knew the couple in that house in Indianapolis had recognized not him but his father.

Joe moved away from the dresser. With tears slipping down his cheeks, he pulled down the window shades of the bright, too-optimistic windows. Without taking off his shoes, he rolled into his double bed with its blue-green plaid bedspread laid out so perfectly. He sobbed.

****

"Fix a plate for Joe, please," Grayson said to Ruth as they stood at the kitchen counter. "I'll take it up and try to get him out of his funk."

After a worried look to her husband, Ruth prepared a ham salad sandwich, pickles, corn chips, and a glass of iced tea. Grayson added a set of silverware and a paper napkin to the tray and left to go up to Joe's room. His hard-set mouth reflected his determined thoughts.

Ruth knew immediately that her stepson was sliding like down a steep, rock-strewn hiking trail. Perhaps that eleven-hour trip from Bloomington gave him too much time to think about what had happened with that kid in Indianapolis. She sat at the kitchen table in front of her untouched plate, straining her ears to hear something, anything. She wiped clammy palms on the edge of the tablecloth, forgetting her napkin. Whenever problems arose with Joe or his sister,

Irene, she had always felt useless. Her only way to help them had been through Grayson. But as hard as he had tried to include her in his children's affairs, the nagging sense of interfering kept her emotionally apart from them. For that, she had loathed herself. She had felt that even when she had been sitting in Joe's apartment last week.

Irene had been a lost cause. Since meeting Grayson's daughter when she was sixteen, their relationship had been cool at best and strained at worst. Ruth never confronted her; she never challenged that defensive, calloused personality to examine what was underneath, although she had an astute idea. Having observed the old women in the Pierce mansion, Grayson's mother, Nina Cassandra, and his older sister, Mildred, she had deduced that Irene had been abused as a child. She saw it in Irene's defensive body language when she was around the malicious grandmother and the brick-hard aunt. She could scarcely imagine Irene growing up with such emotional cruelty. Sometimes Ruth would play out conversations in her head, talking to Grayson about her observations of Irene's deeply scarred psyche. But that was all it was—conversations in her head.

Ruth herself had suffered unkind words from them when she had been introduced to the family. Grayson had apologetically referred to them as the "Spanish Inquisition." It had been so much of a noxious situation that she had almost regretted marrying into this severely dysfunctional family.

But that trip to the grocery store while in Indiana had seemed to soften their estranged relationship. How unfortunate, however, that it took a suicide attempt by Joe to break the ice.

Grayson trudged slowly down the stairs without the meal tray. Looking defeated, he sat at the kitchen table and began his supper.

"Well? How is he?" Ruth asked.

Grayson shook his head. "He says he's just tired." He glanced at Ruth, bags showing under his sad, deep-set eyes. "I'll go back up a little later."

They ate quietly.

"He's depressed again, isn't he?"

Grayson nodded and sighed. "He's had some time to process what happened in his apartment, and he's back in that black hole again. I'm afraid I have to pull him out . . . one more time."

Ruth reached over. They held hands tightly.

"He's stubborn. I'll need to come up with a better plan to get him out of this." Grayson pushed his plate away.

CHAPTER SEVEN

Grayson decided he and Joe would explore the Robert H. Treman State Park. Located in and around Ithaca, the park was an easy twenty-minute drive from the Pierce home. However, they had not visited it in years, and Grayson wanted to see some new trees and creek beds. Joe only shrugged with indifference as he swung his backpack and hiking boots into the back of Grayson's brand new 1964 wood-paneled Country Squire Ford station wagon.

After parking at the entrance, the two "saddled up" with their packs and walking sticks and headed out on a treacherous, downhill trail that led to a magnificent waterfall called "Lucifer Falls." Since it was a hot July afternoon, they frequently stopped to swig water from their thermoses. A few other hikers passed them with youthful ease.

"Are we there yet?" Joe whined, wiping sweat from his forehead.

Grayson turned back to face him. "There yet? Where's 'there?' We've only been out here forty-five minutes. What's the matter? You getting tired already?" Grayson's face was flush, his breathing hard.

Joe didn't answer. He knew Grayson would only dismiss him and press on.

Once they arrived at the edge of the bottle-green pond, Joe shed his backpack and dropped his walking stick. "Grayson, let's stop and rest here," Joe said, lowering himself on a damp, uncomfortable ash log.

"Okay." His guardian almost collapsed next to him. "Whew! This hiking is hard work if you haven't done it in a while." He patted his perspiring neck and his high forehead with a red bandana. "We should come out here more often to get ourselves back in shape." He removed his Cornell University baseball cap and waved it in front of his face.

Joe said, "There're a lot of state parks around Bloomington. The most popular one is Brown County. I haven't been there yet. I hear it's beautiful. Lots of trails and lakes."

"Isn't it near that little tourist village, Nashville?"

"Uh, huh. Not a place to go to during the holidays. That town gets packed with visitors from all over." Joe rubbed his shirt sleeves carefully.

"Are your scars itching?" Grayson asked. "When we get back, I'll look at them."

Joe didn't like that plan. He didn't want any attention given to his arm and wrists. Feeling embarrassed, he lowered his eyes.

As if not seeing his ward's reaction, Grayson went on. "Yes, it's hot out here today. If the wind picks up, we might get some spray from the waterfall. Sure is loud enough." He eyed Joe. "Do you remember when we took that two-week camping trip when you were little? We went to Niagara Falls?"

Joe remained quiet. He slapped an insect on his neck.

"We went to Taughannock Falls State Park and the Finger Lakes. I think maybe even Cayuga Lake." Grayson looked up at the dense tree canopy. "That was a good trip."

Joe looked at him. "What? That was a horrible trip! I have bad memories of it."

"Well, we had some stressful times along the way. But we had fun, too. I taught you how to speak English, and you showed me how well you knew how to read and write in German. And remember the band concert in Rochester at that fall festival? That was your first experience of listening to a live concert. You positively loved it. I think that was the first time I saw how happy you were. You were practically giddy." Grayson grinned. "You know, I think we still have that stuffed giraffe I bought for you from one of the street vendors."

"You do?"

"I think it's in an old toy box in the basement at the mansion. Irene's toys are still in there, too."

"Why would you keep that old stuff?"

Grayson's smile broadened his face. "Sentimental value. Maybe you'll give those toys to your children."

Fat chance. Joe thought. "Grayson, I have the suspicion you had something else in mind coming out here. I think you're setting me up for something I'm not going to want to hear."

Grayson became somber. "You know me pretty well, son." He put his cap back on and put his elbows on the knees of his very long legs. Overhead, Canadian geese honked their way across the pale sky.

Joe slid down to sit in the muddy grass, crushing a few wild mushrooms. He took out his thermos to drink some water. He would not meet Grayson's penetrating eyes.

"Joe, I think you should go back into therapy."

Joe wiped his mouth. He turned down his mouth and stared out into the messy underbrush of the woods.

Grayson continued. "This would be a good time. Here in Ithaca, there's no pressure on you. By that, I mean you've put your dissertation on hold. Ruth and I will give you space to do what you want. Just hang around, sleep as much as you want, eat your way through the refrigerator. Perhaps you can work at the Ithaca library shelving some books. That would get you out of the house and give you something to do. I think old Mrs. Potts is still there. She'd loved to have you back. Maybe you can stop by the mansion and visit your Aunt Mil and . . ."

Joe gave Grayson a look of "you've got to be kidding."

"Or not. I didn't get a chance to tell you Aunt Elvie's living in a nursing home in Rochester. That's where one of her daughters, Phoebe, lives with her husband. She has breast cancer, so Phoebe wants her close. She had a mastectomy last November. I should have told you and Irene about her over Christmas. Aunt Elvie has had some other health problems, also. You may want to take a drive over there to see her. She might not recognize you. She has dementia."

"No, I didn't know, Grayson." Joe cringed. Aunt Elvie was Gramma Nina's sister-in-law by marriage and had moved in the Pierce mansion after her husband had died. He remembered her as a sweet but clueless member of the Pierce household. He would have an obligation to see her, although it would be a not-so-happy visit.

"How long would I stay here . . . with you and Ruth babysitting me?"

Grayson took a deep breath and looked toward the pond. The white, foamy Lucifer waterfall crashed with a powerful roar. "As long as you like. When you're up to it, you can pick up where you left off on your dissertation. Remember, we talked about this at your apartment. I'm sure your advisor will work with you. Besides, living here in Ithaca, you're close to New York City, and you can do your research in all the big libraries down there. And there's even Washington, D. C., and Philadelphia. Just think how much research you can get done using those libraries as well, Joe."

Grayson absently moved a stick around in the dead leaves. "Joe, your stepmother and I are very concerned about your health, physically and mentally."

Joe picked up a small stone and angrily threw it.

Grayson spoke quickly. "Son, you need to face facts. You got so spooked seeing that couple in Indianapolis that you tried to kill yourself. If Irene hadn't checked up on you, you could have died, and Lord knows how long before someone would have missed you. With classes out for the summer, no one would have expected you to be somewhere. I wished you would have called me. I'd have been there in a heartbeat. I told you that back at your apartment."

"I'm a big boy now, Grayson. I can take care of myself."

"Really?"

Joe turned his head away. He put a hand on his breast pocket, reaching for the pack of cigarettes he had left in the station wagon. "Grayson, I don't want to talk about this. You said staying here in Ithaca will give me a break."

"Yes, but what I am also saying is seeing a psychiatrist will help you to deal with what happened in Bloomington. Maybe we can look up Dr. Montgomery. I can make a referral. I'll even pay the bill. Even if he is a child psychiatrist, he might take you because he knows your—"

"Are you kidding, Grayson? He'll just stir up those, those bad memories again, and I'll right back in the hospital!"

"Maybe not this time. You're an adult now. You even said yourself that you have a better understanding of how to handle this."

"This is bullshit."

Grayson suddenly grabbed Joe's T-shirt and pulled him close. "What else would you have me do, Joe? Give in to your plan to destroy yourself? Back at the apartment, you mentioned hanging yourself. I have to take that seriously."

Joe pulled off Grayson's hand and scooted a few inches away. "So, you're going to watch me twenty-four hours a day?"

"If I have to. I know what you do. You stop eating, you don't sleep, and you don't take care of yourself. You just give up. This is history repeating itself. I'm surprised you were even willing to come out here today. What you have is called clinical depression. You had it when you were seven and again when you were fourteen. Do I need to remind you that you nearly killed yourself on both occasions? Depression is difficult to treat. There's no decent medication for it, and it is lethal. People die from it. They commit suicide! That's why you need treatment. You need to see a psychiatrist."

"You don't know what you're asking me to do—"

"Of course, I know what I'm asking you to do!" Grayson grabbed Joe's shoulders to turn toward him, his eyes blazing. "God blast it to hell! I've had it with you, boy! I'll do anything to keep you alive. Do you understand? Do you?"

Joe shook himself loose. He rose, grabbed his stick and backpack, and began walking away from the pond. Grayson hurried to catch up. After several hundred yards, they stopped in a treeless field. A cloud of gnats hovered, forcing them to move on to the next grove of trees. They stopped again.

Grayson struggled to catch his breath in his exasperation. "Joe, I don't care who that guy was you saw in that kid's house there in Indianapolis. There's nothing to be afraid of. He can't touch you. But as always, you're blowing this all out of proportion. Don't think that the Nazis are going to get you. That thinking is just like what you did when you were seven years old!" Grayson put his big hands on Joe's shoulders. "You're not in any danger. Get that notion out of your head!"

Willing himself to relax, he went on in a kinder voice. "Son, you're so close to finishing your doctorate. You have history books to write, future students to teach, a full life to live because you've got the smarts to make it happen. And there's probably a future wife out there waiting for you. I've been so proud of you, Joe, I just want to burst." Grayson tapped his walking stick on the ground. "God wants you to live. He has a purpose for you, not just to survive but also to make a life for yourself.

"You had an unfortunate setback. A bad case of circumstances nobody could have foreseen. Remember what Dr. Montgomery said? Focus on what's meaningful to you, what gives you joy, like playing your clarinet, doing research, going hiking."

"Yet, you want me to see a psychiatrist."

"Yes, I do. You have to talk with a professional to put this incident to bed."

Joe looked around him, seeing the quiet leaves and a lone squirrel disappearing behind a tree trunk. He took off his glasses and wiped his brow. Tiredness made him hang his head. He didn't want to argue anymore.

He put his glasses back on. "Will you let me think about it?"

Grayson took him into his massive body. "That's a start, Joe." He hugged his ward and kissed the top of his head.

"I've told you before I wish you wouldn't do that, Grayson. You make me feel like a little kid."

"That's because you are a little kid. You're my little kid. Now, let's head back to the car. It's too hot out here."

CHAPTER EIGHT

Two white-coated residents laughed as they walked into the doctors' chart room. "Oh, boy, that guy shoulda known better," said one of them as he sat next to Irene at the long counter and opened his patient's file.

The other doctor chuckled. "He thought putting a ring on his dick would, quote-unquote, 'enhance his performance!'" He wiggled his fingers, indicating quotation marks.

The first one poured a cup of coffee. "Well, now he knows better. He's gonna be in so much pain he won't be able to walk for a week! Hee! Hee!"

"So, how did you get it off?" Irene asked, looking up from her stack of files.

The first resident lit a cigarette. "We had to call a jeweler. It took two hours to get the ring off. The guy was as embarrassed as hell."

"I bet his wife was none too happy, either." The second resident giggled.

While the two gleeful residents bantered, Irene looked at the wall calendar to make sure she had the right date—8/29/64. Last week she had made the gravest of errors notating the wrong date on a chart. She never heard the end of it from her supervisor, Dr. Cyrus F. Mellencamp.

The door opened with a knock. The nurse spoke quickly. "Dr. Pierce, we've got another one for you in room two."

Irene sighed and put down her pen. With so many charts to

complete and interruptions with emergency patients every hour, she'd be here well past her shift, which would end in two hours. "So, what do we have, Ann?"

"White male, late teens, with head trauma, possible rib fractures, and contusions on his torso. And he's got a laceration across his throat. He arrived by taxi. But one of the orderlies said a woman just dragged him out of the cab and left him lying on the sidewalk."

"Is she with him now?"

"No. She just took off in the taxi. Didn't even bother to come in to tell us he was out there."

Irene pulled back the curtain and looked at the ill-fated new patient. "Notify security, Ann. Maybe they can track down the cab," she said.

On the gurney lay the young man, eyes glazed in shock. He looked like a wounded deer, freshly hit by a car, panting and struggling to stay alive. He had to breathe through his mouth as his swollen nose seeped blood. Swollen, purple bruises spread under his eyes.

He was immediately placed on an exam table and covered with a sheet. Irene and another resident, Dr. Phil Baker, threw on their gowns, gloved up, and began their work. Nurses took his vital signs and poked his inside elbow to find a vein to draw a blood sample.

"Pulse is ninety, BP one forty over eight-five." A nurse took off the blood pressure cuff.

Dr. Baker shone a penlight in the patient's eyes. He slowly waved his finger in front of his eyes. "Can you follow my finger?" The patient only blinked. "He may have a concussion. We'll get some films on his head." In a voice a bit too loud, he asked, "Did you get hit in the head?"

"Yeah." The young man's voice was hoarse.

"Did you lose consciousness? Did you black out?"

"I don't remember. Yeah, I did. I can't breathe."

"It looks like you have a fractured nose."

"No, I can't breathe from my lungs." The poor young man looked around in panic. Drool seeped out of his open mouth.

Nurses carefully cut away his blood-soaked shirt, revealing vicious red welts on his sides. "He looks like he's been kicked," one of them commented.

Dr. Baker looked closely. "Yeah, he probably has some broken ribs."

"We need X-rays on his torso as well as his head," Irene said to another nurse. She examined the horizontal cut on his neck while a nurse dabbed the congealing blood. The laceration was just deep enough to require stitches. She adjusted her stethoscope and listened to his heart. Other staff members moved about the room, opening a suture kit and gauze packages, calling X-ray, moving tray tables, setting up an IV line.

"Hello, I'm Dr. Pierce. Can you tell me your name?" She studied his face.

"I'm . . . Rob . . ." He squinted at the large, overhead light fixture as he tried to focus on the petite, blonde-headed doctor standing over him.

"What did you say? What's your name?"

"Robert Stangarden." He had trouble forming his words as if his tongue was two sizes bigger than usual. "I'm gonna throw up!"

Someone pushed him onto his side and held a metal pan to his mouth. Robert retched but brought up nothing. As a nurse laid him on his back, he cried out in pain.

"Stangarden?" Irene repeated. "Who was the woman who brought here by taxi?"

The patient only closed his eyes.

The nurse with the medical chart said, "I'll tell Carol to try to track down his family." She turned and left.

"Dr. Pierce, let's turn him over and see what his back looks like." Dr. Baker removed the sheet covering him. "Lydia, Karen, can you get his pants off?"

Someone tugged down his trousers. Irene had stepped back to watch the nurses and Dr. Baker turn the patient on his side. She stood without moving, gripping her stethoscope, and staring.

The patient suddenly screamed.

Dr. Baker observed, "Look at this. See these marks? Like somebody hit him with some round object." Rolling the patient back gently, he said, "Robert, is that your name? What happened to you? Did you get beat up?"

When Robert didn't answer, the doctor went on. "Let's get a blood transfusion . . . Irene, what's wrong? You look like you've just seen a ghost."

Irene ignored the question. She could not take her eyes off the young man on the table. In a wooden voice, she asked, "What happened to you?"

"Car accident."

Irene almost dropped her exam gloves as she peeled them off. This young patient, despite his facial wounds, looked like Joe. He had the same square face, smooth, arched brows, and deep brown, intelligent eyes. However, while Joe's hair was black, Robert's was a dark brunette.

"Are you telling us the truth?" Dr. Baker asked accusingly. "A car accident would not make these kinds of injuries. And somebody cut your throat." He looked around the room. "Did anybody call the police yet?"

"No! Please. Please don't call the police. Ah, it hurts." Robert's head turned to one side. His breathing was rapid.

Another nurse offered, "BP is now one sixty over one ten. Pulse is 144."

Dr. Baker examined his eyes again and said, "Pupils fixed and dilated. He's going into shock. Let's move him to ICU. We'll get his films upstairs. Stat."

The now motionless patient was put back on a gurney and swiftly wheeled away.

Dr. Baker pulled off his gloves. "Irene, are you all right?"

Her voice trembled. "Yes. Can you take it from here? I need to make a phone call."

"Okay." He hesitated. "Are you sure you're all right?"

"Yes . . . yes, I'm fine."

Exiting the room, Irene threw her gloves into a trash can and walked quickly to the ladies' room. She splashed cold water on her face. After turning off the faucet, she patted her face dry with a paper towel. She gripped the edge of the sink and stared at her reflection in the smudged mirror. Have to think, think. Was this patient who she thought he was? Was he the kid Joe had talked about in his apartment back in June? The freshman music student whose parents he had recognized from Buchenwald? She wrung her hands, just like her father did in a moment of anxiety. Joe needed to know about this. But maybe she should talk to her father first. He'd know best how to break the news to Joe about this kid whom he had fled from four months ago and who now was being wheeled to the ICU.

Apprehension gripped her. What about this kid's parents? The alleged Nazis from Buchenwald? They'd want to know who had beaten up their son. But the most upsetting part of this was that when they would be notified and come to the hospital to see their son, Irene would have to talk with them. She couldn't do that. Maybe she could stay incognito and let Phil Baker and the ICU doctors see them.

Who was the woman who brought him to the hospital in a taxicab instead of calling an ambulance? His wounds were severe, possibly life-threatening. The tests and X-rays would reveal how badly he was hurt. Why did this woman dump him right outside on the sidewalk like a bag of trash and then leave in such a hurry? Why wouldn't she stay to talk with the doctors about what had happened to him? Surely, she wasn't his mother. A mother wouldn't leave her son like that.

Irene walked out of the restroom, feeling as if she had left her body. She stopped at the reception desk. "Carol, did you find a phone number for Robert Stangarden?"

"I've found a Henry Stangarden, 5051 West 46th Street. I've called, but there's no answer. I'll try again in a few minutes."

Irene's mind was numb. Her eyes rested on the rack of medical charts on the counter without seeing them. "Y—yes. I suppose you should."

She turned slowly to go to the front lobby to make a collect call to Ithaca. However, Dr. Baker stopped her.

"I had the hospital security call the police, Irene. Since the parents haven't shown up, I think the police need to get to the bottom of this. Did anybody at reception look up a phone number for them?"

"Yes," Irene replied. "Carol found an address and phone number for a Henry Stangarden. Maybe he's the father." She looked down, frowning. A sense of dread made her palms clammy.

Dr. Baker went on. "They need to be here. Robert's in bad shape with a punctured lung and bruised kidney, so he's going to stay awhile." He looked behind him. "I've got to get back to the intake rooms. Make your phone call quick. There was a fire at an apartment complex on the east side of town. Some burn victims, maybe even firemen."

After he left, Irene entered the busy lobby of Marion County General Hospital. She went to a phone booth next to the entrance doors. She called collect and waited for a connection.

"Yes, operator, I'll accept the call. Hello? Irene?"

"Joe?"

"Hey, my favorite sister. How's it goin'?" Silence. "Irene? Are you there?"

"Yes, Joe, I'm here." Why couldn't her father have answered the phone? "I've . . ."

"Okay. What's up? You sound different."

Irene twisted the phone cord around her finger. She very much did not want this conversation with her brother. "Are you busy?"

"Like right now or in general?"

"Right now. No, I mean in general. What are you doing?"

"Well, I'm taking hikes with Grayson and eating lots of Rose's good cooking. You know she still brings over food from the mansion. She can't get out of the habit of cooking for an army even though it's just her and Aunt Mil.

"I got a part-time job back at the Ithaca library shelving books. Those old ladies love me. Every time I come in, they've got these homemade treats for me. They know I have a sweet tooth. I've contacted my advisor, Dr. Reed, about my dissertation. I told him I'm planning to go to New York City next week to do research at the NYC Library and the National Archives. He was excited about that. I have about ten chapters finished, but I will need to revise them now that I can access more materials. It's much better doing my dissertation here than in Bloomington. I should have done this from the start."

Irene heard him take a deep breath. "And I've made inquiries about what teaching positions might be open next school year at some of the local colleges in the area. Some of these small liberal arts colleges will hire teachers ABD. That means all but dissertation. I'm hoping I can land something at Ithaca College. I need the teaching experience."

He paused. "But that would mean I'd be away from you." He spoke in a lowered voice. "I miss you like crazy, Irene. I wish I could screw you right now. I'd start by kissing your mouth and working down to your neck and shoulders. Then I'd spend time with your breasts. Ah! I'm getting hard just thinking about you."

Irene said nothing. Her finger let go of the phone cord and found its way into her hair, twisting a lock.

"We'd be on your bed in your apartment in Indianapolis, and I'd lay you on your back and open those soft legs. I'd start pushing inside your pussy and wrap my arms around you and kiss your sweet mouth."

All the while Joe was talking, Irene shut her eyes, but the tears spilled anyway. She had to ignore his enticing words. "That's great, Joe." She wiped her dripping nose with a tissue from her lab coat pocket. "You sound like you're getting back on your feet." Uneasiness tinged her voice.

"What? Yeah. Um, sure." He paused as if trying to remember the first questions Irene had asked. "Grayson took out my stitches. I'm feeling much better, but he wants me to go into psychotherapy again. He said he'd pay for it. He wants me to see Dr. Montgomery."

"Oh, well, maybe you should, Joe."

"I'm trying to convince him by doing the library job and working on my thesis that I've put things behind me. I guess time and distance made the difference."

An awkward silence hung between them.

Joe said, "Is there another reason why you called? Irene, are you crying?"

She blurted, "Joe, I don't have a lot of time to talk. Can you come back to Indianapolis?" She stopped herself from twirling a lock of her hair, a life-long nervous mannerism she could never entirely control.

"Huh? Do you miss me?"

Irene put her face in her hand, shutting out her surroundings. "A new patient came in this afternoon. Robert Stangarden."

"What?"

"He's been badly hurt."

"Oh. How? What happened?"

"That's the mystery. Apparently, some woman dropped him off by taxi around three o'clock, and she just disappeared. He was able to tell us his name but not who beat him. He said he was in a car accident, but his injuries don't match that. I recognized him from the pictures you had shown us at your apartment, and I remembered that you had said his name was Robert Stangarden. The secretary found the name Stangarden in the phone book. She's called the number, but there's been no answer." Irene paused. "I don't know the address, but it could be the same one you and Robert went to in May."

Irene heard nothing on the line for several moments. "Joe? Are you still there?"

"Yeah . . . Irene. Why did you call me? I can't do anything."

"That woman just dumped him like a bag of old clothes. I'm worried about him, Joe."

Her brother said nothing.

Irene pressed on. "We're waiting for the blood test results and X-rays. We ordered a tox screen, but I doubt anything will show up. He didn't appear to be drunk or high. He's in the ICU right now." She paused. It didn't seem the right time to tell him about the cut across Robert's neck. "Joe, I know you planned to let him go and get on with your studies, but—"

"No, no, and no! I will not come back to Indianapolis. I am done with him and his family. Who knows? Maybe his father beat him up. He could do it, you know."

"That's not fair, Joe. He could have gotten into trouble with somebody else. The police have been notified, but the parents need to know about him."

"Fine. Let 'em. I don't care, Irene. I'm not his keeper."

"But we don't know who else he can turn to. We don't know if he has any other relatives or friends."

Joe's voice hardened. "Do you *really* think I'm going to come back to see him in the hospital when his Nazi parents are going to be there with him? Are you that insane?"

"Please, Joe!"

"Look. Things are going well for me right now. I'm motivated and focused. I'm all healed up, and I've got my head on straight to start on my dissertation. If all goes as I've planned, I expect to finish it next year, maybe by late spring. Then I'll come back to I. U. to do my oral defense to a bunch of old farts, and then I'll be done. After that, I'll be looking for a university job. I'm not going to take a detour and get into something that put me on the kitchen floor of my apartment to begin with. I won't do it."

"But—"

"Irene, why are you so concerned about this kid? Can't you just treat him like any other patient and let the police handle it? You need to stay out of it, particularly when that Nazi couple comes around."

Tightening her grip on the phone receiver, Irene shifted her weight. In front of her mind was how much Robert looked like Joe, like a younger brother.

"I told you before I'll be back in a couple of months to meet with my advisor. I'll come to Indianapolis to visit you. But I will steer clear of this Stangarden kid."

Irene felt her knees shaking. She needed to sit. "Oh, you're just being stubborn and selfish!"

"No, it's self-preservation. And don't call Grayson to tell him about this. He'll put the pressure on me, and I don't want to have to fight him about this."

Irene's mind was a nervous jumble. She couldn't decide if she should get mad and push him harder or continue her almost childish pleading.

"This discussion is finished. You know how much I love you, and I miss you. But my answer is still 'no.' Good-bye, Irene."

He rang off before she could answer. Hearing the dial tone, Irene hung up the receiver and stared at the rotary dial pad. There was a single clink, and her quarter landed in the metal tray at the bottom of the pay phone.

Joe was as unreasonable as always. Irene had had too many drag-out fights with him throughout the years growing up with him not to know that he could be pig-headed. But, as she walked away from the phone booth, she decided Joe wasn't in charge of her. He did not control her decisions and actions. With renewed determination, she decided to call her father. She didn't care how mad Joe would get.

However, she dreaded seeing that Nazi couple enter the hospital lobby, asking the receptionist to see their son. One of the doctors in the ICU would have to come down to meet them. They'd be here at any minute. Irene decided to "hide" back in the chart room. The phone call to Joe's guardian would have to wait until she got off her shift and was safely sitting in her apartment.

CHAPTER NINE

Irene approached the white curtain that concealed the patient. She pulled it back and then closed it. With barely veiled trepidation, she asked, "Are you comfortable?"

Robert's head was wrapped, a cumbersome bandage on his nose. Tubes attached from his arms and side to machines kept him immobile in the hospital bed. He slowly turned his head to look at her. "No, not really."

"Are you cold?"

"Yes."

"Well, I'll get you a blanket. It's always chilly in these rooms." Taking a thin, white blanket from a nearby storage closet, she spread it over him. "The blankets aren't too warm. Did Dr. Manning talk to you about your injuries?"

Robert blinked. "Yeah. I guess I'm pretty beat up. How long have I been here?"

"You were in the ICU for three days." She put the chart back on the hook.

"Are you my nurse?"

Irene had heard that question many times. Because of her sex, patients assumed she was a nurse. Never mind her petite stature and her china doll face that made her look like a schoolgirl instead of a legitimate physician. "I don't know if you remember me. I'm Dr. Pierce. I treated you when you first came into the hospital." She took the medical chart that hung on the end of his bed and scanned the notes.

Robert seemed not to have heard her last statement. He turned his face away.

"You were sedated, so you probably don't remember anything." Irene paused, then said, "Robert, do you remember the other doctor asking you about what happened, and you said you were in a car accident?"

Robert finally met her grey, wide-set eyes. He blinked again as if trying to focus. Irene's heart skipped a beat. She had seen those same liquid brown eyes as Joe had lain on the kitchen floor in a stupor.

"We both know that really didn't happen. Your injuries aren't consistent with a car accident. Besides, we would have been contacted by the police about it. They would have called an ambulance. A woman brought you by taxi. Was she your mother? It's important to know how you ended up like this." Trying to keep her voice steady, she went on. "The receptionist found a phone number for a Henry Stangarden. Is he your father?" She took a small piece of paper from a side pocket of her doctor's coat. "The address is 5051 West 46th Street. Is that your address?"

"Yes," Robert croaked.

"We kept calling that number while you were in the ICU, but nobody has answered. The police are trying to get a hold of them. Tell me about your parents. Why aren't they here for you?" Irene felt she was floating above her body. No Nazis. No Nazis.

Robert exhaled. Amidst the red marks and bruises on his face, Irene saw tears running down the side of his head.

She put a light hand on his knee over the blanket. "Who did this to you, Robert?"

"Please, don't ask! Why are you here? You're not my doctor now, are you?"

The strain in his voice made Irene inhale sharply. She drew back her hand. "Robert, we've never met before you came to the hospital, but I've known about you before this happened."

"Huh?"

Irene settled into a visitor's chair. "I'm Joe Kaufmann's sister. Joe has talked about you quite a bit. He even showed me a picture of you with your French horn."

"What?"

"He thinks you're a wonderful musician."

Robert hesitated, then asked, "Where is he? I want to know why he left so suddenly when my parents came home. He acted like he couldn't get out of there fast enough. After he was gone, my mom and dad got very upset. They were yelling at each other and slamming doors, and my dad was pounding his fists on the kitchen table. But they wouldn't tell me what was going on. Then my dad left the house. I guess he needed to cool off. My mom went upstairs to her bedroom and shut the door. She was in there for hours. I've never seen my mother so shaken up." He frowned despite the tender bruises on his face. "Mr. Kaufmann. He's the one who started this."

"This is a complicated situation, Robert. Let's just wait. The first order of business is for you to get healed. I was told that a detective would be here today. He wants to ask you some questions about how you got your injuries." She kept her voice even and calm despite her trembling stomach.

"My head hurts." His voice was weak. "I don't want to talk anymore."

"All right, Robert. Will you let me check in on you again?"

"I can't stop you, can I?"

"Actually, you can. If you don't want me to come around, just say so. I just want to help you because you're Joe's friend. He thinks very well of you." Irene allowed herself a smile. "You two look a lot alike. You look like his kid brother."

"Yeah, that's what everybody says."

Irene could not disagree.

CHAPTER TEN

Detective Charlie Benson held a palm-sized, wire-bound pad of paper and stubby pencil against his ample stomach and briskly pushed the questions to no avail. He saw the bruises, the bandages, the wrapped chest, the IV lines. His experienced eye saw a beating, and this was a bad one. The wide gauze strips around the kid's throat indicated that somebody had indeed tried to kill him, and he was going to find out who. But this was a most uncooperative victim.

"C'mon, kid. Who did this to you? Are you afraid whoever it was is going to come after you again?" Small, frustrated eyes shone brightly out of flushed cheeks. The stout detective kept hiking up his belt, but his large stomach kept pushing it down.

"No. Yes. I'm afraid."

"Where're your folks, Robert? We've been calling your parents for three days now while you were in the ICU. We even went to their house and left messages on the front door. Are they out of town or something?"

Robert tilted his chin down, averting his eyes.

"Fine. By the way, there're going to be some big medical bills. Who knows how long you'll be in the hospital. Somebody has to come to show proof of insurance. So, your parents are going to have to come around sometime."

"Leave them out of this."

"Where were you when this happened?"

"Please, leave me alone. I'm not feeling well."

"Who was that woman who dropped you off at the ER? Was she your mother?"

Robert said nothing.

"Okay. The woman brought you in a taxicab. What was the name of the cab company?"

"I dunno."

Detective Benson let out a loud sigh and wrote in his little notepad. "Fair enough. I suppose you were too far out of it to know. Where does your father work?"

Without catching why the detective asked that question, Robert replied, "He's an accountant at Allison Transmission." He didn't realize that the detective could find his dad at work.

The detective wrote down, "Allison Transmission." He asked, "What about your mom?"

Before Robert answered, there were two soft knocks on the door, and Joe Kaufmann walked into the room in a white polo shirt, shorts, and a pair of deck shoes. His five o'clock shadow was more of a midnight shadow. He had filled out by a few pounds, thanks to the Pierce family cook's meatloaf, mashed potatoes, and chocolate brownies.

The day before, Joe had left a worried guardian and stepmother in the driveway of their home when he had shoved off for Indianapolis. As he drove non-stop across three states, he kept going over in his mind the heated argument he had had with Grayson. Despite Joe telling her not to, Irene had called her father. After describing Robert Stangarden's injuries and still unknown cause, Grayson agreed that Joe had an obligation to help this kid. He offered to go with him in case Robert's parents showed up. But Joe would have none of it. He planned to give Robert some moral support, spend some time with Irene, and then drive back to Ithaca with a clear conscience. He kept telling himself he was only doing this as a favor to his sister. Grayson's final stern words were, "You are not going to handle this on your own, son. Irene knows to keep close tabs on you. Any sign of trouble and I will be there forthwith. Understand?"

In the hospital room, Joe went to the other side of Robert's bed. He looked at the tubes and machines and IV pole with a clear plastic bag hanging on it.

The detective looked up. "Who are you?" he asked, annoyed at having to been interrupted.

"Joe Kaufmann. I'm a friend of Robert's." Moving closer, Joe barely recognized the young patient in the hospital bed for all the welts and bandages. The considerable bandage on his nose and the purple and red and black discoloration on the kid's face was downright scary.

Eyeing the two, the detective said, "Friend? Do you know his parents? I've been tryin' to reach them for days."

"No, I don't," Joe replied. To Robert, he said, "How are you doing, kid?"

Robert frowned as best he could at Joe.

"He's doing shit. That's what he's doing," the detective snapped. "He's been hammered like a nail, and I can't get him to say who did this. There's going to be assault charges filed, maybe attempted murder with that cut throat. I'll be notifying the assistant DA."

Detective Benson stood and began walking toward the door. Then he stopped and turned around. "Hey, wait a minute. I just thought of something. Robert, it was your mother who brought you to the hospital by taxi, right?"

Robert answered in a trembling voice, "So?"

"Where were you when you were assaulted? And how did your mother know you were hurt? How come she didn't call an ambulance?"

The overbearing detective took a step closer and pointed a finger at the pitiful figure lying in the bed. "You got beat up at your house, didn't you? Was it your father who assaulted you? Or maybe a brother or an uncle or somebody else?"

"No. Please!" Robert tried to sit up, but the pain was too much. "This was all a misunderstanding! I'll be all right. It's nothing."

The rude detective was losing patience. "Nothing? Like hell. Are you mixed up in anything? Something illegal? Maybe that's why you're not cooperating."

Joe spoke up. "Sir, I know this kid. He's a music student at I. U. He wouldn't be mixed up . . . ." But he hesitated. Perhaps he didn't know Robert well enough to say that.

Opening his pad, the detective said, "What's your mom's name? Does she work? I need to get a hold of her." He wrote hurriedly in his pad.

"Please don't ask me any more questions. I think I'm going to be sick."

"Of course, you're going to be sick. Somebody's pummeled you like a jackhammer and left you for dead." Detective Benson impatiently pushed his notepad in the breast pocket of his polyester suit coat. "Well, if you're not going to give me the answers I need to help you, I'll find out what happened another way. I'm going to make some calls. I'll be back with my partner tomorrow, kid." By the stale odor on him, he left, probably to grab a smelly liverwurst and onion sandwich on the way out.

"God, I need more pain medicine." Robert fumbled for the call button wire on the side of the bed stand. "Mr. Kaufmann, why are you here? I thought I'd never see you again." He flinched, holding his left side. "Are you still in Bloomington?"

"No. I drove down from Ithaca."

"How did you know I was in the hospital?"

Joe pulled up a chair and sat. "You remember the woman doctor who treated you when you came in?"

"Yeah."

He scratched his jaw. A good day's start of a beard itched. "Dr. Pierce is my sister. She called and told me about you. She asked me to come down to see you and maybe help you if I could." *Fat chance of that happening. I'm outa here as soon as I swing by the apartment to get some stuff to take back to Ithaca.*

"Oh, she's been coming to check up on me."

Busybody. She's stirring a pot that should be left alone.

Robert looked confused. "How can she be your sister? Is she married?"

"Well, she's not my sister officially. And she's not married. Maybe I can explain it later."

Robert looked dazed.

Joe peered at him. "Are you all right? Should I call a nurse?"

"Yeah. It's just that my head hurts. I hurt all over." He found the call button and pressed it.

Joe held his tongue about Robert's parents. "How long will you stay in the hospital?"

"I dunno. The doctor said he needs to keep an eye on my kidney. He said it was bruised. I have a concussion and a punctured lung, too."

Joe looked at Robert's bandaged neck. "How many stitches do you have?" He pointed his finger at his neck.

Robert turned away slightly, clutching the call button. "Twenty-two."

Joe's heart jumped. Now he realized Irene had been serious about how badly Robert had been hurt. And he understood why the detective was so hard on him for answers. Someone had, indeed, tried to kill him. However, Joe did not want to make any speculations. Not yet. He told himself that the detective would handle this.

Robert touched his lip, then looked at his finger, expecting to see blood. "I don't understand why you ran out as you did when you saw my parents in May. My parents went crazy after you left. But they wouldn't tell me why they were so upset. Where've you been, Mr. Kaufmann? I tried several times to call you, but you never picked up."

"I told you I went back to Ithaca, Robert. That's my home. I didn't need to stay in Bloomington." Joe thought that was a good enough explanation.

Grimacing in pain, Robert went on. "Why did you lie to that detective about not knowing my parents? You looked like you recognized them, and you ran out of the house so fast I didn't know what was going on. God, I'm so confused. My head is killing me." He lightly touched his cut lip again.

Joe knew the kid probably was worried that he wouldn't be able to play his French horn for a while. He asked, "Why did your mother leave after she dumped you in front of the hospital? Was it because she wouldn't have to answer questions from the doctors as to how you got beaten up and by whom?"

"I want my pain meds."

Joe took off his glasses and rubbed his eyes. Putting them back on, he said, "Robert, all this is going to come out. The detective—"

Robert's voice rose as he lifted his head. "The detective doesn't need to know anything. This is my business."

"Why, Robert? You've been badly assaulted. The police have to find out what happened. Someone has to answer for this."

"Stop yelling at me." Robert exhaled. He closed his eyes as if to concentrate on his stiff, throbbing neck.

Joe sighed as he considered this miserable kid. Maybe it was best to stop the grilling. "Okay, Robert. You need some rest." He looked at the empty, crisply made bed on the other side of the hospital room. He was exhausted from the non-stop eleven-hour car trip. But more importantly, the stress of talking with this pathetic young man and his

Nazi father drained his mind. "I wonder if anyone will be using that other bed."

A middle-aged nurse with blue-grey hair waltzed in on rubber-soled shoes. "Mr. Stangarden?"

"Can I have some more pain medicine?"

Unfortunately for Robert, the miserly nurse refused to give him any more relief for his pain for another two hours. He managed to talk her into a sleeping pill, and after a few minutes, he fell asleep. While the nurse attended to Robert, Joe moved to the tempting bed. He couldn't resist sitting on it. When she left, he leaned over to rest his head on the cool, starched pillow.

****

Glaring slivers of light from the window framed the thin drapes on the east wall. Joe focused his bleary eyes on his watch: 6:20. He heard talking, something about breakfast and Detective Benson coming later to take pictures. Too sleepy to pay attention, he turned over away from the window and went back to sleep.

****

"He needs to get up," a female voice whispered.

"Yes. It's ten-thirty. We have to change the bed."

Small, feminine hands shook his shoulders.

"Joe, wake up. It's time to get up. Joe? I brought you a sandwich and some juice." Irene sat on the bed, forcing him to move his legs. "Were you here all night? Get up. The nurses have to change the bed." She turned to the two nurses patiently holding crisp, new sheets. "Please give us a minute," she said. They left after setting down the bedding.

Joe rubbed his well-established beard and ran his fingers through unruly bed hair as he sat up. He then moved to a chair to drink the orange juice. He saw the white curtain surrounding Robert's bed.

He forced himself awake. "Where's Robert?" he asked as he unwrapped the cheese sandwich. He looked for his shoes.

"That detective took him to a room to take pictures of his wounds. He's determined to find whoever assaulted him and arrest him. I overheard him saying he's already gone to the assistant district attorney, whoever that is. Listen, I have to get back to the trauma room. You know it's against hospital policy for you to take a bed like you did last night. You're lucky we didn't need it. If you're going to stay, the orderly will get you a roll-away."

"Oh. Okay. Wait. Did anybody get hold of his parents? Are they coming? I need—"

"No, they're still not answering the detective's phone calls. Since you're still here, why don't you take a shower? The nurses might find a razor for you." Irene looked at her watch. "I've got to go. I've got three more hours on my shift."

Joe thought for a moment. "Okay. I'll take a shower first, and then I'll go to Bloomington and check my apartment."

Irene said, "Joe, you're taking this almost too calmly."

"Yeah, well, I'll hit a wall sooner or later. By the way, I was going to yell at you for telling Grayson about Robert, but now that I've seen him, I'm glad I came."

"I told you so."

"Hey, before you go, will you do me a favor?"

"Sure."

"Would you tell the nurses to let me know if his parents show up? I want to be out of this hospital before they come up to this room."

"Yes, absolutely, Joe. And you'll let me know when you're leaving."

They looked at each other.

"Don't worry, Joe. I love you." Irene kissed his cheek before leaving the room.

Joe went into the bathroom to start his shower. He didn't find a razor. While the water heated, he removed his clothes and then stepped into the shower stall. Rubbing the minute bar of soap into a washcloth, he began to think.

His life had been quieting down for the past six weeks. He was eating well, taking hikes, sleeping late, and teasing sweet, elderly ladies with severely-coiffed hair at the Ithaca library. He had already written outlines for the next several chapters of his dissertation. He had expected to see Robert Stangarden never again.

His well-thought plans had been cruelly ripped apart by this bloody assault on this innocent kid. Despite Robert's unwillingness to admit it, he knew who the assailant was. It had to be his father who had beat him and had cut his throat. And, with nauseating clarity, Joe knew he was part of this awful situation. He just didn't know the exact details of how all this went down.

He had to admit that he was responsible for setting this calamity in motion. Pandora's Box of tragedy had been opened with virtuous intentions when he had proposed to move Robert back home at the end of that third week of May. When he thought about that terrible scene in the Stangarden's kitchen, he shuddered as the hot water sprayed on his shoulders. Now, Robert had paid a life-threatening price for that innocent offer.

To assuage his guilt, Joe could point his finger at his old friend, Frank Oneida, as the real grandmaster of this catastrophe. He had brought the two of them together at that Beethoven opera performance last fall. "I swear. You two look like brothers!" What baloney! Joe's life would have been so much simpler if he and Frank just had a meal at the Gables by themselves after the opera. He would never have met Robert Stangarden.

Joe turned off the shower, stepped out, and began toweling himself dry. He had a choice to stay or to leave. He could easily abandon this naive, confused I. U. student who didn't even know he lived in the shadow of a Nazi ogre. By going back to Ithaca, he could enjoy peace of mind with the distance of 700 miles between him and this ugly, ugly man.

If he stayed, what could he do for Robert? As long as that fat Nazi was out roaming Hoosier streets, Joe could not help him. That Nazi monster was alive and well! Oh, how those deep-rooted feelings of utter dread made him tremble. If he stayed here in Indiana, that meant continually looking over his shoulder. The prospect of that was exhausting.

And what about Robert's mother? Shouldn't she take care of him? Joe had remembered her as being kind-hearted and caring. She had been so pleased when he had eaten her cookies and apple strudel and . . .

No! I'm not going to think about that!

A not-too-small finger of indecision poked his brain.

Instead of waiting for Robert to come back to his hospital room, Joe decided to leave now. He had files, winter clothes, books, and his clarinet at his apartment in Bloomington to pack in his trusty, powder-blue Ford Falcon.

CHAPTER ELEVEN

"Hello?"

"What's going on down there, Joe?"

"I went straight to the hospital in Indianapolis. I didn't stop except for gas and making a pit stop."

"What's the situation?"

"Well, Irene was more than right about Robert Stangarden. He's a mess. He's got bruises all over his face. His nose is broken, and there are bandages on his head and his hands. On top of all that, he has a big dressing on his throat. Irene said it looked like a knife wound. He's got tubes everywhere and machines all around his bed. He was in the ICU for three days."

"My goodness. That's what Irene said. Who assaulted him?"

"He wouldn't tell the detective—"

"Detective? Are the police involved?"

"Grayson, this was—"

"Who, Joe? Who tried to kill him? Get to the point, son."

"Robert wouldn't say."

"That's ridiculous. Why wouldn't he tell the police? When did this happen?"

"This past Saturday, I guess the 29th."

"Did Robert tell you what happened after you had left their house in May?"

"He said his mom and dad went crazy. But they didn't tell Robert why they were so upset about seeing me. And I sure wasn't going to tell Robert how I knew them."

"That makes no sense. What about the mother? What happened to her?"

"I'm not sure. I guess she had to have been there during the attack since the detective figured out she brought Robert to the hospital. Grayson, I think Robert's father beat him. Do you believe me now that Nazi thug is dangerous?"

"Son, I believe you. But what happened to their son changes everything."

"You mean about me?"

"Yes. I know you were planning to live here in Ithaca and finish your dissertation, but you're going to have to stay there in Indiana to help Robert."

"Why? I can't! I don't want to! There's nothing I can do for him."

"Joe, listen. When the police start digging around about this family and, assuming that this brute did attack the kid, they're going to ask questions. Your name is going to come up. The detective is going to want to talk to you. And if this Nazi goon gets arrested and put on trial, you bet that the district attorney will want to talk to you, maybe even put you on the witness stand. If you come back to Ithaca now, you'll just have to turn around and go back. If you don't, you might get subpoenaed. You have to stay there at least for a while."

"No! We had all this figured out in June. I was going to—"

"This is not your fault, Joe. You did nothing wrong."

"But I did, Grayson! If I hadn't taken Robert back—"

"You can't think like that. There was no way you could have known about this kid's parents. I am going to call Irene and tell her to stay close."

"I don't need to get involved."

"Joe, you're involved whether you like it or not. I should come down."

"Grayson, no. You're making me feel like a child again. Like I can't handle this."

"Joe, you couldn't handle this back in June! This isn't like holding your hand to get you through your doctorate exams. And you know as well as I do that I'm the best person to give you the support you need. Are you there, son?"

"All right. I'll stay. Maybe the detective won't need to talk to me."

"Joe, that's wishful thinking. You have to be practical about this. I understand how distressing this is. Maybe, in the long run, something good will come out of it. Just lean on Irene for now. She needs to know what's going on. If you feel like you're losing control, call her. Please, call her."

"Okay, I will."

"And I am going to call you again, often. You're staying there at your apartment?"

"Yeah."

"If you need me, son, I will take a plane down there ASAP."

"Thanks, Grayson."

"I love you, Joe."

"I love you, too, Grayson."

CHAPTER TWELVE

Detective Benson and his partner, Detective Dave Peterman, were finally able to track down the cab company that Ada Stangarden had hired to bring her son, Robert, to the hospital. A nurse thought she had seen the cab as it motored through the drop-off drive as being yellow. After talking with the dispatcher at the Yellow Cab Company, they were able to identify the cabbie as a Mr. Ralph White. In his interview, he had described the scene at 5051 West 46th Street when he had arrived—a very distraught woman and a bleeding kid on the living room floor. The detectives had enough evidence to obtain a warrant to search the Stangarden home. With Mr. White in tow to show the detectives what he had seen in the house, a trip to the Stangarden's residence commenced.

When Detectives Benson and Peterman, plus two uniform policemen and several crime scene workers, entered the Stangarden's home with a search warrant in hand, their timing was perfect. The couple was eating lunch at the kitchen table on this sweltering Labor Day, September 2nd. They were shocked at the arrival of all these strange people. While the technicians set up their equipment and brushing black powder on door frames and walls, and police photographers taking pictures, Henry and Ada were strongly encouraged to come down to the police headquarters to answer some questions. The innocuous German couple was escorted out of their house in plain view of their neighbors and put into the back seat of a squad car. They put up a fuss all the way to downtown Indianapolis.

The only window in the otherwise empty interrogation room had no curtains. The heat from the late summer afternoon sun was kept at bay only by a stand-alone oily fan turning slowly in a corner. The middle-aged, overweight couple sat in metal folding chairs at a long, scratched table. The woman took out a small handkerchief from her lime-colored vinyl pocketbook and pressed it on her face. The man scowled, bracing for a fight.

Both detectives entered. They wore shiny brown suits, white shirts, skinny black ties, and disgruntled looks on their sweaty faces. Detective Dave Peterman opened the first volley. "You know, you two are pretty hard to get a hold of. You never picked up when we called you about a hundred times over the last couple of days." He narrowed his already narrow eyes. "Any reason why you've been avoiding the police?"

The sweating, corpulent man only stared back with contempt.

Detective Branson opened a thin file and studied a sheet of paper. "Do you have a son, Mr. Stangarden?" He clicked a ballpoint pen. The other detective also took out a pen and a small notepad from his suit breast pocket.

"Ya."

"I'll take that as a 'yes.' Will you please speak English, sir? My partner, Detective Peterman's not too good with foreign accents. So, no German. Does your wife speak English?"

"She say nothing." The piggish man's accented voice vibrated deeply in his heavily padded throat. He crossed his flabby arms over his substantial stomach. His hooded, blue eyes watched the detectives with suspicion.

Detective Peterman, a wiry man with thinning, slicked-back black hair, a prominent Adam's apple, and Elvis Presley sideburns scribbled in his notepad. His greyish pallor suggested too many cigarettes for too many years. "Is his name Robert?"

"So?"

The woman whimpered, darting her round, hazel eyes to the lard of a man sitting next to her. Her double chin dripped perspiration. Her tight pin curls shook about her uncertain face.

"Don't play games with us," said Detective Peterman. "Is your son's name Robert? He's nineteen, has brown eyes and brown hair, maybe five-ten or eleven, about one-fifty?"

"Ya."

"Do you know where he is right now?" asked Benson. His combed-over hair was saturated with perspiration and perfumed hair tonic.

The woman looked as if she wanted to speak but said nothing, perhaps out of fear. Unfazed, the fat man answered, "I dunt know where he is, and I dunt care."

"He's been in the Marion County General Hospital for the past five days. Mrs. Stangarden, didn't you drop off your son at Marion County General Hospital in a taxi and then immediately leave?"

The rotund man held up his hand to stop his wife. "She has nothing to say. You talk to me."

"We're asking your wife, Mr. Stangarden."

"Nein. You ask me all your questions."

"All right. Did your wife drop off—"

"What my wife did vas our business."

"Wasn't he hurt? That's why your wife took him to the hospital. And how come she didn't stay with him while he was being treated?"

"He gets into fights."

The woman looked at her husband with widened eyes.

The detectives looked at each other, realizing the sudden turn in the interrogation. "Tell us about that. How does he get into fights?" Detective Peterman asked. He was not afraid to move closer to his interview subject.

"He is always in trouble. He fights, steals, cheats at school."

"Henry!" the woman squeaked.

"Ruhe!" her husband snapped.

"Do you have something to say, Mrs. Stangarden?" Benson asked, now interested in this very frightened woman.

After a look from her husband, she murmured, "Nein." She cast her eyes downward.

Detective Peterman leaned back and crossed his knees under the table. "We did a background check on him, Mr. Stangarden. There's no record of any run-ins with the law."

"Check his school. He's had plenty of discipline problems. Talk back to teachers. He got kicked out."

"Which school?"

"You know die Oberschule. Vat it is, Pike School?" He turned to his wife.

She nodded, melting into her handkerchief. She took off her Coke-bottle bottom glasses and wiped her eyes nervously. Her curls of grayish-brown hair dampened around her ears.

Detective Benson said, "Your wife seems upset, Mr. Stangarden. Perhaps we can put her in another room to let her settle down. Would you like some water, ma'am?"

"No! Say nothing to her!" The man pointed an angry finger at the detectives.

Detective Peterman continued. "Mr. Stangarden, we believe you're not telling us the truth about your son. We will be making inquiries at his high school to see what he did there, like his grades, attendance, friends, and activities he was in. Let's see. He graduated in 1963—"

"You dare to tell me about my son? I raised that good for no'ting . . ." Henry Stangarden seemed to run out of words. Then he waved his finger in defiance. "I know him better than anyone."

"Okay. Okay. Take it easy, Mr. Stangarden."

He sneered. "You detectives think you are smart. You think you can trick me. Well, you not so smart. We were superior in getting information. You are like Grundschule compared to us."

"'Like us?' Who is 'us?'" asked Benson, his hands firmly on the table as he began to rise. Peterman was writing as fast as he could.

"No one. No one."

Ada Stangarden glanced fearfully at her husband.

Standing, Detective Benson slowly laid out eight photographs showing Robert's injuries that he had taken at the hospital. "Who did this to your son, Mrs. Stangarden?"

Ada Stangarden began to cry as she saw the pictures. Her husband did not look at them.

"Look at these!" roared Benson, hitting the table with his fist.

After a careless glimpse at the photos, the obese man put a hand casually on the side of his face. "Did I tell you he also involved in, how you say, fencing? He steals things and sells them. Money, that's all he cares about."

Ada Stangarden put her hands over her face. She sobbed. "Oh, mein Sohn! Mein kostbarer Sohn!"

Detective Peterman tapped a finger on the pictures. "Sir, aren't you the least bit concerned about what happened to your son? Look at these injuries. He has four broken ribs, a punctured lung, a concussion, bruises all over his back, and he may need surgery to repair a kidney if he doesn't lose it. Somebody tried to kill him because he's got a gash on his throat that required twenty-two stitches! And you didn't even come to the hospital to check on him?"

"He run mit bad crowd. No one kill him . . . yet."

Peterman eyed him carefully. "Is that a threat, Mr. Stangarden?"

The podgy man squinted. He took out a white handkerchief and slowly wiped the top of his balding head and bulldog neck.

Benson paced the room. "God damn." He twisted his head and rolled his shoulders to relax his tense muscles. Although it was against official policy, he took off his suit coat. Then he sat back in his chair. "Okay, enough with the lies and the bullshit, Mr. Stangarden. You know how this happened, and we're giving you the opportunity to tell us before we go to the assistant district attorney's office. We know that the Yellow Cab Company made a run to 5051 West 46th Street at approximately 2:15 p. m. on August 29. The cab driver told us he advised your wife to call an ambulance for your son because the boy was badly injured. But she insisted that he take her and your son to Marion County General Hospital. He also stated that after your wife dropped off Robert in front, the cabbie took her back to the same address. So we know the kid got beaten up at your home. Do you deny this?"

Henry Stangarden looked impassive. "Maybe some hooligans beat him."

Detective Benson's face was crimson with rage. "Where? In the house?" The detective paused to catch his breath. "Let's say for argument's sake that he was beaten up by these hooligans somewhere else. He certainly wouldn't have been in any condition to walk home. And even if he did, why wouldn't you or your wife have called an ambulance? Why did your wife take him to the hospital by taxi? Where were you during all this?"

"I tell you the truth! He is a bad boy. He needs to be taught a lesson! No more of this. We go." He pinched his wife's arm to pull her up as he rose. She gave a cry at the painful twist.

Detective Peterman said, "We're not done here yet. Please sit."

Reluctantly, the couple sat.

"We have just started our investigation Mr. Stangarden. Let me remind you that our technicians are at your house now collecting evidence. There's this chemical called luminol. You spray it on something like a couch or a rug, and with the lights off, it'll glow if there's been any blood there. It doesn't matter how much the spot had been cleaned before. Are our techs going to find anything like that in your house?"

Ada Stangarden lost it. Her howls could be heard in the hallway.

Detective Peterman raised his voice over her. "The cab driver is in your house as we speak, Mr. Stangarden. We interviewed him a couple of days ago, and he said he went into the house and saw Robert face down on the floor in the living room with blood all over the place. Is he going to find the weapon you used to beat your son? Is he going to find the knife? Please, ma'am. Can you quiet down?"

Henry Stangarden rose again, roughly pulling up his distraught wife. "No more questions. We leave now."

"All right, Mr. Stangarden. Have it the way you want. But you are not to leave Indianapolis. We'll be in contact with you again."

Flailing his arm, the stout man retorted, "Gehen Sie zur Holle!"

Mrs. Stangarden held back. "Ven my son can see?" Her German accent thickened with anxiety. Copious tears dotted her blouse.

Detective Peterman gathered the photos and stood. "Nothing is stopping you from seeing him in the hospital, Mrs. Stangarden. But we will tell his doctors no other visitors, including you, Mr. Stangarden."

As the couple neared the door, Detective Benson called after them. "Again. Do not leave the city. We will be in contact with you sooner than you think!"

The wooden door banged shut. Both detectives sat and took out their smokes. "That kid doesn't deserve parents like that." Benson organized the papers in his file. He scowled, deepening the wrinkle between his shaggy eyebrows. "That Stangarden guy is lying, and he's so arrogant he doesn't give a rat's ass. He's a piece of work."

"But the wife seems to care." Detective Peterman gazed at the pictures of Robert's injuries before putting them back in the folder. "This is horror-movie stuff. If the father did do this, what kind of a monster is he?"

"Well, we can't make that assumption just yet. We should talk to the missus by herself. She's ready to tell us what happened. I want to know why she didn't stay at the hospital with her son."

"She's spooked. That husband of hers has her under his boot like a SS officer in a Nazi prison camp. Yeah, we have to get her alone. Since this guy works at Allison, we can catch her at home during the day. I'll set the pick-up date with Officers Lynhurst and Jones."

Detective Benson inhaled deeply on his cigarette. "Maybe the cab driver will find the assault weapon."

"Unless they hid it or threw it away."

"That's a possibility."

Detective Peterman tapped a ponderous finger on his sharp chin. "There's got to be a boatload of blood in that living room if what the cabbie said was true when he saw the kid on the floor."

"Yeah, but he could have been beaten up somewhere else in the house and maybe dragged into the living room."

"That wife seems like she'd be a pretty good housekeeper. She's probably cleaned up a lot of the blood already. It's a good thing the techs have the luminol."

Detective Benson looked at his watch. "I'll bet a stack of silver dollars that that bastard beat his son. Hey, we've got time before they have their report ready. Let's go back to the hospital and see how our victim is doing."

CHAPTER THIRTEEN

In the hospital waiting room, the two detectives sat in lounge chairs in front of Robert, who was in a wheelchair. He looked better. His bruises were beginning to fade, and the dressings had been removed from his chest. Now only a small bandage covered where the chest tube had been inserted. The thickly layered gauze around his head was also gone. But he still had a bandage on his nose as well as a bulky dressing on his throat. To the detectives' questions, he offered little beyond "I don't remember. I don't want to get my parents in trouble." He would not admit that his father had assaulted him, only that they had argued about him returning to school. Benson and Peterman were convinced more than ever that the father, indeed, had beaten his son. Why the kid wouldn't say so was illogical.

Detective Peterman decided to change tactics. "Robert, let's back up. Can you tell us what kind of relationship you've had with your father growing up?"

Sensing a trick question, Robert replied, "I don't know what you mean exactly."

"Okay. Were the two of you close? Did you spend a lot of time together? Did he take you fishing or to ballgames? Maybe take you to the Indianapolis 500?"

Robert frowned. "No. He worked a lot. When he came home, he was usually pretty tired."

"So, typically he'd eat the dinner your mom made for him, watch a little TV, and then go to bed. Right?"

"Yeah."

Detective Benson asked, "How 'bout your mom? Are you close to her?"

"Oh, yes."

"How so?"

Robert smiled shyly. "She taught me how to play the piano. Later, when I was older, she took me for piano lessons at the Jordan College of Music. I took lessons all through high school. She also took me to my French horn lessons."

This information perked up the detectives. Detective Peterman said, "Oh, so you play the French horn. Were you in the band in high school?"

"Yeah. I played in the concert band. At the basketball games, I led the pep band. I was also the drum major of the marching band."

"Good for you, Robert." Detective Benson wrote in his small writing pad. "What other activities did you do?"

"I was on the gymnastics team. I was pretty good, and I won a couple of trophies. But I wasn't as good as I was in music. I got three scholarships to I. U. I'm a double major in horn performance and music education. I want to be a band director and maybe play professionally on the side."

The other two nodded approval. Detective Peterman asked, "Robert, how were your grades in high school and college?"

"Well, I was second in my class at Pike, and right now I have a 3.9 GPA at I. U."

"You're a damn smart kid, Robert," said Detective Benson.

"I'm certainly impressed," added Detective Peterman. "I bet you've worked hard for those grades, too. You seem like you've got your head on straight."

Robert looked away, a little embarrassed.

Shifting in the chair, Detective Peterman softened his voice. "Robert, I'm going to ask you a couple of questions that may be a little uncomfortable. We want you to be completely honest, okay?"

"Sure."

The men exchanged glances. Detective Peterman said, "Were you ever involved in anything outside of school that might be, so to speak, unsavory?"

"What?"

"Like running with kids who dropped out of school and doing

drugs or stealing."

"What? Of course not. I didn't know anybody like that."

Detective Benson asked, "Have you ever been in any fights? Ever been suspended for cheating or talking back to the teachers?"

Robert's voice rose. "What? That is categorically not true! How can you even ask that? Who told you those lies about me?"

The detectives did not answer. After a pause, Detective Peterman spoke, his eyes soft with admiration. "Robert, you seem like the kind of young man who's going to have a great future. You're articulate, you're mature, and you're ambitious. You've got your career all planned out, and you have the drive to be successful. You've convinced us that you've done nothing to provoke this senseless attack."

Detective Benson said, "We have techs at your house gathering evidence. With what we'll find, we'll most likely have enough to arrest your father, Robert. The ADA should be able to charge him with at least attempted manslaughter. Isn't he the one who hurt you?"

"What? No! Leave him out of this," Robert said, panic rising in his voice. "If I don't file the complaint, then nothing happens, right?"

Sighing loudly, the detective shifted his uncomfortable body in the orange lounge chair. "If the ADA has enough evidence to file attempted manslaughter charges, it won't matter whether or not you make a complaint, son. You won't have any say in that. And with what your dad did to you, with all your injuries, and what we'll find at your house, you can pretty much assume he'll be arrested."

Detective Peterman offered, "Robert, it would help us out a lot if you could tell us what weapon was used to make those bruises and that cut across your throat."

Robert looked as if he was about to cry.

Detective Benson pressed on. "We have a witness besides the cabbie who saw you being dumped on the sidewalk by a woman. A nurse saw the cab driving off. That's when she saw you layin' there next to the curb." He leaned over, putting his beefy hands on his wide knees. "When we interviewed your parents, your mother seemed to want to speak up, but your old man kept shutting her down. I've asked you before, Robert. Who beat you up? Where were you attacked? If your mother brought you to the hospital, she had to have known where you were and what condition you were in."

"I don't want her to get involved."

"Sorry, Robert, she already is. Son, you're making this way too hard. What are you afraid of?"

Robert's voice shook slightly. "If he goes to jail, then we won't have any money."

The two detectives let out collective sighs. Benson said, "So it was your father."

Robert kept his head down.

"Well, does your mom work?" asked Detective Peterman.

"She's a cook at Central Elementary School in Pike Township. But she doesn't make near what my dad makes. I don't know how we'd get by without his paycheck. I may have to drop out of school and get a job." Robert looked sad at the prospect of that.

"Robert, these things can be worked out. Do you have a church you and your mom can go to for help?"

"We go to First Trinity Lutheran. They might help us," Robert murmured.

Detective Benson chimed in. "Look, you've admitted that your dad attacked you. He's not going to get away with it. When we arrest him, we'll take him down to the police station and book him. Then he'll go in front of a judge for his arraignment. If he makes bail, he'll be free to go back to your home. You can't be there if he does. Maybe the ADA can convince the judge to hold him without bail. Then he'll be locked up in the county jail. By the way, where will you go when the hospital releases you?"

Robert slumped in the wheelchair. "I don't know. I guess I'll go home."

Detective Peterman said, "We can't let you go home if your father makes bail. Is there somewhere else you can stay?"

Robert's troubled face reflected his worry. "I don't know."

Benson said, "We have to keep you safe."

"No, this isn't happening!"

Detective Peterman put a calming hand on Robert's knee. "Son, look. You have to accept that things have changed now."

Robert clenched his fists. "All I want to do is go back to school. I've got these scholarships, and I'll lose them if I don't go!"

Detective Benson said, "Robert, you are in no shape to go to school. It starts when?"

"It starts tomorrow. September third."

Detective Peterman said, "You haven't even been released from the hospital, Robert. With your injuries, it's going to take time for you to recover. There's no way you can be gallivanting around that big campus any time soon. You'd better plan for next semester."

Robert looked down to his lap, crestfallen.

Detective Benson brightened. "What about that guy who was here a few days ago. Tell us more about him. He had black hair, mustache, glasses?"

"Oh, he's just somebody I met at I. U."

"What's his name?"

"Joe Kaufmann. I don't know him all that well."

"What's his interest in you? Is he a casual acquaintance?"

"Sort of. He's a friend of the French horn teacher I had last year."

"He said he didn't know your parents."

Robert looked down, his hands clenched.

"Where does he live?"

"He . . . I guess he lives in Ithaca, New York. He's a doctoral student in the history department."

Benson wrote down "Joe Coffman" in his notepad, misspelling Joe's surname. "So, he came all the over here to see you? He must be more than just a casual friend. Maybe he can help you find a place to live."

"Your mom wants to see you, Robert. How 'bout it?" Dave Peterman lit a cigarette.

"Yes, but what will I say to her?"

"Anything you'd like to talk about." The detective smiled through the wafting smoke showing yellow teeth. "Detective Benson and I will set up the meeting. Let's get a nurse to take you back to your room."

Detective Peterman went into the hall to notify a nurse. After Robert was wheeled out of the waiting room, the two detectives conferred.

Peterman said, "We should look up Robert's high school records, talk with his teachers and any of his friends who might still be around. We could get a yearbook. We need a recent photo for the ADA."

"Yeah. And I'll check with I. U. to see what he was up to this past year. Look at his grades and talk to his professors. And let's see if he's had any run-ins with the Bloomington police while he was down there."

"You know, Charlie. I suspect we'll find a squeaky-clean kid just trying to go to college to get his degree. Naw, he didn't do any of those things his pop accused him of. That guy's a liar and a thug."

"I agree. But we still need to get the real lowdown from the wife."

CHAPTER FOURTEEN

Despite her insistence that her husband would be furious if he found out, Ada Stangarden allowed two police officers to take her back to police headquarters for another interview. Only when she was told that she would see her son did she quiet down. However, the assurances that nothing bad would happen did not convince her otherwise.

At one-thirty in the afternoon, while her husband was at work, Mrs. Stangarden entered the headquarters building escorted by the officers. The headquarters connected to the brand new, twenty-eight-story City-County building on Market Street in downtown Indianapolis. She sat in a first-floor room filled with filing cabinets, a rectangular table, three folding chairs, an industrial-size coffee urn, Styrofoam cups, and bulletin boards covered with most-wanted posters and graffiti-marked rules of the room. Curtains that looked pre-World War II hung over a north window which appeared to have never seen a cleaning rag. In the corner, an exhausted, fingerprint-smeared refrigerator woke up intermittently with complaining hums.

After accepting a paper cup of water from a female clerk who immediately left, Ada waited alone. She was more frightened than she had been when she and her husband had boarded the bus in Weimar, Germany, nineteen years ago that had taken them to a makeshift airport bound for Buenos Aires. What would be worse: being questioned by the detectives now or facing her husband later at home? He was already raging about the disarray and black smudges on the doorframes and kitchen cabinets and bedroom dressers. She had to scrub her house from top to bottom.

As she thought about this, the door creaked open slowly. A police officer in short sleeves wheeled Robert into the room. Ada rose to greet her precious boy, crying his name. Robert closed his eyes in pain as his mother tightly hugged his shoulders. His face reddened with emotion. In German, he whispered, "Mom, why didn't you stay with me at the hospital? Why did you leave? I needed you. I don't know what's going to happen. I want to go home."

Before his mother could answer, the two detectives on the case walked in and sat around the big table.

"Vat goes here?" She began to move Robert's wheelchair toward the far side of the table.

"Please sit, Mrs. Stangarden," said Detective Peterman. "We have a lot to discuss."

"I am arrested? I am in trouble?"

"No, ma'am. We only want to ask you some questions."

Still holding on to her son's arm, she sat in a chair.

"Mrs. Stangarden," said Detective Benson, "we have done extensive background on this incident and—."

"No'ting happened. It vas a mistake!"

"Mrs. Stangarden, please try to control yourself," said Detective Peterman. "Getting upset isn't going to help you or your son."

Robert sat motionless in his wheelchair except for blinking his eyes.

"Can you tell us what happened on August 29 in the afternoon at your house?"

Ada Stangarden's voice quivered. "I know no'ting. No'ting happened."

"When we interviewed you and your husband, you should remember that he implied some hooligans beat up your son. Robert was running with the wrong crowd. He was involved in fencing stolen property."

Robert nearly got out of his wheelchair. "What? You're lying! You're making this up! My father would never—"

Detective Benson pulled out his notepad. "I have it all down right here. He said—"

"I don't believe it! Why would he say such things? I've never been in trouble! I made straight A's in school! I was salutatorian in my class at Pike! I told you that in the hospital yesterday!"

"We know that, Robert. Your father was lying."

Robert turned to his mother. In German, he cried, "Why, Mom? Why would he say such things?"

Before his mother answered, Detective Peterman said, "Please speak English, Robert."

Switching back to English, Robert whined to his mother, "Why would he betray me?" He folded his arms protectively against his chest.

Detective Benson's voice rose. "Because he's more interested in saving his own skin than telling the truth, Robert! That's why we need you and your mother to tell us what actually happened last Saturday afternoon and why you ended up in the ICU!"

His mother took a tissue from her pocketbook and began twisting it. She would not look at her son.

The detectives watched them. No one said anything for several moments.

Detective Benson finally spoke. "Mrs. Stangarden, we know of a gentleman who knows your son. He came into the hospital a day after Robert was out of the ICU."

Ada Stangarden looked at the detective. She missed a beat.

"Do you know anything about this man?"

"Nein."

Letting that dubious answer pass, Detective Benson read from the file in front of him. "His name is Joe Coffman."

Ada Stangarden rocked back and forth, her plump hands hiding her face. She wailed, "Nein! Nein! I never him know! Nicht wahr! Nicht wahr!"

Robert looked at his mother, trying to make eye contact with her. "Mom! What are you saying? He brought me home in May when school was out. He was in the kitchen when you and Dad came in with the groceries. You saw him!"

The panicked woman fidgeted, moving her hands around the table nervously.

Robert frowned in disbelief. He turned to the detectives. "She did! And my dad saw him, too. They seemed to recognize each other. And then Mr. Kaufmann ran out of the house after that. He got in his car and just took off. I never heard from him again all summer. I don't understand any of this." He pounded his hands on the arms of the wheelchair.

The detectives wrote hurriedly. "When was this? How come this is the first we've heard about it?" said Detective Benson.

Robert looked down into his lap. "It was in May."

"So, what happened?" asked Detective Peterman tersely.

"He helped me moved back home after finals week. While he was there, my mom and dad came in. They had been out buying groceries."

"And?"

Robert's mother continued to wail.

"He left, and that was it." He looked back and forth from his mother to the detectives. He was too confused to explain any more details of that bewildering scene.

Detective Benson moved around in his chair in exasperation. He said, "When I spoke to this guy in your hospital room, Robert, he said he didn't know your parents. Now you're saying he saw your parents at your house and knew them. Why would he lie about that?"

Detective Peterman turned to Ada Stangarden. "Mrs. Stangarden, why are you so distressed? Is there something we should know about you and your husband meeting this man?"

The terrified woman opened and closed her mouth as if she couldn't think of the correct answer. Her round eyes behind her smeary glasses darted like Ping-Pong balls around the room. "Nein! Nein! Ve gut volk!"

Robert watched in utter amazement his mother's antics. But before he could say anything, Detective Peterman went on.

"What happened after Mr. Kaufmann left? Robert?"

Robert looked pleadingly at his mother. But she let out full-throated wails. He said to the detectives, "They got mad. My dad left the house, and my mom went up to her room."

Ada Stangarden's shrieks escalated in volume.

"So, they knew each other, right?" Detective Benson nearly shouted to be heard.

Robert's mother appeared ready to fly to the ceiling.

"Okay, Mrs. Stangarden. Please settle down." Detective Peterman spoke over her. "Please. We'll talk about that another time." He glanced at his partner, who nodded once. "Let's talk about something else."

The detectives allowed several minutes for the woman to compose herself. She pressed her tissue into her face and inhaled deeply.

"When did you and your husband immigrate to the United States?"

asked Detective Peterman.

Ada Stangarden seemed caught as if a car she was riding in suddenly swerved into a different direction. Finally, she exclaimed, "Neunzehn achtundviertzig." She shifted in her seat, discreetly pulling her dress down over her knees.

"Nineteen forty-eight," said Robert. "Speak English, Mom."

Detective Benson asked, "Straight from Germany?"

Returning her attention to the detectives after looking around the room, she replied, "Nein . . . Buenos Aires."

"When did you live there?" asked Detective Peterman.

"1945 to 1947. Warum asking me questions?"

"Just some background information, ma'am. So, your son, Robert, was born in Buenos Aires?"

Ada flitted her hands again about the table. "Ya, ya. Can now I go?"

"Please, just a few more questions, Mrs. Stangarden," Detective Peterman spoke kindly.

"Under what circumstances did you and your husband come to Indiana?" Detective Benson asked. His voice revealed scarcely veiled impatience.

Confusion on her face required clarification with the question. "Why did you come to Indianapolis?"

"My husband got job mit Allison Transmission. They make truck parts."

"Yes, we are familiar with Allison," said Detective Peterman. "Did you have Robert with you?"

"Ya."

"How old was he at the time?"

She had to remember. "Three years old, I think. Ya."

"When was he born?"

"Two February 1945. Nein. Zweite Februar neunzehn sechsundvierzig."

Robert said, "February second, 1946." To his mother, he said, "Mom, how can you get the date mixed up?"

Ada Stangarden lowered her head and began to whimper.

"Calm down, Mrs. Stangarden," Detective Peterman said in a warning tone. "Where was he born?"

The woman sniffed and wiped her eyes. The room became still, albeit the old refrigerator humming in the corner.

After a moment's pause, Ada Stangarden put her head on the table on top of her hands and began sobbing again uncontrollably.

Detective Benson rose. "All right, Mrs. Stangarden. I think we've had enough for today." He opened the door and went into the hall to call for the two police officers to take Robert's mother home. But before she left, she sputtered terse words to Robert in German. She clutched his arm hard, seeming not caring that he winced in pain.

"Tell them nothing. Just say it was all a mistake, a misunderstanding."

"That's what I've been saying, Mom. You know I don't want you or Dad to get into trouble. But, Mom, I'm confused about Mr. Kaufmann."

The woman straightened and then leaned back over to Robert. "What did you say to that man? Have you talked to him?"

"He came to the hospital. I spoke to him."

"Oh, God in heaven!"

"Let's go, Mrs. Stangarden." Detective Benson took her arm. As Ada Stangarden reluctantly moved away, he said to Robert, "We'll call the ambulance to come and pick you up. Another officer will take you to the front entrance."

Robert's head began to pound.

CHAPTER FIFTEEN

With the technician's report of finding copious amounts of blood in the living room using the luminol, and the cab driver finding the top of a bloodied glass candy dish, the detectives had enough to arrest Henry Stangarden. What sealed their decision: Mr. White identified the butcher knife hanging in a rack on the kitchen wall, perfectly clean and polished, yet glowing bright with the luminol. At the police station for booking, Henry's protestations could be heard up and down the hallways, and he fought every fingerprint, every mug shot, and every snap of the handcuffs. His wife was beside herself. What should she do now? A sympathetic police clerk suggested that she call a lawyer. But who? Poor Ada knew no one, and she was so upset she couldn't even pick up a phonebook. But she had enough presence of mind to call her good friend, Gladys Mikkelson, who called another friend, a Mrs. William Anthony. Her husband worked in the legal department at American Fletcher National Bank, and he would know just the right lawyer.

Enter Mr. Edward Moscowitz. As an experienced attorney, Mr. Moscowitz worked with the law firm of Dudley, Young, Moscowitz, and Bernhart. He was a well-dressed gentleman, fond of wearing tailored, double-breasted suits, silk ties, natty little handkerchiefs in a breast pocket, shiny gold cufflinks, and European-made shoes. With a pencil-line mustache and heavily perfumed black hair, Mr. Moscowitz looked more like a well-heeled manager of a five-star New York hotel instead of a Midwest defense attorney. He took the Stangarden case after receiving a desperate call from Mrs. Anthony. She convinced him to take the Stangarden case pro bono. He would be doing the Lord's work, she had said. How could he refuse? Mr. Moscowitz considered the potential publicity for his firm.

Henry pled not guilty in front of the arraignment judge. The prosecutor, Assistant District Attorney Wilbur Morris, asked for $10,000 bail. The judge settled on $5,500. Since the final amount was beyond the defendant's means, he was dragged kicking and shouting to a jail cell.

Marion County General Hospital released Robert three days after his father's arrest. Against the stern advice of Mr. Morris, Robert went back to live at his parents' home. The attorney said if in the future, someone posted his bail, he'd be out. Robert could not be at home if that happened. However, Robert's mother, Ada, insisted that he needed her care.

Reluctantly, Robert accepted the fact that he would not be going back to I. U. Over the next several months, his mother helped him continue his recovery with plenty of pillows and German chicken and dumpling soup. Being an active member of First Trinity Lutheran Church, she received support from her two closest church friends, Velma Sheely and Gladys Mikkelson. They went with her to the grocery store and took Robert to his medical appointments. When Robert insisted he was well enough to be left alone, his mother resumed her job as a Central Elementary School cook. She didn't want to go back to work, but they needed her income. Robert started looking in the newspaper for a job.

Ada visited her husband many times at the county jail. A pleasant experience it was not. When she came home, her son Robert always had a cold washcloth for her face, a box of tissues within easy reach, and a comforting arm to put around her quivering shoulders. When they talked about why his father had been arrested, the story they agreed on was that it was nothing but a big misunderstanding. By not saying it out loud what actually had happened, they believed if they kept telling themselves this dubious story, it would be convincing enough to the powers to be to allow Henry to be released and returned to his loving family. The hard part was waiting for something to happen.

A meeting was set up at the police headquarters between Mr. Wilbur Morris and Mr. Ed Moscowitz to discuss a possible plea agreement. Henry Stangarden and the attorneys sat in the same interrogation room. The air in the room was heavy and close.

"Photographs don't lie, Mr. Stangarden." Mr. Morris turned around the file photos to show to Mr. Moscowitz and his client. "Do you remember these pictures from the last time the detectives spoke with you?"

Without even looking at the pictures, Ed Moscowitz replied, "We don't dispute the assault, Wilbur, but to accuse my client of trying to kill his own son is ludicrous. It was just an argument that got out of hand. The kid's got a hot temper, that's all. Mr. Stangarden was only trying to calm him down."

Henry Stangarden folded his arms across his barrel chest, watching and listening.

"Oh, so now he admits he committed the crime. No more hooligans, eh? Now the excuse is he was just trying to calm him down? Let's see. The medical report says that he suffered four broken ribs, a bruised kidney, a concussion, a punctured lung, bruises on his face and back, and, oh, let's not forget, a cut across his throat that required twenty-two stitches." Mr. Morris shook his head, smiling tightly. "No, Ed. This wasn't a friendly spat between a father and son. This was an assault with intent to kill. Besides, his wife was an eyewitness. She saw the whole thing."

"You will never get that in. She'll claim spousal privilege. She won't testify against her husband."

"Even to get justice for her son? Your client is a bully and a thug. He tried to kill his son without any provocation, and he has to answer for that."

"Without provocation?" Henry spoke up, unfolding his arms and putting his menacing hands on the conference table. "Dere vas plenty—"

Ed Moscowitz put a hand on his client's arm. "Please say nothing, Henry. You don't have to respond."

Wisely, Henry closed his mouth.

Mr. Morris said, "See? He admits it."

"Yes, but I've heard that the victim, his son, won't even admit that his father assaulted him. If I get him on the stand, he'll deny everything. But let's say he does admit it. He'll corroborate that it was just a minor argument that got out of hand. I only need one jury member.

Reasonable doubt."

Mr. Morris met eyes with his opponent. "Are you so sure about that? I've got another witness. His name is Joe Coffman."

"Who?"

Suddenly, Henry Stangarden became agitated. His beefy face became crimson. "Nein!" He stood and struck his fist on the table, making it rock. "Nein! Nein!"

Both lawyers stared at him.

"Mr. Stangarden, do you have something—?" started Mr. Morris.

"Wilbur, let's bring this meeting to a close." Mr. Moscowitz shuffled his papers while eyeing his client with some trepidation. After Henry slowly sat, he said, "So can we plead this down to third-degree battery, probation for first-time offense?"

"Not on your life, Ed. When the jury sees these pictures, they'll convict your client in fifteen minutes."

"Well, then I guess this meeting is over." Ed Moscowitz shoved files into his briefcase. "We'll see you in court." He hurriedly pushed his client out of the room.

CHAPTER SIXTEEN

Joe had never been to downtown Indianapolis. Since Irene's apartment was on the near northwest side close to the hospital, he had had no reason to explore this part of the city. He had trouble finding a parking space on East Ohio Street, and he had to dig under the car seat to find enough change for the parking meter. He entered the two-story brick office building and took the elevator to the second floor. He found Suite 201 and gave a quiet knock on the door.

"Come in."

Joe entered the room.

A trim, middle-aged man beaming a friendly smile held out his hand. "Hello. I'm the assistant district attorney for Marion County Wilbur Morris." His welcoming eyes showed an eagerness to put a potential witness at ease.

"Joe Kaufmann." Joe shook firm hands with him. He couldn't help but stare at the other man's sandy-colored hair. It was so luxuriously thick and well-combed that he wondered if it was a toupee.

"Thank you for coming, Mr. Kaufmann. Please. Make yourself comfortable." Mr. Morris gestured to a padded chair in front of his desk. He absently adjusted his horn-rimmed glasses over his slender, slightly crooked nose as he seated himself behind his desk.

Joe sat and looked around the attorney's office. Distinguished-looking law books covered two walls from floor to ceiling, reminding him of the old medical textbooks packed on the shelves in Grayson's home office. Shadow boxes displayed badges, medals, and military ribbons. Gold framed documents and certificates shared space with prints of nineteenth-century English hunting scenes and steeplechases. A black and white photo showed a beaming Mr. Morris holding a shiny plaque in one hand and shaking hands with an elderly, important-looking gentleman. A leather nailhead couch was positioned against the east wall, accompanied by two matching chairs. On a polished walnut coffee table sat a silver tray with a flask of water and glasses along with a green marble ashtray. Scattered throughout the room were cardboard boxes with lids, topped with more file folders. An American flag stood in one corner behind the attorney's desk, the Indiana State flag in the opposite corner. Most prominently displayed on the south wall was a colossal graduation certificate from the Indiana University School of Law.

"Do you mind if I smoke?" asked Mr. Morris, holding a black pipe.

"No, not at all, if you don't mind if I smoke with you," Joe replied, looking at him over a brass banker's lamp on the desk.

He forced himself to join the other man's chuckle as they both pulled out lighters. As they busied themselves, the glass-paneled door opened and another man in a grey wool suit entered carrying a briefcase.

Mr. Morris rose. "Mr. Kaufmann, I'd like to introduce my colleague, Mr. Johnny Wells. He's another ADA with this office who will assist in this case."

Joe stood and shook hands with the dumpy, moon-faced man. "Pleased to meet you, Mr. Wells."

"Same here," replied the other man, attempting to pull back his baby-doll mouth into a smile. He sat in another chair and put a delicate ankle on his tiny knee. He rummaged through his large briefcase in his lap. "Now, where's my pen?"

Mr. Morris handed him one from the center drawer of his desk. "I want it back, Johnny." He gave a grin and a wink to Joe. "He's always losing his pens."

"Hey, somebody keeps stealing them from my desk," retorted the other man defiantly. He took out a small comb and ran it through his thin feathery hair over the top of his round head.

Joe wasn't sure if these two men were being serious or not.

While Mr. Wells situated himself, Mr. Morris continued. "Mr. Kaufmann, this case is one of the saddest I've ever come across." He opened a generous file and changed out his glasses for a pair of half-glasses. "I hardly know where to start." He knitted his brow as he looked at the papers before him. "Nothing's worse than violence that occurs in the home."

"Amen to that," offered Mr. Wells.

Both Joe and Mr. Morris looked at him.

Joe willed himself to stay calm, but he shifted in his chair. He scanned Mr. Morris's desk for an ashtray among the piles of folders on it. The door behind him opened. He turned to see Detective Benson and another man walk in who he didn't know. They pulled up chairs around the ADA's overloaded desk,

Mr. Morris stood. "Mr. Kaufmann, this is Detective Peterman and Detective Benson."

Joe shook their hands. He remembered the fat one, Detective Benson, from that first unpleasant meeting with Robert in the hospital.

The lawyer took out a legal-sized notepad and uncapped a fountain pen. "I don't know how closely you've followed this case in the news. A Mr. Henry Stangarden was arrested and charged with attempted voluntary manslaughter against his son, Robert. The detectives had told me that you had visited Robert when he was in the hospital after the assault, and the two of you seem to know each other. Can you tell me about that visit?"

Joe cleared his throat and drew on his cigarette. He tried to keep eye contact with the assistant district attorney, which was difficult because the man kept shuffling papers and other things on his desk. "Um, I got a call from my sister, Dr. Irene Pierce, who is a resident at Marion County General." He watched the attorney write the date of the interview and Joe's name in large capital letters.

"Umm, my name is spelled K-A-U-F-M-A-N-N. K with two n's."

Mr. Morris gave a short laugh. "So it is." He gave a knowing look to Detective Benson, who had given him the incorrect spelling.

Detectives Benson and Peterman pulled out their little notebooks with irritated resignation and began scribbling.

ADA Morris scratched out the name "Coffman" and wrote "Kaufmann." "Where were we? Oh, yes. When did you receive a call from Dr. Pierce?"

Joe paused to think of the right date. "August 29. She asked me to come back to Indianapolis from Ithaca, New York."

"Why from Ithaca?" asked Mr. Wells in an incredibly juvenile-pitched voice. He also held a legal pad.

"That's my home. I'm a doctoral student at I. U., but I stayed with my guardian and his wife, Drs. Grayson and Ruth Pierce during the summer."

"Doctors? Must run in the family." Mr. Morris looked up. He seemed not to have noticed or perhaps not cared that Joe had said the word "guardian."

"Yes. Dr. Irene Pierce is his daughter."

"Are you in medicine, too?" asked Mr. Wells.

"No. I'm studying history. I'm working on my dissertation."

Mr. Morris said, "Very well. Please continue. You got a call from your sister."

Joe decided not to mention their argument about him coming back to Indianapolis. It didn't seem pertinent. He heard nothing yet from the detectives, although their presence unnerved him. Maybe he could pretend they weren't in the room. "I came to Indianapolis four days later. Irene said she had a patient come in whom she thought I knew. His name was Robert Stangarden."

Mr. Morris did not look up as he wrote on his pad.

"He had been severely beaten. He had a punctured lung, concussion—"

"Yes. I have the medical report." Mr. Morris took another file and handed it to the other ADA. "He was lucky to be alive. Let me stop you for a moment, Mr. Kaufmann. The reason why we're filing attempted voluntary manslaughter is not only because of his extensive injuries but also because Robert had a laceration across his throat. The person who did this meant to kill him." He switched his glasses. After puffing on his pipe thoughtfully, Mr. Morris continued. "This Henry Stangarden fellow. You know him?"

"What? I'm sorry. No." Joe's voice seemed not his own. He felt the severe, unforgiving eyes of the other two gentlemen sitting on each side of him. He heard matches being struck.

Plus, he heard a whistle from Mr. Wells. "Wow. Get a load of these pictures. That guy sure had it out for the kid."

Joe wasn't sure he wanted to see the vivid color photographs of Robert's wounds. He jumped at an unfamiliar voice.

"Why did Dr. Pierce call you in the first place? How do you know Robert, and why would your presence be needed at the hospital?" asked Detective Peterman.

"Ah, I had met Robert last fall at I. U. through a mutual acquaintance, Frank Oneida. He was Robert's horn instructor. You see, Frank and I went to concerts there on campus. Frank got us together after an opera performance. Robert played in the pit orchestra. Frank wanted us to meet because he thought we looked related."

Mr. Morris shifted papers and found another photograph. After removing his glasses and putting on his half-glasses again, he studied it. "Hmm. Yes, I see the resemblance."

The diminutive Mr. Wells stood and leaned over the desk to look at the black and white picture.

Joe tried to see the picture, which from his angle was upside down. It was Robert's high school graduation photo. He was curious about how the lawyer had gotten it.

"Do you know how we can get in touch with him?" asked Detective Benson.

Joe hesitated, thinking. "He's from Washington state. You could probably contact the I. U. music school to get his address and phone number." Joe had his phone number, but it was buried somewhere in his desk at his apartment. He was not keen on offering to give it to these heavy-handed detectives.

"We'll do that." The overweight detective started writing in his little notepad. "We went down to I. U. a few weeks ago to talk with the kid's professors. I don't know how we missed this guy. But we'll check him out." He flicked ashes from his cigarette in an ashtray on the desk.

Mr. Morris said, "Please go on about your relationship with Robert."

"We saw each other from time to time throughout the school year."

"Yes."

Joe had a sudden vision of walking dangerously close to the edge of a precipice. He decided to look at the law books along the wall.

Mr. Morris referred to his notes. "According to the detectives, you had more dealings with Robert at the end of the school year. Care to tell us about that?"

"I-I'm not sure what you mean."

Detective Benson spoke. "We had a chat with Robert and his mother. Robert said you drove him home at the end of finals week." He flipped pages in his notepad. "It was the third Friday of May."

Joe desperately wanted another cigarette but was afraid these unfriendly interrogators might notice him if he lit up.

Detective Peterman spoke. "He said you went into his house and you saw his parents, Henry and Ada Stangarden. Their reaction was most peculiar. His parents started screaming and shouting, and you supposedly ran out of the house."

The ADA peered at him over his half-glasses. "Is that an accurate description of the event?"

Joe's shoulders twitched. "I . . . I saw them, and then I left."

"Did you speak to them?"

"No."

"Did you recognize them?"

Now Joe couldn't control his hands. He shoved them into his pants pockets. The room was warm and humid. "No."

The tall, skinny detective, Peterman, stood and slowly walked around behind Mr. Morris's desk. "Mr. Kaufmann, are you positive?"

Joe felt his glasses slipping. He quickly pushed them up and pushed his chair over a little from the other ADA, Mr. Wells, who took great interest in him. "Yes, I'm sure."

"Hmm. According to Robert, it appeared his parents recognized you, and you dashed out of the house like a bat out of hell." Detective Benson sounded more and more accusingly.

Mr. Morris said, "Were you in contact with Robert after that incident?"

"No. I went back to Ithaca for the summer. I just saw him that one time at the hospital at the end of August."

"What did you and Robert talk about in the hospital?" Again, this bothersome little Wells character.

Joe glanced at him, noticing his odd, tawny eyes. He cleared his throat. "We, ah, just talked about how he was doing, you know, with his injuries. Why are you so interested in me? I'm beginning to feel like I'm the one about to get arrested."

"Mr. Kaufmann, we are just trying to gather all the facts about this case," Mr. Morris explained patiently. "If this, indeed, goes to trial, we have to be ready for anything. This man has a good defense attorney who may put you on the stand. We have to know what your answers will be. We can't help Robert if we get caught unaware of any pertinent facts. Do you understand?"

"W-what would happen if I refuse to testify?"

"Well, you might get subpoenaed, and you would have a legal obligation to take the stand," explained Mr. Morris. Kindly he asked, "Mr. Kaufmann, why would you refuse to testify?"

Joe sat straighter. "I've never had to do anything like this before. Fear of the unknown, I guess."

That answer seemed to satisfy the ADA. "Fine. Let's not get ahead of ourselves. We are just gathering the information. Your cooperation is greatly appreciated. Now, I will ask you again. Do you know this man, Henry Stangarden?"

All four men waited. Joe crossed his arms and knees protectively, and he averted his eyes. "I'd rather not say at this point. It's a long story." His voice was flat.

The fat detective, Benson, gave an angry sigh.

"Is that all, Mr. Morris? I'd like to leave. I've got an appointment back in Bloomington, and I need to get on the road." Would his lies never end? He rose quickly.

After a pause, the attorney said, "Yes. That's all for now, Mr. Kaufmann. But please be aware that we will be in touch."

"What happened to Robert's father after he was arrested?"

Detective Benson rose and stood closer to Joe. "He got arraigned, and he's sitting in a jail cell. Bail was set high enough that he couldn't meet it."

"How long will he stay in jail?"

Standing, Mr. Morris answered, "Maybe until the trial. It depends on whether or not someone posts his bail."

"How long will it be before he goes to trial?"

"These things usually take a year."

"A year?"

"Unless we reach a plea agreement," offered Mr. Wells.

"Okay." Joe hoped the other men didn't see the beads of sweat on his forehead. He turned toward the door.

Detective Benson stopped him. With a blatant look of intimidation, he said, "Don't leave the city, Mr. Kaufmann."

"But I live in Bloomington. I have to work on my dissertation."

Mr. Morris said, "That's okay, Mr. Kaufmann. Just be available."

Joe nodded once. He walked out slowly, trying to act casual despite his racing heart.

CHAPTER SEVENTEEN

"What happened at the District Attorney's office?"

"Irene, the proper title is the Assistant District Attorney's office."

"Okay. How did it go? How long were you there, Joe?"

"About half an hour. It was nerve-wracking."

"What was the assistant district attorney's name?"

"His name was Wilbur Morris. They kept asking me questions I didn't want to answer."

"They? Were there other people in the room?"

"There was also another ADA, a Mr. Wells. He was annoying. Two detectives were there, too. I think their names were Benson and Peter-something.

"Peterman?"

"How do you know that?"

"I got a call from a Detective Peterman yesterday. He asked me to come to the police headquarters for an interview."

"Well, let's hope he only asks you about Robert's injuries and nothing else."

"Maybe. Phil Baker has to talk with him, too. He was the other doctor on duty when Robert came in. Joe, will you please sit? You're pacing around like a caged tiger."

"I can't help it, Irene. I'm nervous, and I'm scared. I hate being in this situation."

"I understand. And put that cigarette out. You know I don't want you smoking in my apartment."

"All right. Happy now? Do you have anything I can eat? Chips or something?"

"Yes. Come into the kitchen, and I'll make some popcorn. There's Coke in the fridge."

"This is turning into a nightmare."

"Will you stop beating around the bush and tell me about your interview?"

"Okay. They asked me what my relationship was with Robert and if I knew his parents. I said Robert was just a friend. Robert told those detectives I took him home in May, and I saw his parents. I told them I didn't know them."

"You lied to them!"

"Yes, I did. I'm trying to stay out of all this."

"Well, I guess you can blame me for getting you involved."

"I wasn't expecting to get wrapped up in this fiasco. It all started when Robert was in the hospital. When I saw him, this Detective Benson was asking all sorts of questions about how he got injured and who did it and where and when."

"Yes. And?"

"Well, Robert kept evading his questions. He wouldn't say what happened. The detective asked if he was involved in something illegal like drugs or something."

"Which he wasn't because his tox screen came back clean. He didn't even have any alcohol in his system."

"Of course not. Robert's too naïve to get into things like that. If he has any bad habits, it's spending too much time in a practice room with his French horn."

"Fine. Go on."

"Is that popcorn ready yet?"

"No."

"As soon as that detective left, I asked Robert who assaulted him, but he wouldn't tell me. But I suspected it was his father. But obviously, the police figured it out because they arrested the old man, and now he's in jail, awaiting trial. They're itching to know why Henry Stangarden assaulted Robert. I think I know why he did it."

"Here's some ice. Go on. Why do you think he beat up Robert?"

"Henry Stangarden has everything to lose if Robert finds out who he really is. That Nazi bastard knows I'm around and—"

"He's afraid Robert will run into you again at I. U. He thinks you'll tell him who his father is. And he can't take that risk."

"He could have just told Robert that he wasn't going back to school. He didn't have to pound him to smithereens and cut his throat. I think there's more going on between the two of them than anybody knows."

"But Robert doesn't know that you knew his parents from Buchenwald. Oh, my!"

"Of course, I didn't tell him! And I made sure I didn't see him or talk to him after that."

"I remember you said when you came back to your apartment after that, you wouldn't answer your phone."

"Robert told me in the hospital that he had tried to call me several times. But I didn't want to talk with him. I didn't want him to know how I knew his parents. Should I have told him that his mother was a cook at Buchenwald, and she gave food to my father and me at night for months? That his father was a Nazi civilian? His disgusting secret would be out.

"By the way, I remember their real names: Rikkert and Matilda Steghausen. They must have changed their names to get into the United States. Henry and Ada Stangarden. What a crock! Their whole lives here have been just one big deception!

"Do you see why I'm so upset? Irene, I'm the lynchpin in this whole mess. And the detectives and this ADA are breathing down my neck to open up. They know I know something. Irene, these guys are smart. They know how to interrogate witnesses. They'd ask me to speculate on why Henry Stangarden assaulted his son. I could tell they didn't like it when I sidestepped their questions. But I couldn't let them take me down that road."

"I don't know why you're so stubborn and uncooperative about all this."

"It's called self-preservation! If he did that to his son, what do you think he'd do to a Jew like me? Once a Nazi, always a Nazi."

"He's in jail, Joe. He can't hurt you now. You have to tell them! Otherwise, this monster is going to get away with what he did to Robert!"

"Oh, he's not getting away with it. There was enough evidence to get him arrested and charged with attempted voluntary manslaughter. He'll get convicted and put in prison regardless. Then Robert can go back to school, I can go back to Ithaca to work on my dissertation, and life will go on. End of story . . . except . . ."

"Except what?"

"The ADA said I might get subpoenaed."

"Yes, you couldn't lie on the witness stand."

"But explaining how I know this monster would cause an explosion like an H-bomb."

"Okay. Let's say that you don't get subpoenaed. No one knows about what you know about this man. If he does end up in prison, he'll get out sooner or later. He'll come after his son again! And maybe you, too!"

"Robert will just have to take care of himself. I, on the other hand, will be safe and sound living seven hundred miles away."

"Joe Kaufmann! How can you be so callous and selfish! Robert can't get on with his life with this hanging over his head! He'll always be looking over his shoulder. He won't be able to live without fearing for his life! If you abandon Robert like this, how could you live with yourself knowing that you allowed him to be trapped under the shadow of his father who's out to kill him? And Robert wouldn't even know the real reason why!"

"So how would I be able to protect him? I'm not his brother. I'm not his keeper! If I stick around and he gets out of prison, he would try to kill me just as he tried to kill Robert."

"Maybe you could get an order of protection."

"You think that would stop that guy? Now, do you understand why I was so damned scared out of my mind this past summer? Irene, I can't . . . I don't want to go on with this! What about my career? I just got back on my feet living at home. I'm ready to start working again to finish this doctorate."

"Joe, I understand that you want just to leave and put all this behind you."

"No, you don't. You don't know what I went through."

"Okay. You're right. But that doesn't mean I can't sympathize and support you. Maybe if you tell the truth to this ADA, this awful man and his wife will be deported back to Germany. You can help Robert then. You could be like his new big brother."

"What? There's no guarantee they'll get deported. I just hope he gets convicted and put away for a very long time."

"And I'm sure Daddy and Ruth would help him, too. They'd treat him like another son. They would be thrilled."

"Irene, you're not listening. Are you suggesting that Robert cut off his mother, his only blood relation, and suddenly be willing to be folded into a perfectly strange family who lives three states away? C'mon, Irene. Get real."

"What's the alternative, Joe? Don't you think Robert deserves to know who his parents are?"

"That would destroy him."

"And getting his throat slashed didn't already nearly do that? You know you're going to have to speak up. The wheels of the justice system will not stop turning just because you don't have the courage to face this couple. If this goes to trial and you get put on the witness stand, you can't lie and say you know nothing. If you have to face that Nazi monster in court, so be it. You have me and Daddy and Ruth to support you. We'll be right there with you. If I call Daddy, I'm sure he and Ruth would come to Indianapolis."

"No. I don't want to keep leaning on Grayson. I'm twenty-six years old now, and I can face my demons on my own. If Grayson comes, he'll just get all weepy and wring his hands and yell at me about being brave. I'm not in the mood for that."

"Yes. And your way of facing your demons is to try to commit suicide."

"I don't need you telling me that!"

"Joe, you've got a friend who desperately needs you. Please don't give up on him. And your guardian has to be in the loop."

"Stop pressuring me, goddammit!"

"Oh, that's the phone."

"Don't answer it! It's probably Grayson. I don't want to talk to him."

"I gotta get it. Joe, you can stay here tonight."

"Okay. Can I smoke a cigarette while you're on the phone?"

"No. Here. Eat your popcorn."

CHAPTER EIGHTEEN

With an impasse on a plea deal, Wilbur Morris spent numerous hours preparing for trial. The detectives interviewed potential witnesses, assisted by Mr. Wells, the other ADA on the case. Besides interviewing Irene and her colleague, Dr. Phil Baker, the detectives knocked on Henry and Ada's neighbors' doors. The most they could say was that the Stangardens were pleasant and quiet, and they had never caused any trouble. They claimed they saw Henry only when he mowed the lawn in the summer and shoveled the sidewalks in front of the house in the winter. Sometimes his teenaged son, Robert, came out to help. Ada occasionally came over for coffee on Saturdays. However, no one had seen or heard anything on that sunny afternoon on August 29.

They interviewed Robert's high school teachers and his gymnastics coach. Robert had been an exemplary student, they had said. Curiously, none of them had ever met his parents. Then the detectives took a scenic trip down to Bloomington to speak with Robert's professors. Much to their unhappiness, ADA Wells went with them, talking up a storm on the seventy-five-mile trip. As with Robert's high school teachers, his music professors had glowing reports about this musical wonder boy. They were disappointed that he had not returned this school year and were dismayed to hear that he had some family issues.

An almost too-good-to-be-true picture of the Stangarden family emerged. Since their arrival in Indianapolis nineteen years ago, Henry and Ada and their toddler son, Robert, had assimilated into American

Midwestern society with apparent ease. Claiming to be German refugees by way of Argentina, they had gained U. S. citizenship, dutifully learned the language, found jobs, bought a home, joined a church, and paid their bills on time.

Detectives Benson and Peterman talked with Ada's co-workers at the elementary school who said they had liked the cheerful, German lady who loved to sing while preparing the students' lunches. She talked with the children as they filed down the cafeteria line, always smiling at them, and asked how they were doing in their classes. And sometimes she brought baked treats to the teachers' lounge.

Likewise, Henry's supervisor and upper managers at the Allison Transmission factory praised Henry as an excellent worker. Mr. Bryon Whitaker, Henry's immediate supervisor, commended his work ethic, his detailed attention to the numbers he crunched, the speed and accuracy of his typing skills. He had sat at the same desk on the second floor for the last nineteen years; no knick-knacks or pictures of his family, only a company-issued calendar on the wall behind his desk. Henry brought his lunch in a paper sack and ate by himself in the employee lounge. He never smiled or even said "Good morning" unless spoken to first. One could count on his routine like clockwork. Laughing, his boss had said, "German efficiency."

Ada Stangarden had two loves: music and cooking. She had told her friends in her church's women's circle that she had played the piano since the age of five, and she had won music contests when she was a teenager in Leipzig, Germany. She had even participated in music festivals in Hamburg and Vienna. When the organist at First Trinity Lutheran was on vacation, she filled in on the piano at the services. And of course, she loved to sing in the choir.

More importantly, she lived her music through her son Robert. How pleased she had been when he had picked out melodies on the piano when he was only four. Twelve years of piano lessons followed, including ten years with a piano professor at the Jordan College of Music in downtown Indianapolis. Showing off his talent to visitors in her home had been her greatest pleasure. Of course, she secretly hoped that he would become a concert pianist. However, when he started junior high school in Pike Township, the school band's lure pushed that dream aside. He took up the French horn. So, Ada drove him to music contests, band concerts, football games where he had led the marching band, and pep band rehearsals. She always sat in the front row at all his performances. When he got ready for college, she boasted to her friends about the scholarships he had won at the Indiana University School of Music. He was training to become a great musician and teacher, she had said.

As to her other passion, Ada eagerly showed off her fine German cooking. Her recipes were always in demand. Of course, many of her church activities included bringing her best dishes to such events as potlucks, Christmas dinners, picnics, craft bazaars, and Easter brunches. She adopted many American-style techniques: deep-pan frying, pressure-cooking, broiling, and toasting. The only time she argued with her husband was when she had wanted to buy a new kitchen appliance at the Sears store. Sometimes he gave in, and the unique culinary delights she had set before him at the dinner table smoothed over the discord.

What was pointedly missing in all this was Robert's relationship with his father. When the detectives and lawyers discussed this issue, no one seemed to know much about it. Of course, his mother was a constant support in his life. She would talk about him to anybody who listened. Henry Stangarden stayed incognito in the shadows of their living room.

****

The most crucial task for ADA Morris to build his case against Henry Stangarden was getting Robert's account of the assault. At his insistence, Ada brought in Robert for a deposition to nail down the event. With his mother tearfully sitting in the waiting room, Robert finally broke and described to Mr. Morris and Mr. Wells what had happened on that Saturday afternoon in August.

"I was getting ready to go back to school at I. U. I had all my stuff packed in the car, and my parents were going to take me down to Bloomington. But at the last minute, my dad decided that he didn't want me to go. He wanted me to stay home and get a job."

"How did it escalate into the physical confrontation?" asked Mr. Morris.

Robert sighed. He didn't want to talk about what had happened next, but he knew he had to.

****

The last suitcase, filled with etude books and some French horn solos, took the far corner of the trunk of his dad's Chevrolet Impala. Robert shut the lid and went back toward the house to tell his parents he was ready to go. As he walked up to the front porch, he heard shouting in German through the screen door.

In the living room, his mother sat on the end of the sofa, her smooth, heart-shaped face in her hands, her shoulders shaking. His father, dressed in his usual white shirt and baggy, ill-fitting trousers, panted with a reddened scowl on his bulldog face. He stood on the other side of the coffee table.

In German, he said, "You will not go to the university. You will stay here and get a job."

Replying also in German, Robert answered, "What? What are you saying? I'm already packed!"

"No!" he said sternly. "This is final. Unpack and go upstairs."

His heart beating fast, Robert turned to his mother. "Why? I don't understand."

His mother said, "Listen to your father." Her clipped German voice was thick with angry acceptance.

Robert exclaimed, "No! You never said anything all summer about me not going back to I. U."

"I'll explain it to you, you ungrateful boy." Henry Stangarden took a step closer to his son. His breath reeked of beer. "We have no money to pay for that university. You will stay here and get a job."

"How can you say that? I. U. renewed my scholarships! All my tuition is covered. Didn't you see the letter I got from the School of Music back in July? You just have to pay for my dorm room and my meals. But I'm going to get a part-time job to help pay for that. This school year will cost you almost nothing!"

His mother spoke. "I can help, too, Henry. I will use my paycheck from the school job to help."

Henry roared, "No! That is a degenerate, disease-ridden sewer of disgusting undesirables. I will not spend money on you to be in a filthy place like that. You will stay away from that cesspool down there and get a job here in this town."

"I don't believe this! You know how hard I've worked to get into this music school. All those private lessons, the recommendations I got from my music teachers. I just can't give it all up! I'm going to become a music teacher!"

"Bah! It's just a pipe dream. You need a real job. Maybe I can get you into a bank or maybe at the company."

Ada stood. To her husband, she cried, "This is what he wants to do! Let him go!"

"Keep your mouth shut, Ada. I rule this house."

"He's my boy, too! Oh, how can you be so unreasonable?"

Robert turned to his mother. "That's it. Mom, you can drive me down. Let's go." Then he hesitated. He stood in front of his father, meeting his granite eyes. Shaking with anger, he said, "You're afraid I'll run into that man you saw in May in the kitchen. I'll stay away from him. I promise. I didn't know him that well anyway." He turned toward the door.

He felt something round and solid strike his shoulder. After he turned around, another blow from the hard object smashed his nose. Blood burst out, and he tasted it on his lip. He instinctively put up his hands to protect himself. He heard his mother cry out. His father had in his hand the palm-sized glass top of a candy jar, a favorite piece in the living room, always filled with candied orange slices and malt balls. But now the thick glass top was a weapon raining blows on his face. They pounded too quickly for Robert to fend off. With an extra bit of effort, his father finally brought him down with a blow to the left side of his head.

Robert saw black. When he awoke, he was on the carpet between the coffee table and the couch. His ears roared, and he saw his mother's feet and heard her screaming and his father shouting and cursing. The attack continued with bone-cracking kicks to his sides. When he turned over on his stomach to try to crawl away, the glass jar top pummeled his back from his shoulders to his waist. Finally, he heard a thud. His whole body was drowning in pain, and he started to retch. He spit blood.

He heard footsteps leading to the kitchen. Silence. Then they grew nearer. He felt his head roughly lifted by his hair, and he saw his mother's heavy-duty butcher knife in front of his bleeding face.

"You will obey me, or you will feel this knife deeper across your throat," his father growled. He lingered, holding the knife close. Then, while his wife looked on, he drew the blade slowly across Robert's throat. Robert began to groan through his teeth, holding out his hands to grab it. But he cut his fingers on the blade. Then he heard a clunk on the coffee table. Robert heard the front door open and close with a bang. His mother would not stop shrieking.

****

Robert's body shook as if the room's temperature was below zero. "He was just trying to make his point that he was serious about me staying home. And . . . I guess I have to do what he says." He put his head down on the table, cradling it in his arms.

"Robert, is that all there is to your story? Are you telling us everything?" asked Mr. Morris.

"Y-yes."

Johnny Wells spewed his questions. He seemed to have forgotten about the woman stenographer sitting in a corner recording this deposition. "Your father talked about filthy, disgusting people down at I. U. Do you know what he meant by that? And you said you'd stay away from your friend. Did you mean Joe Kaufmann? Does your father know him? Does Mr. Kaufmann know him?"

Robert lifted his head. He met the attorney's strangely colored eyes then looked away. "No. Yes. I don't know." He quickly wiped his face.

Mr. Morris motioned the stenographer to stop recording the deposition. He said, "Robert, I can't do my job to convict your father if you don't tell me everything. Can you please explain what he meant when he didn't want you to go back to I. U.?" His voice hardened.

"I don't want you to convict him! I don't want him to go to jail. I just want us to be a family again. I've learned my lesson. I'll stay home and get a job. Can't you just stop all this?" Robert sounded like a petulant child.

Wilbur Morris set his mouth hard in exasperation. He exchanged a look with his colleague, who nodded his head in concurrence about this difficult young man. He asked, "Who are these 'undesirables' your father was referring to?"

"Please! Just let me go home."

There had to be more, but Wilbur Morris couldn't pry it out of Robert. "All right, Robert. We're finished. You can use the phone at the front desk to call a cab to take you home." He sighed and rose, closing his files. Mr. Wells followed him out, along with the stenographer.

After parking on East Ohio Street near his office building, Wilbur kicked the front tire of his ten-year-old Pontiac Catalina in frustration. This case was taking on the elements of a Miss Marple whodunit. Too many holes in a story that at first had appeared a slam dunk. He was working harder than he should have to on this obvious attempted voluntary manslaughter charge. The proof was there that this brute of a man had attacked his son. And he didn't have to prove motive, although he knew from experience that juries loved to have it presented at trial. But even so, when he had offered a lesser charge of third-degree battery just to avoid the hassle of a trial, the accused was too arrogant and too stupid to take it.

But it was this uncooperative victim who stymied Wilbur. He knew the kid was holding something back. But he thought about the interviews with the Stangardens. Why did they fly off the rails whenever the other character in this bizarre calamity, Joe Kaufmann, was mentioned? Despite the son's evasive answers, the couple, indeed, seemed to know this mysterious man from Bloomington. Yet, at the same time, he suspected Kaufmann was also not telling everything he knew. He flatly denied knowing this couple even though Robert thought that he did. There were secrets here that everyone involved seemed desperate to keep at all costs. Wilbur knew he had to have the answers. He had to be prepared for Ed Moscowitz's defense strategy.

He debated about taking another run at the enigmatic Mr. Joe Kaufmann. Could he get to the bottom of this, or would it just be a waste of time?

CHAPTER NINETEEN

Grayson and Ruth stood in the back of the packed, strepitous courtroom. After taking off their coats, they settled in for a long morning. Grayson held his wife's white-gloved hand. As Joe sat with his guardian and stepmother, his churning stomach could not be relieved by the antacids he took by the handful. He kept watching for the defendant but didn't see him. Then he saw the courtroom double doors swing open.

Ada was flanked by two stoic, middle-aged women with defiant chins held high. Adorned with perky tea hats with netting veils over their faces and walking in no-nonsense, low-heeled pumps, they kept Ada moving forward. In her brown print dress with matching jacket and carrying her new JC Penny black clutch purse on her arm, she held her head as if she wore blinders, never looking right or left, not unlike a reluctant bride walking down the aisle to meet her husband-to-be by an arranged marriage. One would almost expect a triumphant fanfare from a church organ. The spectators were hushed as all eyes were on this little-known wife of the defendant.

Ada sat immediately behind her husband in the gallery. Her two companions sat on each side of her, their arms folded in the manner of resolute bodyguards. They eyed the courtroom with mouths turned down.

At the defense table, Mr. Ed Moscowitz, resplendent in a navy blue Botany 500 single-breasted suit and stoplight-red Armani tie, sat next to his client, Henry Stangarden. The lawyer bent his head toward him, whispering. However, Henry sat with crossed arms over his tight suit coat, staring straight ahead as if not listening. At least he appeared subdued. Perhaps he was being told to keep his behavior under control.

Among the spectators were men in suits and fedoras, scribbling in tiny notebooks similar to those the detectives used. One curious man was busy drawing sketches of the courtroom. Grayson noticed all of them and whispered to Ruth, "Those are reporters. This trial is going to get a great deal of publicity."

"Where's Robert?" she whispered back.

Grayson twisted his head to look around. "Maybe he's out in the hall."

"All rise!"

Like a congregation reluctantly standing for the first hymn, the spectators rose. The judge, the Honorable Leonard E. Campbell, a lantern-jawed, gray-haired gentleman, took his seat on the dais.

"Be seated!"

The first witness was Dr. Irene Pierce. Having had no experience sitting in a witness box, she was understandably nervous.

"Please state your name and address." ADA Morris stood and came around his table.

"Irene Pierce, 201 West 38th Street, Apartment 3-E, Indianapolis."

"Thank you." Mr. Morris gestured to the overweight, orange-haired court reporter sitting to the left of the judge's bench. With thick-veined, bejeweled hands still poised over her machine, she gave a fleeting smile to the witness.

"Miss Pierce, will you please describe Mr. Stangarden's injuries when he arrived at Marion County General Hospital on August 29 of last year?"

Irene explained in layman's terms what his condition had been. While she spoke, Mr. Morris organized several large, color photographs that he had taken from a thick folder.

"If it pleases the court, I would like to enter into evidence these photos, People's exhibits one through eight."

"Objection, Your Honor!" Ed Moscowitz was on his feet. "These pictures are highly inflammatory and will be prejudicial to the jury!"

Wilbur Morris countered, "Your Honor, these photographs reveal much more the extent of Robert Stangarden's injuries than what Miss Pierce could describe in purely medical terms."

The judge held out his hand to take the pictures. He put on his black-framed half-glasses over his hooked nose and examined them, lips pursed in a downward grimace. "I'll allow them. Objection overruled."

The jury eagerly studied them. One woman gasped. Maybe she was looking at the raw gash on Robert's throat held together with nasty black stitches.

"Did you happen to see who brought him in, Doctor?" asked Morris.

"Objection! The prosecution first referred to this witness as Miss Pierce. Now she's a doctor. Which is it? Does she even work at Marion County?" Ed Moscowitz was undoubtedly on his game.

A muffled tittering rose from the gallery. In the back, Ruth noticed her husband had let go of her hand and squeezed his knees. His mouth was a thin, hard line.

"My apologies to the court. Let me back up." Mr. Morris covered his error with a disingenuous smile to the judge. "Dr. Pierce. Would you please tell the jury your qualifications?"

Irene frowned as if insulted that she had to explain herself. "I am a resident physician at Marion County General Hospital. I graduated from the Indiana University School of Medicine in 1960. My title is Dr. Irene Pierce."

"Thank you for that clarification. So, on the day in question, where were you when Robert Stangarden was brought in?"

"I was working in the doctor's chart room."

"Did you see Robert come into the hospital? Did he walk in, or was he on a stretcher?"

"I don't know. I didn't see him when he was brought in." Irene courageously looked out at the gallery. She saw Joe sitting in the back-left side of the courtroom with her father and stepmother. She hoped he could not see the defendant, Henry Stangarden.

"Was anyone with him?"

"No. He was alone."

"What were his injuries?"

Irene looked at the jury members who were still studying the photos. "He had a concussion, broken nose, four cracked ribs, a bruised kidney, and a punctured lung."

"How long was Mr. Stangarden hospitalized?"

"Seven days."

"What did Mr. Stangarden tell you about what had happened to him?"

"He didn't. We, the other resident doctor, Dr. Phillip Baker, and I had to ask him."

"Didn't he say at first he had been in a car accident?"

Irene was ready with her answer, as she had been prepped earlier by Mr. Morris. "Yes."

"But that wasn't consistent with his injuries, correct?"

"Correct." She paused and then went on. "He looked as if someone had beaten him."

"Objection!" announced Ed Moscowitz. "Calls for speculation."

"Your Honor, as a trained physician, Dr. Pierce would be knowledgeable as to what such injuries would reveal an assault rather than a car accident."

The judge said, "Sustained. Rephrase, Mr. Morris."

"What made you think he had been assaulted rather than injured in a car accident, Dr. Pierce?"

"He had several hematomas on his back—circular bruises, like something round had been used to hit him. When we looked at his scalp, we saw the same bruising."

"How many times had he been struck?"

Irene had to think fast. "Eighteen times, counting all the similar shapes of the bruises."

Mr. Morris went back to his table. He took an object out of a cardboard box. He held up the softball-sized item for both Irene and the jury to see. "Would he have been hit with something like this?"

Mr. Morris gave the object to her to examine. It was a round, thick glass piece with a sloping edge on one side. She wasn't sure what it was as it was the first she had seen it. "Yes. This could have caused the hematomas." She handed it back.

Facing the jury, Mr. Morris asked, "Do you know what it is?"

"It looks like the top of a piece of glassware."

"People would like to enter into evidence exhibit number nine, Your Honor." Mr. Morris held up the glass piece to the jury, walking slowly so all could see it.

The judge squinted. "So be it."

"Thank you, Dr. Pierce. No further questions." The assistant district attorney put the glass ball back in the box and sat.

Defense Attorney Moscowitz buttoned his suit coat as he approached the witness stand. "Dr. Pierce, you said that Robert said he had been in a car accident. But that wasn't true, was it?"

"No." Irene could feel heat coming up from the neckline of her dress.

"And we know there was no police report of an accident. Correct?"

"Yes."

"So, Robert had lied to you about what had happened."

Unsure, Irene said, "Well, yes."

"In fact, he continued to lie and deny what had caused his injuries, didn't he?

"He was too trama—"

"No more questions for this witness."

Irene hesitated before stepping out of the witness box. She wanted to describe more about Robert's emotional state, having suffered that horrible flogging. But the court waited patiently for her to step down.

Next up was a Mr. Ralph White.

Dressed in a frumpy, over-sized checkered suit, the small man climbed into the witness box after taking the oath. The deep lines in his face suggested ample life experience.

"Please state your name and address, sir." Mr. Morris studied his open file, appearing uninterested in the man's answer.

"Melbourne Ralph White. 882 East Rural Street, Indianapolis." The slight man moved around in his chair, a bit too fidgety. "Folks call me Ralph."

"Very good, Mr. White. What is your occupation?"

"I'm a cab driver for Yellow Cab Company."

"And you've been employed with this company for how long?"

"Goin' on twenty-five years." He grinned proudly at the jury, showing crooked, cigarette-stained teeth. Unable to sit still, he rocked from side to side.

"Mr. White, would you describe your movements on August 29, 1963?"

Mr. White kept his foolish grin. "Well, that was almost a year ago, so I'll have to think."

In a tight voice, Mr. Morris said, "Please tell us what you remember." He gave a stern look at the witness, thinking, We went over this three times in prep. You very well remember what you did that day. You said you'd never forget it!

"Ah, well, I got a call from dispatch to go to 5051 West 46th Street."

"What time was this?"

"Around 2:00."

"What did you see when you arrived?"

"I saw all these boxes and clothes and books and such in the driveway and on the sidewalk. It looked like somebody just threw it out like garbage. Then there's this big lady who was coming out of the house screamin' and hollerin' like the house was on fire. And the worse part was she had all this blood on the front of her dress. My, oh my!"

"Go on."

"She was speaking in a foreign language and broken English, so I couldn't quite get what she was sayin'. So, I get out of my cab, and she grabs me by the arm and pulls me into the house."

Mr. Morris moved closer.

The courtroom was still, except for Henry Stangarden tapping a benign forefinger on his folded arm.

"So, I go in and, boy, I've never seen anything like that in my life!"

"Please describe what you saw."

The man lost his grin and replaced it with raised eyebrows and widened blood-shot eyes. "It looked like a tornado hit it."

"It being?"

"The front room. The living room, I guess. There were chairs overturned, and the davenport was settin' crooked. Then there was the blood."

"Where did you see the blood?"

"Oh, it was on the davenport and the coffee table, and a lot of it on the carpet."

"What else?"

"All the time, the woman kept yellin' and cryin'."

Out of the corner of his eye, Wilbur Morris saw Mrs. Stangarden behind her husband, worriedly rocking with her hands tightly clasped under her ample bosom.

The cab driver scratched the back of his head nervously. "Then I saw the kid."

"Are you referring to the victim, Robert Stangarden?"

"Yeah. He was layin' on the floor on his stomach, not movin'. The woman, I guess she was his mother, wanted me to help get him up and into my cab. She kept saying somethin' like 'kranen.' Maybe she meant the hospital.

"I could tell right away that this poor kid was hurt bad. He wasn't movin' or nothin'. So, when I stooped down to turn him over to get him on his feet, Lord, he was bleedin' like a stuck pig from his neck! Then I saw . . . I saw that round thing on the coffee table."

Mr. Morris quickly took the glass object from his colleague, Mr. Wells. "Is this it?"

"Yeah, only it had blood on it. Not much but—"

Ed Moscowitz was on his feet again. "Objection! Calls for speculation as to exactly what was on the piece of glass!"

"Rephrase, Mr. Morris."

"Mr. White, how would you describe what was on the glass ball?"

"Looked like blood to me. But then I saw right next to it a big butcher knife. Now I know for sure what that was. That was blood!" He leaned forward and pointed his finger for emphasis.

The gallery came to life. The judge banged his gavel hard. "Quiet!"

Meanwhile, Mr. Morris went back to the prosecution table and exchanged the round, glass ball for a large, black-handled kitchen knife from the other ADA. "Mr. White, do you recognize this knife?"

Before Ralph White could answer, female wails erupted from behind the defense table. The defendant turned around to speak to his distraught wife.

Mr. Moscowitz was too busy trying to break up his client and his wife to object.

No one seemed to bother watching the jury's reaction. They moved about in their seats, straining to see the alleged weapon used to cut the victim's throat.

Judge Campbell pounded his gavel again. "Order in the court! Order!"

Ed Moscowitz stood. "Your Honor!"

"I will clear the courtroom if you don't all be quiet!"

The volume in the room settled.

"Mr. Morris, continue!" the judge barked.

Slowly, for the sake of drama, Mr. Morris carefully held the knife pointed down with two fingers on the handle as though it were alive and dangerous. He held it up for the jury. "I will ask you again, sir. Do you recognize this knife?"

"Yeah! That's the one I saw on the coffee table."

Over the scuffling gallery, Mr. Morris nearly shouted, "I submit to the court People's exhibit ten!" The notorious knife went back in the box.

"So ordered." Judge Campbell scowled, still angry with the boisterous gallery.

More loud sobs and wails came from behind the defense table, drawing the judge's attention. "Ma'am, if you cannot control yourself, I must ask you to leave." He shook his gavel at Mrs. Stangarden.

"She'll be fine, Your Honor," said Mr. Moscowitz. He spoke hushed but terse words to his client's wife. She seemed to understand, albeit reluctantly. Her two female "bodyguards" patted her shoulders with reassuring, lace-gloved hands.

Mr. Morris resumed. "Mr. White, let's continue. You say you saw Robert on the floor lying on his stomach. He wasn't moving."

"Yeah. So, I turned him over real slow, and I'd never seen anyone look like that before! I couldn't believe my eyes! He had all these bruises and marks on his face, and he had a bloody nose. But the worse was this cut on his neck. He was bleedin' somethin' fierce. And I told the lady to go get some towels. But she just stood there like she was in shock. I said, 'Lady, we need to call an ambulance.' But she kept sayin', 'Nein, nein.' She insisted that I get him into my cab to take him to a hospital. Well, I hate to say it, but I didn't want him bleedin' all over my backseat. You know, what would my boss say? Besides, I wasn't sure that he wasn't already dead. We'd have to get the police involved, and they'd probably impound my cab, and who knows when I'd get it back."

Ada Stangarden had had enough. She pushed her way to the center aisle and hurried out of the courtroom, her two female bodyguards in close pursuit.

Mr. White mumbled as he watched the women leave, "If it was a crime scene or somethin'."

During the testimony, Robert's father sat motionless, staring straight ahead as he had admonished to do.

The prosecuting attorney continued with this witness. "Mr. White, what happened next?"

"Well, I had to do what the lady said, as much as I didn't want to. As soon as I lifted his arm, he came to. So, I thought, Thank God, he's still alive. I kinda picked him up and dragged him through the front door, and the missus tried to help me. Somehow, I managed to get him in the back of the cab. I hope I didn't hurt him any more than he already was. I needed some towels as I was getting' blood all over my hands and my shirt. The lady grabbed her purse, shut the front door, and away we went. Since she didn't tell me which hospital to go to, I figured Marion County would be the best one to take him to.

"When I pulled up to the front doors. I figured I'd go in and tell somebody that I had a hurt passenger and that he needed help right now. But the lady got out and started pulling the kid out of the cab. I helped her get him out, but as soon as he hit the sidewalk, she just pushed me back toward my cab, and she got in. She told me in her broken English just to drive away. I tried to tell her that we needed to alert the docs and the nurses, but she kept sayin' to get goin'. So, I did. I thought surely somebody would see him. I felt real sorry for him. I couldn't understand how a mother could just leave her son like that."

"Objection! The witness has not been asked to editorialize the scene."

"Sustained. The jury will disregard that last statement by the witness."

Mr. Morris turned slowly to face the jury. "Did you notice anyone at the entrance who may have seen you take this unfortunate young man out of your cab?"

Mr. White thought. "No, I don't think so. For a place as busy as that hospital, you'd think somebody would have. I'm not sure."

"What happened when the woman got back into your cab?"

"Well, I took her back to her house. She paid my fare, and I left. I got another call for a pick-up downtown." The cab driver frowned. "But I had to stop at a gas station to clean up the back seat." He frowned and added, "I even had blood on the steering wheel. I had a heck—"

"Did you tell your supervisor about what had happened?"

"Well, yeah. But we figured since the kid was in the hospital, the doctors would look after him. We decided to let the police figure it out. Then about a week later, I got called by some detectives."

"No further questions." Mr. Morris sat.

Ed Moscowitz approached the witness. Mr. White looked a bit confused, not sure why he was being asked more questions.

"Mr. White, your testimony is that you got a call to make a run to 5051 West 46th. Is that correct?"

"Yeah."

"And when you arrived, other than seeing some items in the driveway, everything looked normal."

"I suppose, except when the lady came out like she did."

"Did she identify herself?"

"No."

"So, you didn't know who she was."

"Well, I assume—"

"Please, don't assume anything, sir. So, you followed her into the living room where you saw the disarray, the glass piece, the bloody knife on the coffee table."

"Yes. That's what I told—"

"Mr. White, did you know the young man on the floor?"

"No."

"Did you know his relationship with the woman?"

Mr. Morris popped up. "Your Honor, the defense is trying to muddy the waters when it is clear that the cab driver didn't know either the woman or the victim."

"Move it along, Mr. Moscowitz," said the judge.

"Mr. White, did you go into any other room in the house?"

"No."

"Did you see anyone else in the house?"

"No."

"Did the woman say if there was anyone else living there?"

"No." Mr. White frowned.

Abruptly, Ed Moscowitz turned around. "No more questions for this witness."

The judge said wearily, "You may step down, sir."

Mr. Morris called two more witnesses, a nurse, Susan Block, who had found Robert outside the front doors, and Dr. Phil Baker, who corroborated Dr. Pierce's account of Robert's injuries. The defense attorney, Mr. Moscowitz, had few questions on cross-examination.

Judge Campbell looked at the big wall clock at the back of the courtroom and called a recess for lunch. The trial would resume at 1:30.

Having sat in the back row, Joe, Grayson, and Ruth were among the first to enter the large hallway. After the crowd passed through the double wooden doors, Mr. Morris and Mr. Wells came out and joined them. Reporters began pumping questions which Mr. Morris ignored.

They lost interest when they spotted their next easy prey, Ed Moscowitz.

Joe kept a wary eye out for Robert's mother. Thankfully, he didn't see her. To Mr. Morris, he asked, "Who were those women who followed Robert's mom when she left?"

Mr. Morris lit his pipe. "I don't know, Joe. I didn't see them."

Robert stepped up to them from behind. "They were some of her church friends. She told me they'd be here with her."

Joe turned sharply to his right. This was the first time since the hospital visit almost eight months ago that he had seen Robert. His heart suddenly beat faster. His palms felt clammy. He hardly knew what to say to him.

"I guess that's nice of them," said Ruth.

Turning to Mr. Morris, Irene asked, "How did I do? I tried to answer the questions as we rehearsed."

"You did fine, my dear." The prosecuting attorney put a condescending hand on her shoulder. "You laid a solid foundation for our case."

"Yes, indeed," Mr. Wells added.

"But that defense attorney wouldn't let me finish my answer about Robert fibbing about how he got hurt."

To this, Robert bowed his head and turned away.

"That's a lawyer's tactic," Mr. Morris replied. "The trick was to leave in the jury's mind that the victim, Robert, is a liar. No matter that it was taken out of the context of the situation." He watched Robert wander toward a water fountain. "Excuse us. Johnny?"

Before Joe could introduce Robert to his family, the two lawyers moved away to talk to Robert. Ada Stangarden and her entourage joined the troupe. Joe watched intently, not realizing that he had stood behind Grayson as if the big man could keep him from being discovered by the woman who had been so kind to him so many years ago.

CHAPTER TWENTY

"The prosecution calls Mrs. Hermadine Wilson."

While the audience murmured, a heavy-set woman in a yellow, polka-dot shirt dress approached. She wore a tidy, Juliet hat and a sweet smile. After being sworn in, she took her perch beside the bench. She looked confident and prepared.

"Mrs. Wilson," Mr. Morris began. "How do you know Robert Stangarden?"

The woman's voice rang with clarity. "Robert was a student of mine while he was in high school."

"And where was that?"

"Pike High School."

"What class did he take with you?"

"He was in my junior advanced grammar class and American literature class his senior year."

"How did he do in those classes?"

"Very well. Robert was one of my best students. His essays and book reports were well-organized and articulate. He did very well on his grammar tests, too, as I remember."

Mr. Morris smiled. "What more can you tell us about him? Was he punctual? Did he get along well with the other students? Did he turn in his assignments on time?"

"Oh, goodness. Robert was always on time for class. And he got along well with the other students. I've never had a more serious, dedicated student. He always tried his best. And he was very, very polite. It showed good parenting." She smiled as if pleased with her answers.

After her last statement, Mr. Morris jumped ahead, hoping that the jury hadn't heard it. "Mrs. Wilson, we appreciate your assessment of this young man."

"Oh, I forgot to say that he knows what his goals are. He told me that the grammar class was to help him sharpen his writing skills for his college classes. This is a young man who has his head on straight."

"Thank you, Mrs. Wilson." Mr. Morris returned to his table. "Your witness," he said to the defense table.

Ed Moscowitz rose and buttoned his suitcoat. "Just a question or two, Mrs. Wilson. You described Robert as being courteous and well-disciplined. And you noted that that was because of good parenting. Would you expound on that, please?"

Mrs. Wilson replied, "He was much more mature and well-mannered than the other pupils. He had to have learned that from been reared in a home that values self-discipline, hard work, and respect for authority."

"Thank you, Mrs. Wilson."

The judge asked Robert's English teacher to step down.

The next witness, hurrying up to the witness stand like the busy man he was, was Mr. Olin Mitchell, Director of Bands at Pike High School. He eagerly answered Mr. Morris's questions, almost before he finished asking them.

"Yes, I've known Robert since he was a sophomore. But I knew about him when he was in junior high."

Mr. Morris matched his enthusiastic smile. "Oh? How so?"

"The junior high school director, Matt Stevens, just raved about him. He had started Robert on the French horn in beginning band, and he told me this kid was a natural at it. I was excited to have him in my band program.

"Please tell the court of your observations of Robert. Was he a good student?"

"Oh, I wish I had a hundred students like him. Smart as a whip, focused, hard-working. I can't say enough good things about him. And as Mrs. Wilson said earlier, polite as can be."

Mr. Morris continued to smile, pleased to have such an exuberant witness.

"But the best thing about Robert is his musical talent. He told me that he had been taking piano lessons since he was four, and he continued all through high school. I made him drum major in his junior and senior years because he was good at conducting. He led the pep band at the basketball games, too. He was quite popular.

"He took horn lessons with a professor at the Jordan College of Music. It didn't surprise me that not only did he get into the I. U. School of Music, just about the hardest in the country, but that the school awarded him so many music scholarships. He could just about skate his way to graduation."

Suddenly, before Mr. Morris could dismiss him as a character witness, the music teacher blurted out, "It's a damn shame his father never appreciated him. Beating him up like that! Robert never deserved—"

"Objection!" Ed Moscowitz was on his feet. "Witness was not asked his opinion on the relationship between the defendant and—"

Judge Campbell interjected. "Jury will disregard that last statement by the witness." He turned to Mr. Mitchell, who was glowering at the defense table. "Sir, only answer the questions put to you. No outbursts, please."

Reluctantly, the band director returned his attention to the prosecuting attorney.

"No more questions, Your Honor."

Ed Moscowitz declined to cross.

****

The trial resumed the next morning. The victim, Robert Stangarden, was the first witness.

"Mr. Stangarden, can you please tell us exactly what happened on the afternoon of August 29, 1964?" asked Mr. Morris.

Robert felt extremely uncomfortable in his too-big black suit, the one his mother had bought for him to wear for his band concerts at I. U. He had worn it just three times during his freshman year. He could only wish that he would be able to wear it again for the same purpose soon. "I was packing my dad's car to go down to I. U."

"That's where you go to school?"

"Yes. My dad was supposed to drive down with me, unload the car, and then he would drive back up to Indianapolis."

"By the way, was this your first year at I. U.?"

"No. I was ready to start my sophomore year."

"Thank you for that information. So, what happened as you were getting the car ready?"

Even with twenty feet between them, Robert felt his father's cold, hooded eyes. The left side of his head, where that candy dish lid had struck him, began to ache. His eyes wandered about, settling on the heavily rouged court reporter. Her experienced fingers, adorned with various gold and stone-set rings, waited over her machine.

"Mr. Stangarden?"

"Yeah, um, I went into the house, and my father told me I couldn't go to back to school."

"Why? Hadn't he seen you pack the car? Seems an odd moment to tell you that." Mr. Morris walked about, hands in pockets.

"Well, he decided that it wasn't the best place for me to be."

"Why not?"

Robert shrugged. "I don't know. He just didn't."

Warning bells in Wilbur Morris's head made him tighten his shoulders. To buy time to think, he went back to his table and pretended to read some notes. "According to what you said in your deposition on November 13 of last year, didn't he say at first he couldn't afford to let you go to college anymore? That he wanted you to stay at home and get a job to help support the family?"

"Yeah, he said that." Robert absently brushed his dark brown bangs away from his eyes. He had been told not to fidget.

"But isn't it true that you had won three music scholarships last year, and the school had renewed them for your sophomore year?" He put three pieces of paper in front of Robert. "You received the John Phillips Sousa Foundation Scholarship, the Dean's Scholarship, and the Premier Young Artist Award."

Robert sadly looked at the papers.

Mr. Morris paused to allow the jury to see Robert's reaction. "So, that excuse about not having money didn't hold water, did it? Did your father know about these scholarships?"

Robert had told himself before he got on the witness stand that he would not break down. But now he couldn't stop his trembling chin. Weakly, he said, "Yes, he knew."

"Could you repeat that, please, Robert?"

In a louder voice, he said, "Yes. He knew about them."

Mr. Morris feigned confusion. "So, that couldn't have been a reason for keeping you at home." The attorney stopped in front of the jury. "Then you said in your deposition that if you went to I. U., you might become involved in undesirable groups, people he didn't approve of?"

"I guess. I dunno."

"Mr. Stangarden, you are aware that you're under oath to answer the truth, all of it."

"Objection! Asked and answered." Ed Moscowitz half-rose.

"Sustained," came the weary-voiced answer from the bench.

"Did you know what he meant by 'undesirables?'"

Robert would not meet the other man's eyes. "To be honest, I didn't. I was confused."

Morris looked back and forth between the father and the son. "Robert, what kind of relationship do you have with your father?"

Robert truly felt ill. He wanted his father to stop intimidating him with those cruel eyes. "All right, I guess."

"Have the two of you been close?"

"Yes. No."

A couple of the jurors frowned. What was of no confusion to Mr. Morris was Robert not sticking to the prepared answers he had prepped him on. "Did he support you, take you to ballgames, perhaps attend your band concerts at school?"

"No. But that doesn't mean he wasn't a good father."

Morris let out a quick breath. "Let's get back to the day of the assault. You went into the house, and your father told you that you weren't going back to school. Then what happened?"

Robert looked as if in real physical distress. *Oh, please, why can't he just stop this?* "We got into an argument." He saw his mother sitting behind her husband, anxiety clouding her wonderful, caring face.

"And?"

"That's it, just an argument."

Morris had a feeling he was entering an episode of *The Twilight Zone*. He took a paper-clipped stack of papers from Mr. Wells and flipped several pages. He quickly put on his half-glasses. "Robert, you stated in your deposition that your father beat you because you refused to stay at home. Isn't that what happened?"

No answer.

"You do remember telling us about the beating?"

"Yeah."

"Can you tell the court what happened?"

"Uh, huh." Robert could not stop his restless leg from bouncing up and down, a mannerism that he used to cope with high-stress situations.

To the judge, Morris said, "Your Honor, a word with the witness, please?"

With no objection from the defense table, Morris hurried up to the witness box and whispered curtly to Robert, "What are you doing? This isn't helping us." He backed up before Robert could answer him. He debated if he should ask to make Robert a hostile witness. But that would also make him an unsympathetic witness to the jury.

"Is the man who assaulted you in the courtroom, Mr. Stangarden?"

Robert did not want to do this. He studied the wood paneling inside the witness box. "Yes."

"Will you please identify the man who beat you within an inch of your life?"

"Objection!"

"I'll rephrase. Will you point to the man who tried to kill you, Mr. Stangarden?"

"Objection, Your Honor! Leading the witness!" Moscowitz stood.

"Mr. Morris, let's keep our perspective," warned the judge.

When nothing happened, Judge Campbell turned to Robert. "Son, you must answer the question," he said with patience.

Thinking that if he just closed his eyes, this would all go away, Robert pointed a frightened finger toward the defense table. He opened his eyes to see his father slowly shaking his head, warning him with a threatening glare.

"Let it be entered into the record that the witness identified the defendant, Mr. Henry Stangarden, as his assailant. No more questions." Morris knew as he sat at his table that tonight would be a three-martini evening.

"Just a couple of questions, Robert." Ed Moscowitz approached the witness box, then pivoted to the jury box, floating confidant eyes over the jurors' faces. "Do you love your father?"

"Yes."

"Do you believe he loves you?"

"Yes."

"Has he ever done anything other than provide you a good home, a supportive hand, a solid Christian foundation upon which you could conduct your life?"

"No." Robert wished he could sound more decisive in his answer.

"Did he suggest that you stay in Indianapolis and help you get a job, say, in a bank?"

"Yes." Robert looked out at the spectators. Through the onlookers' immobile faces, he noticed in the back Joe Kaufmann, elbows on knees and his face hidden in his hands.

"And how would you describe the incident that happened in your parents' house that day?"

"It wasn't anything to get worked up over. We just had a disagreement. I know that I haven't been the best son in the world. I can be pretty headstrong sometimes."

A jury member, a fortyish woman wearing cat's eyes glasses and a bouffant hair-do, tilted her head slightly and frowned.

"Have you had arguments before?"

"Yes. But afterward, I always knew my father was right. I love my father. I have to obey him. He's head of the house."

"Thank you, Robert."

Joe exited the courtroom enraged. A white-shirted policeman followed him down the hall. Irene was right behind them, with Grayson and Ruth trailing.

Joe stomped away down the hall, swearing a blue streak.

"Shhh! Sir, please lower your voice."

Joe and Irene walked to the far side of the corridor next to the marbled railing. Grayson and Ruth looked on as they were in deep conversation. People began streaming out of the courtroom. Then, when Mr. Morris came out, Joe went to him.

"I'm ready to testify, Mr. Morris." He rather rudely pushed the other attorney, Mr. Wells, out of the way.

"Joe, I'm not sure that's a good idea. It's late in the game." The ADA set down his briefcase. "Remember, when we had our interview, you seemed reluctant to tell me how you fit in with this case. Do you have more information now?"

Joe's hard face reflected his brave determination. "I've made my decision to tell you everything. Robert didn't help himself on the witness stand. He practically excused his father for what he had done to him. Right, Robert?"

The young man standing behind Mr. Morris looked as though he was about to melt into the floor. "Mr. Kaufmann, you don't understand."

Joe's barely controlled voice reflected his fury. "I understand a lot more than you think." He turned back to Mr. Morris. "I know you must prepare your witnesses, sir. Can we go somewhere and talk?"

CHAPTER TWENTY-ONE

On the morning after Robert's testimony, the audience filed back into the courtroom, speculating animatedly about what would happen today. Outside the courtroom doors, reporters from the local newspapers, radio, and even television stations gathered in tight, oppressive circles around the parties involved. Although Mr. Morris's answers to their aggressive questions were brief and evasive, Ed Moscowitz exercised his oratory skills in defending his client, Henry Stangarden. Yes, his client's son had suffered some injuries as a result of a "disagreement." But it was nothing more than a family argument that had gotten out of hand. The son even said so himself. The kid wanted to be back with his family and move on with his life. There was nothing more than that.

When Ed saw Joe Kaufmann's name as the next witness, his heart dropped. He knew he made a mistake. Having seen this man's name on the witness list provided to him by the prosecution earlier, he should have interviewed this shadowy man from Bloomington, But his client had bullied him into not speaking with him. They nearly came to blows when Ed tried to reason with him. Curiously, Henry refused to explain why this witness should not be contacted. And for some odd reason, his wife, Ada, also had begged him not to talk to the man whose name they would not speak. Today, regrettably, Ed conceded that he'd have to "wing" it.

The assistant district attorney waited after Joe took the oath and sat in the witness chair. Mr. Morris quickly glanced at his notes, thinking this has to be done exactly right. He turned to the defendant and studied him. Did he see an almost imperceptible uncertainty in how the man patted the top of his shiny head? Did he see him blink once? His lawyer, Ed Moscowitz, did not even appear to notice that his client was sitting next to him. But he was ready with his pen and legal pad, prepared to take notes. The whole courtroom was hushed under a sense of anticipation, but not knowing of what.

"Mr. Kaufmann, please state your full name and address for the record." Mr. Morris's tenor voice echoed up to the high plaster ceiling.

"Joseph Kaufmann, 7154 State Street, Ithaca, New York."

"What is your occupation, sir?"

"I'm a doctoral candidate in history at Indiana University. I've been a teacher's assistant part-time."

"How long have you lived at the address in New York?"

"Approximately twelve years."

"Approximately?"

"I've lived in Bloomington, Indiana, for the past five years working on my master's degree and doctorate. The Ithaca address is my permanent one."

Mr. Morris walked around slowly in front of the witness box with his hands in his suit coat pockets. Then he stopped and put his hands to his sides. "Mr. Kaufmann, do you know Robert Stangarden?"

"Yes."

"Can you tell the jury how you know him?"

Joe remembered to talk to the jurors, nine men and three women. All of them looked about middle-aged and reasonable.

"I met Robert through a friend of mine, Frank Oneida. Frank was a doctoral candidate in music, and he was Robert's French horn teacher."

"When did you first meet him?"

"It was in October of last year. I believe on the twenty-sixth. Frank and I attended an opera performance at I. U., and Robert played in the pit orchestra. The three of us went out for a meal afterward."

"So, you were living in Bloomington at the time?"

"Yes."

"Did you stay in touch with Robert after that?"

"Occasionally. We'd meet from time to time in a practice room in the music annex building. I play the clarinet as a hobby, and since Robert played the piano, we'd get together for fun. Frank and I also attended one of his band concerts."

"So, the two of you have a mutual interest in music."

"Yes."

While Joe spoke, Mr. Morris let his eyes wander to the defense table, checking the mood of the defendant. He asked, "Would you consider Robert a good friend?"

Joe was ready for this. "Not really. I'd have to say Robert was too busy to be a good friend with anybody. His priority was studying and practicing his French horn."

"Yes. At a prestigious school like I. U., he'd have to. Can you describe for the jury your assessment of Robert?"

Joe looked directly at the jury, meeting as many eyes as he could. "Robert's relationship to music is practically a religion. He loves playing his French horn. His goal is to become a public school band director and play professionally on the side. Not to be able to pursue his dream would devastate him. He picked I. U., not because of its vicinity but because he knew that was where he would get the most rigorous training anywhere in the country, perhaps in the world. He has no interests other than music. The fact that Robert was awarded three music scholarships demonstrates his value to the school as an extraordinarily talented student. They don't give out those awards unless the student is truly worthy."

"Thank you, Mr. Kaufmann, for your observations." Mr. Morris smiled.

Joe did not return it. He met eyes with Robert, who was sitting deep in the gallery on the prosecution side. They stared at each other for a passing moment.

The assistant district attorney changed gears. "Did you see Robert when the school year end?"

"I helped move him back to his home in Indianapolis at the end of finals week. After that, I went back to Ithaca."

"When was the next time you saw him?"

"Dr. Irene Pierce, who is my sister, had called me on August 29 to say that Robert had been in some sort of altercation and that she wanted me to come back to see him. I saw him in the hospital."

"Because you two were friends?"

"Yes."

"Describe the visit when you arrived."

Joe allowed himself to shift a little. "I was shocked. I'd never seen anyone in such bad shape in my life. He had tubes and machines around him, and his nose was bandaged as if someone had smashed it. He had nasty bruises on his face and bandages on his hands. Even his lip was cut. He just laid there in the hospital bed like he couldn't move because he was in so much pain."

"Did you know the extent of his injuries?"

"Irene, Dr. Pierce, had told me when she had called me three days prior."

"Did you get an opportunity to talk with Robert?"

"Yes."

"What did he say?"

Ed heard his cue. "Objection, Your Honor. Hearsay!"

"Sustained." The judge said with sleepiness in his voice.

Joe purposely didn't look at the defense table where Henry Stangarden sat with his fists on top of it. His wife, Ada, leaned forward.

Undeterred, Mr. Morris continued. "Have you seen Robert since that day in the hospital?"

"Only here at the trial."

A pause.

Judge Campbell asked, "Any more questions for this witness, Mr. Morris?"

"Yes." The attorney for Marion County, Indiana, rubbed his pointed, sharp chin thoughtfully. "Mr. Kaufmann, do you know Robert's parents, Mr. and Mrs.—"

"Nein!" the defendant shouted and got on his feet. He began pounding the defense table.

Judge Campbell shouted, "Mr. Moscowitz, control your client!"

"Objection, Your Honor! Relevance!"

The audience began to stir. Henry Stangarden shook off his lawyer's hands, trying to pull him back into his seat. Two courtroom guards gathered near.

"Ich werde dich toten sie Jew Schwein!"

"Mr. Moscowitz! Tell your client he must be quiet!"

Joe's heart raced. He grabbed the witness box railing, ready to jump over it and flee for his life. But Mr. Morris stood right in front of him, staring at him, willing him to stay calm.

Robert stood without realizing it. He looked right toward the defendant's table. What was going on with his father?

In the back row of the gallery, Grayson grabbed hands with his wife and daughter.

The gavel pounded over the din. "Mr. Moscowitz. Please tell your client to sit! You, too, over there." The judge pointed his gavel at Robert.

The big, heavy man finally sat. One could almost see the steam shooting out of his red ears. His wife began her usual rocking and moaning, putting her hands together as if in prayer. Her friend on her right held her shoulders and whispered to her.

Robert sank back in his seat.

Mr. Morris said to the judge, "This line of questioning goes to the defendant's state of mind at the time of the assault, Your Honor."

The judge tilted his grey head to think. "I'll allow it. But make it a straight line, Mr. Morris. No detours."

"Thank you, Your Honor." Mr. Morris stepped back and put his eyes back on the witness. "Let me ask you again, Mr. Kaufmann. Do you know the defendant?" He pointedly stood where Joe could not see the defense table.

"Yes."

"Do you know his wife?"

"Yes."

"When did you first see them?"

Talking as fast as he could, Joe replied, "While I was there at Robert's house, his parents walked in with some grocery bags."

"Had you seen them before that day?"

"Yes."

"And where and when was that?"

"I knew them from the Buchenwald concentration camp from 1944 through 1945."

Chaos exploded in the courtroom. The defendant was on his feet again. The police guards tried to restrain him, but he was as strong as a heavyweight prizefighter and would not yield. While Ed Moscowitz threw a fit and the gavel knocked incessantly like a jackhammer, Joe sat motionless, as though pretending to be a baby rabbit hiding from a lurking feline predator. He felt his body go numb, his mind blank. He closed his eyes, forcing himself to shut out the commotion around him.

The judge ordered the courtroom cleared, and the jury sequestered.

After throwing his weapon of choice on top of his bench, he called the lawyers into his chambers. He disappeared.

Joe opened his eyes and looked to see who would tell him to step down. The bailiff motioned him. But he waited to watch the guards take that minacious bulldog of a man out of the courtroom through a side door. Only then did he slowly rise and take the three steps down from the witness stand.

Joe wasn't sure where he was supposed to go. He asked a guard, "Should I wait in the hall?"

"You can stay there, but don't leave. The court attendant will tell you when to come back in."

Before Joe knew it, he felt arms around him from behind, pulling him into that familiar, comforting body. He smelled faint cherry pipe tobacco on the moist breath.

Grayson would not let go of his ward.

Others waited around him, understanding tears filling their eyes.

"I love you, Joe," Grayson said in a low voice. Finally, he let go and turned him around to gaze into those liquid brown eyes.

Joe exchanged tight hugs with his stepmother and his sister. A few yards away, he saw Johnny Wells walking toward him.

"Mr. Wells," he said. "What's happening?"

The dumpy little man said, "The opening shot across the bow, Mr. Kaufmann. Wilbur is duking it out with Ed Moscowitz in the judge's chambers."

"What does that mean?" asked Ruth.

"They are arguing about whether or not Mr. Kaufmann's last statement is inflammatory enough to declare a mistrial. Ed Moscowitz just got slammed with a curveball. Most likely, he never knew about your connection with the defendant. Even if it's not true, just the inference that he's a Nazi is enough to throw the trial."

Grayson shook his head. "But would the jury even know about Buchenwald? It's not common knowledge."

Mr. Wells shrugged. "Maybe. If the judge rules a mistrial, you'd better believe Wilbur will file charges again. He's almost counting on it. But he's got Moscowitz over a barrel and can get a better plea deal for Robert. Way to go, Mr. Kaufmann!" He tapped Joe on his arm.

"Just wait. I gotta get into chambers." The little man darted away.

Joe didn't know what to think. Johnny Wells had no idea the gravity of his statement about how he knew the defendant. To nobody, he said, "Is there anywhere I can sit?"

Judge Campbell's office looked much like Wilbur Morris's, but it was bigger and much more crowded with furniture and the requisite cardboard boxes and stacks of files on the floor. He had a penchant for greenery as potted plants took every available space on his desk, bookshelves, and filing cabinets. Two spider plants and a Boston fern hung from gold link chains at his spacious window. In front of his desk sat the three opposing counsels, Mr. Morris, Mr. Wells, and Mr. Moscowitz. The court reporter with the coiffed, bright orange hair sat in a corner with her little stenograph machine.

With arthritic, age-spotted hands clasped together, Judge Campbell began. "Gentlemen, I don't like surprises like this." He held up his hand before Ed Moscowitz could speak. "Mr. Moscowitz, I know what you're going to say, that the declaration from this witness that the defendant is from a Nazi concentration camp is the very epitome of a reason for a mistrial. I am inclined to grant your request. However, Mr. Morris, please explain what this is all about."

Wilbur Morris could hardly contain himself. "Your Honor, Mr. Kaufmann came to me yesterday afternoon asking to be put on the stand to give his take on this heinous attack on Robert Stangarden. He has a direct connection with the defendant and also his wife. He will reveal the real reason why this bully of a human being bludgeoned his only son and cut his throat."

Ed Moscowitz leaned back, rolling his eyes. "Your Honor—"

"Save it, Ed. Wilbur, we're not in the courtroom. So, what is this direct connection?"

"When Joe Kaufmann was six years old, he and his parents were prisoners at Buchenwald from 1944 to the end of the war. He saw Henry Stangarden, and he and his father were given food by his wife, Ada. And the defendant knows Mr. Kaufmann because, ironically, Mr. Kaufmann is the spitting image of his father, Hans Kaufmann. You saw the outburst from him when Mr. Kaufmann was on the stand. I believe he called him a Jew something or other."

Ed Moscowitz countered, "Of course there was an outburst from my client! Wouldn't you be a little perturbed if someone accused you of being a Nazi?"

Judge Campbell shuffled some papers on his desk. "Was this man on your witness list, Wilbur? This smells suspicious."

"Actually, he was. Until yesterday, he wouldn't testify because I felt I had enough testimony and evidence already. I wasn't planning to ask him originally."

Ed held out his palms in feigned innocence. "But, Your Honor, I need time to prepare. This is so sudden!" He crossed and uncrossed his knees. He would postpone kicking himself until later for giving in to his client's insistence on not interviewing this Kaufmann guy. He should have gotten a deposition.

Holding up a piece of paper, Judge Campbell said, "Here is the name: Joe Kaufmann. And the date on the list is October 30, 1964. And today is March 19, 1965. You've had plenty of time to interview this witness before the trial. No excuses, Ed."

"But Your Honor—"

"I didn't say I wasn't going to grant you a mistrial." The judge looked at Wilbur. "But if I do, I suppose, Wilbur, you will refile the charges. Correct?"

"Your Honor, the People will, indeed, refile."

"So, we'd be right back where we are now. Gentlemen, I must deliberate on this for the rest of the day. We will reconvene tomorrow morning at 8:30 here in my office for my decision."

****

Joe and his family left the City-County building to eat dinner at a popular downtown restaurant called St. Elmo Steakhouse on South Illinois Street. No one had much of an appetite. Grayson and Ruth left in their rental car to stay at the historic Omni Severin Hotel in downtown Indianapolis. Joe accompanied Irene to her place in the recently built Meadows Apartments on Indianapolis' northwest side.

As they got ready for bed, Irene tried to keep Joe's spirits up.

"I am so glad you decided to speak up, Joe," she said as she came out of the tiny bathroom in her nightgown.

Joe was turning down the covers of her double bed. "I can't believe how tired I am." He rolled into the bed and lay on his side.

Irene got in on her side and turned out the yellow ceramic light on her nightstand. She began rubbing Joe's back. "I know this is probably the hardest thing you've ever done in your life. Just remember it will be over soon. Maybe there'll be that mistrial, and you won't have to testify again."

"But, the ADA will just file the charges again."

She stared out in the darkness of her bedroom. "Joe, what did Robert's dad shout after you said you knew him?"

Without turning to face her, Joe replied, "'I will kill you, Jew pig.'"

Irene stopped her hand. "Then, you were right. You had every reason to be scared after you saw him last May." She sat up, drawing the blanket over her knees.

"Uh, huh." Joe turned over on his back. "Irene, I've thought about that dream I had the night after I came home from the hospital."

"I remember you waking up and moaning. I asked if you were having a nightmare."

"Yes. It was a nightmare. It's stayed in the back of my mind ever since then. I remember more of how I felt rather than what happened. I was scared. I had to get away from a woman. I think I was running away from Ada Stangarden. There was a man in a SS uniform. He hurt my arm when he pulled it. I remember how much pain I was in."

"You were waking up and moving your arm. That was what caused your pain."

"Yeah. That was it."

Joe said no more. Irene put her hand into his. Her mind raced as she laid back and stared at the ceiling.

CHAPTER TWENTY-TWO

The trial continued the next day. The judge told the attorneys in chambers that the defense would have ample opportunity to cross-examine the prosecution's star witness about this "Buchenwald" statement. The jury would decide whether or not to believe it.

At 9:40 a.m., The judge reminded Joe that he was still under oath as he climbed back into the witness box.

Mr. Morris began. "Mr. Kaufmann, you said yesterday that you knew the defendant and his wife from, what was it called, Buchenwald?"

"Yes."

"Before we explore that, let's fast-forward to the present. Please tell the court again when you had seen them recently?"

"At the end of the school year last year, in May, I offered to move Robert back home to Indianapolis for the summer."

"What was the date?"

"May twenty-second. It was the end of finals week at I. U."

"So, you helped him pack his gear, and you drove him home."

"Yes."

"What happened then?"

"After we unloaded his things in the living room, we went into the kitchen for some Cokes. He offered me cookies that his mom had made."

"At this time, you didn't know who his parents were? You had not met them before this day?"

Joe knew to make his answer precise. "Not here in this country, not in Indiana."

Rumblings stirred from the gallery.

"How did you meet them at the house?"

"A door opened, maybe from the laundry room, and a woman and a man walked in carrying grocery bags."

"Did Robert introduce them to you?"

"No. His mother came in first, took one look at me, screamed, and dropped her groceries. I think something broke, like a bottle. Then I saw the man behind her, and he saw me. I immediately ran out of the house. I got in my car and drove back to Bloomington."

"Did this couple recognize you?"

"Yes. We recognized each other. We had seen each other in Buchenwald. But I was six years old at the time. My mother and father were with me."

"But if you were a young child, and you're an adult now, how would they have recognized you?"

Joe straightened his shoulders. He looked only at Mr. Morris. "I look very much like my father. To that couple, I must have looked as if my father had risen from the dead."

More rustling from the gallery.

Joe forced himself to stay calm. Mr. Morris had coached him to pretend he was an actor in a play. It was a ploy to focus his attention and keep his emotions in check. Joe knew the smartest way to get through these questions was to disengage himself while explaining his experiences at Buchenwald. Besides, it would take every bit of acting skill for the inevitable cross-examination.

Mr. Morris slowly moved about, keeping a covert eye on the jury. "That scene in the kitchen must have been a shocking experience for you."

"To be honest, I was terrified."

"Terrified of what?"

"That the man, Robert's father, was going to come after me. I thought he would hurt me." Just like he hurt his son.

Mr. Morris waved his hands and turned toward the jury. "I guess you'll have to explain further, Mr. Kaufmann."

Ignoring the crimson-faced defendant who looked like he was ready to explode like a volcano, Joe answered, looking at the jury, "If that Nazi monster could go after his son and nearly kill him, he is just as capable of killing me as I am a Jew." Amidst the rising tidal wave from the gallery, Joe went on, "He has to stop me from exposing him to the authorities."

Over the clamor in the courtroom and the jackhammer pounding of the gavel, Ed Moscowitz rose and shouted, "Objection! Non-responsive!"

The police guards stepped nearer to the defendant.

Mr. Morris kept a straight face.

"Objection sustained! The jury will disregard that last statement by the witness. Mr. Morris, rephrase your question!" Now the judge looked angry, apparently put out by these verbal shenanigans.

Mr. Morris waited for the storm winds to settle. "Mr. Kaufmann, tell the court the circumstances in which you knew the defendant at this Nazi concentration camp."

Joe readied himself. "Buchenwald was a major slave labor camp near Weimar, Germany."

Raising his voice above the excited murmurs from the audience, Mr. Morris asked, "When were they there at this camp?"

"I know they were there from the summer of 1944 through early spring 1945 because that was when my family and I were at the camp."

"Were they slave laborers at this camp?"

Joe had to control himself. "No."

"What were they doing there?"

"The man, Henry Stangarden, a.k.a. Rikkert Steghausen, was a civilian in the Nazi party whose job was to document the prisoners when they arrived at the camp. I saw him when my parents and I had gotten off the train. He was sitting at one of the tables with several other Nazi civilians outside a big building. I was hiding behind my mother's skirt when I watched him process my parents."

"How do you know of his Nazi affiliation?"

"He wore a swastika armband."

More agitation from the audience. Joe kept his eyes directly on Mr. Morris.

"What about the woman you saw at Robert's house?"

"She, Ada Stangarden, a.k.a. Matilda Steghausen, was a cook for the SS officers who were in charge of the camp."

Behind the defendant, Ada made a little, tortured noise.

"And you know this how?"

"At night, she gave food to my father and me. Sometimes the same man who I'd seen at the processing table would be with her. I realize now that he was her husband."

"So, you're saying they had different names while at the camp. How did you know their names?"

"My father told me."

"Why do you think they changed their names?"

Leaning forward ever so slightly, Joe recklessly looked at Henry Stangarden. "You would have to ask him."

It appeared to take all the effort of a Hercules for the defendant to stay in his chair.

"Mr. Kaufmann, can you tell the court how you and your parents came to Buchenwald?"

"My father, my mother, and I hid in an attic above a clothing shop in Berlin during the war. As Jews, we were lucky not to have been discovered for as long as we lived there. But in the early summer of 1944, we were discovered and sent by train to Auschwitz, a huge death camp in Poland. But we didn't stay there. The Nazis forced us to get on another train, and we went to Buchenwald. I believe workers were desperately needed to keep the German war effort going. So that's why we were taken there."

"What happened when you and your family arrived?"

"My father and mother were processed by this Rikkert Steghausen. As I said earlier, I managed to stay hidden behind my mother. If a guard had discovered me, I would have been taken away immediately and sent back to Auschwitz. There, most likely, I would have been gassed to death along with hundreds of thousands of other children."

Mr. Morris paused to allow the audience to absorb Joe's testimony. He took stock of the jury's reaction. A few of them looked confused, and others looked skeptical. "You said this woman who was a cook gave food to you and your father. What happened to your mother?"

Joe wanted to look at the whimpering Ada Stangarden, but he focused on Mr. Morris. "A Nazi officer took her away after she and my father were separated."

A cry erupted from the overweight woman who sat right behind Henry Stangarden.

Mr. Morris ignored the outburst. "How often and how long did the woman feed you and your father?"

"Once each night until early spring of the next year. I don't know what month."

"What happened? Why did she stop?"

"You have to see this in a larger context. By early 1945, Germany was on the verge of collapse. The Russians were closing in from the east, the Allies from the west. The camp was becoming very chaotic. The Nazis were trying to decide what to do with the prisoners and the camp itself. But they were losing control. Prisoners were getting restless, and they got bolder with the guards. The woman, this Matilda Steghausen, just stopped feeding us. We didn't know why. Looking back, I suspect she and her husband were trying to get out of the camp before the Allied troops arrived."

"But you're only speculating. You don't know for sure."

"That's right. But being a historian, I've studied what happened at the end of World War II in Europe, specifically in Germany. Thousands of Germans fled to South America, whether they were refugees or Nazi criminals pretending to be refugees. Some went directly to the United States."

Twisting his mouth as he paused to think, Joe added, "When I first met Robert at I. U. back in October 1963, he told me that he was born in Buenos Aires and that his parents came there from Germany in 1945. It would be a reasonable deduction that they fled Germany pretending to be refugees, and that they changed their names to keep their Nazi affiliation secret."

Ed Moscowitz spoke up angrily. "Objection! Facts not in evidence!"

"Sustained."

Mr. Morris was undeterred. "Mr. Kaufmann, to be clear, do you see in this courtroom the man whom you saw not only in Robert's house on May twenty-second, 1964 but also in this slave camp in 1944 and 1945?"

"Yes."

"Will you please identify him?"

Joe pointed at the defendant. "That's him over there, the man now calling himself Henry Stangarden."

Mr. Morris started to turn but halted. "By the way, Mr. Kaufmann. What happened to you and your father after the woman stopped giving you food?"

Joe didn't even blink. "We starved. We were no better off than the miserable, pathetic souls in that hellhole."

"Did your father survive?"

"No."

"Care to explain?"

"I'd rather not revisit that memory, sir. It's enough to say that he died right before the American troops opened the camp."

"How did you survive?"

"When the American troops liberated Buchenwald on April 13, 1945, they were followed a few days later by army medical units. An army doctor found me in one of the barracks and took me to the evacuation hospital set up at the administration building. He had to move on with his unit to follow the troops going east. I was taken to an orphanage by a priest with the Red Cross in Zurich, Switzerland. But the doctor did not forget about me. After the war was over, he came to Zurich a few months later to take me to live with him and his family in Ithaca, New York. He became my guardian."

"What is his name?"

"Dr. Grayson Pierce."

"Very good, Mr. Kaufmann." Mr. Morris casually walked about in front of the jury box. "Sir, you heard Robert Stangarden's testimony that he said his father didn't want him to go back to college because at first, he said there was no money. Then he said he didn't want Robert to be in contact with undesirable elements down there. Would you speculate on what he meant by 'undesirable elements?'"

"Objection. The witness cannot know what was in the mind of my client."

"Your Honor, this goes directly back to the incident in May when Mr. Kaufmann saw the defendant and his wife in that house. Mr. Kaufmann has ties with both Robert and the defendant. He knows more than anyone else in this courtroom as to the motive of the assault on Robert Stangarden."

"This has no relevance, Your Honor. The prosecution is only trying to confuse the jury."

Judge Campbell intertwined his crooked fingers and looked down in thought. Both attorneys held their breath.

"I'll allow the witness to answer. Mr. Moscowitz, you are free to challenge the response in your cross."

Turning back to Joe, Mr. Morris said, "You may give us your opinion, Mr. Kaufmann, as to what is going on here."

Joe had to choose his words with care. He looked again at Robert, slumped pitifully on the other side of the gallery. This kid needed him. He deserved justice. Joe realized that Robert had been more than a punching bag for Rikkert Steghausen, a.k.a. Henry Stangarden. There was a further motive here than a father insisting that his son stay home in Indianapolis.

It came to him. Maybe this cruel, barbaric Nazi civilian took the opportunity to beat up an innocent young man to take out his frustration for not being able to wear a Nazi SS uniform. Perhaps he couldn't pass the requirements to become a Gestapo or even an army officer. His inability to serve his country by being on the front lines rounding up the noxious population that threatened the Fatherland must have gnawed at him for years. As a lowly administrative minion, he couldn't even carry a pistol! All he could do was sit and write down the names of these feculent degenerates in his big green ledger books. Joe clearly remembered this man's demeanor—his impatience, scorn, and bad temper. He simmered with rage while his wife ladled out the dumplings and the gravy and the cooked vegetables into the tin bowls for Joe and his father. And when the cook took his father aside to talk, Rikkert Steghausen stood there in front of him, looking as dangerous as one of those SS guards' police dogs, baring blood-thirsty teeth at this little child who was trying to gobble as much food as he could. One wrong move and that monster would have beaten Joe just as viciously as Robert had been or worse.

"Mr. Kaufmann?"

The courtroom was hushed.

Joe looked at Henry Stangarden. "I know what he meant. The word 'undesirables' is a euphemism for describing Jews. And, of course, he knew I was a Jew. He recognized me in the kitchen, although he thought he was seeing my father. And he knew that I knew him. He is afraid I would go to the authorities and expose him. He knows he could get deported, or at the very least, lose his job and his reputation. And he knew I would go through Robert to get to him. He was willing almost to kill his own flesh and blood to keep us apart."

"Objection!"

"Overruled."

"Go on, Mr. Kaufmann."

"This Rikkert Steghausen or Henry Stangarden was so determined to keep Robert away from me that he nearly killed him."

"Objection! Move to strike!"

Joe spoke directly at the jury. "The cut on Robert's throat was just a warning." Then he turned his eyes toward Rikkert Steghausen. His heart pumped so hard he thought it would burst through his dress shirt. But he willed that Nazi goon to look back at him. Joe decided he would face this demon with grit and determination.

As the gallery exploded, Judge Campbell was on his feet, pounding his jackhammer. "Order! Order!"

"Your Honor, move to strike! The witness's statement is nonresponsive!"

The defendant sat motionless, cold as a steel trap.

"That last statement is to be disregarded by the jury."

Above the animated discussion amongst the spectators, Mr. Morris said, "Thank you for your testimony, Mr. Kaufmann. No more questions."

The judge announced it was time for a recess. The trial would resume at two o'clock. Joe calmly kept his eyes forward as he walked back to join his family.

****

Mr. Ed Moscowitz gave Joe a too-disarming smile across his narrow, acne-scarred face. He wore a dark, pin-striped suit with a waistcoat perfectly fitted. One would see a tiny gold stickpin topped with a seed pearl in his red tie if one looked carefully. All that was missing was a carnation in his lapel.

"Mr. Kaufmann, you tell a compelling tale." His voice revealed no sarcasm, yet. "It's almost a rags to riches story."

Before Joe could react to the brunt of that insult, he heard Mr. Morris shout, "Objection!"

"Sustained. Ask the witness a question, counselor," said the judge.

"This is all quite a heroic tale about hiding in an attic during the war, being sent to Auschwitz only to be sent back to this alleged slave labor camp."

"There is nothing alleged about Buchenwald, sir. I was there!" Joe blurted out. He'd forgotten that Mr. Morris had told him not to volunteer anything, only to answer the questions put to him.

Ed Moscowitz smiled as if pretending to apologize. "Yes, as you say. And somehow, you managed to be overlooked by Nazi guards." Mr. Moscowitz flailed his slender hands about for emphasis. "You and your father getting fed by some benevolent, soft-hearted cook who seemed to know to pick out you and your father from hundreds and even thousands of prisoners. How do you think she did that? Why would she choose you and your father?"

Joe had to think fast. "I believe it had something to do with my mother."

"Your mother. Hmm. Now, what was her story? Did you say somebody took her away?"

There were moans from behind the defendant.

"Yes. I saw her being taken away by a Nazi officer." Joe knew his face was reddening, a thick vein in the middle of his forehead appearing. Irene had told him that happened whenever he was under stress.

"So, how is that connected with you, your father, and this cook?"

This time cries rang throughout the courtroom. Judge Campbell said sternly, "Ma'am, please settle down. You have to be quiet. If you don't, I'll have a court attendant escort you out."

Ada Stangarden apparently could not control herself. Even her son, Robert, stared at her from across the aisle.

The female attendant and the two women who had sat next to her helped her out of the courtroom.

"To be honest, I'm not sure. My father never told me."

Ed Moscowitz decided to let that pass. "Mr. Kaufmann, do you really expect this court to believe what you are saying about my client, Mr. Stangarden? Are you accusing him of being a Nazi?"

"I'm not just accusing. I am asserting the truth about him. He was a Nazi because he wore a swastika armband. His wife was, at the very least, a Nazi collaborator."

"And what makes you say that?"

"Because she prepared the meals for the SS officers who were in charge of the camp. She fed those sadistic monsters." Joe again spoke to the jury. "Rikkert and Matilda Steghausen didn't torture the prisoners with whips and dogs, or hang or beat them to death with clubs. They didn't force them to work in rock quarries and railroad yards until they succumbed to exhaustion. They didn't starve them or make them stand in below-freezing temperatures for some fake roll call in the middle of the night. They didn't make them live in rows of

drafty, disease-ridden shacks with no proper plumbing except a board
with holes in it over a trough overflowing with bloody excrement. They
didn't laugh at them like the other Nazi brutes as they watched them
kill each other, trying to get a piece of apple core or a rotten potato.
And they didn't carry the stacks of dead bodies to the crematoriums to
be burned up like old newspapers."

He stopped. The courtroom was silent. As Joe passed his eyes over
Henry Stangarden's attorney, he saw an almost split-second of
compassion on his face. But perhaps that's what Joe wanted to see.
Instead, he had the smug, disbelieving demeanor of a man who dressed
as if he were going to a cocktail party after the trial. "Yes, Mr.
Moscowitz. Your client and his wife didn't do any of those things. His
wife put warm food in the bellies of those criminals dressed in their
sharp, smart-looking uniforms. She fed those monsters who beat, shot,
starved, and worked to death thousands of innocent people, to say
nothing of the brutal, useless medical experiments. Mr. Steghausen was
just a pencil-pusher sitting on the sidelines. He wrote down the names
of all the human beings who were pushed out of the trains like cattle
and made to line up under Nazi guards who kept firing their pistols in
the air. They were both parts of the Nazi machine. They are not
without culpability."

Ed Moscowitz suddenly turned and faced Joe squarely. His voice
was resolute. "And where is your proof, Mr. Kaufmann? Where is the
physical documentation that my client was there? Or better yet, where
is the documentation for your presence in the camp? Any papers, any
certificates, any photographs? You say that you were only six years old.
You're how old today?"

"Twenty-seven."

"That's a lot of years in between. And being just a little boy, how
could you remember what even happened in this camp, let alone
remember those two people and who you see today?"

"You don't forget the face of the person who kept you alive for
months, Mr. Moscowitz. Or the man who was with her."

"How do we know you're not just describing what you had read in
your history books? After all, you did say, as a historian, you've studied
Nazi Germany."

Joe rose slowly and leaned into the other man's face. He spoke
through gritted teeth. "If you want proof of me being in that place,

he's sitting right over there in the left-hand corner of the gallery. Dr. Grayson Pierce." He pointed to his guardian. "He's an eyewitness. He and his medical teams had to clean up what those contemptible villains left behind! He rescued me! He saved my life!"

Mr. Moscowitz discreetly backed away. He smiled. "I don't care, Mr. Kaufmann, about this doctor who allegedly rescued you." Then he lost his smile. "But, I do care about the irresponsible insinuations you are making about Mr. Stangarden!"

Mr. Morris jumped up. "Objection, Your Honor! The defense counsel is badgering the witness!"

"It's the truth!" Joe declared, still on his feet.

Judge Campbell intervened. "Objection sustained. Please sit, Mr. Kaufmann. We will have civility in my courtroom. The jury will disregard that last statement from the witness! Mr. Moscowitz, do you have any more questions for this witness?"

"No more questions." Ed Moscowitz returned to the defense table. "Your Honor, I move to strike the entire testimony of this witness from the record. It is inflammatory, speculative at best, and is too prejudicial for my client." His clipped voice carried over the noise in the courtroom.

"Clear the court! Chambers!"

The spectators and reporters slowly began to exit amidst loud discussion. Some of the jury members lingered, looking at Joe and then the defendant. Joe stepped down from the witness stand. As he walked toward the railing that separated the gallery, he saw someone in his peripheral vision come from behind him. But a guard stopped the figure before he could land a blow on his back.

"Jew Schwein!"

Swift handcuffs clicked around Henry Stangarden's wrists before his fists made contact with Joe's back. Joe hurried on without looking behind him. The last two jury members who saw what happened lingered, then followed the others out of the courtroom.

CHAPTER TWENTY-THREE

The Pierce family collapsed in their luxurious Omni Severin hotel room. Grayson took off his coat and hat, throwing them on the end of the sprawling, king-sized bed. He loosened his tie and took off his shoes and lay back in the king-size bed. Irene went into the bathroom, which appeared bigger than her entire apartment, and shut the door. Ruth removed her double-breasted camel hair coat and sat at the polished walnut desk. She took off her hat and rearranged her lovely honey-blonde hair with her fingers. Taking off his dress coat and black wool fedora, Joe found an ashtray and lit up.

Nobody wanted to say anything yet, as if not talking would dissipate the tension they all felt.

Irene came out and poured a glass of water. After a swallow, she went to Joe and kneaded his shoulders.

"You were incredibly brave, Joe," said Ruth. "You got through it in one piece." She kicked off her high heels and rubbed her feet.

"That damn defense lawyer!" Irene took Joe's cigarette out of his mouth and smashed it in the ashtray.

"Sweetheart, he was just doing his job defending his client." Grayson sat up. He went to his suitcase to look for his pipe. He stopped to look at his ward.

Joe said, "I feel like I'm in a waking nightmare. I volunteered to get on the stand to tell the truth—all of it! But I said a lot more than I planned. And that defense attorney ridiculed me! He had the sheer audacity to imply that I was making it all up! And that's what the jury will believe." He went to the half-size refrigerator to look for a can of pop. He took out a can of 7-Up. He popped it open and drank.

Grayson found his pipe and lit it. But he stayed far enough away from Irene, knowing she would take it away from him. (Her doctor's training had its drawbacks, including learning the health hazards of smoking.) "Joe, think about it. These people, the jury, they're all fine Midwestern folks who know about the world only through what they read in the newspapers or what they watch on TV. This Nazi business, what they did to the Jews. They've heard very little about such things. What you said was so outlandish, so shocking that they're not likely to take your word for it."

He held out his hand to stop Joe from speaking. "We know Ed Moscowitz believes your description of the camps. He's been around long enough to be aware of Nazi concentration camps. Who knows? He might have fought in Europe during the war and saw or at least heard about the atrocities. But he's playing the jury for the benefit of his client. He's got to convince them that Henry Stangarden is not the man you say he is. And the way he's doing it is to poke holes in your testimony. In other words, to discredit you. And, frankly, I can understand that."

"But—"

"Now, Joe. I hate to say it, but all the jury has is your testimony. The defense attorney was correct. There's no physical evidence to back up your story." Grayson watched his sullen ward while puffing on his pipe. "Moscowitz has to keep the focus on what went down between Stangarden and Robert last August. You just temporarily got in the way. When it's his turn to present his case, he has to minimize the assault on his son." He puffed away thoughtfully. "Although that's a tall order."

"Fat chance with that," Irene said. "That physical evidence is so strong. I don't understand why there's a trial in the first place. Everybody knows he tried to kill Robert. You can't look at his injuries and think otherwise."

"But there's always more than one way to look at a situation," Grayson said patiently. "That's why there are defense lawyers. Their job is to make twelve presumably unbiased people look at the crime differently, say, from the accused's perspective. What's his angle? His motivation?"

The big man poured a glass of scotch from the bar. "What Joe did was try to make clear that Henry Stangarden's real motive was to stop Robert from seeing him and putting their heads together. Joe is the real threat to this guy, not Robert. As we all know, he has everything to lose if Joe and Robert talk to each other."

He took a step closer to Joe. "I am proud of you, Joe. Frankly, I would have never thought you had the courage." He stopped, thinking to choose careful words. "And we, your family, will always support you. You will never have to shoulder this weight alone. You know that, right?"

"Yeah, I do, Grayson," Joe replied. "What I did on that stand was an act. Wilbur Morris told me to pretend I was describing what had happened to another person. He said not to personalize it. And to always keep my eyes on him. I had to remove myself mentally when I answered his questions. But then I got carried away with Ed Moscowitz. Not to bring up a cliché, I didn't tell the whole truth." He reached for another cigarette in his shirt pocket. When Irene put out her hand, he snapped, "Leave me alone, Irene. Let me have something to calm myself. Just stop playing doctor, okay?"

She retreated.

"I've got more to talk about." Joe lit up and wiped the sweat from under his heavy glasses. "Sorry, Irene."

His sister crossed her arms and huffed.

After giving his daughter a look, Grayson finished his drink. He refilled his tumbler. "Go ahead, Joe."

Joe sat in a chair beside Ruth at the small hotel table. He met quick eyes with her as if for reassurance. She put her hand briefly on his arm. "Both the lawyers asked about my mother. But they moved on to other things, and I never fully explained what had happened when we got to Buchenwald. So, I want to tell you now." He looked at Grayson. "I'm ready to tell you, Grayson. You've never heard this before."

His guardian sat in a cushioned chair with his knees crossed. He took a sip.

"We lived in an attic above this clothing shop on Bonn Street. This was in Berlin. I can't remember living anywhere else before that, so I must have been born there. There was a small window, and I remember climbing up on a chair to look out. The streets were very busy, and I saw a lot of soldiers and police officers. Sometimes there was screaming, and I watched them take people away against their will.

I didn't understand why, and my mother and father didn't explain it to me.

"My mother worked downstairs in the store during the day. My father stayed with me and helped me learn things like reading and writing, some Jewish rituals, and history. Grayson, do you remember when I was seven, and you took me on that road trip around the state to get away from the old women?"

"Yes, I do. I remember being so surprised how well you could read and write, in German, of course. I still have that little story you wrote about our cat, Mr. Henry. I think it's in a scrapbook in a closet."

"That was my father's doing. Besides German, he also taught me some Hebrew and Yiddish. And my mother sang songs to me. Those were good times for a while. But it all ended when the Gestapo came and took us away. I'm surprised they didn't shoot us on the spot. Someone must have said something. I was terrified. Looking back, I realize it was so close to the end of the war. If only we could have lasted one more year." He stopped. "But we could have just as easily been bombed to smithereens by the Allies."

No one said anything to this remark.

Joe went on. "The Gestapo had us. We had to get into this big covered military truck already crowded with other people who were just as scared as we were. I had to sit on my mother's lap. I don't know if they were also Jews." He twisted his mouth as he thought. "This is what I learned in studying those library books I hoarded last summer. Berlin was virtually devoid of Jews by the time the war started in 1939. The businesses, the synagogues, the shops, everything had been destroyed or taken over. My family was very, very lucky they were missed.

"We were taken to this train station and crammed into a big boxcar filled with many strange people. I know now it was a cattle car. We were all scared out of our minds, and all I could think about was holding my parents' hands. These other people were speaking languages I didn't know, and they were crying and moaning. And the smell was suffocating. They had defecated and urinated on the floor, but they couldn't help it. Who knew how long they had been on that train? On top of that, it was completely dark. Some tiny cracks at the top of the wall on one side let in some light, but that was it. Finally, the train started moving. No one knew where or for how long. After a long time, the train stopped, and more people were pushed into the car. We were packed so tightly I had to stand on someone's feet. The air was getting hotter and hotter, and we couldn't breathe. But the train never stopped."

Joe furrowed his brow. "There was this one man. He had a watch, and he kept looking at it. I heard him talk to a woman, maybe his wife. But I didn't understand the language he was speaking."

Joe's family said nothing. They stared at him, mesmerized.

"Eventually, the train stopped. By this time, everyone had been sleeping or at least trying to. We woke up. After a long time, the door slid back. We were suddenly terrified. There were all these Nazi soldiers. I found out later they were SS guards. They started dragging everybody out and yelling, 'Schnell! Schnell!' That's German for 'hurry,' 'quick.' My father held me as we had to jump. Some older people couldn't jump that far. When they fell, they didn't get up fast enough, and a few of the guards dragged them away. One of them couldn't walk. I think she hurt her ankle. I heard gunshots close by. Just 'pop, pop, pop.' One after another.

"After everybody was off, some of the men had to get back into the car to push out the dead bodies. There were a lot of them."

Irene gasped. Ruth got up suddenly and went to her purse to get a tissue.

Joe stood. He wandered back to one of the hotel room windows, the small sun beginning to disappear behind some moving clouds. One could see the expansive vista of the downtown skyscrapers and the flat, hazy landscape beyond. With his back turned away, he continued.

"This situation of us getting out of the train car was not just us but the whole train itself. There were hundreds and hundreds of people getting out. They were screaming and crying, and the guards kept firing their weapons in the air to keep order. They shoved everybody around, separating the men from the women. All the children were rounded up and immediately taken somewhere else.

"I tried to see what was around us. There were these massive brick buildings everywhere. Something dead was burning because the air was smoky and had this putrid odor. I heard this word over and over again, 'Auschwitz. Auschwitz.' I guessed that was where we were.

"Before the guards came up to separate me from my parents, some other guards came up and told us to get back on the train. My father was quick, and he practically threw me on first. He pointed to a corner, and I went there to hide. Then he helped my mother get on. He was next, along with all these other people, some who had not been on it before. The door slammed shut, and we waited.

"Nobody knew what was going on. All I remember is the crying, the moans, and wailing. People were trying to pray, but there was so much noise you couldn't hear yourself even think. There was sheer panic, but because we were packed so tightly, nobody could move. I felt like I was suffocating.

"Finally, the train started to move. My father talked to someone in Yiddish. He told my mother that the train was heading to a place called 'Buchenwald.' There was work to be done there, and that's where we were going. Again, we didn't know how long we were traveling to this new place. On the way, people began dying. We had no food or water, and it was so hot people died from dehydration."

Joe turned around. He lit a fresh cigarette. "The train stopped once. The door opened, and we saw a big, open field. Some Nazi guards told the men to pull out the dead bodies and push out the waste with their hands. That gave us more room, and with the door opened, we could breathe fresh air. But it didn't last. They shut the door again, and we moved on.

"I remember my mother holding on to me, kissing me, and telling me it was going to be okay. She sang songs to me. My father joined her. I think I was the only child in the train car."

Joe broke down. "God, I miss my mother! She was . . ."

Joe's shoulders shook as his tears fell. He collapsed into a chair. And put his cigarette and glasses on the nightstand. Ruth went to him and offered him a tissue.

Grayson stood and paced the room. He closed the curtains at the windows.

"That's okay, Joe," Ruth whispered. "It's okay."

Joe took a tissue to wipe his face and eyes. He put his glasses on and looked to his guardian. Yet his tears streamed. "This is why I didn't want to go to Temple Beth-El when I was a child. I didn't want to say Kaddish for my parents. I wasn't ready. It just hurt too much."

Grayson pulled Joe up and against his big, comforting chest. "I can't begin to understand what you went through. It's too much to bear. Your parents loved you deeply."

"Here's some more water for you, Joe." Irene offered a glass.

Joe took it, choking as he swallowed.

"I wish I could say something to make you feel better," she said, wiping her eyes.

"There's nothing you can say, Irene. Nobody can. Remembering that moment is . . . painful." He handed the glass back. "But, I need to explain more about this couple at Buchenwald."

Joe sat at the table. He gripped the edge of it. "I remember it was raining. And there was this awful, nasty smell. It was different from the smell at Auschwitz. It smelled like a sewer. Everybody got out of the train cars again and, of course, the Nazi guards were trying to keep control of the crowds. There were police dogs, too. We couldn't see many of the buildings because it was dark. But there were lights.

"I saw this vast building, like a headquarters or something. And there was this lone tree in the middle of this courtyard. There were long wooden tables and men in civilian clothes sitting at them. But they were still Nazis because they wore the swastika armbands. People stood in lines in front of each table. So, we got behind the last person. My mother told me to stay behind her so that the guards wouldn't see me. But more people came and stood behind us, so the guards didn't notice me. When we got up close, I could see small metal contraptions and big green books, and stacks of long yellow notecards on the tables. The Nazi civilians were writing down things as they talked to each person. When we finally got up to a table, my mother and father had to give them their names and ages and whether or not they were Jewish to this fat man in a white shirt. I got a good look at him."

Joe closed and then opened his eyes. "He was fat, kind of bald, and mean-looking. After he talked with my parents, we were quickly pushed aside so the people behind us could be processed. There were hundreds of people there, many with suitcases they had to give up. It sounded like the Tower of Babel with all the different languages spoken. And those dogs kept barking, and the guards kept shooting their pistols in the air.

"They separated the women from the men. My father tried to hold on to my mother, but the crowds forced him back. I screamed for him, but my mother put her skirt around me and told me to stay quiet. We walked away with the women, but I kept trying to keep my father in sight. Despite all the chaos, he was able to follow us. Then suddenly, I got pushed, and I lost my mother's hand. I tried to catch her, but there were too many people. She was wearing a red scarf with flowers on it, so I kept seeing her. Then, all of a sudden, this tall Nazi soldier came up to her. He wore a lot of insignia and medals, and there was some decoration on the brim of his hat that was much more elaborate than the other SS guards. He stopped behind my mother and took down her scarf. She turned, and they looked at each other. I saw the shock on her face. Then this officer grabbed her arm and took her away. I screamed for her, but she was gone."

Joe took deep breaths, reliving the incident in his mind. "I think my father heard my screams because he was right there. He picked me up. We went back to join the big group of men. The guards didn't seem to care about me, or maybe they didn't see me. They kept pushing us and telling us to hurry up. We walked down this wide, muddy street. It had a lot of potholes filled with yellowish water and mud. I realize now it was urine and feces. There were rows and rows of these long, wooden buildings. As we walked, I could see bodies lying around, some of them in piles. None of them were wearing any clothes. They looked as if they had died from starvation. There was a tall, barb-wired fence in the distance and this tower with a light shining out. Once, as we were walking, a gunshot went off from that tower. That frightened me."

Joe looked at Grayson, Ruth, and Irene. "I know how difficult all this is to hear. It seems incomprehensible. The sheer terror of being in a situation where you have no control, you don't know what's going to happen to you, you see all those dead bodies and the dogs are trying to bite you, and the guards just keep pushing and pushing you, making you run, but you don't know where to. And they had whips and wooden batons, and they beat the slower ones. As we walked, we saw all these skinny men wearing black and white uniforms with hats. Some wore civilian pants or shirts, but they were basically in rags. And the shirts had tags with numbers sewn on the front and these little colored patches. They were pink or red or brown. But most of them were yellow. I know now they were the Jews. They wouldn't look at us. There were always some Nazi thugs milling around, keeping them in line.

"We came up to another part of this camp that had barbed wire all around it. We had to climb over it. Later, I learned it was called 'Little Camp.' It was exclusively for Jews. It was truly the worst place on Earth. We had to go in one of these dilapidated shacks with nothing but wooden beds stacked up to the ceiling. There was no running water, no heat, nothing but a long board that ran the barrack's length in the middle on top of these stinking buckets. It had holes in it just big enough for a man to sit to relieve himself. The smell was enough to make one faint. There were no lights except a couple of small windows that didn't even have glass or plastic covering. That's where I stayed with my father."

All the while Joe described the "Little Camp" and the barrack, Grayson continued to pace and chew on his pipe.

"My father pushed me into a corner to stay hidden. He and the others went out for a long time. Like what I had told you last summer at my apartment. When he came back, his hair had been completely shaved off, and he had some cuts that were bleeding. He wore those black and white pajamas. I don't know what they did with his clothes. The clothes he had on now were dirty, and the shirt had holes and stains on it.

"Prisoners came in and started piling up in these wooden beds. Some had to be helped into them because they were so feeble. They looked like they hadn't eaten in weeks or months. I saw two of them collapse. And the shocking part was that immediately they were stripped and just dumped outside. And nobody acted as if anything was wrong. All those men, their faces were just blank. It was business as usual. I was terrified.

"My father was able to lay on the edge of the bunker closest to the center of the barracks. I laid on top of his chest, and I was so tired. I think I fell asleep at once, even as men were shouting and crying because they were so hungry. When the weather got colder, I'd unbuttoned the top buttons of my father's shirt, so I could lay my head against his skin to keep warm. And every morning, he had to help the others drag out the prisoners who had died during the night. New men arriving every day made the barrack always crowded.

"On the second day, my father dug a hole with his bare hands behind some boards at the floor. That's where I would hide most of the time during the day. The next day when the guards took him away, I stayed in that hole. When it started to get dark outside, he came back and took me out of that hole. He told me that he'd been assigned to work in the kitchen of the officer's building. We still hadn't been given any food or water. I was ravished by then.

"After the third day, my father told me to stay in the hole at the end of the workday. The other prisoners were coming in, and he didn't want them to see me. When they weren't paying attention, he took out some bread and radishes to give to me. I was so hungry I practically gulped them without chewing them. But it was the best food I had ever tasted. Then we got into the wooden bed.

"A couple of nights later, my father and I sneaked out of the barrack. A guard was waiting for us. We had to follow him quickly out of the 'Little Camp' and toward the camp entrance. There was this big, brick building that we went around to the back. An overweight woman stood at a door. She wore her hair in a bun, and she had a round face. She was holding a black iron kettle. While the guard looked on, she gave us the boiled potatoes that were in that pot. And she even had a small glass bottle of milk for me. I couldn't believe our luck. We were so grateful for the food that we both started crying. But we had to eat fast.

"On the way back to the barrack, I wanted to ask my father how this could have happened. But I knew not to speak in front of that SS guard.

"So, this went on day after day. My father told me that the woman was the head cook for whom he worked. She gave him leftover food to give to me. Some of it was mushy like it was leftovers from plates or dishes. But I didn't care. I had to eat it in the hole because if the other prisoners saw it, they would have killed me for it. Then at night, we'd go to the back of that building. The food was delicious, and it was fresh. Sometimes, while I was eating, my father went with the lady a little ways off to talk. My father never told me what they talked about, and I never asked.

"Then, this fat man started coming with the lady. I figured out he was her husband. And I recognized him as the same man who had processed us when we had arrived at the camp. He was in a bad mood, always mad and impatient with us. But the woman was kind. She seemed worried about me, maybe because I was a child, and there were no other children in the camp. She told my father to be careful not to let me wander around. If the guards didn't see me, the other prisoners, especially the kapos, the prisoners who were in charge, might, and that would be very bad for me. So, I stayed hidden as much as I could.

"When winter came and the snow was over my knees, we didn't have any warm clothes. My dad managed to steal a dead prisoner's shirt, and he put me in it. It was strange, though. My father's number on his shirt was 72001, and the number on my shirt was 72003."

Joe's mouth began to water. "I remember how wonderful that food tasted. She made corned beef and cabbage and buttered noodles and corn. One time she had chicken and cooked vegetables. And she always had cookies. Oh, I've never eaten food that tasted that good!"

He sniffed and wiped his mouth. "Eventually, the other prisoners figured out that we were leaving at night to get food. They tried to go after my father. But strangely, the Nazi guards always intervened. They threatened to shoot anyone who would hurt us. And they made an example of one man. They shot him right in front of everybody.

"Sometimes, when all the prisoners were out during the day, I sneaked out to see what was going on. There was some commotion, and I hid behind some empty barrels to watch. There was a big kettle that looked like it had water in it. The prisoners were all crowded around it. Some of them were punching and tearing at each other. Others were stepping over each other, trying to get at that pot. They had these tin bowls and spoons. Two or three men dipped out the water or broth into their bowls. Some of them had only one bowl between them, and they were all eating out of it. Another man sat close to where I was hiding, and I could see what was in his bowl. It was grayish water, and it had two or three lumps in it, like a potato. And I saw a big bug in it, too, like a spider. But the man didn't seem to care. He drank every last drop of that water and ate the lumps like it was a gourmet meal. He was so skinny. He turned and saw me. Then he got up and walked away.

"They stopped giving us food when the weather was getting warmer. Just one day, my father came back to the barrack with no food. He said he wasn't working in the kitchen anymore, and he was picking up dead bodies and carrying them to the crematorium. The woman who had given us food must have left. We didn't know why."

Irene asked, "Did you know why that woman gave you and your father food in the first place?"

Joe shrugged. "I don't know." He frowned. "It may have had something to do with the conversations my father had with her."

"Did you know what they were talking about?" asked Grayson.

"No. They were too far away. Besides, I was too busy gulping the food and keeping a safe distance from Rikkert Steghausen."

Ruth spoke. "Did you ever find out what happened to your mother?"

"No. I asked my father once, and he said she was in a better place. I didn't know if he meant she was dead or just somewhere else. I didn't ask again."

Irene frowned. "That Henry Stangarden was so angry seeing you on the witness stand. He shouted something in German at you. What did he say?"

"'I will kill you, Jew pig.'"

Ruth inhaled. "What?"

Joe looked at his stepmother. "Now, do you believe me when I said that man is out to kill me? Why I was so scared in my apartment?"

No one answered him. Grayson rubbed his forehead, his face clouded.

After a few moments, Joe turned to his sister. "Irene, do you want to know why I broke that bathroom mirror?"

She met his soft, liquid brown eyes.

Joe kept his face blank. "When I looked in that mirror, I realized how much I look like my father. Seeing my image like that, I couldn't look at myself without remembering him. So, I smashed the mirror to stop seeing him." He turned away to look at the large hotel windows. "That's why I kept this mustache. My father didn't have one." A pause. "He didn't wear glasses either."

Sitting in a corner hotel chair, Grayson rested his face in the palm of his hand. He closed his eyes.

Joe looked at his guardian. "Grayson, I'm sorry. I didn't mean to upset you like this."

His guardian roused himself. "No. I'm so sorry that you had to go through that ungodly affair." He looked pensive, maybe thinking how inadequate his words were. Slowly, he set his empty glass on the table. He gave a long sigh.

Ruth said quietly, "What happened to you and your father after that couple left?"

"We starved like everybody else." Joe released himself from Grayson's arms. "There was a lot of chaos, and the Nazis were leaving. My father died, and Grayson rescued me. You know the rest of the story." Exhausted, he dropped on the bed.

The room was as silent as a mausoleum.

Finally, Ruth said, "I don't think I'll be able to sleep tonight. I'm afraid I'll have nightmares."

Joe remarked bitterly, "Join the club. Well, that's the whole story."

To Irene, he said, "I want to go back to your apartment, Irene. I'm tired, and I don't want to drive back to Bloomington."

Grayson stared at his ward. "Joe, you going to be okay for the rest of tonight?"

"I don't know. I'm so tired I just want to go to sleep."

"Yes. You need a good rest. Your sister will take care of you."

Irene picked up her coat and purse. "Well, let's go."

Joe put on his coat and hat. When they entered the hall, he turned back to see his guardian and stepmother holding each other and standing at the threshold of the hotel room door. They looked at him with worry.

"See you in the morning, I guess." Joe followed Irene to the waiting elevators.

CHAPTER TWENTY-FOUR

After the court took a recess after Joe's testimony, the two ever-loyal church women, Gladys Mikkleson and Velma Sheely, drove Ada Stangarden and her son Robert to their two-story house at 5051 West 46th Street. It had been an extraordinarily tense day. All three women sat wearily in the living room while Robert disappeared upstairs.

Velma watched her dear friend sit motionless, completely spent. "Ada, we know what a hard day you've had. We want you to know we won't give up on you. We're going to see this through to the end."

"Yes, we will," Gladys agreed. "You poor thing." She reached over to give a comforting squeeze on Ada's hand.

Ada took a deep breath. She tilted her chin down and closed her eyes.

"Try to stay brave," Velma said. "By the way, just last night, I got a phone call from the choir director, Pete Vandivier, asking how you're getting along. He said the choir misses you, and they say a prayer for you at every rehearsal."

Blinking back tears, Ada said in a weak voice, "I dunt know what to do. I am worried about my husband. I think he vill go to jail. I am so frightened!" The thought of being separated from Henry was too much to bear.

Velma reached in her purse to get a tissue for her friend. "You must have faith in the Lord, my dear. He will take care of you and your family."

Gladys said, "And have confidence in the defense attorney, too. He knows what he's doing. He put that Kaufmann fellow in his place today." She angrily rummaged through her purse. "The vile things he said! None of it's true. He was just trying to confuse the jury."

"He certainly has a wild imagination," said Velma.

Gladys found her billfold and counted the bills inside. "Yes. The very audacity of him accusing Henry of being a Nazi! He's as bad as they come."

Ada was mute. What she had heard today from Joe Kaufmann on the stand cut terror into her heart.

"Let's see. I've got enough, Velma." She put away her billfold. She and her friend stood. "We're going to the store to buy you some groceries. Is there anything in particular you want us to get?"

Ada also rose, albeit with effort. Her face reflected despondency, almost defeat. "Nein. You dunt have to go if—"

"Of course, we do!" said Velma. "We want to help you and Robert." She nodded to Gladys. "You don't deserve to be in this situation. Along with everybody else, we know this whole thing was just a disagreement that got a little out of hand. Henry is a good father, a good husband—"

"And a good Christian," Gladys finished.

Both women turned toward the front door. "We'll be back in less than an hour," said Velma. And they left.

Ada did not move from her spot. In front of her feet lay the braided throw rug under the coffee table. It didn't match anything in the living room. She had bought it at a Montgomery Ward's store after the taxicab had brought her home. But she had to wait until Henry came home to use the car. She remembered how she was on her hands and knees, scrubbing as hard as she could to get the stains out. But the ugly black spot remained. So, the rug had to hide it.

Ada looked at the stairs and then mounted them, pulling on the handrail to help her climb up. Robert's room was at the end of the upstairs hall next to the bathroom. When she entered, her son was sitting on his impeccably made bed, staring at the two-shelf bookcase overloaded with record albums. He did not acknowledge her presence.

Ada spoke in German. "Son, I . . . I . . ." She sat in a wooden dining room chair next to his dresser.

Robert said in German, "I don't understand. I can't believe it. Why would he say those things? I've never even heard of Buchenwald. Is it a real place? I know about World War II and Nazi Germany. But what he described wasn't anything I read about in my social studies classes in high school. The teachers never mentioned the things he described. Is any of it true?"

He turned to face his mother. "Mom, were you and Dad in that place?"

But his mother turned away. "No. We lived in a town called Eppingen. It is in the district of Heilbronn in Baden-Wuttemberg. That's southern Germany. It's on a map."

When Robert continued looking at her, she went on. "Your father worked at a factory called Dieffenbacher. He was an accountant. It's an old company. But the enemy came and overran the town. American soldiers they were. After the war, we decided to move to Buenos Aires for a little while."

"But why? Why not just stay in Germany?"

His mother rose and faced the bedroom window. She didn't realize she was wringing her hands. "You don't know about the devastation. The enemy destroyed everything. We just couldn't stay. We didn't have a place to live anymore. We went to Buenos Aires."

"But why there?"

"It seemed the right place to go. Everyone else was going there, and the government seemed willing to take us." She swallowed hard. Taking a white sweat sock from a dresser drawer, she began dusting everything on top of it—anything to keep her shaking hands busy.

"So, how did you and Dad come to America?" Robert watched her, frowning. "Mom, what are you doing?"

A little too quickly, she replied, "I'm cleaning your room. What does it look like I'm doing? I can't depend on you to keep it clean." She opened his closet door to check his dirty laundry basket. "Do you need clean clothes?"

"Mom, you're making me nervous." Robert went to her. "Are you all right?"

His mother slammed the door shut and commenced dusting the top of his nightstand. "I'm fine. You don't need to ask me so many questions!"

Robert sat on his bed and watched her as she went back to the closet. She pulled down a set of fresh sheets and pillowcases from the shelf. Then she began stripping his bed, making Robert stand up. "We made a good life for you. We want you to go to school and be successful."

Ada didn't realize her mistake.

Robert said, "Wait a minute. Mom, that wasn't what Dad wanted. He got mad because I argued with him about going back to I. U."

"Your father is a passionate man. You know that. Sometimes he loses his temper."

"So, he does want me to go back? For sure?"

Ada pushed him out of her way to get to the other side of the double bed. "When this is all over, we will sit and have a good talk. I think we can reason with him. He'll come around. You will go back to school. We will call the university to get you set up in your classes. Maybe they'll give you the scholarships again." She fluffed a pillow and stuffed it into an ironed case. "You deserve them. You're the best music student there!"

"I'm not so sure about that," Robert replied. "What about Mr. Kaufmann?"

"You just forget him. He's nothing to you. He'll go back where he came from, and that will be it."

"Yeah, I guess so. He's from Ithaca, New York, you know."

She threw the bedspread back onto the bed and straightened it. "See? Nothing to worry about. Your father has the best lawyer in this city. Mr. Moscowitz will convince the jury that he is innocent, and he will be back home soon. Then we'll have that talk, and you will be back at Indiana University. All right?"

Robert seemed not quite able to believe her. "But why were you so upset when Mr. Kaufmann was on the witness stand? And Dad just about had a heart attack." He shook his head in disbelief. "I'm still confused about when he came to the house and you and Dad—"

"Robert. Don't worry about it. He's nobody. Think nothing of him." She would not look at him. "Trust me, Robert. This will pass. We must be brave and support your father. He is head of this house. He is your father."

Robert thought for a moment. "Mom, I almost forgot to ask you. When we talked with those detectives last September, you know, at the police headquarters, why did you tell them that I was born in 1946?"

His mother gathered the dirty bedsheets. "Never mind. It was just a mistake."

The doorbell rang.

"Oh, that must be Velma and Gladys. They're back so soon."

Ada quickly stuffed the sheets in the hamper. She gave a quick kiss to her son and went back downstairs. She decided she would not think any more about this conversation.

CHAPTER TWENTY-FIVE

"The prosecution rests, Your Honor."

"Mr. Moscowitz, present your first witness."

"The defense calls Mr. Albert Wentworth."

The tall, ram-rod straight man took the oath with the demeanor of a seasoned military man. When he sat in the witness box, he did not unbutton his dark gray suit coat but only pulled it down to keep his precise appearance. His square, chiseled jaw with the cleft chin looked sharp enough to intimidate the most disorderly subordinate under his command.

"State your name and address, please, for the record." Mr. Moscowitz didn't bother looking up from the papers on his table.

"Albert J. Wentworth, 2247 Bristol Court, Carmel, Indiana."

"What is your occupation?"

"I am the OEM Accounts Manager at Allison Transmission."

"How many employees do you supervise?"

"Approximately twelve, depending on sales and market projections. We are a growing company, and we have contract employees from time to time."

"How many years have you been with Allison?"

"Twenty years."

"And what did you do before that?"

"I was captain of the 244th unit of First Division, Marine Corps, 1941 through 1945."

"Very good, Mr. Wentworth. On behalf of all Americans, your

service to your country will always be appreciated and never forgotten."

Mr. Wentworth nodded once.

"Let's get back to your job at Allison. As part of your duties as manager supervising your men, do you give assessment reports as to their job performance?"

"Yes. We have bi-yearly and year-end reports that determine whether or not the employee will be promoted, demoted, put on probation, or in the worst-case scenario, released from his job."

"Were you a manager in Henry's Stangarden's area?"

"Yes."

"How long has Mr. Stangarden worked at Allison?"

"Twenty years. I know that because I came into the company at the same time."

"But you were his boss. How did that come about?"

"When I applied to work at Allison, there were openings in management."

"What job did Mr. Stangarden have?"

"He was hired as an accountant."

Ed Moscowitz handed a thick, brown file folder to the witness. "This is the personnel records of Mr. Stangarden. Are you familiar with it?"

Mr. Wentworth opened the file and looked through the top two pages. "Yes. I wrote most of the reviews."

"Can you give the court a summary of those reviews?"

The witness put the closed file on top of the witness stand rail. "Excellent reviews. He consistently met all the criteria of his job."

"Criteria such as?"

"Accuracy of his accounts, attendance, promptness, ability to get along with other employees, typing skills, completion of projects, taking the initiative to see areas that need improvement, and making suggestions, just to name a few."

"And Mr. Stangarden's performance reviews?"

"All exceeding expectations. Henry Stangarden is first-rate employee."

"Anything else?"

"If I was to evaluate him in one area that he could do better is his social skills. He seems a bit standoffish. Maybe it's because of his language. He's from Germany, you know, and with English such a difficult language to master, he may not feel confident in conversing with others."

Still holding his smile, Mr. Moscowitz said, taking the file folder, "Thank you, sir."

As Ed Moscowitz took his seat, Mr. Morris walked to the witness box, knitting his brows as if in deep thought.

"Mr. Wentworth, you said your employee, Henry Stangarden seemed standoffish."

"Yes," the witness replied a little cautiously. "Polite but not very social."

"Hmm . . . . Have you ever seen any pictures of his son, Robert, on his desk? Or even of his wife? Any family photos?"

Mr. Wentworth titled his head. "Well, no."

"Does Mr. Stangarden ever talk about his son? His good grades, his band concerts, his gymnastics activities? Or getting in the I. U. School of Music and being awarded all those scholarships?"

Mr. Wentworth looked puzzled. "Well, no. To tell you the truth, I never knew he even had a son until this trial came up. And I don't remember hearing any of his co-workers talking about his family."

"Thank you, Mr. Wentworth. No other questions."

"Reverend Thomason, you've known the Stangardens as members of First Trinity Lutheran Church for how many years?"

"Eighteen." The pastor sat comfortably in the witness box as if he had had plenty of experience being in it. He casually crossed his legs and clasped his hands over his knee.

"And how would you describe the family?"

"Oh, they are most devoted to the Church. Mrs. Stangarden is active in our women's groups, and she sings in the choir. And if our organist is on vacation or is ill, she's eager to volunteer to play the piano for the services."

"That's nice," commented Mr. Moscowitz. "So, she is a well-loved member of the congregation."

"Indeed."

"And what about her son, Robert?"

"When the Stangardens became members of our church, Robert was three years old. When he was ready for preschool, he began attending Sunday school. He was confirmed at age thirteen. But, like a lot of teenagers, once he was in high school, his activities in the church tapered off except on special occasions, such as Christmas Eve or Easter when he'd play his French horn in an instrumental group. He received many compliments for his musical talent."

"I see." The defense attorney pretended to hold great interest in the religious activities of the Stangarden family. "Is Mr. Stangarden active in the Church?"

"Hmm, not as much. Mostly he attends Sunday services."

"So, overall, what is your assessment of the family?"

The Reverend uncrossed his legs and put his fingertips together as he spoke. "They were an immigrant family who found a home in Christ at our church. They are devoted to God. Faith is very important to this family."

"Thank you, Reverend Thomason."

Mr. Morris approached. "Did the defendant interact with congregants? Did he attend the adult Sunday school classes?"

"Maybe once or twice, as much as I can remember. I can't answer that with certainty."

"In all the eighteen years he and his family attended?"

"Well, yes."

"Did he attend a prayer group or men's breakfast group? You have those at your church, don't you?"

"Yes, we do. But no. I don't believe that he participated."

"How often does he attend your services? Is he there every Sunday?"

"Well, no."

"How often?"

"Perhaps once a month."

"Does he take communion?"

"Yes."

"Has he ever asked for a meeting with you to discuss any problems or spiritual needs?"

The minister sighed. "No."

"Have you seen him interact with anyone in the church?"

"Maybe just a few."

"Any speculation as to why that is?"

"Objection! The witness is not a mind-reader."

"Sustained."

Mr. Morris turned to the jury. "So, the defendant goes to church at most once a month, does not participate in any church activities, doesn't even interact with any other church members. It almost sounds like he goes to church only as a cursory gesture to appease his wife."

"Objection!"

"Withdrawn. No more questions."

Decidedly not as confidant as he was before, Reverend Thomason stepped down.

CHAPTER TWENTY-SIX

Henry Stangarden gave the court officer a rare smile as he took the oath, as much as a bulldog could. This was a good day. He thought about perhaps taking his wife out to dinner when this was all done; someplace nice like a steakhouse. He pulled his too-tight suit coat together as he sat in the witness chair. Skin bulged over his shirt collar, making his neck perspire. His skinny black tie threatened to strangle him like a noose. He had even gotten a haircut while waiting in his jail cell, though it was hardly needed.

Ed Moscowitz knew he had to muster his best performance as a defense attorney as his difficult client's freedom depended on it. The day before, he got into a shouting match with Henry about whether or not he would take the stand in his own defense. Repeatedly, Ed had told him to do so would be a fatal mistake. It was just too risky. Inwardly, Ed was not confident that his client would stick to his prepared answers.

Moreover, he knew his opponent, ADA Morris, would have a field day with him. And Henry's belligerent demeanor during the trial would not make him a sympathetic witness to the jury. But stubbornness and sheer arrogance ruled. Henry wanted his day in court to clear his name.

Later, while sitting at a local watering hole with his files in front of him and nursing his second highball, Ed regretted taking this case pro bono. If he had had to do it all over again, he would not have gone near it at any price.

The jury was seated. Judge Campbell nodded to Mr. Moscowitz.

"Please state your name and address for the record."

"Henry Stangarden, 5051 West 46th Street. Indianapolis, Indiana."

"Mr. Stangarden, where are you and your wife from originally?"

"Eppingen, in the district of Heilbronn."

"In Germany?"

"Yes, Baden-Wuttemberg." Henry had been admonished to speak only English words.

"You lived there all your life?"

"Yes."

"And what did you do there? What was your occupation?"

"I was an accountant at Dieffenbacher."

"And what did that company make?"

"Oil presses."

"Then, after the war, you and your wife and son immigrated to the United States by way of Argentina?"

"Yes."

"Mr. Stangarden, how long have you and your family lived in the United States?"

"Twenty years, give or take a few months." Henry folded his arms over his barrel chest, a familiar pose.

"Where do you work?"

"Allison Transmission."

"Do you own your home?"

"Yes." Henry Stangarden spoke with care.

"Ever been in trouble with the law?"

"No."

"Bankruptcies? Money troubles?"

"No."

"You and your family are members of First Trinity Lutheran Church?"

"Yes."

Ed Moscowitz took inventory of the jury's attention. So far, so good. "Tell the jury if you would please what happened on Saturday, August 29, 1964?"

Henry unfolded his arms. "My son, Robert, thought he was going to university. I decided it was not right for him to go."

"And why was that?"

"Too many bad elements down there. People there do not think the way I do or my wife. They would be a bad influence on Robert, and I wanted to keep him away from that." Henry remembered to speak slowly and to enunciate his English well.

"Okay. So, what happened at the house?"

He shrugged with a look of total indifference. "I told him 'no,' and he argued with me. I had to set him straight. It is like in the old country: the father's word is the law. That's how my father raised me, and that is how I raise my son." He remembered to look at the jury. "You know, in this country, children are spoiled, no discipline, no respect for their elders." He noticed some of the older jury members nodding. "I want the best for my son. I want to keep him safe. Look at him." Henry gestured to Robert, who was now sitting with his mother. "He's fine. No harm was done. He's a healthy boy, and a wiser one."

That drew some murmurs from the gallery.

"Thank you, Mr. Stangarden. No more questions."

Assistant District Attorney Morris leaped out of his metal courtroom chair and almost bumped into the passing Ed Moscowitz. "You say, Mr. Stangarden, that you want your son to be safe? After you were done with him on that Saturday afternoon, he safely landed in the hospital for a week? That's keeping him safe?"

Henry touched his head and then his heart. "Safe up here and safe here."

"Where is your son living now, sir?"

"At home with his mother."

"Is that a safe place now?" Mr. Morris tried to hide his clenched jaw. A scene flashed in his mind. He imagined Robert's blood sprayed on the furniture, the bloody knife on the coffee table, the furniture in disarray. He wondered how hard the wife had to scrub the carpet to try to get the stains out before the crime techs came in to take pictures days later. Her efforts had been fruitless. The techs had noticed the odd-looking rug and had looked underneath it.

"He's with his mother," he repeated.

As Mr. Morris turned his back to go to the prosecution table, sarcastic retorts spewing in his mind made him grimace in anger, which he had to suppress. Wilbur Morris' assistant, Mr. Wells, gave him the palm-sized heavy glass piece from the box.

"Mr. Stangarden, can you identify this object?"

Henry barely looked at it as Mr. Morris held it in front of him. "Some glass ball."

"It doesn't look familiar to you?"

Henry shook his head.

"Please answer the question, sir, for the court reporter."

"Nein."

"Would it surprise you if I told you that this is the lid of a glass candy dish that sat on the coffee table in your living room?"

No response.

"Do you see here on the side where it makes an air-tight seal over the top of the dish?"

No response.

"Mr. Stangarden, I asked you a question. Isn't this the top of the candy jar?"

When the witness stayed silent, a scowl of contempt forming on his sanguine face. Judge Campbell intervened. "Please answer the question, sir."

"Ya."

"This is the lid of a candy bowl that sat on the coffee table. Correct?"

"Ya! Ya!"

Too bad, the wife had washed the darn thing, probably with bleach. The techs could lift no fingerprints from it.

"You heard earlier testimony from Dr. Irene Piece, who had treated Robert Stangarden in the ER, that this object could have been used to make the contusions and bruises on his shoulders, his back, and his head, which caused him to suffer a concussion. Do you agree that that might have happened?"

Ed Moscowitz rose. "Objection. The witness is not a medical professional or a forensic expert qualified to make such a determination."

"Sustained."

Mr. Morris went back to his table and pulled out the knife. "What about this?" He walked to the jury so they could see it again. "This knife was also found on the coffee table with blood on it, according to the earlier testimony of Mr. Ralph White, the taxi driver who picked up your wife and son."

"Is there a question here?" Ed Moscowitz felt he had to do something.

"Mr. Stangarden, do you recognize this knife?"

No response.

"Mr. Stangarden?"

The bulldog of a man growled, "No. I don't recognize it. Knives all look the same."

Mr. Morris returned the item to his table. Mr. Wells put it back in the box.

"Mr. Stangarden, let's say someone told a reasonable person that your son landed in the ER with bruises, a concussion, a broken nose, and a deep cut across his throat. Then that person was told that certain items that could have made those injuries were in your house. Is it reasonable to conclude that those items had been used to inflict those injuries?"

Henry Stangarden's thick neck and his ears turned bright red.

Mr. Morris strolled in front of the tables to allow the witness time to think of a response. When no answer came, he said louder, "Mr. Stangarden. The candy jar lid and the knife were found in your home. A witness testified that there was blood on them. The crime technicians sprayed these items with luminol and found the blood. Another witness testified that the lid and the knife could have been the weapons used against the victim, your son. So, I ask you again. Mr. Stangarden, did you use the candy jar lid to beat your son and use the butcher knife to cut his throat?"

"Yes! I had to discipline him. He was arguing with me. I had to show him who is the boss. I am the head of my family. He does what I say!"

It was time to pivot. "All right. Now let's talk about this argument you had with your son that led to this attack. You didn't want Robert to go to Indiana University because, in your words, there were 'too many bad elements down there?'"

"Ya." Henry forgot his English again. He leaned back and resettled in his chair.

"Can you explain what you mean?"

Ed Moscowitz said, "Objection. Asked and answered."

"I'll allow it," said the judge.

"You know, communists, people not of Christian values." Henry remembered the Christian angle, thanks to Ed Moscowitz's practice sessions.

" 'People not of Christian values.' " Morris repeated this slowly, walking from side to side in front of the jury box. "Are you talking about Hindus, Buddhists?"

"Yes." Henry Stangarden frowned as if wondering what that had to do with anything.

"Well, why not send him to a private Christian school?"

"Too expensive." This drew nods from the jury and a few of the spectators.

"Robert is a music major, isn't he? He was a freshman last year, correct?"

"Yes."

"How likely would it be that he would be exposed to these bad elements if he was in classes with fellow music students and being taught by music professors? Are you saying these people would have a harmful influence on him?"

"He is better off at home."

"Your Honor, will you please direct the witness to answer the question?"

Before the judge could speak, Henry Stangarden growled, "Ya. Dey are a bad influence."

"Have you ever been to the I. U. campus and talked with his friends and his teachers? Were you familiar with his routine? Where he went for his classes? His social activities? Have you attended any of his performances?"

"Nein! But it doesn't matter! I know what goes on!"

ADA Morris asked, "Then why did you allow him to go to I. U. the previous year?"

The witness hesitated.

"Mr. Stangarden?"

"He got some scholarship, and my wife pushed to let him go. So, I let him go for one year. That's it."

The sigh from the defense table was audible.

"Would it be safe to say that there might be Jewish people down there? After all, it's a big university, lots of people from all over the world coming to take classes and earn their degrees. Are Jewish students also part of this bad element you're talking about? How did you say, 'undesirables?'"

"Objection! Relevance, Your Honor."

"No, I vant to answer."

"Go ahead, Mr. Stangarden," said the judge.

Ed Moscowitz shuffled papers.

"Jews, foreigners, they are all alike. We must be vigilant. We are in a war, a cold war! We must guard against anti-American activities at all times. Otherwise, the communists and the big-money corporations will take over. They are stealing right under our noses. We work so hard just to scrape by. Not right that those people make profits off our backs." He swayed his head back and forth, looking for a receptive audience. "They lend money at ridiculous interest rates. That debt to foreign countries was making the country go bankrupt! We needed leadership to throw off those reparations and to make us strong again!" Henry flailed an arm toward the gallery.

"The country going bankrupt? 'We needed leadership to make us strong again?' 'Reparations?' I'm confused, Mr. Stangarden. Are you talking about this country? The United States? Or—"

"Never mind. I say no more." Henry waved a dismissive hand and leaned back in his chair, satisfied with having finished the interrogation. He folded his big arms again and looked passively at the gallery.

"Your Honor, I want to strike that answer as unresponsive," said Wilbur Morris.

"So ordered. The jury will disregard the last statement made by the witness." The gray-haired judge frowned at Henry Stangarden. He was straying away from the questioning in a most peculiar way.

However, Henry had heard the judge's pronouncement. "What you mean by 'disregard?' I am telling you the truth!" He put meaty hands on top of the witness railing.

"Mr. Stangarden, please just answer the questions from Mr. Morris only. We don't need a speech."

"Bah! They should know! I am speaking to truth to all you, to all Americans. Maybe I should talk to the newspapers. The Russians pointed missiles at us in our own backyard down in Cuba. Communism is spreading in the world! Look what is happening in Viet Nam! Inflation is rising, the big banks in the East holding this country by the throat. I know this because I work for a company that does business with them. I see the numbers all the time. Those greedy bastard Jew money-lenders . . ."

He stopped.

ADA Morris halted and faced the jury box. He made eye contact with each one of the jurors. "Go on, Mr. Stangarden. What about the Jewish money-lenders?"

Henry breathed heavily to catch his breath. He surveyed the hushed crowded courtroom. Then he saw the black-haired man sitting next to that woman doctor in the back of the courtroom. His hooded eyes mere slits, he peered at the culprit who had instigated this whole sorry affair for a long time. "As I said, undesirable elements I don't want my son exposed to."

Mr. Morris followed Henry's gaze to the back of the courtroom. Then he turned back. "Who are you looking at, Mr. Stangarden?"

The witness seemed not to have heard the question.

"Are you looking at one of the undesirables you referred to earlier?"

Henry's face filled with frightening hate.

Ed Moscowitz stood. "Your Honor, may I have a moment with my client?"

After an "I-don't-care" nod from Wilbur Morris, the judge allowed Ed to come forward. Hushed, terse words were exchanged.

"Mr. Moscowitz, do you desire a recess?" Judge Campbell asked.

"Your Honor, I object," said Mr. Morris. "I am not through with this witness."

"Mr. Moscowitz?"

Reluctantly, Ed Moscowitz retreated from his client. "No, Your Honor." He returned to his table, trying his best to appear unruffled and confident. At the defense table, he quickly took out a silk handkerchief and dabbed his forehead. He crammed it back in his inner breast pocket, hoping nobody on the jury would see his nervousness.

Wilbur Morris continued. "Mr. Stangarden, do you know the gentleman sitting in the back, Mr. Joe Kaufmann? I will remind you that you are under oath. You must tell the truth. Perjury is a federal offense."

Henry Stangarden hesitated. "No."

The gallery froze.

"Are you sure?"

Another tense moment hung in the air. Wilbur Morris waited patiently.

"Ya. I am sure."

One could hear a pencil snap at the defense table.

"Your Honor, may we have a recess?" Ed Moscowitz began to stand up.

Glaring at the witness, Judge Campbell pronounced, "Recess until ten o'clock tomorrow." He angrily banged his gavel and threw it on the bench. "I want to see counsel in chambers. Now!"

Judge Campbell unzipped his robe. "Is there a plea deal on the table?"

The two lawyers met eyes. Wilbur said, "We will be in discussion about that as soon as possible."

Ed nodded in concurrence.

"Well, I sincerely hope you two can resolve this, so I can bring an end to this trial, which is turning into a circus complete with the peanut gallery!" Judge Campbell shook a finger at the attorneys. "In the meantime, you two put your heads together and come to an agreement."

Outside the judge's chambers, Ed said to Wilbur, "Drinks at the Slippery Noodle? Seven o'clock?"

"Meet you there."

CHAPTER TWENTY-SEVEN

The next morning before the trial resumed, Henry Stangarden was hustled into a conference room by his lawyer. In the corridor, the Pierce family waited. When Joe and Irene saw Wilbur Morris leaning against the marble railing and lighting his pipe, they went to him. Johnny Wells meandered around like a small, bored child. Spectators and reporters crowded the hall.

"What's going on?" Joe asked.

Wilbur Morris smiled. "Mr. Kaufmann, this case is almost over. Like the old saying, when the fat lady sings. Ha! Ha! I'm waiting for Ed." He nodded toward the conference room. "Stick around." He left them to talk with Johnny, ignoring the shout of questions around him from the ubiquitous crowd of reporters.

"God, I can't stand this." Irene sighed with exasperation.

Joe lit a cigarette and began smoking hard. The nicotine only agitated his dancing nerves.

"That man is a mockery of the human race," Grayson snapped. "Son—"

"Something's gonna happen." Joe interrupted. "Oh, there's Robert."

Robert was with his mother, along with the two church women. The three of them were trying to keep her on her feet. They half-guided, half-dragged her to a bench near the women's restroom. The poor woman looked as if she had given up on carrying the weight of the world on her sagging shoulders.

The meeting room door opened, and Ed Moscowitz came out. He motioned to Wilbur and Johnny. Turning to Joe quickly, Mr. Morris said, "Mr. Kaufmann, please don't leave." He conferred with Mr. Moscowitz and then walked with him back to the conference room. Johnny Wells trailed behind them.

Joe smashed his smoke in a cigarette butt container. "I'd give anything to be a fly on that wall."

"Time to present the deal again to your client, Ed." Morris put his briefcase on the floor and sat at the expansive wooden table. He folded his hands. "Your client just cooked his goose. Mr. Stangarden, would you care to elaborate on that answer you gave in court about not knowing Joe Kaufmann?"

With defiant folded arms Henry Stangarden spat, "Go to hell."

"Please, Mr. Stangarden, manners."

"All right. All right. Let's not go down that road." Ed Moscowitz put out his hand. He looked at his client. "Henry, this is the plea deal Mr. Morris is offering: aggravated assault, class C felony. If you accept it, you will be looking at three to eight years. A hearing would determine your sentence. That means aggravating and mitigating factors would be presented so that the judge has all the extenuating information to determine your sentence. Mr. Morris and I will present circumstances about your case that were not presented during the trial both for and against you. Also, we can call character witnesses, and the victim, your son may talk to the judge."

"Vat sentence? I am going to jail?"

"Yes, you are if you agree to this. The plea agreement means you admit assaulting your son, Robert. That's what aggravated assault means. You inflicted grave bodily harm with a deadly weapon, in this case, the top of that candy dish and the kitchen knife. And you will have to allocute. You will have to tell the court what you did to Robert." With intense eyes on his client, he added, "It would help if you show some remorse."

Henry swept the table with his arm. "Nonsense! Like I said out there, I only wanted to control him, to keep him at home." He raised his voice. "I did no'ting to him! I put him in his place. The jury will know that. Look, I am innocent. I am a good man. I go to work. I provide for my family. I mind my own business. I am a good father to my son. I have no trouble with the police ever. How would they understand that not?"

Mr. Morris said, "Are you rejecting the plea agreement? Do you want the jury to decide your guilt or innocence on the more serious charge of attempted voluntary manslaughter? That's ten to thirty years."

Henry looked back and forth between the attorneys, incredulity on his face. "Vat is this? What kind of justice is this in this country?" He turned to Ed Moscowitz. "How can this be? Aren't you supposed to help me? Get them to understand vat I did?"

Mr. Moscowitz said, "Henry, I strongly suggest that you take this deal. It's in your best interest to do so. We're looking at the difference between a prison sentence of three and eight years instead of ten to thirty. Do you really think you have a choice here?"

Mr. Morris said, "And while you're sitting in a prison cell pondering what you did to your son, I'll be passing along this case file to the United States Department of Justice. They will open an investigation into your activities during World War II, namely at the Buchenwald concentration camp. And we'll be looking at your wife as well."

To this statement, the fat man suddenly stood, his face bursting with rage. "Nein! You leave my frau out of it!"

His lawyer put a firm hand on his arm to try to get him back in his chair.

"And we have a pretty solid eyewitness," Wilbur said.

Henry Stangarden pounded his fists on the table. "I vil kill that Jew! He started all of this!"

His shouting brought a police guard into the conference room, his right hand on his belt close to his service revolver. The lawyers saw him and motioned him out.

"I need to speak to my wife. She vill make you understand." Henry fell back into his chair. He wiped his wet face.

Ed Moscowitz asked, "All right with you, Wilbur? Maybe she can talk some sense into him."

ADA Morris nodded.

After a quick word to the guard standing outside the door, He brought in Ada Stangarden. She looked as if she were about to be taken to the gallows. Before she sat, her husband said to her in German, "Tell them this is all a mistake. This—"

Mr. Morris reproved him. "You and your wife will speak in English, Mr. Stangarden, or we will ask her to leave."

Annoyed reluctance crossing his face, Henry Stangarden said to his wife in English, "Tell them I was disciplining that boy. We did no'ting wrong! Tell them!"

Ada Stangarden's usual tiny white handkerchief came out. Trembling, she said, "Ich nicht—"

"English, Mrs. Stangarden." Wilbur Morris's voice said sternly.

"Okay. Okay. I tell the truth." She slowly sat next to her husband and put her new JC Penny leather pocketbook on the table. She sniffed and pressed her hanky against her nose. "I try my best. I try to be a good wife—"

"Sagen sie ihnen!"

"Shut up!" Wilbur snapped, hitting a warning fist on the table. He turned to Ada, who looked as confused and frightened as when her husband had been arrested months ago. Wilbur tried to keep his voice calm. He spoke slowly. "Mrs. Stangarden, we have a plea deal on the table. Let me reiterate what it is because it can be difficult to understand. I am willing to accept Mr. Moscowitz's offer of aggravated assault, which is a C Felony. That's three to eight years in prison. He might be allowed credit for time served for the ten months he spent in jail awaiting trial. It's going to be up to the judge to determine his sentence. He will have to allocute, and if he shows remorse, the judge might be lenient. With good behavior, he could be looking at early release. But he'll be put on probation. Also, he will be ordered to have no contact with your son indefinitely. Do you understand?"

Ada Stangarden looked between the lawyers and her husband, trying to absorb all this. Her dilemma was overwhelming. She had always done what she had been told. That was her job as a dutiful German wife. She had chosen to serve and obey her husband when she had married him, and when the call to help the Fatherland came, she followed him without question. As required by the State for all German women to bring new generations of pure Aryans into the world, she had tried to give children to her husband, but she was unable to. However, she had made up for it when she had joined her husband, who went to work in that labor camp near Weimar. She had volunteered her skills as a cook and was put to work at once. It was all for the Fatherland. It was about making the country strong again; to build a superior race. Or so she believed.

She looked again at her husband to whom she had been married for almost thirty years. Whom she cared for, cooked for, cleaned for. The man with whom she helped build a new life in America.

But now, the world was crashing around her ears, just as it did in early spring 1945. The airplane to Buenos Aires had sat on the tarmac. Oh, how did it all come to this?

Ada said nothing with brimming eyes behind her cloudy glasses; her thin, 1930s brows knitted in bewilderment.

Ed Moscowitz said, "This is a good deal, Ada. If Henry refuses, the original charge of attempted voluntary manslaughter will stand. The jury will decide either his innocence or guilt. If he's found guilty, the judge will sentence him between ten to thirty years in prison."

Ada looked at the defense attorney with widened eyes.

"We brought you in here for you to try to convince your husband to take this deal."

Ada fingered the straps on her purse. "He vill lose his job?"

Mr. Morris answered, "That's pretty much a given, Mrs. Stangarden. If your husband is found innocent, maybe his employer will take him back. But if he's found guilty, he'll be a convicted felon. I doubt he'll find as good a job as he had before if he finds a job at all after he gets out."

The ADA pressed on. "Even if he's acquitted, the Federal District Attorney will be looking into his background as to what he did in Germany during the war. Your background will come under scrutiny, too."

Ada gasped.

With the ever-steadfast attitude, Henry said, crossing his flabby arms, "They vill find no'ting."

Ada didn't know what to do with these baffling choices. It would be unthinkable for her to give him her opinion. Even if she told Henry to take the deal, he wouldn't do it.

But her husband was taking an enormous risk. Thirty years! She and Robert would become destitute without his income. How could they live?

Finally, she said in a small voice, "I do vat my husband say."

The lawyers exhaled. Ed Moscowitz said, "Okay, Wilbur. I guess we'll see you back in court."

Henry Stangarden was put back in handcuffs and led away.

CHAPTER TWENTY-EIGHT

"All rise!"

The Honorable William R. Campbell breezed into the courtroom in his billowing robe and sat in his big office chair on the bench. He did not look happy. As people took their seats, he spoke.

"Any more witnesses, Mr. Moscowitz?"

Ed Moscowitz rose. "No, Your Honor. The defense rests."

"Very well. Is the prosecution ready for closing arguments?"

Mr. Morris was on his feet in an instant. "Yes, Your Honor." He buttoned his suit coat.

"Proceed."

After making sure his co-counsel, Johnny Wells, had put the photographs of Robert's injuries within easy reach, Wilbur Morris approached the jury box.

"Ladies and gentlemen of the jury, this is a tragic, appalling case." He put his hands in his pockets and began to walk.

"Here is a young man, Robert Stangarden. A music student enrolled at the prestigious Indiana University School of Music. A bright, extraordinarily talented student. Recipient of three music scholarships. A double major in music education and French horn performance. At the end of his freshman year, 3.9 point grade average.

"He was salutatorian of his class. He was drum major of the marching band, out there on the field during football halftime leading the band. Moreover, he conducted the pep band at the basketball games. Since the age of four, he has studied the piano and took private music lessons on his French horn at the Jordan College of Music, up on 34th Street and Pennsylvania Avenue. He participated in music contests and won top division ratings. And, if that wasn't enough, he was on the gymnastics team for three years, winning two medals. Robert was a busy kid.

"Ladies and gentlemen, this is an ambitious, focused, achievement-oriented young man. He has had the maturity to know who he is and what he wants in life from an early age. He has never been afraid of doing the hard work it takes to reach his aspirations. A determined young man who has set his career goals at a time when so many young people today hardly know what they want to do for the weekend, let alone for the rest of their lives. Robert wants to be a music teacher, a public school band director. And he wants to play his French horn in a professional orchestra or a community band. He's preparing for it all now . . . or rather he *was* preparing for it."

Wilbur Morris paused, making eye contact with jurors, gauging their reaction. They looked back at him with spellbound attention. He went to his table and picked up the pictures. He handed them to the man sitting on the front left-hand side, who studied them and then slowly passed them on. One woman put a tissue to her mouth and squeezed her eyes as if not wanting to see them. Another man turned his head away.

"This . . . was Robert Stangarden ten months ago." Wilbur Morris spoke with gravity. "I understand how uncomfortable it is to look at these photos. They had been taken after he had been in the ICU for three days with a respirator tube down his throat. Another tube had been inserted into his side for fluid to drain from his punctured lung. These pictures don't show the bruised kidney. They don't show the concussion, forcing him to walk with a cane so he could keep his balance. They don't show the four fractured ribs making breathing as painful as any broken bone. However, one picture does reveal the circular pattern of bruises on his back made by a glass top of a candy dish. And a nurse took off the dressing to show the twenty-two stitches in his throat."

Discreetly observing the grim faces, Mr. Morris collected the pictures. "This was more than just a beating." He waved the photographs. "Someone wanted to kill this innocent young man." He returned the pictures to his table and came back to the jury box.

"Or maybe not. Maybe Robert just needed to be taught a lesson.

To get the message across that, he must stay home and be a dutiful son. To get a job, to help with upkeep around the house perhaps. Maybe to help his mother with the laundry or setting the table for dinner. To do odd jobs like mowing the grass and shoveling snow and cleaning out the garage on the weekend.

"He had his fun at college. He was permitted to indulge in his pipe dream of studying music for a while. But on that Saturday afternoon, August 29, it was time to put away those childish ambitions and join the real world. Get a job. Be a teller at a bank, for instance, or work in a factory.

"Or maybe there was something else going on. Maybe Robert needed protection from unsavory, shady characters who might be lurking behind some maple trees on the I. U. campus. Villainous, stinking, unkempt, liberal-minded, anti-war degenerate professors and students who were ready to pounce on unsuspecting, naïve, freshman music students with their un-Christian, impure views about the world. Oh, no. Robert couldn't be exposed to those kinds of, quote, unquote, 'undesirables,' be they Hindus or Buddhists or Catholics or . . . gypsies or homosexuals or—"

"Objection, Your Honor!" Ed Moscowitz shouted. "He's straying from—"

Judge Campbell pounded his gavel to the outburst from the gallery. "Order! Order in the court! Quiet!"

When the reverberations to the high, wood-paneled ceiling dissipated, he said, "Mr. Moscowitz, you will have your turn at rebuttal. Sit down."

The defense lawyer sat, shaking despite his effort not to. He grabbed a pen and worried it to keep his hands busy.

After a nod from the bench, Mr. Morris continued. "Let's refresh our memories of what the charge is against the defendant: attempted voluntary manslaughter. Voluntary manslaughter means that the killer was under the heat of extreme emotion at the time of the assault, resulting in the victim's death. There was no forethought or planning to commit the deed. That would be murder. Henry Stangarden was so angry with his son that he picked up a candy dish lid and pummeled him over and over and over. He kicked him as if he was a dog that needed to be brought to heel. But it didn't stop there. By taking that butcher knife and drawing it across Robert's throat, the defendant tried to kill him. But because Robert survived, the charge is *attempted* voluntary manslaughter.

"What about the excuse for the brutal assault on this young man? Was Henry Stangarden justified in beating his only son within an inch of his life? Members of the jury, Robert only wanted to go back to school! He wasn't attacking his father. He had no weapon. When you study the pictures of his wounds, you can see that this was a violent, personal act of rage! What made this man so angry that he had to take it out on his own flesh and blood? This attack goes way beyond disciplining his son. That this man did such a merciless deed to another person shows his complete disregard for human life!

"Look at him over there. Is this someone who deserves to be out on the street, minding his own business? Yes, he has a good job. Yes, he goes to church. Yes, he provides for his family. On the outside, he appears benign. He pays his taxes and waves the American flag on the fourth of July.

"But these pictures show who he actually is, a dangerous . . . malicious . . . monster!"

Wilbur Morris caught his breath and paused, letting that last statement ring to the high plaster ceiling. He took careful steps closer to the jury.

"Ladies and gentlemen of the jury, there is no question about what the defendant did to his son. There is no reasonable doubt. This act cannot go unpunished. Convict Henry Stangarden of attempted voluntary manslaughter. Give justice to his son, Robert."

With not a sound in the room, ADA Morris returned to his seat.

CHAPTER TWENTY-NINE

"Mr. Moscowitz?" asked the judge.

Ed Moscowitz knew this trial was the biggest challenge of his career to date. As an officer of the court, his duty was to mount a vigorous defense for his client. He felt he had done so throughout this trial. He had made the appropriate objections. He had put character witnesses on the stand. He had conferred with his colleagues about the case. He hadn't just gone through the motions. He had given his best effort.

The plea offer from the ADA was fair. There was no reason to reject it. But his client was a fool. The arrogance of this man stunk like the smell from an Indiana hog farm. Ed could barely keep down his revulsion.

"Members of the jury, I present to you a different side of this story for your consideration. You must look at this in a broader context. Mr. and Mrs. Henry Stangarden are German immigrants. Although they've been in this country for twenty years, their views of the world, their culture, and their way of living are from a country where the society is quite different. German values can be strict, but they are also admirable. German culture focuses on hard work, perseverance, ingenuity, respect for authority, devotion to church, and family. These are values the Stangardens brought with them when they settled in our fair city. They are living those values now. Mr. Stangarden is an exemplary employee at Allison Transmission. He is well-skilled, committed to his job, consistent in his work habits. His performance reviews reflect a solid, dedicated, loyal company man. His wife, Ada, is a wonderful cook, an active member of her church, and a loving, devoted spouse and mother.

"Henry brings a paycheck home every week. He is the breadwinner of his family. From his salary, Robert could enjoy taking music lessons and participating in band concerts and gymnastics meets. However, there's more to it. Robert's demonstration of hard work, a sense of purpose, strength of character, maturity, discipline—all this came out of a home with good parents who taught him these things. Members of the jury, this goes far beyond just a paycheck.

"In these current times, young people are defying authority, their parents, their teachers, law enforcement. They are acting out impulsively with no thought about the consequences and certainly not taking responsibility for themselves. But today, we have a young man who is the exact opposite. You heard the prosecutor sing Robert's praises. We know for a fact that Robert is a good kid. He doesn't take drugs, doesn't drink or smoke, doesn't run around all hours of the night partying with his friends. He's a straight arrow. I'm sure many of you would love to have him as your son. *I* would love to have him as my son.

"But you have to consider how he became who he is. His sterling character comes from loving but firm parenting. Learning self-discipline. Doing the hard work to get the job done. Willingness to take responsibility. Having integrity. None of these things came out of a vacuum. He grew up in a home where these values mattered. While the hippies and riffraff live in communes or on the streets strumming guitars and dropping acid, Robert prepares for his career. He will be successful in life, not these other flower children.

"So, I urge you to consider where Robert is now today. Return his father to his home to continue the good work of parenting his son. Find Henry Stangarden innocent."

After a survey of his tiny audience of twelve, Ed Moscowitz slowly returned to his chair.

CHAPTER THIRTY

"Members of the jury, this concludes this portion of the trial. I have a few instructions for you. When you go into the jury room, you must first select a foreman. His job is not to add weight or influence you on your deliberations but to keep things organized, such as contacting the court officer, Mr. George Janson, if you need a restroom break. If you have questions or need to have parts of the transcript to review, write them down, and give them to the foreman, who will contact George. If you have any questions for me, I must have it in writing, and I will also answer in writing.

"The most crucial instruction I am giving you now is that you may not discuss any elements of the case outside the jury room. You only discuss the case with each other in the room. You are not to talk about it with friends or relatives, and certainly not with the press. Do not discuss the case when you are on a break.

"As you deliberate, you must consider only the evidence. Do not allow emotion, sympathy, or personal feelings enter into your deliberations. You must be impartial. You must ask the question: Do the defendant's actions meet the criteria for attempted voluntary manslaughter? Your verdict must be fair and just. When you reach your verdict, the foreman will tell George, and we will reconvene in this courtroom. You may now follow the court officer to the jury room."

Ed Moscowitz packed his notes and files in his bulky alligator skin briefcase as the jury filed out. He didn't have the stomach to tell his client to be hopeful that everything would work out. He was glad this was almost over. The inevitable verdict would just be an afterthought to this charade of a trial.

He turned to see Wilbur Morris and Johnny Wells standing next to him.

"Ed, the plea deal's still on the table."

Ed looked after his client shuffling away with an officer. "I could ask him again, but I think it would be a wasted effort."

"Mr. Moscowitz?"

Ada Stangarden touched Ed's arm like a child asking for attention.

"Yes, Mrs. Stangarden?"

She looked between the two lawyers. "I . . . I wish to talk. I vant both you to listen."

The attorneys looked at this exhausted woman with the cloudy glasses and greyish hair and sad, colorless eyes. Her care-worn face revealed a finality of heart-breaking defeat.

"Why, of course, Ada," said Ed.

"Mit my husband. Can ve do dat?"

Wilbur Morris asked, "Where is your son, Mrs. Stangarden?"

"I tell him to go to that man, Joseph Kaufmann, and those people mit him. He vill be okay."

The three attorneys escorted Ada back to the conference room. Henry Stangarden entered the room after a few minutes. Wearing his perpetual scowl, he waited for the cuffs to be removed. He sat next to his wife. "Vas is this? Is dis a trick?"

Ed Moscowitz said to his client, "We're here to discuss the plea deal, Henry. It's not too late."

"Nein."

With courage, Ada spoke up in German. "Henry, listen to them! Did you hear the witnesses? Did you hear what Mr. Morris said when he spoke to the jury?"

Henry waved his hand at her as if he were brushing away a fly.

"Did you see the jury? When they looked at the pictures, they were horrified! They will find you guilty. Henry, you cannot deny what you did to Robert! You will go to jail for thirty years! Oh, why are you so stubborn?"

In German, Henry replied, "I will be vindicated. I put that half-breed in his place. They will understand."

"Henry, these are not our people. These are Americans."

"Ada, we must protect ourselves. We can't allow it to come out!

You abide by my decision."

"And if you get convicted and go to prison, Robert and I will suffer for the next thirty years. How can we live on our own? I don't make enough at the school to pay the bills. Robert will have to drop out of college and get a job."

"I don't care about him and his college!"

"He will be so disappointed. He'll be miserable."

"And so what? He's been a burden on us ever since we left the Fatherland. Now, he's a danger to us. We have to get rid of him."

"Henry! We've reared him as our son! He's our family!"

"He's Carl's spawn."

Ed Moscowitz interrupted. "Mr. and Mrs. Stangarden, Mr. Morris and I would like an answer to our plea arrangement."

Ada said to her husband, "I am going to tell the truth, Henry. I can't live this lie anymore."

"No! It's all that Jew's fault! He—"

"Henry, you beat Robert! You didn't have to hurt him as you did. He almost died. If he had, you'd be in worse trouble than you are now. I am going to speak."

Henry's face became a thundercloud. "If you do . . ."

She met his eyes with defiance.

"Do not disobey me!"

She held her eyes to him for another moment. Then she turned to the lawyers. Over and over, she twisted that handkerchief she had taken out of her pocketbook. She spoke in English. "Ya. My husband tried to kill him. I could not stop him. I saw him beat him vit the candy dish lid." She swallowed; a catch was in her throat. "He hit him many, many times, and when he hit him in the head, my poor Robert fell to the floor on his stomach. Rikkert started kicking his back and shouting at him. Then he hit him on his back with the lid."

She dared not look to her right where her husband sat. "Den, he go into the kitchen and takes my big kitchen knife, what I use to cut cabbage and potatoes. He came back and took Robert by the back of his head. Robert vas still awake and trying to fight him off. He cut his fingers on the knife. Then my husband said, 'This will be your warning to stay away from that Jew pig.' And he sliced the knife on his neck. The blood came out, and I vas screaming. Den Rikkert put the knife on the table and said he vas leaving. He told me to clean up the living room."

Ada hid her face in her hands. Her whole body shook.

Her husband rose, fists ready. In German, he shouted, "You bitch! You betray me like this?"

The lawyers also stood in alarm.

"Henry, sit, or I'll call the guard!" Ed Moscowitz pointed a threatening finger to the door.

Breathing hard, the man slowly lowered himself into his chair. His face poured sweat. His body odor stank in the room.

Everyone else waited. Ada composed herself. When no one spoke, she continued quietly in English. "Ya, ve lived at Buchenwald. I vas a cook for the officers." Shielding herself away from her husband, she went on. "Rikkert vas a clerk at the front entrance. He wrote down the names of the people coming off the trains. I worked in the kasino, how you say, mess hall, where the officers eat."

"Rikkert? Who's Rikkert?" asked Ed.

"Our real names. He is Rikkert Steghausen, und my name is Matilda. We changed them when we lived in Buenos Aires."

Johnny Wells looked through the papers in his file folder quickly. "I remember those names. Joe Kaufmann said their real names on the stand. Do you remember that, Ed?"

Ed also took out a thick pad of typed papers and searched through them. "Here it is in the transcript. Okay. I'm with you."

Wilbur snapped his fingers. "Then, Joe Kaufmann was right. He knew both of you from Buchenwald!"

Ada nodded. "Ya. We knew him, and his Mutti und Vatti."

Wilbur asked, "How long did you and your husband work in Buchenwald?"

She shrugged. "Three years. Until almost the end of the war."

"How did you leave? Where did you go?"

"In March, we got on a plane to go to South America, to Buenos Aires. Everybody was leaving. We had to get out of there schnell. We took the baby with us."

"What?" asked Ed. "What baby?"

Wilbur and Johnny looked caught off guard as well. "What did you say?" asked Johnny.

Bravely ignoring the dangerous glare from her husband, Ada replied. "Ina's baby, Carl's baby."

Henry Stangarden turned away from her, still breathing hard. He angrily slapped his hand on the table.

"Who is Ina?" asked Ed Moscowitz.

Ada took her handkerchief and clenched it. "She vas Karl's pretend Frau."

The lawyers shuffled their feet under the table. Wilbur Morris said, "Can you explain to us what you're talking about? Start at the beginning. Who is this Karl, and who is this 'pretend' wife?"

"The Jews got off the train at night. Rikkert—"

"Your husband's real name?" asked Ed.

"Ya. He is Rikkert Steghausen. My name is Matilda."

"Go on, Mrs. . . . . Steghausen."

"Karl is my brother-in-law. Rikkert's younger brother."

"My stupid brother," Henry muttered under his breath.

"He saw Ina, this Jewess, and took her away in the front of the camp. Her last name vas Kaufmann. She vas so beautiful, Karl fell in love mit her and took her to be his Frau."

Henry spat. "My foolish, idiot brother! Good-looking, empty-headed brother. He is Vater's favorite. He is the one who gets into the SS-Totenkopfverbande. He comes back after the invasion of the Low Lands. He rises through the ranks to become second in command at Buchenwald. He is the one who organized the labor force to work in the quarry and railroads. He brings in the doctors to do the experiments. He is the one who has the power und I get no'ting! I am only a, how you say, zivilian. I get the lowly job of just processing the prisoners. Just dumm papierkram. I vanted to do more! I vanted to join the SS. Organize the work details! I vanted to drive the slaves! Make them work harder!"

Henry Stangarden spoke with sour bitterness. "He could have had any Jew-bitch he wanted. Raped them if he wanted to. No one would care. Nein, he sees this Jew-whore and brings her into his home. This Judenscheisse!"

"Rikkert!" Ada admonished him.

All three lawyers were writing furiously on their legal pads.

Ada turned to her husband and said, "Rikkert, your broder vas in love with her. She was so gentle and sweet." She turned back to the attorneys. "She vas the most beautiful woman I had ever seen. She vas the model of Aryan womanhood. Tall, vite-blonde hair, perfect figure, the bluest eyes, like the ocean. She could have been a movie star. Who would think of her as being a Jewess?"

She turned back to the lawyers. "Karl wanted to start a family with her. With his handsome looks, their children would be perfect models of de Deutsche Rassen. Isn't that right, Rikkert?"

"Bah!"

"And she could sing and play the piano. A voice like an angel! She entertained the other officers at parties."

Henry said, "It vas dangerous for Karl to take her and pretend she vas pure Aryan. I could not convince him that she was a Jew-slut no matter how blonde her hair, how blue her eyes."

"The plan vas Ina would go along with Karl and be his new Frau. But she asked dat Rikkert look in his ledger book and find her husband and child. We would feed them and protect them, and Ina would go along pretending to be a woman he had found in Berlin. Dey got married. Karl vas so in love. He would do anything for her.

"So, at night, a guard brought the Jew husband and child to the back of the kitchen. I gave them food. It vas arranged for the husband to work in the kitchen, and I would give him more food."

"Und Karl made sure they stayed alive," said Henry, still seething. "The guards were ordered to keep the other prisoners away from them. Such a risky, foolish thing he did."

Wilbur Morris asked, "What were the names of the husband and child?"

Ada readily answered, "His name was Hans Kaufmann, und the Kind vas Joseph." She allowed herself a tiny smile. "He vas cute."

"Joe Kaufmann," said Ed Moscowitz, tapping his pen. "But I don't understand. If Joe was a child when you saw him, how was it that you recognized him in your house back in May of last year when he was an adult?"

Henry said, "He looked like that Jew pig husband. Ven I saw him in the kitchen, I thought, how can this be? He is still alive! And he looks the same! Nineteen years go by, and here he is!"

"So, what happened next?" asked Mr. Morris.

Ada replied, "We fed them through the vinter, but things were getting bad. Deutschland vas losing the war. The enemy vas coming from both the east and west. The prisoners still kept coming, but it vas harder to control them. They knew it, too. By now, Ina vas showing."

"Showing?"

"She vas pregnant. The baby came in February."

Ed said, "What a minute. Is this the same baby you claimed as your child? Is this Robert you're talking about?"

"Ya." Ada's face became reflective.

Henry said, "So, ven it vas time to leave Buchenwald, Karl wanted his baby safe. So, even though I didn't vant to, we took his baby, my half-nephew, with us on the plane to Buenos Aires. That vas in March, '45."

"What happened to your brother and Ina?" asked Wilbur Morris.

"Karl had to go to Berlin to help with disbanding the other camps. But he would nicht leave behind the Jew-bitch. She vent with him. The plan vas they would go to Buenos Aires when the war was over." He paused, then added with contempt, "And take back that half-breed Kind."

Ada said sadly, "Aber, we never heard from them again."

"So, that's how you kept the baby," said Ed, writing as he spoke.

"Ya. When we got to America, we said he vas our child and gave him the name Robert. It vas easy to get false papers in Buenos Aires." She looked at the attorneys. "I always vanted children. I love kinde. We could not have them. So ven Karl gave the baby to us, I had a chance to be his Mutti for a while. Then ven they never came to Buenos Aires, we pretended he vas our own. He is my child. I love him. I always vill love him."

"I make this sacrifice for my brother!" Henry snarled. "I raise his Kind for him. This halbe Rasse!"

Ada straightened her back in an act of courage. "Rikkert, Robert ist nicht our nephew," she said in a rush of words.

Her husband turned to her. "Vat?"

"Robert is not our nephew."

"Vat? Vat are you saying?"

"Ina, that Jewess, vas already pregnant ven Karl took her. She told me."

Everyone in the conference room stared at her.

"She said she vas a little pregnant, maybe three weeks. And ven I gave food to her husband, he said that too. He vas so worried that Karl would find out and do away with her. And I said, 'Nein.' She vas safe, and we kept the secret. Karl always believed the child vas his. He treated her like a queen."

"Nein, dat cannot be right." Henry began counting with his fingers.

"They came in June 1944, Rikkert. He vas born in February."

With this new revelation, Henry could not find his words.

Johnny Wells said with excitement, "So Robert is the true brother of . . . Joe Kaufmann! Of course! That explains why they look so much alike. And if my memory is correct, the detectives said that's how these two got together at I. U. This friend of theirs, and I can't recall his name, claimed they had to be brothers. That's how this all started!"

Ed Moscowitz exclaimed, "Unbelievable!"

"Would you think of that?" said Wilbur Morris.

But Henry Stangarden stared at his wife in utter disbelief.

Ada Stangarden held herself fearfully. She knew better than anyone her husband's capacity for violence. Although he had never laid a hand on her, at this moment, she knew he was liable to do anything, regardless of the lawyers sitting at the table. This secret might cost her dearly.

In German, he shouted, "You tell me that kid is a full-blooded Jew? That stinking parasite who lived in my home for nineteen years?"

His wife replied, also in German, "But Rikkert! Robert is a good boy! You raised him too!"

"Why didn't I kill him when I had the chance?" he roared. He stood, knocking over his chair.

Ada closed her eyes and rocked. "He's a good boy! He's a good boy!"

Suddenly the door opened. "Jury's back," said the bailiff.

The attorneys began collecting their legal pads, papers, and file folders. "That was quick," said Ed.

"Yes. That might be a record." Wilbur Morris and Johnny Wells gathered their papers. Mr. Morris said, "Mr. Stangarden, the plea deal was obviously something you are not willing to take." He went to the door and motioned the guard. Impulsively he said, "You shouldn't count on acquittal."

Before he had a chance to react, Henry Stangarden was cuffed and led out of the conference room. His wife, Ada, followed with heavy steps.

CHAPTER THIRTY-ONE

"All rise! This court is in session. The Honorable Judge Leonard E. Campbell presiding."

"Please be seated." The judge, still donning his half-glasses, gathered his robes, and sat. When the courtroom settled, he announced, "Bring in the jury."

The twelve jurors solemnly marched in from a side door and took their seats in the jury box. Their eyes were downcast. Their faces were dour.

"I understand that a verdict has been reached."

The foreman, a lanky old man who looked as grizzled as a weather-worn Indiana farmer, stood. "Yes, Your Honor."

The bailiff took a piece of paper from him and handed it to Judge Campbell. He unfolded it and looked at it. Without any facial expression, he folded it and gave it back to the bailiff. "You may read the verdict."

Ed Moscowitz stood. He motioned his client to stand also.

The bailiff spoke with vigor for all to hear. "In the matter of People versus Henry Stangarden on the charge of attempted voluntary manslaughter, we, the jury, find Henry Gunter Stangarden guilty."

No one else in the courtroom expressed as much surprise as Henry Stangarden. "Vas is this?" he shouted. His head swiveled to his attorney, then the judge, the jury, his wife behind him, and back to the judge. He shook his fist. In German, he bellowed, "This is an outrage! You cannot find me guilty of putting that Jew vermin down! That

Jewshit! That bloodsucker! That . . ."

The gavel came down hard. "Order! Mr. Moscowitz! Control your client!"

It took not only Ed but also two guards to push Henry back into his chair. No one seemed to notice that Ada Stangarden seated two rows behind him was moaning, her face in her hands, her body swaying. Her "son," Robert, sitting next to her right, put his arm around her heaving shoulders. Her ever-devoted church friends looked on in dismay.

Henry roughly shook off the hands, restraining him. His burst of wrath frightened the juror sitting closest to him. She leaned back, expecting a blow.

Judge Campbell said, "Pre-sentencing hearing will be set next Thursday at nine o'clock sharp. Court is adjourned. Guards, take the prisoner away."

Before the judge turned to exit the bench, he heard a commotion. He looked up to see Henry Stangarden climb over the rail behind him. He pushed his way around his wife and lunged at his "son." He grabbed him by his suit coat and landed a swift blow to his face. People quickly got out of the way, calling out in surprise. Robert lost his balance and tumbled backward over the courtroom bench. Even as he tried to hide under it, Henry reached for him and managed to grab his ankle. Violently pulling him out, he hit him over and over about his face. And all the while, Ada Stangarden screamed in German, "Leave him be! Stop this, Henry! Stop hurting him!" These were the same words she had shouted ten months earlier in the middle of her living room.

Henry Stangarden began cursing in German, shouting and spitting as the courtroom guards pulled him away from the poor kid on the floor. With much effort, they had him in handcuffs and pushing him toward the side door. Above all the fracas, Ada Stangarden's ear-shattering screams echoed in the courtroom.

Like Moses parting the Red Sea, Dr. Grayson Pierce elbowed the crowd to get to Robert, who was still on the floor, holding himself in a fetal position. "Let me by! I'm a doctor," he barked. There was so much disorder no one seemed to hear him. He knelt and gently cradled Robert's head in his hands. Seeing the red marks all over the kid's face and the blood dripping from his mouth, he nodded to his daughter, Irene. "See if you can find an ice pack. And call an ambulance." Irene disappeared with his wife, Ruth. To the crowd, he shouted, "Everyone, back away! Give him some air!" He began loosening the kid's tie.

The court officers tried to push people away, including the reporters who were busily peppering questions to everybody involved. And on top of that, flashbulbs were exploding like fireworks. Somehow a TV camera appeared.

Robert opened his eyes to see a wrinkled, gray-haired man in black staring at him upside-down. "Are you all right, young man?" His question sounded like a stern pronouncement.

Robert recognized him as the judge. "Yes, sir," he mumbled. He allowed his shoulders to relax, his head still resting in the stranger's big, soft hands. He heard the judge say, "You're a doctor?"

"Yes. Dr. Grayson Pierce."

"You related to Dr. Irene Pierce?"

"I'm her father."

"Nasty piece of work," the judge spat. He straightened and left to talk to the bailiff and some police officers.

Ruth returned with ice dripping in a towel. She gently held the cold compress to Robert's cheeks. "Oh, dear. You sweet boy. We're going to get you to the hospital. Don't worry. Grayson and I will stay with you. I'm a doctor, too."

Robert's mother pushed her way to her son. She stroked his arm, her face damp with tears. In German, she lamented, "My son. My son."

Grayson carefully lifted Robert and laid him on the bench. For Robert, the shock of being struck so many times gave way to bitter, familiar pain. While Grayson dabbed the blood around his mouth, he said to his mother in German, "Why, Mom? Why did he do this again? Why is he so angry at me?"

Through her tears, she replied, "We will talk, Robert. We will talk."

No one noticed that Joe Kaufmann, his back pressed hard against the back wall in a corner, trying his best to stay hidden from that dangerous Nazi thug.

CHAPTER THIRTY-TWO

In handcuffs and chained twice around his waist and chained at his ankles, Henry Stangarden stood before the judge. Having interviewed all the parties involved, the probation officer had presented his written report to the judge several days earlier. Defense attorney Ed Moscowitz had made an earnest speech about his client's positive attributes, such as his good standing in the community, his clean record, and his sterling employment history. Assistant District Attorney Wilbur Morris countered with the heinousness of the crime, Henry's lack of remorse, and his behavior during the trial, such as verbally assaulting one Joe Kaufmann twice. Most importantly, this man's monstrous attack on his son after the verdict had been read had revealed his true character. The defendant did not allocute to his crime, nor did he speak on his own behalf for leniency. And Robert did not give a victim impact statement. He was hardly brave enough to sit in the gallery, let alone tell the judge how the assault ten months ago had affected him physically and emotionally.

"Will the defendant please stand?" requested Judge Campbell.

Both Henry Stangarden and his lawyer stood at the defense table.

"I have read all the reports and listened to both sides. Having considered all this, I hereby sentence you, Henry Stangarden, to serve twenty-five years in the Indiana State Prison. Furthermore, at the end of your sentence, you will be turned over to the Special Prosecutor of the U. S. Justice Department for further investigation as to your affiliation with the Nazi Party and possible deportment."

The spectators in the gallery began to talk eagerly amongst

themselves. The gavel went down twice.

The tired-faced judge interlaced his arthritic fingers. He peered over his silver half-glasses at the defendant.

Henry Stangarden kept his chained hands on the table. He glowered defiantly at the judge.

"Sir, your attitude and behavior are beyond despicable. Yours is the most sickening display of contempt of these proceedings I have ever seen from a defendant. I can surmise by the smug look on your face your true take on this matter. You believe you were justified in the ruthless assault on your son. You were waiting for the perfect excuse to unleash your hatred of him. And then you had the audacity to think that there should be no consequence to your abominable actions."

The judge studied the spectators and rested his eyes on Robert Stangarden sitting next to his mother. Robert's bruises had blossomed into their full, ghastly colors on his face, and he had a black scab on his upper lip. Judge Campbell looked back at Henry. "Let me make myself clear. You and your wife were granted the privilege to come into this country even if under false pretenses, as ADA Morris stated in the hearing. You were given citizenship and were allowed to live and to prosper in our city. To attend the church of your choice, gather with friends of your choice, and speak freely without fear of censorship. Those are the rights of every American citizen as put forth in our constitution." He leaned forward. "You have given up those rights by your actions in which this American justice system considers illegal. Whether or not you accept it is your choice."

He halfway stood, his hands pressing down on his bench. "It has never been made clear to this court why you assaulted your son. I have my theories. Perhaps when more information comes to light with the federal investigation of your ties with the Nazi Party during the war, that will finally bring some answers to this whole sad affair. I will be following this investigation closely."

He hesitated as if deciding whether or not to say more. But he finished with, "Court is adjourned." After a quick rap of his gravel, he rose and speedily exited a back door, banging it after him.

A familiar cry cut through the din as people rose to file out of the courtroom. Ada Stangarden was in the front row, weeping uncontrollably. She held out her hands as if trying to touch her husband. But a guard led him away. Henry Stangarden did not look back at her.

She turned and looked around forlornly, her wails turning into quieter sobs. Her two devoted church friends, Velma and Gladys, patted her arm to console her. But Ada's shock overwhelmed her. Her husband was gone. She was suddenly all alone for the first time in more than forty-nine years of her life. There was no one to take care of her; no one she could depend on.

Picking up her pocketbook, she slowly went around the railing to Ed Moscowitz. "Herr Moscowitz," she said. "Vat happens now? Vat do I do?"

Gently he replied, "I suggest you get a lawyer, Ada. You will be contacted by the Justice Department soon. They have offices here downtown on Market Street."

A greater sense of dread restricted her heart. "Aber, I did no'ting wrong. I am not a Nazi. I vas never in the Party."

Ed Moscowitz picked up his heavy briefcase. "But your husband was, and as his wife, and that fact that you worked in the Buchenwald concentration camp, your status is uncertain. I really can't answer any more questions." He began to move past her.

"Aber, bitte. How do I get a lawyer? How do I pay for a lawyer?"

He replied, "Call my office in a couple of days. I'll try to find someone who can help you. I'm sorry. I must go."

He hurried out of the courtroom.

Ada's shock and fear turned into complete numbness. Her mind was blank in her distress. She looked around. She stared without seeing ADA Morris pack his files. He never looked toward her.

"C'mon, Mom."

Her son, Robert, held out his hand. She collapsed into his arms and bawled.

Robert gently led his mother out of the courtroom and into the corridor. Her church friends followed. People walked around them but did not seem to notice them. The gaggle of reporters was waiting to get statements from the ADA and the defense attorney. Ada allowed her son to guide her to a bench.

"I'm sorry, Mom," said Robert. He unbuttoned the top button of his white shirt and loosened his narrow, blue and red-striped tie. He sat next to her and held her hand.

"Vat vill we do? Was werden wir tun?"

Robert looked on to see Joe Kaufmann and his sister, Dr. Irene

Pierce, standing on the other side of the hall next to the marble railing. He recognized the petite, blonde lady as his ER doctor as he had not seen her when she had taken the stand. As a witness, he had had to stay out of the courtroom during her testimony. The other tall man, Grayson Pierce, stood next to the sweet-faced lady who had put the ice pack on his face. Maybe she was his wife. They all were watching him and his mother.

Joe Kaufmann's gaze made his heart quicken.

"I don't know yet, Mom. I think we should go home and have supper and rest. We don't have to do anything right now." He added, "We should look at your financial situation. I should stay home and get a job."

"Nein! You have your schooling!" she exclaimed.

Robert held her shoulders. "That's all right. Maybe later, I can go back. But we both know we have to find some way to support ourselves. Things can't go back to the way they were." He suddenly had a sense of déjà vu. He had heard that statement from one of the detectives so many months ago.

Ada looked across the hall to the small clutch of people still watching her and Robert. She knew she had to make a decision.

She unexpectedly met eyes with Joe Kaufmann.

"Ada, let's get you home," said Gladys. "You've had a long day, and you must be tired."

"Ya," Ada replied listlessly.

Indeed, there had been enough upheaval for the day.

CHAPTER THIRTY-THREE

Two days after the sentencing hearing, Ada called Ed Moscowitz's office to meet with her and Robert to recommend a new lawyer and talk about legal matters. She asked if the Reverend Eugene Thomason could come to give her support. She also requested that Joe Kaufmann be present. But since she didn't have any way of contacting him, Ed Moscowitz's secretary said she would handle it.

On Tuesday, March 29, Ada was escorted by Reverend Thomason into a three-story brick office building on 3345 North Delaware Street. A stately, imposing structure that was in a neighborhood filled with grand, old mansions, it had been built in 1868 by a business tycoon, Wallace Harding, to be home to his large family. Today, it was the law offices of Dudley, Young, Moscowitz, and Bernhart.

A stylishly dressed young woman greeted Ada, Robert, and the reverend and took them into a spacious, wood-paneled conference room. Large oil paintings of dark, scenic landscapes hung on the walls that were divided by maple-varnished wainscoting. Planters of real philodendrons, Mother-in-Law Tongues, and Boston ferns stood in corners. A floor-to-ceiling set of bookshelves were tightly packed with law books. A brass chandelier hung directly above the center of the sleek, glass-topped conference table. Underneath the table laid a plush blue and pink oriental rug over a walnut floor. Cut-glass decorative knick-knacks sparkled in open cabinets, and an occasional table presented colorful Chinese vases and gold-trimmed ceramic lamps. A wood antique wall clock ticked quietly. One could smell old money in this room, along with the faint attic smell of a hundred-year-old house.

On one side of the table sat the Pierce family. Ada was startled to see them. She was expecting only Joe Kaufmann.

"Please be seated, Mrs. Stangarden," said the secretary. "I will bring coffee if anyone wants some." A tray of crystal glasses and a pitcher of water sat in the middle of the massive table.

To cut the tension, Reverend Thomason reached over the table, his hand out to Grayson Pierce. "Hello. I'm Reverend Eugene Thomason. I'm the minister at First Trinity Lutheran." He appeared to be about the same age as Grayson and perhaps an inch or two shorter.

They shook hands vigorously. With a good-natured smile, Grayson replied, "I'm Grayson Pierce." He stood. "This is my wife, Ruth, and my daughter, Irene. That's my ward, Joe Kaufmann, over there." He pointed to Joe, who had his face in his palm and trying to look disinterested.

"Yes. I recognize Dr. Pierce from the trial. And Joe. So good to meet you and your family."

Ruth and Irene smiled and nodded to him. Ruth offered, "You are Ada's minister, is that correct?"

As a stranger spoke her name, Ada looked at the younger woman for the first time.

"Yes, I am. Ada is one of my favorite congregants. She sings in the choir, you know."

The two men sat, hands folded on the table. Reverend Thomason said, "I'm here just as a visitor, to support Ada." He gave a cordial smile to her.

To end an awkward pause, Grayson said, "Robert, how are you feeling? Taking some aspirin for those headaches?" He couldn't help wearing his doctor's hat. "It'll take a couple of weeks before those bruises will fade. Warm compresses will help."

Unsure, Robert replied, "Ah, okay." Nobody had told him about the compresses. He kept his eyes down.

Ruth spoke, a little nervousness showing through her tight smile. "I'm not sure why we are here. Mr. Moscowitz invited us to this meeting. We assumed it was for Mrs. Stangarden to discuss her affairs."

A door opened, and the secretary carried a heavy tray of cups and saucers, spoons, and a white porcelain coffee pot decorated with tiny flowers. Another woman followed with a tray of matching bowls filled with cream and sugar and napkins. Busy hands poured coffee and stirred spoons in cups.

"I guess we're waiting for Mr. Moscowitz," Irene said. She watched her brother Joe slide an ashtray toward himself. He lit up, then sipped his coffee. If he was at all ill at ease, he didn't show it. However, he wouldn't look at Robert, either.

Ada Stangarden frowned to herself, dismayed. Maybe this wasn't such a good idea. She was almost ready to rise and ask Reverend Thomason to take her home. She searched her pocketbook for her hanky.

Ed Moscowitz entered with as much confidence as if he owned the room. "Welcome, all," he said in a loud voice. Today he wore a seersucker tan suit, sans waistcoat. Another man, younger and wearing a conservative gray suit, followed him. "This is Mr. Douglas, my paralegal. He'll be taking notes." At seeing the men begin to stand, he said, "Please, don't get up." He and his assistant took their chairs at the end of the table.

"I see everyone is here, and you've all been served coffee. The restrooms are out that door and down the hall to the left. My secretaries are standing by if anyone needs assistance."

No one spoke. The tension level raised a notch, although seemingly not noticed by Mr. Moscowitz. He opened a legal-sized, leather-bound notebook and unscrewed a fountain pen. Mr. Douglas did, likewise. Only he clicked a ballpoint pen. Looking around the table, the attorney started, beaming a clueless smile.

"I want to thank Joe and his family for coming. I understand that you are from New York, and you are eager to return. Needless to say, we've all had a pretty rough ride this year, and I'm sure you all want to move on and return to your lives." He paused for comments. As none were made, he continued. "I have invited you here to go over some issues that were not resolved during the trial."

"Issues?" Grayson asked. "As in legal issues?"

"Umm, not exactly. However, it may lead to some legal actions down the road." He looked at Ada, who was a study in anxiety. "Ada, would you like to begin, or would you rather I start the ball rolling?"

Swallowing hard and choking, causing her to have a coughing fit, Ada pressed her handkerchief to her mouth. She blew her nose and took off her glasses to wipe her eyes. Reverend Thomason gave her a glass of water, which she accepted eagerly.

Ruth said, "Are you all right, Mrs. Stangarden? Would you like me to help you to the restroom?"

Ada looked at her with startled eyes. Then she dissolved into a crying spell. The Reverend patted her hand.

Everyone sat patiently except Joe. He blew smoke toward the ceiling and extinguished his cigarette. He moved about in his chair and rapped the table twice with his knuckles.

"Mom, we should go," Robert said. "This isn't working. Maybe we can come back another day and have a private meeting with Mr. Moscowitz." He took her hand.

Breathing deeply, Ada stayed her tears. Trembling, she said, "Nein. Ve must do dis." After sweeping her eyes around the room, she said, "I vil speak English. Dey must all understand."

She closed her eyes and knitted her pencil-lined eyebrows. "My son, I . . . I have something you should know. It is about you and dat man over there."

"You mean, Mr. Kaufmann?"

"Ya." Ada Stangarden opened her eyes. She took a deep, slow breath. "Robert, you are not our son."

"What? What are you talking about?" Robert let go of her hand.

"My brother-in-law, Karl, your father's—I mean, my husband's brother, took a Jewish woman after the train came in and unloaded the prisoners. He fell in love mit her and took her to his house."

"Who? Who is this Karl?"

"Karl Steghausen. He vas second commandant of Buchenwald. He had much power and authority. Rikkert vas his older brother, and he worked at the front of the administration building and processed the prisoners. He wrote down the names of dat man's father and his mother, Hans und Ina Kaufmann. I dunt think he wrote down the name of their son."

Robert's mouth hung open. He shut it and frowned angrily. "Who is this Rikkert? Mom, you're not making any sense!"

"Dis man, Kaufmann. It vas his wife Karl took. He pretended he found her in Berlin. Dey got married."

"What?"

"She vas so beautiful. Und she could sing and play the piano. She entertained at parties. She vent along with Karl if he promised to take care of her real husband and her son."

Robert looked at Mr. Moscowitz for help.

The attorney stepped up to the plate. "Robert, maybe I can explain this more coherently."

Robert stared at him and then at the people sitting across the table. All were as motionless as statues, their faces betraying nothing except Joe. He stood and reached over to pour a glass of water. Alas, his hand slipped, and the water spilled on the beautiful wood table. But since the glass top protected it, there was no real damage.

Irene grabbed some napkins to clean the water. She poured more water for Joe. Then she discreetly moved closer to him. He ignored her.

Grayson Pierce kept protective eyes on his ward.

"Robert, let's start at the beginning." Ed Moscowitz put his Montblanc pen next to his writing tablet. He flipped through a couple of pages and found his notes. "We have to make clear who were your real parents. I know how difficult it is to hear this. This set of events was alluded to during the trial by Mr. Kaufmann's testimony. But your parents' real names, or should I say the couple who reared you as their son, are Rikkert and Matilda Steghausen."

The attorney paused, referring to his notes. "The Steghausens worked at the Buchenwald concentration camp during the war. Rikkert, a member of the Nazi Party, documented the prisoners when they came into the camp. His wife, Matilda, worked as a cook for the SS officers and was not a member. Rikkert's younger brother, Karl, was the second commandant of Buchenwald. Just as a side note, the Steghausens had no children."

Ed waited for this to sink in. Robert stared at his mother, his face frozen.

"In June 1944, a family of Jews, the Kaufmanns, arrived at Buchenwald. But they were from Berlin, and they had managed to hide until then. His father's name was Hans, and his mother's name was Ina. Joe was six years old."

Robert looked at Joe as if for the first time in his life.

"According to your mother, after Rikkert Steghausen processed them, Ina was taken by Karl Steghausen, his younger brother, to become his new wife. She became Ina Steghausen, and the ruse was that he had found her in Berlin. Because of her coloring, she could easily pass as a—"

"What do you mean, 'coloring'?" Robert asked.

Ed Moscowitz cleared his throat. "She had blonde hair and blue eyes." He looked about uncomfortably. "She looked like a pure Aryan woman."

Ada jumped in. "He loved her so much he would have done anything for her! He verehrt her."

"Worshipped her?" said Robert.

"Ya. De plan vas she would go along mit all this as long as her real husband and her son would be taken care of. I gave them food at night. Und Rikkert came out mit me sometimes. Karl made it so the guards would harm them."

Joe lit another cigarette, trying very hard to act nonchalant. He became obsessed with flicking ashes into the glass ashtray.

"But der ist more," said Ada. She twisted her hanky, her face contorted in angst. "This woman, Ina, vas already pregnant ven she vas mit Karl. Just a little bit, she told me. Aber Karl thought the baby vas his. He vas so pleased ven she got with child so quickly."

This bit of information perked Joe's attention. Irene put a steadying hand on his arm.

"When I fed the man and his boy at night, I talked mit him. He wanted to know what vas happening to Ina. I told her she vas fine. She vas getting along well. Aber, she did dat for her family to be taken care of in the camp. She pretended to love Karl." She added breathlessly, "She vas very brave."

Robert said, "Are you saying that . . . that . . . ?"

Ada could not speak.

Ed Moscowitz said, "You are the second son of that man, Hans Kaufmann, and Ina, his wife."

Robert looked at Joe and then back at his mother. "This can't be right! This is insane!" He stood and said to Joe, "Does that mean we're . . . brothers?"

Joe bore daggers into the other young man's eyes. One could see his jaws clenching, that thick vein bulging in the middle of his forehead. Then he turned to the woman.

"You're lying,"

"Nein. Ist true," Ada replied in a halfhearted voice.

Robert sank into his chair.

Grayson asked, "So, what happened after her baby was born? How did you and your husband end up with Robert in the U.S.?"

"Robert vas born 2 February 1945. Things ver terrible in the camp.

Everybody knew Germany vas losing the war. We had to make plans to get out before the enemy came. So in March, Karl vas called away to Berlin to help disband the camps. He decided it vas safer for the baby to go mit Rikkert and me to Buenos Aires on a plane. He would not leave Ina behind, and he took her with him. They ver going to meet us in Buenos Aires after the war ended. But they never came. Ve kept watching for their letters, but der vas no'ting. Rikkert and I pretended the baby vas our son. Ve renamed him Robert. We got papers to immigrate to America."

Grayson asked, "Did he have another name? What was his original name?"

Ada looked at the big man across the table for the first time. "Ina vant a good German name to hide him from being a Jew. She named him 'Maximillian.' 'Max' for short."

Ruth said, "So, his real name is Max Kaufmann?"

Ada replied, "Ya. That vas the name she chose, and Karl vent along. They go to a church in Weimar, and he vas baptized with that name."

Robert frowned. "Mom, you said I was born in 1945."

"Ya. Two February 1945."

"Then why did you always tell me I was born in 1946? That makes me a year older than I thought I was! Then I'm 20 instead of 19! Mom, how could you do this to me?"

"Ve had to lie about you ven ve ver in Buenos Aires. We pretended dat you ver our son."

Grayson said, "You and your husband falsified your papers to get into the United States."

She replied, sighing, "Ya. We came here as refugees. It vas easy to get papers. Everybody was doing it."

Stillness held the room for several moments. Robert focused his eyes on the table, his face a study in suppressed fury as he thought about what his mother was saying. His whole body trembled.

"Ven I tell Rikkert about all this with the lawyers, I thought he would kill me. He always thought Robert vas his half-nephew, but ve had to act like he vas our son. But he vas never close to him. He vas never interested in Robert's music."

Robert put his face in his hands, realizing at last what his father's relationship had been to him. Indeed, he had been no father at all. Such a bitter epiphany!.

Ada went on. "Rikkert vas a good provider and had a good job. He paid the bills, our food, and clothes. But ven Robert vas little, he disciplined him too hard. Robert learned fast to stay out of his way. I tried to protect him." She felt Robert's eyes on her. "Since Robert vas good at music, I helped him. I paid for his piano lessons and then band lessons."

Grayson said, "No wonder he hated you, Robert. You were never his son. You were his half-nephew, and half-Jewish to boot!"

Robert grimaced at this blatant observation.

Ed nodded to Robert. "And when Henry and Ada saw Joe in your kitchen last May, they recognized him. Henry could not allow their cover to be blown. Joe knew that Henry Stangarden was a Nazi. So, Henry did what he felt he had to do to keep you away from Mr. Kaufmann, even to the point of almost killing you. That was his real motive."

Ada said, "Rikkert took out his rage at his brother on you, Robert. He vanted to be an officer like Karl. He said he wanted to drive the prisoners in the quarries and on the railroads. You ver, how you say, a reminder always of vat he could never be in the camp."

Robert shook his head violently. "No. It's not true. He's not a Nazi. How could a Nazi have raised me?"

Joe spoke with impatience. "This is all well and good, but I'm not listening to this. Robert, there are some things your mother is telling you that are true. Yes, she did feed my father and me, and the SS guards kept the other inmates from hurting us. That was no small task." He glanced at his guardian, Grayson. "Yes, her husband was a Nazi. And, yes, I did see a SS officer take my mother away. But I didn't know he was Henry Stangarden's brother. How could I? My father and I never saw my mother again. I kept asking Vater what happened to Mutti. He said she was okay. She was being taken care of." Joe pointed an accusing finger at Ada. "But my father never told me that my mother was already pregnant before we arrived at Buchenwald. He would have told me."

Ada spoke fast in German. "Maybe you were too young to understand."

Joe looked away, his anger smoldering. Then he turned back to her. "No, I don't believe you. I'm done here." He quickly lit a cigarette. "Grayson, let's go. This meeting is a waste of time." He gestured to Robert. "You have a good life, Robert. Good luck dealing with your

Nazi parents."

He stood, but his family stayed in place. Ada looked forlornly at Ed Moscowitz.

Ed took a manila envelope from his paralegal, Mr. Douglas. "Mr. Kaufmann, I have some pictures you might want to see."

Joe stopped.

Ada said quietly, "Look, bitte."

Joe stubbed out his cigarette and blew out smoke. He hesitated, then took the envelope and sat again.

The first photograph was a four-by-six professional portrait of a stunningly beautiful woman. Although in black and white, one could see that her eyes were light-colored, and her wavy hair was shoulder-length and blonde. Her sparkling eyes were set wide over her prominent cheekbones and straight, slender nose in an exquisite, perfectly symmetrical face. She looked directly at the camera; her voluptuous lips closed in seemingly forced detachment. She wore a buttoned-down, dark-colored dress with a white rounded collar. A tiny, gold-lettered name, "Grimmel," in the bottom right corner indicated the photographer.

Joe turned over the photo. Someone had written, "Ina Steghausen, 24 Juli 1944." He turned it back, staring. His body was so rigid that it could have been broken with nothing more than a stern look.

He slowly laid out the next picture. A larger eight-by-ten, this had been taken at the altar of a church. Standing in the middle was a black-robed minister of some denomination. To his right stood the same woman well-dressed in a suit and wearing a small, flat hat. She held a baby wrapped in a white, lace-trimmed blanket. A man dressed in a German officer's uniform, complete with medals and a swastika armband, rested his arm around the woman's shoulders. He was the tallest person in the picture, with blond hair, severely cut in the usual German style. A strong cleft chin and square jaw suggested authority. However, here, he beamed a proud smile. On his left side stood the same couple whom Joe had known in the concentration camp as Rikkert and Matilda Steghausen, dressed in their Sunday best. Matilda smiled slightly, but her husband did not. He also wore a swastika armband.

With a shaking hand, Joe turned this one over. Taufe auf Maximillian Richard Steghausen, Nicklaikirche, Deutschland 28 Februar 1945

The third paper was a birth certificate in German. Vater: Karl Steghausen. Mutti: Ina Steghausen. Kind: Maximillian Richard Steghausen.

Joe could no longer focus his eyes on the paper. All he knew was that he couldn't breathe. His hands shook so hard he couldn't put the pictures and the certificate back in the envelope. As someone took them from his hands, he closed his eyes. He heard loud voices despite the roaring in his ears.

"This is my father?" Robert shouted. "He's wearing a swastika! That's me as a baby?"

"Ya, Robert," Ada replied.

"Then . . . that means you were there, too, at Buchenwald?"

"I am sorry, my son. I—"

"You're not my mother? This is all just a fake? A deception? All my life I thought I was . . . . You were my parents. None of it's true?"

While Robert barked his questions, the envelope was discreetly passed around the table.

"My mother is your mother?" He pointed his finger at Joe.

Joe nodded. He blinked back unwanted tears. "Yes. That is my mother. And that is the SS bastard who took her." He quickly wiped his eyes.

"But . . ."

Joe was gone.

CHAPTER THIRTY-FOUR

"I . . . just don't know what to do."

Joe sat in the back seat of the Grayson's rental car with Irene. Through the windshield, they watched for everyone to come out of the office building. But it had been a long wait. Joe dreaded seeing Robert and his mother. Of course, that minister would be with them. At least he had had the good manners to stay quiet during that meeting.

Joe rolled down the window as it was getting hot even in this late March air. He felt Irene's head against his shoulder, her hand rubbing and squeezing his arm. Even with her embracing comfort, he could not stop shaking.

Quietly, Irene said, "Your mother was beautiful."

Choking back a sob, Joe replied, "She was." He lifted his head, blinking to keep the tears from falling. "I loved her so much. She was so good to my father and me." He paused. "Even though we lived in that cramped attic for those few years, we were happy because we were a family."

Irene took a tissue from her purse and wiped her eyes. "Hearing you say that makes me miss my mother even if I never knew her."

"Yes. I suppose I should be grateful for the time I had with her."

They held each other and wept.

Joe released Irene. "She must have kept those pictures all these years. I wonder if there're more." He pushed up his slippery glasses. "Man, I've got a terrible headache."

Irene dabbed her tissue to her nose and sniffed. "Daddy probably has aspirin in his suitcase. We can get it back in the hotel room."

"Maybe he's got something stronger I can take. I'm just so tired. I know I won't be able to sleep tonight, if I'll ever sleep again." He was thinking about sleeping pills.

But Irene wasn't taking the bait. "I feel sorry for Robert. To suddenly know he's not who he thought he was, his family isn't his family. And this is on top of getting beaten up so badly last year and then again three days ago. What he must be going through!" Her voice hardened. "I hope that Nazi brute rots in hell."

Joe said, "That baptism picture is the best evidence that that stinkin' scumbag was a Nazi. Rikkert Steghausen is locked up for now, and then maybe he'll get deported back to Germany. What a relief! I don't know if his wife will be deported with him, but if even if she isn't, she'll probably go with him."

"And leave Robert? What a choice she'll have to make! But even if she leaves, it's not as if Robert will be alone. He has you now." Irene sat up straight, but she kept her fingers intertwined with Joe's. "Don't you realize you're his family now? Aren't you happy about that?"

Joe shrugged. "I barely know him."

"But you showed me those pictures, your friend, Frank Oneida, took. You went to Robert's concerts. He's not a perfect stranger."

Joe let go of her hand and stared out the window. "I didn't tell you about the time we were in a practice room at the music annex building there on campus. He had told me he could play the piano. It's almost serendipitous. He took piano lessons since he was a child just as I did." Joe frowned. "We were both in band, too."

"Tell me about that, Joe."

Joe looked at her. "It started in the music library . . ."

****

The I. U. School of Music library was situated on the third floor of Merrill Hall, the music building. Joe had made a few visits to this large, crowded room from time to time, mainly to see if he could supplement his research papers for his doctoral classes. Besides the long Formica-topped tables, metal chairs, rows, and rows of bookshelves and periodicals, listening to carrels, complete with portable record players, filled the north end. Thousands of record albums lined the wall. Students taking music history classes were tasked to identify music pieces for their tests, and the vast amount of music to learn was daunting. "Drop the needle" was the dreaded term. If Joe found an empty carrel, he gave in to temptation, checked out a set of headphones, and whiled away his time listening to some favorites and maybe a few unfamiliar pieces. He kept a notebook handy to write down titles of albums he liked but didn't own.

On a late Saturday afternoon in December, he had sat at a table thumbing through a rather pedantic book on American music at the turn of the century. His doctoral thesis was on American business and labor unrest in the early 1900s. On a whim, he thought the music of the time might provide a social context. But this book focused too much on the music itself, such as the development of early popular music, Broadway tunes, sheet music for the piano, ragtime, and the early years of jazz. Nothing he could use. So, he left the book on the table and got up to wander toward the records area.

He walked past a familiar figure seated in a listening carrel. Robert Stangarden's eyes were closed with a set of headphones over his ears. With a slight smile, Joe quietly moved on to check out another set at the front desk. He pulled up a chair, trying not to disturb the hard-at-listening music student. He managed to push the jack into a second socket without Robert noticing. He put on his headphones.

He clicked a pen and wrote on Robert's notepad, Bach, Second Orchestral Suite, third movement. Robert read the note, frowning. Putting his headphones around his neck, he looked into Joe's grinning face. "How did you know that?" he whispered loudly.

Playing innocent, Joe only shrugged. Robert stopped the record and replaced it with another one from the stack next to the phonograph. He dropped the arm in the middle of the spinning vinyl disk. He drew a big question mark on a blank notepad. Without hesitation, Joe wrote, Haydn, *The Heavens are Telling, the Creation*. Happily, he waved a finger in the air, keeping time.

Irritation shadowing his face, Robert took off that record and put it in its jacket. He got up and searched through a middle shelf of albums along the wall. He pulled one and returned. Hiding the record jacket under his chair, he put on the record and dropped the needle again. This time, Joe pretended to listen hard. After about twenty seconds, he wrote Mendelssohn's *Reformation Symphony*, first movement, Philadelphia Symphony Orchestra, Stokowski. Showing irritation, Robert quickly got up again and pulled one from the bottom shelf. Joe tapped his finger on his chin, his face screwed in mock heavy thinking. Stravinsky, *Symphony in C,* fourth movement, Cleveland Orchestra, George Szell, I think.

Robert stopped the record and threw down his headphones. Standing, he growled, "How the hell do you know all this?"

The librarian at the desk said, "Shhh!" Some other students looked their way.

Joe put his hand over his mouth to stifle his laughter. He took off his headphones. "You don't know who you're dealing with, Robert. I grew up listening to all that," he whispered.

Robert's anger simmered in his low, terse words. "Damn. I've got to learn all this music in three days, and you're sitting here naming all of it like it was nothing. That's not fair."

"Don't feel bad. You're not the only person who gets mad at me for knowing all the answers."

"Huh?"

Joe noticed the librarian's warning eyes. "Let's get out of here. We're annoying the house Frau."

After returning the headsets and gathering their things, Joe and Robert went out and sat on a bench in the hall. Joe lit a cigarette. They watched students walk by, two of them attractive females carrying textbooks and music. Joe bit his tongue to not comment on them. He had observed Robert enough to know he wasn't interested yet in the opposite sex. He was all work. A "Jack" who was, indeed, a dull boy.

Robert started the conversation. "Who are you? I thought you were a history major. You seem to know more about music than the music majors."

Joe smiled. "Yeah, well, I guess I should let you in on a little secret. It's something I try to keep to myself because I get into trouble if I don't. I've got a pretty high IQ."

Robert frowned, confused. "I don't understand. What does that have to do with you knowing so much about music?"

"I know a lot about everything." Joe dragged on his light. "It's just that music has always been a hobby. I grew up with music."

"So, what's your IQ?"

"I was tested when I was eight. I think it was 194. I don't remember."

"Really? That's genius level, isn't it?"

"Yes."

"Why haven't you been tested as an adult? Don't you want to know?"

Joe stubbed out his cigarette on the floor and crossed his knees. "No, I don't. It wouldn't change anything, at least regardless of what I'm doing now, which is finishing this doctorate."

Robert pondered his next question. "Mr. Kaufmann, there's a lot I don't know about you. You told me when we were in that practice room back in October that you have a sister, and who was it, a guardian?"

Joe lit another cigarette. "It's complicated." He was hesitant to say more, but perhaps it was okay to share some background with Robert. "At the end of the war, I was rescued from a camp in Germany by an American army doctor, Grayson Pierce. He became my guardian. He lives with his second wife, Ruth, in Ithaca, New York., which is where I grew up. He has a daughter, Irene. She's a year older than I am.

"How old are you?"

"I'm twenty-six. My guardian is a surgeon at the local hospital, third generation. Irene is a resident at Marion County General in Indianapolis." He dragged on his smoke.

"Did you ever want to be a doctor?"

"Never. Even if I were his biological son, I wouldn't. Too much real-life tragedy to deal with. I prefer tragedy that happened five hundred years ago."

Not catching Joe's witty remark, Robert took some moments to reflect on all this. "So, how did you find out that you were a genius?"

"When I started second grade at the beginning of the second semester, my Aunt Mil, Grayson's older sister, found out from another parent that I was helping the other kids in the class. I told him I already knew the lessons, and the teacher was trying to keep me busy. Not that I would get into any trouble, of course. The principal suggested having me tested. So, Grayson took me up to Rochester. That's when I learned my IQ. It's been a burden ever since."

"How so? I think it would be a good thing."

Joe gave a cynical smile. "Yeah, that seems obvious. But it just caused me a lot of grief, especially with the other students when I was in junior and senior high school. And at home, too, with Irene. She was so jealous of me she couldn't stand it. She'd see me breeze through my classes, making straight A's on tests without studying. But she had to work at it, hard. To her, it was just so unfair that I didn't even have to lift a finger when we were in college. She was a sophomore when I was a freshman at Cornell University. I was able to test out of all the courses, so I took sophomore-level classes at the same time she did. I had to be very careful for the rest of undergraduate school not to take any classes with her."

"Where was this again?"

"Cornell University. That's where I got my bachelor's degree. Your horn teacher, Mr. Oneida, went to Ithaca College. We met through a mutual friend, Alex Greene. I've known Alex since we were kids. His family was Jewish, and they took me to Shabbat services and had me over to celebrate the holidays. He played the alto sax, and we were in the band together from seventh grade through high school."

"Why didn't you have Jewish services with your own family?"

Joe grinned sardonically. "That is a big can of worms. Grayson and his family were devout Catholics, especially his mother and his sister, Mildred. When he brought me to his home after the war, he wanted me to keep my Jewish faith out of respect for my parents and my heritage. That didn't go over well with my Aunt Mil. She insisted that I convert to Catholicism. She taught me behind Grayson's back. They had fights over me for years." Joe reflected on those chaotic times. "Nasty ones. The equivalent of major Civil War battles."

"What about his mother? What was her name?"

"Mrs. Nina Cassandra Pierce." Joe shook his head. "She wanted Grayson to stick me in an orphanage. I remember one time overhearing a phone conversation she had with somebody who ran one for Jewish kids in New York. She was already making the arrangements. She hated me."

"Why?"

"Because I was a Jew. She was a closet anti-Semite." Joe exhaled smoke. "She was as cold and mean as a witch's kiss."

Robert blinked.

"But Grayson stayed the course. He wasn't about to give in and get rid of me. He reared me as if I were his son."

"So, you two are close."

Joe looked away. "As close as a father and son could be. I wouldn't be here if it weren't for him." A pained expression crossed his face. "I love him. He has been everything to me since I was seven years old."

They both fell into silence. After looking at his watch, Robert stood.

Joe also got up. "You want to get something to eat? It's dinnertime. Then maybe we could swing around my apartment to pick up some of my old clarinet music, and we'll go to the music annex building and play through them. You can accompany me. You said you play the piano, right?"

Robert hesitated.

"Oh, c'mon. You need a break from that awful dorm food."

"Yeah. That food's pretty bad."

"Institutional grub. Gives you heartburn every time." Joe tapped his fist to his chest.

"Well, okay, as long as I pay for my meal. I won't be a leech like Mr. Oneida."

Joe threw back his head and laughed.

In the practice room, Robert flipped through the piano accompaniment to Mozart's *Clarinet Concerto,* K 622. Joe had chosen this solo as he had studied it in junior high school and had performed the second movement at a music contest. He had played it by memory and had received a perfect score.

"This looks pretty straight forward," said Robert. He put the music on the piano rack.

"Well, it's not like the Debussy. Remember when we were in a practice room back in October, and you helped me with a rhythm problem on the third page of *Premiere Rhapsodie?*"

"Yes."

Joe closed his clarinet case. His face reddened.

"What? Why are you looking like that?"

Joe burst out laughing. "I've got to tell you something, Robert. I played a joke on you."

"Huh?"

"I already knew how to play that section. I studied that piece when I was taking lessons in high school. I was just messing with you."

"What? Why did you do that?" Indignant anger made Robert raise his voice.

Joe continued to laugh. "C'mon. It was a ploy to get you to loosen up. You were so uptight I thought if I gave you a chance to show what you know about music, you'd relax and have some confidence in yourself. You did teach me well. You know your stuff about music."

Robert balled his hands into fists. "But you deceived me! You . . . you . ."

Joe couldn't control his giggling. He put his hand over his mouth.

"You think you're all high and mighty with your genius IQ. You can just boast about how much you know about music and everything else! Well, some of us down here on planet earth have to work at what we do. I'm one of the normal people who don't know everything! I bet your sister would agree with me, and I don't even know her!"

The mention of Irene brought Joe out of his mirth. He turned his attention to putting the reed on his clarinet mouthpiece. "You're right, Robert. I'm sorry. I shouldn't have tricked you. You have every right to be mad at me." He stood and put his music on the stand. "You are a gifted musician. I've heard you enough at your concerts to know you carry the horn section. I could tell that even if Frank had never said anything about you." He paused. "I bet you've been called a perfectionist. Right?"

Robert said, "I suppose. I just want to do what's right. I'm not afraid to work hard." He turned slowly back to his music. Under his breath, he muttered, "I earned those scholarships."

"Huh? You're on scholarships? That's fantastic." Joe regarded the young man at the piano. "There's nothing wrong with being a perfectionist, Robert. I know you work your tail off. I bet you'll whip through the Mozart without blinking an eye. Can you play an 'F'?"

After tuning to the piano, Robert began the long introduction. Although trying to count the rests, Joe was distracted by Robert's intuitive musical and technical skills. This young musician nailed Mozart's delicate style, even if he was sight-reading the music. Joe, feeling strangely intimidated, doubled his concentration as he begun the solo part, determined not to embarrass himself by tripping over the arpeggio and scale passages. Fortunately, his fingers had enough "muscle memory" to negotiate the numerous sixteenth notes in the brightly paced first movement. They kept a solid tempo, or rather, Robert's accompaniment forced Joe to keep a steady beat. To his pleasant surprise, they made it to the end of the twelve-minute Allegro without stopping.

"Whew! That was fantastic, Robert!" Joe took out his handkerchief to wipe the sweat from his forehead. "You are a great pianist!"

Robert was already turning the page to the second movement.

"Thanks. You're darn good on the clarinet, Mr. Kaufmann. Mr. Oneida was right about how well you play. You're better than the seniors in the band."

Joe grinned. "Besides being burdened with a genius IQ, I've had to deal with my musical talent. My Aunt Mil, my guardian's older sister, wanted me to major in music in college. She wanted me to go to Julliard. And she would have paid every dime for it, too. I may have told you I started piano lessons with her when I was eight. After two years, I took from a teacher at Ithaca College through high school. But the clarinet has always been my first love. Aunt Mil bought me this Buffet clarinet when I was a freshman in high school."

"I bet you're good on the piano, too."

"No. Not as good as you. I stopped playing when I was at Cornell."

"I'd like to hear you play."

"Well, I would need to practice for at least a month. I'm pretty rusty." Joe chuckled. "My Aunt Mil was one scary dame. She pushed me in music like an Egyptian slave driver. I remember when I first came into the Pierce mansion. I was seven. She set me down in front of the radio every Sunday evening to listen to the New York Philharmonic. Those were wonderful times. She wanted me to live up to the quote-unquote 'God-given talent' I had not only in music but also in everything else. When I was little, I called her Frau tot Fishaugen. Ha!"

"Mrs. Dead Fish Eyes?" Robert grinned.

"Yeah! How did you know that?"

"I grew up in a German house. My parents are German. I know German as well as English."

"Oh, I forgot you told me that before."

"Why did you call your aunt Mrs. Dead Fish Eyes?"

Joe smirked. "Because her eyes were hard and black like a fish's eyes. There was no, absolutely no emotion in them, no expression. It was creepy, especially to a little kid like me trying to cope in that big mansion."

"Mansion? What mansion?"

"That's where I grew up. The Pierce family is loaded."

"Oh? How so?"

"That family had more money than what you and I will ever see in ten lifetimes. They still do. Besides, Grayson, having money because he's a doctor, his mother, Nina Cassandra, had money, although I've never found out how much. She passed away a couple of years ago. It's my Aunt Mil who has the serious cash. You see, she's a widow. Back in the 1920s, her husband owned a big office supply company in New York that had been in the family since before the Civil War. He was killed in an auto accident, and his estate, including the company, went to Mildred. There may have been some life insurance money, too. She got some good advice from a financial advisor, and she sold it right before the stock market crash in '29. She made a killing."

"How much?"

"I don't know exactly, but it was in the seven figures. It's all tied up in investments."

"Oh."

Joe said, "Okay. Enough chitchat. Ready for the second movement?"

Starting quietly, Mozart's Adagio opened like a fragile, pure white orchid, small and elegant. Both the clarinet and piano expressed the unfeigned simplicity that was Mozart's signature. The melodic line's gentle strength climbed with restrained dynamics until it finished at its satiated conclusions at the cadence points.

Beyond inborn talent and well-trained skill, Joe and Robert demonstrated an inner connection to music that was so personal, so deeply felt that to speak of it would destroy it. There was a connection between them that neither of them had felt before. It was as if they shared the same blood, the same genes that let them communicate through sound and emotion. Joe realized this as they finished the last peaceful chords of the slow movement.

As if they were performing in a recital, Joe nodded and took off on the pick-up notes of the third movement. This music was typical playful Mozart in a brisk, light, six-eight meter. Measure after measure of sixteenth notes kept him scrambling to keep looking ahead. His heart pumped, and his glasses began to slide down his perspiring nose as he played. But he was determined to stay the course in this lengthy movement. It seemed an eternity of pulsating, non-stop energy. And Robert's dogged tempo gave no ground.

At last, just when Joe felt he was losing the grip of his mouth on the reed, the end was in sight. He was on the bottom third of the last page. After finishing the last repeat of the opening theme, Robert continued the piano reduction of the orchestral accompaniment with driving vitality. He completed the movement with three vigorous, proud chords.

Both of them applauded each other. "Bravo!" Joe exclaimed, catching his breath. "Well done, maestro!"

Robert beamed. "That was fun!" He laughed wholeheartedly.

"I think we're ready for Carnegie Hall. Do you know any agents who can get us a date? Ha!"

Robert laughed harder. Then he settled a bit and said, "I'm serious. If you give me some more accompaniment parts, I'll work on them, and we can do this again."

"It's a deal, Robert."

"And if you want, I'll give you some horn pieces, and you can accompany me."

Joe gave a thought to this offer. "Yeah, I'd be willing to give it a try. Only let's stick to eighteenth- and nineteenth-century composers. Any twentieth-century music is going to have too many accidentals and weird rhythms. I don't want to crash and burn after every two measures. We'd never get through the music."

"Yeah, but I can 'help' you with the rhythm." Robert made quotation signs saying the word "help."

They both burst into even harder laughter. Joe took back the Mozart and searched his briefcase for another solo. He found Brahms's *Clarinet Sonata*, opus 120. "Here. Chew on this." He handed the piano accompaniment to Robert.

The other young man looked through the pages quickly. "No problem. I can handle this."

Joe rolled his eyes. After licking his reed and adjusting the music stand, they began.

****

Sadness cast a shadow over Joe's face. "We had some good times last year. It's hard to accept how everything went so downhill after that. I wish I could go back in time and start all over."

"But, but, Joe. Look what has come out of this. You have a brother! You have a family all your own."

"You and Grayson are my family. Even those old women were my family. Even Ruth's my family."

"Yes, but not like having a blood relation. Doesn't that mean anything to you?"

Joe seemed to ignore Irene's question. "Maybe he'll get some help from that minister. He'll survive."

"Huh? What are you saying?" Irene asked with alarm.

"He's got his mom."

Irene glared at him. "His mom? You just said she'd go back to Germany once her husband gets deported. Where does that leave Robert? Joe—"

"I want to go home back to Ithaca. I don't want to be here in Indiana anymore."

Irene slapped his shoulder. "And abandon Robert? How could you even think like that?"

"Too many bad memories. Oh, here come Grayson and Ruth."

Behind his guardian and stepmother, Reverend Thomason walked with Ada Stangarden, holding her arm. Robert brought up the rear with his head down, following his mother and the minister to another car. Joe studied him, lighting the last cigarette in his pack.

Ruth entered the rental car on the front passenger side. Grim-faced, Grayson slammed his driver's side door and started the engine.

"So, what happened, Daddy?" Irene asked, her hands gripping the top of the front car seat.

As he pulled out of the parking lot, her father replied, "There was some talk about what Robert should do now that he knows who his parents were—changing his name, how that might affect the Stangardens' will, if they have one. The lawyer is going to take care of that. But mainly, we just sat and let him take in all these revelations." He eyed his ward in his rearview mirror. "I'm a bit surprised you left, Joe."

Irene asked, "So is he going to change his name?"

"We don't know. Robert said he has to think about it. Of course, his mother, um, Ada, is ambivalent about it. She's a bit upset right now." The car stopped at a red light. "Honey, which way do we turn? Do we want to have lunch somewhere?"

Before his daughter could answer, Joe said, "Turn east, Grayson. I want to go home."

Both Ruth and Grayson twisted their heads to look at him. Then Grayson drove through the intersection.

Ruth said, "Are you talking about going back to Bloomington?"

"No, I mean, Ithaca."

"Surely, you're not going to leave Robert all by himself."

"Yes."

"Son, you need to think about this." Grayson turned south at another stoplight toward downtown.

"My lease is month-to-month, so I'll tell my landlady I'm moving out at the end of next month. That'll give me time to pack and move my stuff. I'll close the apartment and get the utilities shut off. I'll sell my furniture or give it away. Maybe, if Frank Oneida's still around, he'll take it. He takes everything else from me."

When nobody spoke, he went on. "I'll call my advisor to tell him I'll finish my dissertation in Ithaca and come back to defend it next year."

Irene said, "You are making a big mistake, Joe. I can't believe this is what you want to do. You're making this decision on impulse."

"Yeah, well, it's my impulse," he retorted.

"You're acting like everything is going back to the way it was before any of this happened. Like it's no big deal."

Grayson pulled into the hotel parking lot and shut off the engine. He and Ruth sat and listened.

Irene said, "But it's not the same as it was before. I'll say it again. You have a brother, and he needs you. But your attitude is like, well, I've gotten over that hump. I made it through this crisis without killing myself. It's time to move on. Stay in the present. Think about the future. Nose back to the grindstone. Just like what Aunt Mil would say. Forget the past. It's over, and there's nothing you can do about it."

"Irene, enough!" Joe threw out his cigarette.

Irene shook her head. "This is different, Joe. I don't understand how you can be so, so insensitive and downright cruel. Don't you think your parents would want—?"

"Irene, I think we should stop this discussion for now," said Grayson. "Joe needs some breathing room. Why don't we have lunch and think about what to do next in the hotel room?"

Irene moved away from her brother. The Pierce family exited the rental car.

CHAPTER THIRTY-FIVE

Grayson placed four gentle knocks on Joe's bedroom door. Hearing nothing, he opened it and stepped into the silent room. Bright sunlight framed the ivory-colored shades pulled down over the twin windows. The darkened stillness seized his heart—a reminder of past nightmares, worriment, and missed opportunities that had nearly cost the life of his precious boy.

He turned on a dim lamp on Joe's old dresser. The antique quilt that had originally belonged to Grayson's mother covered Joe completely as he lay on his back with half-closed eyes. He had arranged the quilt about his head and tucked under his chin, making it a shroud. His grey-white pallor suggested death.

Grayson gingerly sat on the edge and pulled down the cover.

Without opening his eyes wider, Joe tried to pull the quilt up. But Grayson wouldn't let go.

"Joe . . ."

"Go away."

Grayson looked around the dismal room, trying to think.

"Just leave. Please . . . Grayson."

"Joe, I've been patient with you. I've let you indulge in your melancholy for two weeks now. It's the depression again." Grayson sighed and scratched the back of his neck. "We need . . . . Dammit, I want to talk about this. The least you can do is give your old man the time of day." He didn't like the irritation in his voice, but recklessly he didn't care. "C'mon. Get up."

No response.

"So help me, I'll pick you up out of this bed and set you on the floor. I'm still bigger than you are, you know." He looked over the world at six foot five. Joe was a measly five foot nine.

After a moment, Joe slowly pushed aside the cover and sat up in his tank top undershirt and boxer shorts. He rubbed his days-old beard and tussled his unruly hair. After putting on his glasses, he looked into the shadows cast by the lamp.

Joe's guardian set his feet apart and put his fists on his hips, ready to channel his older sister, Mildred, who would have scolded Joe for giving into his doldrums and not picking himself up by his bootstraps, or in this case, his brand-new tennis shoes under his bed. However, he hesitated. That approach would not work. He sat back on the bed next to his ward.

"Talk to me, Joe."

Joe moved his hands about helplessly. "I have this-this overwhelming sadness. It's like I'm suffocating in it. I'm drowning in quicksand, and I'm too tired even to try to fight my way out." He sniffed and rubbed his nose. "I feel like it's time to give up. I can't even cry. I can't think." His voice cracked. "I'm just numb." His shoulders slumped. "I don't know why I'm still on this earth. I should be dead. I shouldn't exist anymore. I can't keep trying and trying to stay in the moment. It's . . . I don't want to live anymore. It just takes . . . too . . . much . . . work."

He inhaled quickly. "But I've said that before." He looked intensely at Grayson. "You know what I mean." He folded his arms. "This is déjà vu all over again."

Grayson put his arm around Joe's shoulders and hugged him. "Yes, it is. It's okay to feel like you want to give up." Impulsively, he kissed the side of Joe's head and smoothed his thick hair. "We've been down this road before. And looking back at this past year and a half, it's understandable how you've come to this point. I think all the stress and fear and being forced to relive your experiences at Buchenwald has caught up with you. It's no wonder you're exhausted. I can't begin to understand what you've gone through.

"When we were in that hotel room in Indianapolis, I was honestly shocked to hear you describe what had happened to you and your family, crammed in a boxcar, going to Auschwitz and then to Buchenwald—talking about how people died on the train and pushed out like trash. Being put in those shacks with nothing but boards to sleep on, no toilets except another board set up with buckets underneath.

"Joe, do you remember when I came into the barrack, and you were hiding in that dirt hole behind the broken board? When I met your eyes, it melted my heart to see your fear, your acceptance that you were finally going to die, just like everyone else. I will never forget that moment."

The big man trembled at the memory.

"You told us how you got into that hole your father had dug for you to hide in. How that woman fed you and your father, keeping you both alive all those months." Letting go of Joe, he shook his head in disbelief. "How can you rectify the brutality you and your father endured in the camp when at the same time, one of those Nazis monsters stole your mother, taking her as his bride and, in a twisted way, sparing her life? I don't know how you can come to terms with that.

"The courage it took for you to share with us what had happened to you and your family is beyond me. But through it all, you've kept yourself together. You faced down that Stangarden character in that courtroom. I am so very proud of you, Joe."

The two of them said nothing for a moment.

"Joe, I know why you're reluctant to go back to Indianapolis and see Robert again. You can't look at him without thinking about your mother and your father. It hurts too much."

He rubbed Joe's shoulder.

"Joe, you're grieving. You're mourning the loss of your mother. You know, we never really talked about her when you were growing up. It wasn't until this situation with Robert that you had to confront your memories of her."

Joe waited.

"It had to be a shock to see that picture of her."

Joe drew up his legs and put his head on his knees.

"And then to see her in that church picture."

He could not hold back his sobs.

Grayson took him into his broad chest, rocking him as he wept. The big man stroked his face, holding him as the swell of grief seized his ward's body. He would not tell Joe that he didn't need to cry. He would not say to him that everything was going to be all right. He would not ask him to get over his despair. He knew it was Joe's time to embrace his sorrows.

CHAPTER THIRTY-SIX

The second Saturday in May was pleasurably mild under motionless white clouds. In the Pierce home's backyard, Ruth had tried her hand at putting in a vegetable garden. Her biggest challenge had been keeping a family of rabbits from chewing the leaves of her struggling tomato plants. Joe had mowed the lawn three days ago, but the subsequent rain had made the grass more determined than ever to keep growing at a record pace.

Joe sat at the picnic table with Grayson and Ruth on the back porch, staring through his prescription sunglasses at the Kentucky Fried Chicken and mashed potatoes on his plate. He flicked cigarette ash into a plastic ashtray.

"Joe, put out that cigarette and eat some of that KFC. The colonel would be insulted." Grayson licked his fingers and wiped them on a napkin.

"Do you want some more tea, Joe?" asked Ruth. She reached for the green plastic pitcher. She looked refreshing and smart in her sleeveless tangerine blouse and white pedal-pushers. With her honey-blonde hair held back with barrettes, her face was tan from working in her garden.

"I'll have some," said Grayson. "Where's the sugar?"

As the two of them poured tea, Joe stared out at the black walnut trees that lined the wooden privacy fence, shading the yard. He knew Ruth's garden wouldn't thrive. Having had tended the Pierce gardens at the old mansion years ago under Grayson's mother's severe tutelage,

Nina Cassandra, he knew vegetable gardens needed full sun. Maybe he should tell Ruth, but that would spoil her enthusiasm for her efforts.

He pushed away his paper plate. "I'm not hungry."

Ruth said, "I'll wrap it up and put it in the fridge. You can eat it for supper." She rose to go back into the kitchen.

"So, when are you going to start working on your dissertation, Joe? You've still got a deadline to meet." Grayson noisily rattled a spoon in his tumbler to stir the sugar.

Joe eyed him. "A deadline that's three years away."

"Well, no time to dawdle. Maybe getting back on it will take your mind off yourself."

"I know what you're trying to say, Grayson. You want me to get off my ass and do something useful."

"Well, okay. Maybe you should call your advisor. Let him know where you are and what you're doing."

The backdoor slammed, and Ruth came back carrying Saran Wrap and plastic storage boxes. Grayson watched as she began collecting the leftovers.

"If you want, you can set up in my office with your typewriter," Grayson offered.

"No, thanks." Joe frowned. "I'm just not in the mood yet. I've got to get my head on straight first."

Ruth remarked, "Well, it's a step in the right direction that you've decided to take a shower every day and make your bed."

Joe glared at his stepmother.

She added, "The next project is to shave at least once a day, comb that mop of hair on your head, and eat the nutritious meals I so lovingly bring home from the fast-food restaurants."

Grayson smiled at his wife.

"I suppose mowing the grass doesn't count," said Joe.

Grayson said, "While you're on the phone with your advisor, why don't you call your landlady and tell her you're coming back to Bloomington?"

Joe turned his head quickly. "What?"

Grayson piled the paper plates full of chicken bones and gathered the plastic spoons and forks. "You heard me."

"Are you kicking me out?"

Grayson shrugged. "I noticed you never got around to telling her you were moving out, and you're still paying rent. So, it stands to reason that you'll eventually go back. Time marches on. Your books are getting lonely."

"But I thought I'd stay here to finish my dissertation. Last summer, we had talked about going to New York and D. C. so I can do my research. We were going to make a vacation out of the trips." He watched Grayson follow Ruth back into the house. He picked up the salt and pepper shakers and the iced tea pitcher and went after them.

"Do you want me to help you put all this away?" Grayson asked Ruth, gesturing to the kitchen table laden with filled Tupperware storage containers.

"No, I can finish." She went to the sink to rinse the glasses before putting them in the dishwasher.

After replacing his sunglasses with his regular pair, Joe followed Grayson into the living room. Grayson said, "Since it's such a nice day today, I think I'll call Stan and Morey to see if they're up for a golf game this afternoon." He sat in a padded, upholstered chair next to the end table and picked up the phone. Stan Madison and Morey Allen were colleagues in the surgery department at the Thompkins County Hospital. Grayson had been friends with them for more than thirty years.

Ruth spoke from the kitchen, "Stan's on call today, Grayson. I talked to his wife this morning."

"Oh, that's right. I'll try Ted Abernathy. Since he's retired, he should be looking for something to do. Joe, do you remember your old pediatrician? You want to go with us? I think he'd be glad to see you."

As Grayson lifted the receiver, Joe stopped him. "Wait a minute. We haven't settled this. Besides, you know I don't play golf. I hate golf. That's just a waste of time knocking a little ball around in the grass."

Grayson replaced the receiver. "All right. Let's finish this." He took his pipe out of a drawer of the end table, stuffed it, and lit it.

Joe paced the room.

"Aren't you getting bored, Joe?"

Joe didn't answer.

Ruth came in. She sat on the couch and folded the newspaper to do the crossword puzzle. Little Blueberry decided that it was her cue to jump in her lap and lie on top of the paper.

Grayson pulled out the latest New England Journal of Medicine from a magazine rack and pretended to read the table of contents. Ruth pushed Blueberry as far she could to start filling in the blanks.

"You started this," Joe declared. "You brought it up."

Sweet, blue smoke lifted to the high ceiling. "Yes, I know."

Joe plopped in a chair near the empty fireplace. "You want me to go back to Bloomington. You're getting tired of me hanging around here moping and feeling sorry for myself."

Grayson put the journal on the coffee table and waved his pipe at him. "I never said that. You are welcome to stay here as long as you like. This is your home. Hell, eventually, you'll get the deed to this house."

Ruth gave him a hard look.

"Well, that's something Ruth and I will have to discuss later. But that's not my point. There's another matter waiting for you besides your dissertation."

Joe looked at Grayson. He felt his jaws tightening.

"There's a young man down there who could use a visit from you, Joe."

Joe turned his head away and studied the slate fireplace floor.

"He's probably wondering if he'll ever see you again. I'm sure he's been thinking about all this business for the past couple of months."

"He's fine. He'll manage,"

Ruth said, "You don't know that, Joe. We don't know what emotional state he's in. And with his mother being as unstable as she is, he may need help dealing with her. What are they doing for money? Did he have to get a job? And if he did, does that mean he won't be able to go back to school?"

"All right. You've made your point, Ruth," Joe snapped a little too forcefully. "I'm sorry. I didn't mean for it to come out like that."

Ruth put down her newspaper and took out some cross-stitching from a wicker basket, another new hobby. So far, not so good. "I feel sorry for him. I don't like that you've abandoned him." She pushed Blueberry to the floor, who was trying to eat the embroidery thread.

"Ruth, now remember what we talked about," Grayson said. "Joe has had a rough time, and we can't push him."

"Well, you're pushing me now!" Joe snapped. He turned to his stepmother. "Ruth, you don't know what I've—"

"I do so know. Your guardian has told me everything. I'm not just an innocent bystander, waiting in the wings with a plate of cookies. I'm part of this family, too." She gave a warning look at her husband, who chose to concentrate on relighting his pipe. She gave up on her needlework and stuffed the Aida cloth into a plastic bag. She closed it and threw it toward the basket and missed it. "That trial was a strain on all of us. Horrible, horrible things brought up that none of us wanted to hear. Our lives will never be the same. It's even affected me in my job. I have trouble concentrating on my patients because I'm thinking about you, Joe. I'm so worried about you! And I feel so helpless. I can't do or say anything to make things right."

Grayson moved to the sofa next to her and squeezed her hand. He put his pipe in the marble ashtray.

Joe said sharply to Ruth, "You want me to go back to Bloomington so you won't have to deal with me. Isn't that it? Here I am, sulking around, dirtying the bathroom, and sleeping all day when you want me to get up, so you can change the sheets. You have to do an extra load of laundry because of me. I'm just lying around all day, not doing anything except mowing the grass."

"Joe, that's enough!" said Grayson.

Ruth stood and faced her stepson. "Joe, you've missed what I'm trying to say. I don't care about the lawn or the laundry or the bedsheets. I'm talking about you going back to Bloomington to see Robert. He's your brother. He needs you."

Joe waved his hand in dismissal.

"Joe, I'm serious. Look at me. If need be, I will get in my car and drive to Indiana, pick him up, and bring him here." Ruth's face hardened, her neat, slanted eyebrows knitted in determination. "Irene made a good point in the car after that meeting with the lawyer. Your mother and father would want you to take care of Robert. You owe that to them. He's you're only real family."

Joe covered his ears with his fists.

"Yes, this has been hard to deal with, almost impossible. Grayson's right. You need to get back to work on your dissertation. I don't care if you want to do here or back at I. U. If you stay here, I'll pick up after you as long as I have to. But at the same time, you can't just ignore Robert because he makes you feel uncomfortable. Maybe you're still not ready to believe that he is your brother."

"And maybe he doesn't believe *I* am his brother," Joe retorted.

"Well, go down to Bloomington or Indianapolis or wherever he lives and sort it out with him. Be friends with him. Build on what you have in common. You both love music. Let that be the connection between the two of you."

Joe moved away from Ruth and stared at the grey-painted bricks in the fireplace.

Ruth returned to the sofa, giving a loud sigh. She and Grayson watched him. The living room was quiet except for the slow, muffled ticking of the antique Grandfather clock that stood next to the dining room doorway. It was a softly ticking witness to an aggravated Pierce household.

Joe finally said, "Give me some time to think." He got up and exited the house through the front door, not bothering to close it. Hands in pockets, he hurried down the sidewalk heading east. He kept his eyes down, ignoring the stately, Victorian-styled houses. A cool breeze gusted, blowing his hair out of place.

He stopped at an intersection and watched two cars meet and then pass through. He walked on quickly but stopped again to catch his breath. His poor appetite over the last several weeks had weakened him. The constant smoking didn't help either. His clothes hung on his body. He hadn't weighed himself lately, but he knew he had lost weight.

It was happening all over again. Just as what had happened in the Havensbrook Psychiatric Hospital when he was fourteen, he was starving himself again—an indisputable symptom of depression.

Even while standing on a sidewalk on a warm, June afternoon in the bright sunlight, Joe's spirit crashed. The black hole of nothingness permeated his being. He knew there was only way out of this.

CHAPTER THIRTY-SEVEN

As familiar as an old high school yearbook was Taughannock Falls State Park. Joe and Grayson had hiked in this 750-acre park for years. It was one of the first parks they had visited when Joe was seven back when they had taken a two-week excursion around New York State. Joe remembered the trip with ambivalence. The immediate purpose was to get out of the Pierce mansion and away from the terrifying grandmother and bellicose aunt. They had done their best to bully and subdue a frightened, helpless little boy fresh out of a Nazi concentration camp. But that was in the past.

Joe staggered down the narrow Gorge Trail on an exceedingly steep hill. He took his time, his boots shuffling through the dead leaves and loose rocks and sometimes grabbing hold of a stray sapling branch to keep from losing his balance and sliding down the path on his butt and elbows. He could hear the roar of Taughannock Falls as he edged closer. When he reached the natural rock cataract, fenced off to prevent curious tourists from taking a closer look into the deep, green pond, he took off his backpack and sat on the flat shale rock. Lighting a cigarette, he stared at the water, mesmerized at the spectacular display, the tallest single-drop waterfall in the entire eastern half of the country. He had always been captivated by the unceasing free-fall of foamy water pouring violently into the pool, sending up clouds of spray and mist. Joe remembered to sit back far enough so he wouldn't have to keep wiping his glasses.

He tried to focus on the thunderous water instead of hearing the discord in his brain, hoping that the distraction of doing this hike would dispel the voices in his head—the shouting, the cajoling, the arguing, the arm-twisting, the constant demands. Putting the screws to him, pushing him to do what they wanted him to do, insisting that he be productive, expecting him to do something, say something, write something, be something!

Joe quickly got up, stomped out his light, and hitched his backpack. He took off his Cornell baseball cap to wipe sweat from his forehead. Readjusting it on his head, he turned around and, in a rush of energy, mounted the hill. But the sticky heat overcame him, and he began to slow down as the trail became steeper. At the top of the hill, he bent over with his hands on his knees to catch his breath. Straightening, he saw the distant cerulean Cayuga Lake rimmed with trees and sand and boat docks. Tiny sailboats sat motionless on the water as if part of a picture postcard. Joe moved on but kept his eyes down to watch for tree roots.

He went off the trail (a no-no in the park rules) and bushwacked his way deeper into the forest. He pushed through the low-hanging tree branches into the gloomy, dense woods, crushing vines and ground cover along the way. His walking stick swept a path through the masses of spider webs, freeing hapless tiny insects that flew right into his face. After tramping for twenty minutes, he found a heavily decomposed birch log. He dropped his walking stick and sat on the wet leaves beside it. He took a long drink from his thermos and then closed his eyes.

Surrendering once more to descend into that black hole, he took off his glasses. First, the tears slid down his face, and then the sobs lurched from the pit of his stomach. It was no use. Disconsolation clung to him like the broken spider webs on his face. No matter how hard he wiped it away, the despair always returned. His mind was so immobilized that he couldn't even put a name to what he was feeling. There was no connection of his misery to everything that had happened in his life. None of it mattered anymore. Sheer hopelessness was his only emotion. And it felt as ethereal as the clammy fog created by Taughannock Falls. He couldn't hold it in his hands or see it in his mind's eye, but it squeezed his heart like a vise.

Was this Purgatory? Was he suspended in a state of eternal despair, knowing that he would never get out?

Je's rear end was getting damp from the wet ground. He stared out at the greenery, drinking in the stillness, the loamy, putrefying smell, the cool shade. He could stay here forever with the rocks and the mushrooms and the bugs and the rotting log he leaned against. Yet, he drew no comfort from this verdant place. He felt no spiritual uplifting as he had on countless hikes before. There was no joy, no pleasure, no happiness, no exuberance about being alive.

Joe wiped his hands on the handkerchief he took from his jeans pocket. He unfastened a flap in his backpack and took out a long leather pouch he had bought at a hardware store on his way to the park. He withdrew the hunting knife and laid aside the sheath. He studied the knife with its shiny, 10-inch, clip-point blade, so virginal and ready for the first fast-moving ribbon of blood. It had a sturdy brass pommel and a finger-grip oak handle. The knife was heavy enough to do the job with a mere jerk of the wrist.

Joe looked around. He was a good three miles from Taughannock Falls, and he estimated at least two miles from the trail. He had met no other hikers. So, he figured he could do the deed and not be disturbed as he bled out, ensuring his demise. He had left no note on the kitchen table, saying where he was going for the day. He had parked his Ford Falcon behind an abandoned gas station a half-mile from the state park entrance. No one had seen him on this late-July Tuesday morning save a slow-moving pick-up truck on the highway. It could be hours before anyone would even notice he was gone.

This knife was far more serious than that palm-sized piece of mirror shard. That attempt in his apartment had been just a practice run. He really hadn't known what he was doing at the time. He needed a clear head to do this. He had to follow through on the decision that he couldn't change at the last moment.

Joe ran a light finger carefully along the edge of the blade. He could almost feel love for this knife. It would take away the sadness, the black hole, the desolation, the terror, the nightmares. There would be no more fighting, no more aggravation, no more hassles, no more struggle to get out of bed and put his clothes on. And, most importantly, no more Buchenwald. This gleaming blade was the gate through which he would walk to release himself from Purgatory.

Joe's chin trembled. He didn't want to think. He put the knife in his lap and stared at it. What about all the people in his life he would leave behind? No! They didn't matter. He had to live his life for himself. It was his pain, not theirs. He had endured his suffering for twenty-seven years. Enough was enough. He had to free himself of the steely chains of living that had bound him so tightly like a camp prisoner trussed and ready for the noose. The sweet nihility of death would be a welcome respite!

Joe crossed his arms. With tears streaming, he rocked back and forth. He broke into loud wails. The trees surrounding him blurred. They stood straight, motionless and voiceless. They were deaf to his weeping. They would not give him the courage he needed. Nor would they stop him. They would witness the execution without judgment.

Thoughts about his family emerged despite his effort to keep them out. Anger made his tears stop. *They* were the ones who had driven him to this. Under the sincere and well-intentioned display of concern and sympathy, they had been all too eager to tell him to get past his self-pity. Cynically, he thought their heavy-handed pressure on him was their attempt to alleviate their own anxieties. Upon hearing about piles of naked corpses and bugs in a watery stew and shaved heads that had bled from careless razors, they had mentally turned away their faces. Hands held up to ward off the images. They had wanted to move on, to get back to the business of careers and late-night TV talk shows.

Joe picked up a rock and threw it, hitting a tree trunk. It had been a waste of his time trying to make them understand what he had gone through when he was just six years old in a Nazi concentration camp. Ever since Irene had found him on the kitchen floor in an overdosed stupor, his family had politely listened to his sad Buchenwald stories and then promptly told him to get over it and get a relationship started with his new "brother."

Irene and Ruth had been pushy enough, but it was Grayson who had bossed him the most, bullying him at times. This gargantuan Chief of Surgery at the Thompkins County Hospital was a water-soaked, smelly old wool blanket. The big man wouldn't leave him alone. All the bear hugs and the embarrassing kisses and shaking fingers in his face had made even breathing impossible. And up until now, all Joe could do was to tolerate it. Yet, all the spectacle of wringing hands and phone calls and threats of psychotherapy wouldn't keep him alive. Despite the near misses of bedroom windows and self-imposed starvation and overdoses of sleeping pills and mirror shards, here he sat alone in a remote part of the Taughannock Falls State Park with a hunting knife in his lap.

He had told Grayson over and over to back off. But the old man never listened.

But Joe had to stop. The guilt. This well-intentioned, over-bearing, religiously-faithful do-gooder had saved his life! Grayson had taken him out from under those urine-stained boards in a stinking, decrepit wooden barrack and had put him in that stuffy, moss-covered old Pierce mansion filled with stuffy, moss-covered old women. He said he had always wanted a son, and Joe had filled the bill. Grayson had showered him with everything from toy racing cars to spending money when he had been at Cornell. Joe had never wanted for anything. He could have turned out just as spoiled as Irene. Yes, Joe had to be grateful to his guardian.

But here he sat with the knife. He remembered Grayson telling him that depression kills by suicide. There was no medication, no surgery, no life-saving treatment save a locked psychiatric hospital ward and the suspicious, watchful eye of an orderly.

Holding the knife in his left hand, he brought the flat side of it to the indentation under his right ear and jaw. He pressed in gently, feeling the sharp edge. He thought that was where the jugular vein was. The cut had to be deep enough to cause significant blood loss, meaning he'd have to push the knife in deeply, and then forward and across his throat. And he'd have to do it in an instant before he lost his nerve.

The image of Robert's sliced neck sprang into his mind's eye. He had not seen the laceration in the police photos, only the considerable dressing on the kid's throat. There had been twenty-two black, hideous stitches underneath. What pain he must have endured. The utter shock of feeling his skin open, warm liquid dribbling out. Did that monster draw the knife swiftly, or did he do it slowly to increase his "son's" torture? How much blood flowed? How fast did it slide down his chest? Was his whole shirt soaked? Was there a lot of it on the floor?

A shudder made him drop the knife in the dirt. His imagination was getting the best of him. He put his clasped hands up to his forehead and repeatedly hit it. Moans came up from his own throat. How could he do this? How painful would this be? Could he execute the stroke without stopping? Could he keep his mind blank? How long would he stay alive as his wound bled? Would he lose consciousness first? What would happen if the knife slipped out of his hand? Would he be brave enough to pick it up and try again?

And most frightening of all was that there was no one to stop him; no one to save him from himself.

Joe didn't realize he was holding his breath. His entire body was as hard as a marble statue. He blinked once, and then he exhaled. His body loosened like a deflating balloon. He was too tired to think anymore. There was no energy left to proceed with his plan. He took off his glasses and carefully laid them on top of the log. Using his backpack as a pillow, he laid down on his side and bent his knees up to his chest. He closed his eyes and mercifully fell asleep.

He woke up still curled in a fetal position. Despite the shade under the abundant tree canopy, it was warmer than it had been hours earlier. Joe heard a bird screech. He brought his wristwatch up to his very near-sighted eyes: 3:30. He struggled with stiff arms and legs to sit up. Fortunately, his glasses were still on top of the log. After putting them on, he took another gulp from his water thermos. It was almost empty. He scratched a fresh bug bite on his elbow.

Still feeling a little disoriented, he looked around. He saw the hunting knife just where he had dropped it. With his arms trembling, he sat on one hip, his hands pressing into the damp ground. He tried to remember his thoughts before he had fallen asleep. It was about the knife—his reason for coming out here to the park to begin with. The deed was yet to be done.

Robert Stangarden came into his mind. Joe had loudly protested that this naïve, fresh-faced music student from I. U. was not his sibling. Their similar physical appearance was just a coincidence, despite people commenting that they looked related. Frank Oneida's boisterous, self-assured declaration that they were didn't make it so.

He mulled over the revelation Ada Stangarden had announced in that meeting room at Ed Moscowitz's office. He did not dispute that Joe's mother, Ina Kaufmann, was his biological mother. But what about her statement that Robert's biological father was Joe's father? Could he accept that? Could Robert accept it?

As he gazed at the thick-trunked oak and ash trees surrounding him, Joe fantasized about their relationship. He imagined himself as the older brother. He could help Robert, giving him advice about school and about getting along with his professors. Maybe they could go hiking. There were plenty of state parks and state forests in southern

Indiana. Perhaps Robert could come to Ithaca. If he did, he'd be inundated with attention. And he could show off his musical talent to the family and relatives. Cringing, Joe thought how his elderly Aunt Mil would be ecstatic (in her own stiff-upper-lip way) hearing Robert play the piano.

The one thing Joe had in common with Robert was music. More than anything else, that could be the bridge between them. Ruth had told him that. When they had been together before that fateful Friday afternoon in May 1964, everything they did revolved around music—playing together in a practice room, attending Robert's band concerts, doing that silly "drop the needle" game in the music library. They could be not only brothers but also good friends.

If Joe used the knife on himself, Robert Stangarden would be devastated for having lost his only possible blood relative. The loss of his only family would weigh on him for the rest of his life. He would have nobody except the wife of a Nazi who may end up deported sooner or later. Joe could almost sympathize with Robert's anguish if that happened.

The least he could do was to give the kid a chance.

Here was the possibility of a new, unique relationship beyond having grown up in a family with whom he truly never belonged. He thought how his mother and father would want him to continue the Kaufmann line. Obligation to them made his eyes teary. Unlike so many millions of families destroyed, whole clans and family names wiped out, the Kaufmann family could survive for future generations. It would start with the joining of two brothers.

He looked around at the trees again and then rested his eyes on the knife.

He decided he had to go back to Bloomington. How he would find the kid he'd figure out once he got there. And he did need to pick up where he had left off with his dissertation. Besides, there would be the 700-mile, eleven-hour car trip between him and his busy-body family. And then there would be Irene . . .

The knife didn't look so enticing anymore. Joe got on his feet and put it back in its sheath and into his backpack. As he put the pack on his back and adjusted his baseball cap, he thought he still had the hardware store's receipt in the side pocket. Still tired but determined, he picked up his walking stick. He hoped he could find the trail again without getting lost.

CHAPTER THIRTY-EIGHT

At the end of August 1965, Joe was back in his old apartment. His professors were delighted to see him back on campus. They promptly gave him three classes to teach: two freshman classes of "A Survey of Russian history," and a sophomore class on the "History of London in the Eighteenth Century." Joe was encouraged after his hour-long meeting with his advisor, Dr. Reed, who had been impressed with the ever-expanding bibliography, footnotes, and the fifteen-page abstract of his dissertation. The paper was coming together "splendidly." He anticipated that Joe would be ready next spring to do his oral defense. At the end of the meeting, the ever-sanguine-faced, breathless instructor slid a thick newspaper across his desk, *Chronicle of Higher Education*. It was folded on page two, where several university job ads had been circled in red.

Irene came down to visit on the second Sunday he was back. She hugged and kissed him and said he should look up his new younger "brother." When Joe mentioned his hesitancy to go to his house up in Indianapolis, she suggested that he check out the Registrar's office to see if Robert had enrolled for the fall semester, and, if so, what classes he'd be taking. Joe said, "Yeah. I'll be hiding around the corner waiting to ambush him when he gets out of his music theory class. Get real, Irene."

But Joe didn't need to wait around the corner in Merrill Hall. On a late October afternoon, he decided to go to Bloomington's famous restaurant, The Gables, to sit at a booth for lunch and organize about a hundred notecards. Previously named The Book Nook, this historic restaurant, situated on South Indiana Avenue across the west side campus, was where Bloomington native Hoagy Carmichael had penned one of his most famous songs, *Star Dust*, in 1927. But today, college students filled the dining room, along with harried waitresses and wafts of French fries and fried hamburgers.

Joe worked on his cards. Customers came and went. The dining room was noisy with clinking dishes and boisterous laughing, with a whiney country-western singer he didn't recognize booming over a loudspeaker. Then he stopped and listened. It came back to him. He remembered his old friend, Frank Oneida, saying that was Hank Williams singing *The Great Speckled Bird*. Two years ago, they had brought here a nervous freshman music student after an opera performance to share a meal; Robert Stangarden, a pale, French horn-playing neophyte who couldn't pick up on the jokes between Joe and Frank. It was déjà vu.

Joe looked around. Co-eds giggled and laughed as they sat at tables, spooning thick chocolate milkshakes and picking at their cheeseburgers. For once, Joe felt old. These were kids barely out of high school, happy-go-lucky, and terribly immature. People moved in and out of booths and scraped chair legs under the tables. Pink-uniformed waitresses carried enormous plates of food on their arms. Two pimply-faced busboys in white paper Garrison-styled hats slung big red tubs of dirty glasses, used napkins, dishes, and silverware, making as much noise as they could. Watching the entire dining room was a long-deceased Hoagy Carmichael with a dangling cigarette and sitting at a piano in a black-and-white picture hanging on a wall.

After a table of four women customers stood and walked toward the cash register at the front of the restaurant, Joe caught a familiar head turned away in a booth. Two other young men sat opposite of him, their backs toward Joe. The three of them were talking and laughing and draining their glasses half full of melting ice.

Joe never took his eyes off that booth. A waitress left his check. Quickly, he laid out a dollar and two quarters. The two men with their backs to him slid out of the booth and headed toward the cash register. Joe had a better view of the third one, Robert Stangarden.

But Robert didn't leave with his friends. He took out a book from a satchel. Joe leaned forward to glimpse the title as Robert opened it and held it up to read. *Basic Judaism*. If the kid would just hold still, he could make out the author: Rabbi Milton Steinberg.

Joe hurriedly gathered his notecards and stuffed them in his briefcase. Then he sat and watched. He lit a cigarette. More customers walked by, and a busboy started to clear his table. Joe knew he'd have to leave. But he wanted to keep Robert in his sights. He decided to exit the restaurant and casually hang around on the other side of the street. Moments later, he stood under a giant oak tree near the sidewalk, still smoking. He'd watch for Robert to come out to "ambush" him, as he had suggested to Irene.

He didn't have to wait long. Robert walked out of the diner into the cool fall air, carrying his bag and heading toward the limestone buildings across the street. He kept his eyes down.

"Robert?"

The young man jerked up his head. His face displayed confusion, then surprise.

"Mr. Kaufmann?"

Joe put on a hopeful grin. "How's it goin'?"

Robert did not return his smile. "It's going well."

Joe nodded. "I'm glad to see you again. What have you been up to?" He couldn't believe how calm he was and how stupid his question was. He dropped his cigarette and crushed it with his foot.

Robert's eyes wandered. "I'm back in school." He glanced at his watch. "I've got a band rehearsal at three."

Joe looked at his watch. "That's in twenty minutes. You have time to talk for a couple of minutes?"

"Okay."

Joe shifted his weight. "So, what band are you in?"

"Wind Ensemble. The same one I was in last year." Robert frowned. It was actually two years ago.

"You're a sophomore now?"

"Yes. I got my scholarships reinstated." He held his satchel protectively against his chest.

"That's great. So, what did you do this summer?"

"I had a job working as a caddy at a golf course in Indy. It didn't pay much. I hate golf."

Joe grinned. "So do I. My guardian, Grayson, has tried for years to get me interested, but I think it's a pointless sport if you want to call it that. I like to play tennis, and I do some hiking." Joe realized he and

Robert had never shared their outdoor interests or disinterests. He switched topics to keep the conversation going. "Is your horn instructor, Frank Oneida, still teaching? I haven't seen him this year." Nor had Frank contacted Joe in more than a year. Who knew what that crazy guy was doing now.

"No. I don't think he's come back. I'm studying with Mr. Farkas now."

Joe nodded. He was not surprised. Either Frank ran out of money or was unable to keep his mood swings in check to cope with his doctoral program. Maybe it was both.

"Say, I have to go." Robert started to back up.

"Sure. You don't want to be late."

"I have to warm up before rehearsal."

"Yeah, that's a brass player's MO."

"Huh?"

"Modus operandi."

"Oh. Well, good-bye."

Joe walked after him. "You going to be in a practice room this weekend?"

"Yeah. I'm always there on Friday and Saturday nights." He hurried off before Joe could say any more.

****

"Grayson, you'll be pleased to know I met Robert Stangarden on campus a couple of days ago."

"Well, well. That's great news. How is he?"

"He acts like he did when he was a freshman. Always distracted and in a hurry, as if he's late for something or he's looking for someone. I think he does that to avoid having to hold a conversation, at least with me."

"Is he okay physically? His bruises all healed?"

"Grayson, that was seven months ago. You should know the answer to that. He looks okay. He said he's a sophomore this year, and he got his scholarships back."

"Did you talk about his mother? How is she holding up?"

"We didn't talk about her. He was in a hurry for a rehearsal, and we only talked for five minutes. Grayson, when I first saw him in a restaurant, he was reading a book on Judaism."

"Is that right? Did you say something to him about it?"

"No. I didn't get a chance to bring it up. I need to find the right place and time to talk with him about . . . you know. He said he'd be in a practice room this weekend. I've met him there before. There's a new building on campus called the music annex. It's nothing but practice rooms and some studios, connected to the main music building. If I get up the nerve, I'll look for him there this weekend."

"Oh, Ruth wants to talk to you."

"Hello, Joe? Sweetheart, are you doing well? Are you eating enough and getting a good eight hours of sleep?"

"I swear, Ruth, you are turning into a Jewish grandmother. Next, you'll be asking me why I haven't found a girlfriend yet. Or maybe you're fixing one up for me."

"I will if you want me to, Joe. I overheard Grayson saying you saw Robert."

"Yes. He's back at I. U., still a music student."

"I want you to invite him to come to Ithaca, maybe at Thanksgiving. He needs a family to go home to."

"Ruth, aren't you getting a little ahead of things? I haven't had a decent conversation with him yet. He still calls me Mr. Kaufmann."

"And invite his mom, too."

"Ruth, that would be awkward."

"We could put her up in your room, and you could sleep on the couch. Oh, wait. What about Robert? No, we should put them in a couple of those spare guest rooms at the mansion. Rose would be thrilled to have company to cook for. But we would need to ask your Aunt Mil first."

"Ruth, wait a minute! One step at a time. I don't even know how I'm going to interact with him."

"He's your brother, Joe. I thought we had this settled this summer. He's part of our family."

"But . . . but—"

"And be sure to let Irene know you're bringing him home. She should drive since her car is bigger than yours."

"But she might not be able to get off work."

"Well, we'll figure it out. Just let us know when you firm up your plans."

"But—"

"Goodbye, Joe. We love you."

CHAPTER THIRTY-NINE

Joe decided to drive over to the music annex building on Saturday evening. Although he usually didn't observe Shabbat services at the local university Jewish center called the Hillel, he impulsively attended a Friday night service. It gave him courage for when he would see Robert.

He brought his clarinet and some music, thinking that even if Robert wasn't there, he could get in some practice. When he had arrived in Bloomington a few weeks earlier, he had mused about contacting the music school to ask if he could sit in with the band class designated for non-music majors. He had done this before when he had been an undergrad at Cornell University. But here at I. U., he had never heard these particular students perform, so he didn't know their skill level. It could be a waste of his time if they just wanted to fill a course slot and didn't make a commitment to the music. Maybe one of the more advanced bands . . .

He pulled into a parking lot on the north side of the annex. He was grateful he had spent the exorbitant fee of $75 for a parking sticker that allowed him to park virtually anywhere on campus. The stickers' availability was limited, and he had come at the right time at the campus security office to get one.

He took the elevator up to the second floor of the enormous building. It would take time to find the kid if he was here at all. But, of course, he'd be here. Robert was a workaholic. It would be inconceivable for him tonight to go to a party or a bar to relax with his friends. He was as predictable as a cat.

The practice rooms were unusually full tonight. Joe heard a cacophony of singers, trombones, trumpets, violins, and flutes. He quickly passed by the locked rooms reserved for the piano majors. Of all the music majors, they were the most dedicated and most unhappy students of all. But Joe couldn't feel too much sympathy for them. They had chosen to study the most competitive instrument in the whole wide world of music. Hey, if they had wanted to play an instrument with the most performance opportunities, they should have picked the bassoon.

Joe went up to the third floor, then the fourth, and then the fifth. No luck. He decided on the sixth floor he would find an empty room and set up. He walked through the curved hall, looking for a darkened door window. Then he stopped to listen. He recognized a melody from the fourth movement of Brahms' *Symphony No. 1*. He closed his eyes to visualize a lone French horn's wind-swept call from a distance. He imagined an open plain under heavy clouds ready to drip rain. Yet, orange sun rays peeked through the fast-moving swirls in the vast sky, a hopeful sign of one of the most famous orchestral melodies ever written to set the stage for the rest of the movement. Joe leaned against a wall; his eyes were still closed to put himself on that musical prairie. It was a fleeting vision.

He stared at the door handle. Shouldering the strap of his music bag, he knocked and then slowly entered.

Robert immediately stopped playing his French horn, his face reflecting alarm. Joe put his clarinet case and his black leather bag on the smudged, grimy floor. He pulled out the piano bench of the ancient practice piano and sat. "Can we talk?" he asked flatly.

Robert carefully put his instrument in his open case. He moved it and the music stand off to the side.

"You knew I was going to come here, didn't you?" Joe's question was more of a statement. He took off his leather bomber jacket and laid it on top of the piano.

Robert shrugged. "I wasn't sure."

Joe knitted his smooth brows and crossed his legs. He passed his hand over his shirt breast pocket in the habit of reaching for a cigarette. But in this tiny, poorly ventilated room, the smoke would make breathing difficult. "When I met you the other day before your rehearsal, I saw you first in the restaurant with a couple of friends."

"Yeah. They're in the band with me. One is another horn player, and the other plays alto sax. We were in the Marching 100 two years ago." Robert looked away as if thinking about how much time had passed since he had first stepped onto the I. U. campus. On an impulse, he picked up his French horn, took off the mouthpiece, and began taking out the crooks and emptying them of saliva and condensation on the floor. He turned the instrument around and around. Water dripped out of the lead pipe.

Joe said, "I watched you after they left. You were reading a book on Jewish history."

"Ah, yeah." Robert put his French horn back together and put it in the case. With nothing left to do, now it was his turn to show his discomfort. His right knee began to shake up and down violently, a mannerism he did under stress. His eyes moved around the room; white walls banged up with black scuff marks, sure signs of abuse by instrument cases.

Absently, Joe lowered the keyboard cover of the dilapidated spinet piano. He wiped some dust off the lid. "Why are you reading that?"

Robert shrugged again. "I dunno. I guess I've been interested in it."

"Aren't you Lutheran?"

"Yes, I am. I just wanted to learn more about another religion. That's all."

Joe's eyes blurred. He blinked and sniffed. He said, "So, what have you been up to this summer?" He realized at once that he had asked this question before. *That was stupid.*

"I stayed at home with my mother." Robert looked away as if to avoid meeting Joe's eyes. "I had that first job as a golf caddy. But I quit and got another job at a Sears store stocking shelves. It pays more. The school renewed my scholarships. I told them what had happened to me last year, and they seemed to understand."

"I'm glad to hear that, Robert. And how is your mother?" This conversation was becoming surreal.

"She's . . . okay. The ladies from our church are helping her. She cries a lot."

Joe rubbed his glasses with the tail of his shirt as a stall tactic to give himself time to think about what he would say next. Putting them back on, he stood and walked a few steps around the practice room to get his bearings. He fixated on the acoustic tiles that covered the upper half of the room. They, too, had been damaged by errant instrument cases. Somebody had inked "Kilroy was here" in a corner.

Robert went on. "I think it helps my mom to work at the elementary school. Takes her mind off things." He paused, thinking. "I played with a community band this summer."

"Oh, yeah?" Joe turned around to face him.

"It's called the Indianapolis Symphonic Band. The conductor is this crazy old geezer named Bob Phillips. They had a summer concert series at one of the malls. It was embarrassing to watch him. He worked the audience like they were a bunch of grade school kids. I don't know why I stayed in it. The musicians were pretty bad."

"I'm thinking about joining the band here for non-music majors. Know anything about that?"

Robert shook his head. "No."

"Hmm . . ." It was so easy to talk about music and band.

"Have you lived in Bloomington all this time?"

"Huh? No. I went to Ithaca for the summer. I came back to work on my dissertation." No, he wasn't going to think about sitting next to that old birch log in the middle of Taughannock Falls State Park. That seemed so long ago.

"Are you going to stay here?"

"Yes, at least until I finish my doctorate. I plan to defend my dissertation next May. I'll get my degree after that." He sat back on the piano bench. His nerves were so tight that if he had his clarinet in his hands, he'd break it in two.

"This is difficult to ask, but have you been thinking about that meeting with that lawyer, Ed Moscowitz?" He crossed his knees and folded his arms.

Robert averted his eyes. "I . . . I don't know what to think." His knee stopped bouncing.

"Have you discussed it with your mother while you've been home?" Mother? Robert's mother wasn't his mother.

Now it was Robert's turn to stand and pace. "I can't. It's too painful for her to talk about it. We don't even talk about my father. Sometimes our minister takes her to Indiana State Prison to visit him. Since it's up in Michigan City, it takes all day, and she doesn't get home until almost midnight. Of course, she's wiped out and can't function for the next two days. She's miserable. I know she misses him." He frowned to himself.

"Do you believe what she said about what happened at Buchenwald?"

Robert shook his head. "I—I don't know if I believe her. If it's true, my whole life, my identity has been a lie! Is it true? My real parents are . . . your parents?"

Joe replied solemnly, "Yes, Robert. Ada Stangarden would have had no reason to make up any of that. Think about it. She could have easily said nothing and kept the charade that you were her son. My God, you are the only family she has left!

"But she couldn't live that lie anymore. I think she realized that after she saw you and me together. That picture of our mother and the one of your baptism. She didn't have to show those to us." Joe reflected. "She loved you enough to tell you the truth even if it meant giving you up. She sacrificed her own desire to keep you with her for the truth you deserve to know about who you really are."

Joe stood. "Robert, you are the son of Hans and Ina Kaufmann, German Jews."

He turned away from Robert, steeling himself. If Robert would accept him as his brother, he knew he would have to act like the older brother, someone Robert could look up to, to lean on, to help him. It meant a change in their relationship for the rest of their lives. Joe knew he would have to put away the memories. There could be no more sliding into depression, no more suicidal thoughts, no more sleeping pills, more hunting knives. Robert need never hear about that. Thank God the kid hadn't noticed the scars on his wrists and right upper arm.

"What about your father? Our father. Is it true what my mom said that you look exactly like him?" Robert brought him out of his thoughts.

Joe nodded. "Yes. But I don't want to talk about him. Maybe sometime in the future."

"Oh," Robert said with disappointment.

Joe leaned against a wall. He wanted a cigarette badly. "I can't blame you for being who you are, Robert. For your entire life, you've been the 'son' of allegedly innocent German parents who made a home and a life here in Indiana. You're not responsible for any of this. And the fact that you've suffered by taking that awful beating makes me feel guilty for abandoning you as I've done." He slid his foot to knock an old cigarette butt under the piano. He shoved his hands in his jeans pockets. "I kept running back to Ithaca. My family had to beg me to come back to help you. I didn't want to see you because I would have to face that couple and bringing up bad memories. I'm sorry."

Robert faced him. "But all that wasn't your fault. My father—"

Joe raised his voice. "Yes, it was my fault, Robert. If I hadn't come into your life, if Frank Oneida hadn't introduced us, you would have been down here at I. U. a year ago, still healthy and whole and working like a Hebrew slave on your music degree. I'm the reason you went through all this hell for the past year and a half."

Robert said nothing.

Joe stared at the wall. Then he heard loud sniffs and choking sounds. He turned. Without speaking, he sat back on the piano bench and looked at Robert intently.

With crossed arms, Robert shook as if the room's temperature was below freezing. His face darkened. He ran quick fingers through his thick, brown hair. He blinked as if trying not to cry, but his chin trembled.

"He was so mean to me," he whispered hoarsely. "When I think about how he hit me . . ."

Joe leaned over and put supporting hands on his shoulders. He tried to catch his wet eyes.

"It was so quick. Like my body didn't even have time to feel the pain. And my mother kept screaming and screaming. I remember . . . I remember he said over and over, 'Du wirst es ihnen nie sagen.' 'You will never tell them.' I didn't know what he meant by that. I didn't know who 'them' was."

Robert finally met Joe's eyes. "I couldn't believe how cruel he was. Sure, he was pretty hard on me as I was growing up. But he never hit me, except that one time when I was around four. I don't even remember what I did. But I learned my lesson after that."

He paused. "When we had that argument in the living room, and I asked my mom to take me back to school, it was like an explosion. I'd never seen him lose his temper like that." Unknowingly, Robert put his hand to his neck, rubbing the opened collar of his shirt.

Joe swallowed. The knife.

"I was so scared, even throughout the trial when I knew he was in handcuffs and kept in a jail cell. I was afraid he would break out and attack me again. And he did! Remember? After he was found guilty in the courtroom?"

Joe said, "I was scared, too, Robert. I thought he'd come after me as well. That's why I ran out of your house. I—I ended up running all the way back to Ithaca." He let go of Robert's shoulders and shifted on the piano bench. He looked away, remembering in his apartment, his mind-freezing terror as he had squeezed himself between his bed and the wall to hide from old, familiar swastikas dancing in the faint light from the tiny lamp on the bookcase.

"Is that what you went through at Buchenwald?"

After a long silence, Joe replied, "Yes."

Robert put his hands on his knees. "I'd never been afraid for my life before. I can't imagine what it would have been like for you as a little kid." He thought for a moment. "Then, losing your parents like that." New sobs came up from his throat. "They were my parents! I never knew them, but I miss them! Oh, why did they have to die?"

"Because they were Jews, Robert. To be a Jew meant death in those times."

"The hate I saw in his face. Was that the kind of hate in that place?"

"Yes, Robert."

Joe swallowed. "In a strange way, we've both suffered from that hate. We both have the scars not only on the outside but also on the inside. Yet, we have survived. If we stay with each other, we can get past it. We can lean on each other. Do you want to do that?"

Joe wanted to put his hand on Robert's shoulder again.

After a moment, Robert twisted his head from side to side. He sat heavily in his chair. "This is so hard! I don't know!" He put his face in his hands, crying violently.

Joe bent his knees in front of Robert and took his arms. "Robert, we're brothers. We are the sons of Hans and Ina Kaufmann." He looked deeply into Robert's face. "It's taken a grueling road of hurt to get to this place. Are we going to take that next step?"

Copious tears spilled over in Robert's deep-set, liquid brown eyes, streaking his face. "I . . . I want a family! I want you to help me!"

Joe grabbed him and held him tightly. His deep-set, liquid brown eyes filled. "Yes, Robert. I will help you. Our mother and father would want us to be together. We must do this for them, to honor their memory, Robert. We are the next generation of Kaufmanns."

They wept together, clinging to each other desperately. Their emotion was almost unbearable.

Robert pulled away. He wiped his face with his sleeve. Joe took out a handkerchief to wipe his red eyes and to blow his nose. He smiled at his brother, even as his tears still streaked his face.

"Mr. Kaufmann—"

"Come on. Call me Joe." Joe laughed, wiping wet eyes. "We don't have to be so formal . . . Max." He grinned.

"Max?"

"Maximillian Richard Kaufmann. Your first and middle names were on your birth certificate. That's what Ada said our mother named you. You can call yourself 'Max' for short."

The younger man brushed tears from his splotched cheeks and sniffed hard. "I guess this means I should get my name changed. But I don't know how to do that."

"Don't worry. I'll help you figure out who we need to contact." Big brother for sure. "So, are we good?"

Robert, or rather, Max nodded.

They sat for several moments, breathing deeply to calm themselves. Then Joe reached to grab his clarinet case on top of the piano. "Hey, I brought my clarinet. You up for some music-making? I brought the Debussy."

Max Kaufmann replied, wiping his nose on his sleeve, "Sure, Joe. I think I can handle the piano part." He put on a slightly forced grin.

Joe put together his clarinet and arranged his music on the stand. Max opened to the first page of the accompaniment part to Debussy's Premiere Rhapsody and played a few notes. "Oh, this piano is out of tune."

"That's all right. We'll just have to live with it," replied Joe. He ran a quick chromatic scale to warm up. "Ready?"

Max began the first measure of slow, mysterious open chords. Joe slipped in with a subtone, as subtle as a single watery ripple over a still pond in a deep forest. His restrained musical touch was matched by his brother's weightless, simple grace that was the style of early Twentieth-Century French music. Guided by underlying chords, the melody quickly rose and fell in dynamic bursts. The two brothers continued this dreamy setting for several lines. The agile, horizontal melody floated over quiet, busy triplet patterns. The clarinet range expanded higher and higher, soaring above the sweeping harmonies of the accompaniment. Then the musical scene suddenly evolved into animated jumps like tiny hummingbirds flitting from flower to flower in a brief, improvisational dialogue between the clarinet and the piano.

Having studied this piece for many years, Joe relied on muscle memory in his fingers to navigate through the complicated thirty-second notes. But he became distracted and began to miss some rhythms. His attention strayed from this difficult solo that demanded an inner sense of beat to stay with the equally challenging piano part. He had to stop. He remembered he had not taken the receipt out of his backpack.

BIBLIOGRAPHY

Biber, Jacob. Risen From the Ashes. Borgo Press, 1990.

Black, Edwin. IBM and the Holocaust. Crown Publishers, 2001.

Confino, Alon. A World Without Jews. Yale University Press, 2014.

Dwork, Deborah. Children With A Star. Yale University Press, 1991.

Dwork, Deborah, and Robert Jan Van Pelt. Auschwitz. W. W. Norton, 1996.

Gilbert, Martin. The Boys. Owl Books, 1996.

Gilbert, Martin. The Righteous. Owl Books, 2004.

Gross, Leonard. The Last Jews in Berlin. Open Road, 2015.

Harran, Marilyn, et al. The Holocaust Chronicles. Publications International, 2000.

Helman, Peter. When Courage Was Stronger Than Fear. MJF Books, 1999.

Hemmendinger, Judith, and Robert Krell. The Children of Buchenwald. Gefen Publishing House, 2000.

Hughes, Matthew, and Chris Mann. Inside Hitler's Germany. MJF Books, 2000.

Johnson, Eric A. What We Knew. Basic Books, 2005.

Kaplan, Marion A. Between Dignity and Despair. Oxford University Press, 1998.

Klee, Ernst, Willi Dressen, and Volker Riess, editors. The Good Old Days. Translated by Deborah Burnstone, The Free Press--Simon and Schuster, 1988.

Kogon, Eugen. The Theory and Practice of Hell. Berkley Medallion, 1966.

Konigseder, Angelika, and Judith Wetzel. Waiting for Hope. Translated by John A. Broadwin. Northwestern University Press, 2001.

Koonz, Claudia. The Nazi Conscience. Belknap Press, 2003.

Levi, Primo. Moments of Reprieve. Translated by Ruth Feldman. Penguin Books, 1995.

Lichtblau, Eric. The Nazi Next Door. Mariner Books, 2014.

Lower, Wendy. Hitler's Furies. Houghton Mifflin Harcourt, 2013.

Mullally, David S. Order in the Court. Writer's Digest-F & W Publications, Inc., 2000.

Novick, Peter. The Holocaust in American Life. Mariner Books, 2000.

Rosenberg, Maxine B. Hiding to Survive. Clarion Books, 1994.

Shirer, William L. The Rise and Fall of the Third Reich. Gallery Books, 1990.

Toland, John. Adolph Hitler. Vols. I and II. Doubleday and Company, 1976

Wiesel, Elie. After Darkness. Schocken Books, 2002.

Wiesel, Elie. Night. Hill and Wang, 2006.

Zelizer, Barbie. Remembering to Forget. University of Chicago Press, 1998.

"Historic WW II Nazi Concentration Camps." Quality Information Publishers, 2006. DVD

"Holocaust Ravensbrook and Buchenwald." ArtsMagic LTD, 2006. DVD

"Night and Fog." Criterion Collection, Janus Films, 2003. DVD.

"Naked Among Wolves." Dir. Frank Beyer. IceStorm, 1963. DVD.

ABOUT THE AUTHOR

Anita Tiemeyer was born in Columbus, Indiana. She has been a writer since elementary school. Ms. Tiemeyer received her bachelor's degree in music education and history at Western Illinois University in 1980. She entered the United States Air Force in 1983 and served until 1991 at Lackland Air Force Base in San Antonio, Texas. She was awarded her master of music degree in 1995 from Butler University in Indianapolis. As a music educator by profession, she has maintained a private woodwind studio in Central Indiana for over thirty-five years. Ms. Tiemeyer resides in Indianapolis, Indiana.

Connect with the author at:

Facebook: Anita Tiemeyer Author
Website: www.anitatiemeyer.com
Email: ast4586@gmail.com